THE GIRL FROM DEVIL'S LAKE

Also by J. A. Jance

Joanna Brady Mysteries

Desert Heat
Tombstone Courage
Shoot Don't Shoot
Dead to Rights
Skeleton Canyon
Rattlesnake Crossing
Outlaw Mountain
Devil's Claw
Paradise Lost
Partner in Crime: A Beaumont/Brady Novel
Exit Wounds
Dead Wrong
Damage Control
Fire and Ice: A Beaumont/Brady Novel
Judgment Call
The Old Blue Line (novella)
Remains of Innocence
No Honor Among Thieves: An Ali Reynolds and Joanna Brady Novella
Random Acts: A Joanna Brady and Ali Reynolds Novella
Downfall
Field of Bones
Missing and Endangered
Blessing of the Lost Girls: A Brady/Walker Family Novel

J. P. Beaumont Mysteries

Until Proven Guilty
Injustice for All
Trial by Fury
Taking the Fifth
Improbable Cause
A More Perfect Union
Dismissed with Prejudice
Minor in Possession
Payment in Kind
Without Due Process
Failure to Appear
Lying in Wait
Name Withheld
Breach of Duty
Birds of Prey
Partner in Crime: A Beaumont/Brady Novel
Long Time Gone
Justice Denied
Fire and Ice: A Beaumont/Brady Novel
Betrayal of Trust
Ring in the Dead (novella)

Second Watch
Stand Down (novella)
Dance of the Bones: A Beaumont/Walker Family Novel
Still Dead (novella)
Proof of Life
Sins of the Fathers
Nothing to Lose
Den of Iniquity

Walker Family Novels

Hour of the Hunter
Kiss of the Bees
Day of the Dead
Queen of the Night
Dance of the Bones: A Beaumont/Walker Family Novel
Blessing of the Lost Girls: A Brady/Walker Family Novel

Ali Reynolds Novels

Edge of Evil
Web of Evil
Hand of Evil
Cruel Intent
Trial by Fire
Fatal Error
Left for Dead
Deadly Stakes
Moving Target
A Last Goodbye: An Ali Reynolds Novella
Cold Betrayal
No Honor Among Thieves: An Ali Reynolds and Joanna Brady Novella
Clawback
Random Acts: A Joanna Brady and Ali Reynolds Novella
Man Overboard
Duel to the Death
The A List
Credible Threat
Unfinished Business
Collateral Damage

Poetry

After the Fire

THE GIRL FROM DEVIL'S LAKE

A BRADY NOVEL OF SUSPENSE

J. A. Jance

WILLIAM MORROW
An Imprint of HarperCollinsPublishers

Without limiting the exclusive rights of any author, contributor or the publisher of this publication, any unauthorized use of this publication to train generative artificial intelligence (AI) technologies is expressly prohibited. HarperCollins also exercise their rights under Article 4(3) of the Digital Single Market Directive 2019/790 and expressly reserve this publication from the text and data mining exception.

This is a work of fiction. Names, characters, places, and incidents are products of the author's imagination or are used fictitiously and are not to be construed as real. Any resemblance to actual events, locales, organizations, or persons, living or dead, is entirely coincidental.

THE GIRL FROM DEVIL'S LAKE. Copyright © 2025 by J. A. Jance. All rights reserved. Printed in the United States of America. No part of this book may be used or reproduced in any manner whatsoever without written permission except in the case of brief quotations embodied in critical articles and reviews. For information, address HarperCollins Publishers, 195 Broadway, New York, NY 10007. In Europe, HarperCollins Publishers, Macken House, 39/40 Mayor Street Upper, Dublin 1, D01 C9W8, Ireland.

HarperCollins books may be purchased for educational, business, or sales promotional use. For information, please email the Special Markets Department at SPsales@harpercollins.com.

hc.com

FIRST EDITION

Designed by Michele Cameron

Library of Congress Cataloging-in-Publication Data has been applied for.

ISBN 978-0-06-325263-9

25 26 27 28 29 LBC 5 4 3 2 1

For Jane Decker and Becky Federico
who provided invaluable help when I needed it

THE GIRL FROM DEVIL'S LAKE

PROLOGUE

FERTILE, MINNESOTA
1956

THE VOICES HAD BEEN WITH STEVE FOR AS LONG AS HE could remember. They had been friendly at first. When he was a little kid, living with his divorced mother in a mobile home behind his grandfather's house on a farm in Minnesota, the voices would tell him stories when it was time for him to take a nap or go to bed, and they'd still be there talking to him when he woke up.

His mother worked as a waitress at the little café in town. She'd be gone in the morning before Steve got out of bed, and she didn't come home until almost suppertime, so most of the time he was stuck with his grandmother. In the fairy-tale books Steve's mother read to him at bedtime, Cinderella had an evil stepmother, and so did Snow White. As for Stevie Roper? He had an evil step-grandmother. His mother's real mother, Grandma Joanie, as Gramps called her, had died of breast cancer while his mom was still in grade school. Grandma Lucille, as Steve was taught to call her, was Gramps's second wife.

Steve's mother, Cynthia, and his father, Jackson Roper, had been high school sweethearts. When they learned they were pregnant, they married without either one of them graduating from high school. Grandma Lucille had despised Jackson the first time she saw him, and the fact that Cindy and Jackson "had to get married" hadn't improved her opinion. Jackson had proved her right by running off with another woman when Steve was less than a year old.

At that point, Grandma Lucille had hit the roof, but Gramps had sprung into action. He had purchased a used mobile home and moved it to a pad on his farm so his daughter and fatherless grandson would have a place to live. Gramps was a good man. He took Steve in hand. He taught the boy how to drive a tractor and how to fish for bullheads in the small lake on his property. He taught him how to carve and how to build things with Tinkertoys and Lincoln Logs and how to fly a kite, and although Steve's father never paid a dime's worth of child support, Gramps never said a mean word about him.

Grandma Lucille, on the other hand, had plenty to say about Jackson Roper and about Steve too. As far as she was concerned, Jackson was a no-good, worthless punk. She was forever telling Steve that he was "the devil's spawn." If spawn were baby fish, did that mean Steve's dad was also the devil?

Most of the other kids had mothers and grandmothers who wore housedresses or maybe capris. Not Grandma Lucille. Except for church on Sunday—which she never missed—she wore Oshkosh overalls and a pair of lace-up boots. That's what she wore at home and that's what she wore to the post office or grocery store. Kids at school, mostly the boys, teased Steve, saying that his grandmother wore GI boots. Unfortunately, it was undeniably true.

Grandma Lucille was old-school. She believed that children in general and Steve in particular should be seen but not heard. Nor did she subscribe to sparing the rod and spoiling the child. In that regard she preferred using a flyswatter rather than a rod. And she told him more than once that if he didn't behave himself, she was going to snap his head right off.

Steve believed Grandma Lucille on that score. She raised chickens—not only for the eggs but also for food. She could snap a rooster's neck and chop his head off in the blink of an eye.

What all that really meant was that whatever time Steve had to spend with her—from when the school bus dropped him off until his mother got home—was absolute hell. But then, as soon as Gramps came in or his mother got home, Grandma Lucille did a complete about-face. The mean looks and disparaging words vanished, and suddenly she was nothing but sweetness and light.

But all along, Steve's voices kept talking. They told him stories about a magic owl named Hoot who watched over him day and night. The eagle he called King Kong also kept an eye on Steve and spoke to him from time to time, telling him things he needed to know. That's how Steve learned that a dog named Charlie, who lived on a neighboring farm, was really a werewolf in disguise and not a bluetick hound. Some of the voices were smarter than others, and they bickered a lot among themselves, but the thing they all agreed on was that Grandma Lucille was a witch and had to go.

Grandma Lucille had told Steve often that he was dumb as a stump, but he was smart enough to know that if he was going to get rid of her, he had to make it happen without being caught.

Gramps's place was an old-fashioned farmhouse with a fenced yard all around it. A sunporch had been tacked onto the front of the house, and a short set of six steps with banisters on either side led up from a concrete walkway to the front door.

One day, when Steve was eleven, knowing that Gramps was in town having his tractor fixed, instead of going directly into the house after getting home from school, he stopped by Gramps's toolshed. Once inside, he opened Gramps's tackle box, removed a spool of fishing line, and then used his pocketknife to cut off an appropriate length of fishing string. Back at the house, he secured both ends of the fishing line between the two topmost porch banisters at what he estimated to be ankle height.

Grandma Lucille didn't like most animals—she especially didn't like dogs—but she was fond of an outdoor cat who lived in their barn, one she referred to as Kitty. Once the string was fastened in place, Steve dashed into the house calling, "Grandma, Grandma, come quick. Kitty's been hurt. I think a raccoon must've got him!"

"Where is he?"

"In the barn."

Steve rushed back outside and down the steps, carefully clearing the fishing line on his way. Once on the ground, he turned back in time to see the top of Grandma Lucille's boot catch on the fishing line. For a moment, she faltered, grabbing for the handrail, but she couldn't catch herself. She tumbled headlong to the ground six steps below. She landed face down on the walkway and then lay there without moving. Steve stepped closer, staring at her long enough to see a pool of blood ooze out from under her head and onto the sidewalk. Before he did anything more, Steve hurried back to the steps, where he removed the fishing line and dropped it among the ashes in the bottom of Grandma Lucille's burning barrel.

When he returned to check on her, she still hadn't moved. The pool of blood had widened by then, and he watched in fascination as it gradually spread across the paved walkway and seeped into the grass. That was when Steve realized this was a moment he would always remember. It was also when he spotted the gold band of her wedding ring blinking up at him in the afternoon sunlight. Pulling the damned thing off wasn't easy, but finally it came loose. Then, after slipping the ring into the pocket of his jeans, Steve dashed up the stairs and into the house. He ran to the kitchen where he grabbed the receiver off the wall phone.

"Number please," the operator said.

"I need help," Steve said breathlessly.

"What's wrong?"

"It's my grandma," he said. "She must've fallen off the front steps. She's hurt real bad and bleeding like crazy."

"Is she breathing?"

"I don't know."

"Where are you?"

He gave her the address.

"What's your name?"

"It's Roper—Steve Roper."

"All right," the operator said. "I'm contacting the sheriff's department right now. It was smart of you to call for help."

Steve went back outside and rode his bike out to the county road so he could wave down the cops when they arrived twenty minutes later. A lone deputy showed up first followed by a speeding ambulance. The deputy checked Grandma Lucille's wrist for a pulse and then shook his head at the arriving ambulance attendant. Then he stood up and walked over to Steve.

"I'm Deputy Dan Hogan with the Polk County Sheriff's Department," he said. "You're the one who called it in?"

Steve nodded.

"What's your name?"

"Steve Roper."

"What happened?"

Steve shrugged his shoulders. "I don't know. When I came home from school she was just lying there. Is she going to be okay?"

The deputy shook his head. "I'm afraid not, Steve."

"You mean she's dead?"

The deputy nodded.

Steve knew he couldn't show what he was really feeling. That would give the game away. So he dropped heavily to the ground where he buried his face in his hands. "That's awful," he mumbled.

"Yes, it is," the deputy said, pulling out a small notebook. "Who all lives here?"

"Grandpa and her live in the house. Mom and I live in the trailer out back."

"Where are they now?"

"Mom's still at work. She's a waitress at the Country Inn in Fertile. Grandpa's in town getting his tractor fixed. Grandma looks after me once school gets out until Mom gets home."

"Your grandpa's Orson Hawkins?"

Steve nodded.

"And the tractor's being fixed where—Cooper's Tractor Repair in Fertile?"

Steve nodded again.

Deputy Hogan closed his notebook. "Okay, Steve," he said. "Why don't you come have a seat in my patrol car while I see what I can do to get ahold of your folks."

What happened after that was a flurry of activity. For a while, cops were all over the place. Detectives came, and so did the coroner. After that Deputy Hogan took Steve to the sheriff's office in town where they had him tell his story again and again. Eventually they took his shoes away because they wanted to see if the soles matched the bloody footprints they had found in the kitchen.

Finally, Mom and Steve were able to go back to their mobile, but Gramps, after being questioned by the detective, had to stay in a motel in town for almost a week because his house was considered a crime scene. But much later, that first night, Steve's mother came into his room to tell him good night.

"Are you sorry she's gone?" Steve asked.

His mother sighed. "Not really," she said. "I never liked her much, but I'd never say that to Gramps. She was good to him. Now go to sleep. I'm going outside to have a smoke."

That had been one of Grandma Lucille's rules—no smoking inside the house. Steve's mother smoked like a fiend. Her brand was Lucky Strikes. Gramps smoked cigars—Montecristos. After supper in the evenings, the two of them would sit outside on the steps or, in the winter, on the sunporch to enjoy their smokes. And every year without fail, for Christmas, Steve's mother had given Gramps a box of Montecristo cigars.

The year Steve turned five, Gramps had handed him one of his empty cigar boxes. "Every little boy should have one of these," Gramps had said.

"How come?" Steve had asked.

"To hold your treasures," Gramps had answered.

"What are treasures?"

"The things you want to keep forever."

That's exactly how Steve used it.

Sitting in the bottom drawer of his dresser, it held his pocketknife, the hook he used to catch his first fish, some marbles he'd won at school, a lucky rabbit's foot, a Ten Commandments bookmark from bible school, and a feather taken after shooting his first-ever pheasant. That night, after his mother went outside to smoke her cigarette, Steve dug Grandma Lucille's wedding ring out of his jeans, stuck it on the rabbit's foot, and put them both in his cigar box.

On the day of Grandma Lucille's funeral, Gramps was really upset because he suddenly noticed that her wedding ring had gone missing. When the cops gave him an envelope with her things in it and the ring wasn't there, Gramps hit the roof. He blamed all kinds of people, from the ambulance attendant to the first deputy who had arrived on the scene.

"Just because they're cops doesn't make them saints," he had growled.

At the funeral, one person after another stood up in the First Lutheran Church of Fertile and said what a wonderful, hardworking, God-fearing woman Grandma Lucille had been. Steve didn't say a word. He just sat there, doing his best to look both sad and respectful.

After that things at home were challenging for a while. From what Steve was able to overhear, at first the cops seemed to think that Gramps had been responsible for Grandma Lucille's death because she'd had some life insurance, and he was the only beneficiary. However, Mr. Cooper at the tractor repair shop gave Gramps an airtight alibi, saying he'd shown up with the tractor on a trailer bright and early that morning and had stayed there all day until the deputy called to say Gramps needed to come straight to the hospital.

Eventually Lucille Hawkins's death was declared an accident. A few months later, the insurance money came through. Gramps used that to finish paying off the mortgage on his farm and began buying up some of his neighbors' properties as well. After that, as far as Steve and his mother were concerned, everything changed for the better. Steve and his mom moved into the house to live with Gramps, while the new hired hand, brought in to help Gramps with the chores, ended up living in the mobile home.

Naturally Steve never talked about what had happened with anyone—other than Hoot or King Kong, and occasionally with Casper, Steve's very own friendly ghost. And although that was the first time Stephen Roper got away with murder, it certainly wasn't the last.

CHAPTER 1

BISBEE, ARIZONA
Thursday, November 9, 2023

AS SHERIFF JOANNA BRADY PRESSED THE IGNITION BUTTON on her Ford Interceptor, her husband, Butch Dixon, leaned in through her open window. "Do you have everything you need?"

"I do now, thanks," she answered. As she'd headed for the garage, she had left her freshly cleaned dress uniform, still in its plastic bag, hanging on the doorknob in the laundry room. It would have been there still had Butch not spotted it and carried it to the car.

"Drive carefully," Butch said, giving her a peck on the cheek, "and be sure to tell Jenny I'm proud as punch."

"Will do," Joanna said, putting the SUV in reverse. Butch was still there waving as the garage door slid shut behind her.

Leaving the ranch, she turned first onto High Lonesome Road and then Double Adobe Road before reaching Highway 80. Her office at the Cochise County Sheriff's Department was just a few miles ahead. She had intended to drive straight by her office, but with the situation at the jail currently such a powder keg, at the last moment, she turned off, pulled into her reserved spot on the far side of the building, and stepped inside through her private entrance.

When she walked through her office and into the waiting room outside, Kristin Gregovich, her secretary, looked up in surprise.

"What are you doing here?" she asked. "I thought you were on your way to Peoria."

"I am," Joanna replied, "but I wanted to stop by and see how things are."

"All right so far as I can tell," Kristin answered.

"Where's Tom?"

Tom Hadlock was Joanna's chief deputy.

"Where do you think?"

"The jail?" Joanna asked.

"Where else?" Kristin said with a sigh.

Aware that she was out of uniform, Joanna made her way through the series of security doors that led into the jail's interior. Growing up, she'd loved watching reruns of the Andy Griffith show. When she'd first been elected sheriff, the Cochise County Jail resembled the one in Mayberry where even the town drunk had been treated like visiting royalty. Back then, the jail had been a bit on the casual side and generally filled with a collection of locally well-known but minor offenders—ones charged with DUIs, drunk and disorderly, domestic violence, speeding, driving without a license, etc.—who came and went on a regular basis. Those original frequent fliers had usually been held for a matter of days or weeks at the most.

Over time, all that had changed. Chaos along the Mexican border had brought a whole new world of criminal activity to Cochise County. Now, in terms of inmates, the county jail resembled a regular prison. Offenders who had been arrested for various kinds of smuggling and drug offenses and who were unable to post bail were having to be housed for months or even years while awaiting trial. That meant the jail was usually filled to capacity and beyond. In fact, the situation had become so precarious that several months earlier Joanna had been forced to make arrangements for all jail personnel to wear body cams while on duty.

Two months earlier, one of her patrol deputies had spotted a vehicle that had been cosmetically altered to resemble a UPS van speeding northbound on Central Highway just outside Elfrida. When the officer gave chase, the driver of the van had opened fire. The pursuing officer had radioed for help, but realizing he was mostly on his own, he had finally resorted to shooting out one of the rear tires of the speeding vehicle, causing the driver to lose control. The van had lurched off the highway, plowed into an irrigation ditch, and then rolled three times before coming to a stop.

The driver, who had been wearing a seat belt, walked away from the incident without a scratch and was taken into custody. Unfortunately none of the twenty-three illegal immigrants crammed into the back of the van had had seats, much less seat belts. Five of the passengers died at the scene. Four more later succumbed to their injuries. EMTs and law enforcement officers from all over the area, and even as far away as Lordsburg, New Mexico, had responded to the carnage. Joanna herself had shown up on the scene, doing her best to comfort the less seriously injured who, after being triaged, had to wait their turn while medics responded to those with life-threatening injuries.

The driver, one Antonio Rodriguez-Otero, an illegal immigrant with no valid driver's license, was now being held in the Cochise County Jail, charged with nine counts of felony vehicular homicide, one count of assaulting a police officer, and one count of driving a stolen vehicle. Since he was an obvious flight risk, no bail had been offered, and he had waived his right to a speedy trial. In other words, there was no telling how long he would continue to languish in Joanna's lockup before his court date.

Unfortunately, Antonio was anything but your ordinary, man-on-the-street kind of illegal immigrant. He was a hardened criminal and a full-fledged member of the Sinaloa Cartel, and someone who much preferred his own company to anyone else's. Whenever he was allowed to mingle with the general population, he'd pull some stunt to land himself in solitary confinement. Two weeks ago, he had used a fork to attack another inmate standing in line in the mess hall.

With Mr. Rodriguez-Otero pretty much permanently ensconced in the jail's only solitary-confinement cell, Joanna had been forced to embark on carving out spaces for two more solitary units from an area that had once held a total of ten inmates. The process of obtaining permits for electrical and plumbing for the jail remodel was a bureaucratic nightmare. Not only that, with overcrowding now that much worse, tempers among the inmates were at a boiling point.

After two near riots the week before, Joanna had finally asked the governor for help. Seven members of the Arizona National Guard had been dispatched to the Cochise County jail to help maintain order.

That morning Joanna found Tom Hadlock in the jail's administration office where he was huddled with the new jail commander, Terry Gregovich. For years Terry, Kristin's husband, had served as the department's K-9 officer. Once his knees gave out and he could no longer keep up with his dog, Mojo, Joanna had brought both man and beast inside. With everything that was going on, having a jail commander with a trained K-9 assistant at his side seemed like a good idea.

"Hey, guys," Joanna said, letting herself into the room. "How's it going, Mojo?"

The dog thumped his tail but didn't raise his head.

"You'll notice she didn't ask either of us how it's going," Tom grumbled to Terry.

"How is it going?"

"We made it through breakfast without any incidents," Terry reported. "I guess that's something."

"How are the National Guard guys working out?" Joanna asked.

"Fairly well," Terry said. "Two of them speak fluent Spanish, so that's a help, and our regular guys who've been having to work double shifts really appreciate having a little breathing space."

"What are you doing here?" Tom asked. "Aren't you supposed to be on your way to Peoria for Jenny's graduation?"

"I am," Joanna replied. "I just wanted to stop by to see how things were."

"For right now, we've got it covered. The construction crew is due any day to start digging the trenches for the new water and power lines. Listening to a jackhammer all day will probably put everybody's teeth on edge."

"In that case, I'm glad I won't have to be here to listen to the racket. So I'll head out then."

"And I'll come with you," Tom said.

As they walked back through the security doors, Tom was shaking his head. "I remember when Jenny was just a cute little towheaded kid with her hair in braids. It seems impossible that she's already old enough to be graduating from the police academy."

"Time flies, Tom," Joanna said. "I can barely believe it myself."

"Tell her congrats from me," Tom said. "It's a crying shame she couldn't come work here instead of signing up with Pima County."

"Nepotism and all that," Joanna told him with a smile. "Having her on the job here would never have worked."

Minutes later, Joanna was back in the car and underway. On this bright November day, as she drove through the Mule Mountain Tunnel at the top of the Divide, she looked forward to the flash of bright blue sky that she knew would await her on the far side. On sunny days like this, it was always there, seemingly with a promise of good things to come. In this instance, with Jenny's graduation ceremony scheduled for ten a.m. on Friday morning, good things really were in the offing.

Years earlier, the first time Joanna had made the two-hundred-mile trip from Bisbee to the Arizona Police Officer Academy in Peoria, northwest of Phoenix, things had been far different. As a recently widowed single mom who had just been elected sheriff, she'd had no idea that her stay at the academy would mark the beginning of a whole new life.

Now, with Jenny taking the same course, Joanna's daughter was on track to become the fourth law enforcement officer in the family, following in the footsteps of her maternal grandfather, Cochise County Sheriff D.H. Lathrop; her father, Deputy Andrew Brady; and now her mother, Joanna, too. Although this wasn't an outcome Joanna had ever expected, she was proud of it all the same. She was especially proud that, as an APOA graduate herself, she had not only been invited to speak at the graduation ceremony, she would also be there to pin Jenny's badge on her brand-new Pima County Sheriff's Department uniform.

Joanna had been driving for some time, and the miles had been rolling by, so she was on the bridge crossing the San Pedro in St. David when her thoughts stalled on the word *graduation*, because her graduation from APOA had been Joanna Brady's one and only.

By the middle of the second semester of Joanna's senior year at Bisbee High School, she was already a married woman with a baby bump that was becoming more obvious by the day. Late in April she had received a letter from the superintendent of schools, notifying her that "due to her delicate condition" she wouldn't be allowed to participate in any of the high school ending ceremonies—class night, baccalaureate, or graduation.

Incensed, Joanna had wanted to fight the administration's decision and had gone to her mother for help, insisting that nothing would show under her cap and gown anyway. Unsurprisingly, Eleanor Lathrop had sided with the superintendent of schools. As a consequence, Joanna's high school career had ended with none of the customary rites of passage enjoyed by her classmates, and her diploma had come to her in the mail a week after everyone else received theirs.

As a result, when Jenny had graduated from Northern Arizona University a year and a half earlier, it had been cause for a joyous celebration. The entire family—Joanna, Butch, and Jenny's half-siblings, Dennis and Sage—had all been in attendance at the J. Lawrence Walkup Skydome in Flagstaff to watch Jenny walk across the stage and receive her bachelor of science degree in criminology and criminal justice. After that she'd been offered a coveted yearlong paid internship with MMIV—the Missing and Murdered Indigenous Victims—Task Force based in Denver.

When it came time for her to apply for a job with the Pima County Sheriff's Department, she'd already had a whole year of law enforcement experience under her belt. It also helped that, while still at NAU, she'd been instrumental in helping solve a long-cold homicide case that had originated in Tucson. All of which meant that, unlike her mother, Jennifer Ann Brady was coming into her law enforcement career with a running start.

Butch and Joanna had decided that Jenny's graduation ceremony from APOA would be all about her. Not wanting Dennis and Sage to be a distraction, they had ruled out removing the younger kids from school for the occasion. That meant this trip was strictly a mother/daughter event. Tonight she and Jenny would have a quiet dinner together at the hotel. Tomorrow would be another story. By then it would be a full crowd. Jenny's steady boyfriend, Nick Saunders, would be in attendance as would his mother and her new husband.

Originally Nick had planned to attend veterinary school in Washington State, but once his widowed mother had remarried and the couple had moved from Utah to Arizona, Nick had changed his mind. He was now in his second year of a three-year program at the University of Arizona in Tucson. After finishing her stint with MMIV in Denver, Jenny had focused her job search in Tucson, where she and Nick now shared an apartment. Since they weren't even officially engaged, Joanna wasn't exactly thrilled with that arrangement, but considering her own premarital track record, she kept her mouth shut.

Yes, tonight it would be just the two of them—Joanna and Jenny, mother and daughter. For that Sheriff Joanna Brady was extremely grateful.

CHAPTER 2

PEORIA, ARIZONA
Thursday, November 9, 2023

JOANNA HAD TIMED HER ARRIVAL AT THE HOHOKAM HOTEL so she'd pull up at the front entrance just in time for her three p.m. check-in. As she followed the GPS directions off I-17, she had been stunned by all the changes. At the time she'd attended APOA, the Hohokam had been the only high-rise game in town. That was no longer the case. Another hotel property covered the block where Butch Dixon's Roundhouse Bar and Grill had once stood, because not only had her time at the academy marked the beginning of her long career in law enforcement, it had also been the start of her relationship with Butch.

Butch's restaurant had been the nearest watering hole for APOA attendees. While there, she and Butch had met and hit it off. Later on Butch had used the proceeds from selling his restaurant to build the enviro-friendly hay-bale ranch house where they now lived, having left behind the old farmhouse-style home on High Lonesome Ranch where Andy, Joanna's first husband, had grown up and where Joanna and Jenny had lived after his death. So for Joanna, in many ways, this trip meant revisiting memories from a time that had marked a huge turning point in her life.

Her dinner reservation with Jenny was set for six, so Joanna decided to use the time of relative quiet to work on the remarks she intended to deliver at the graduation ceremony. Many things had changed dramatically since her time at the APOA, and it was difficult to know where to start. Knowing she needed to speak from her heart rather than reading a prepared speech, Joanna spent the next couple of hours putting together a list of the topics she wanted to cover and then saving it in the Notes app on her phone:

How I got here
No Girls Allowed (LeAnn Jessup and me)
Hazing
Shoot/Don't Shoot
Where we are now
First line of defense

By the time her thoughts were organized, Joanna hit the shower. While putting on her makeup, she couldn't help but notice that, as time passed, she was beginning to resemble her mother more and more, except for her hair, that is. Joanna had always been a redhead, but now the red was sprinkled with gray—something Eleanor Lathrop Winfield would never have tolerated. The moment her roots began to show, she had been off to see Helen Barco for an emergency dye job. Joanna, on the other hand, regarded each gray sprig as a non-red badge of courage, and she wore all of them with pride.

Thinking she was early, Joanna headed down to the lobby at ten to six only to find Jenny already seated there, waiting. "It was the last day, so they let us go early," she explained, after giving her mother a hug.

"On good behavior?" Joanna asked.

"I guess," Jenny agreed.

Joanna asked for a quiet table, so the hostess escorted them to the far side of the restaurant where they had a view of the sparsely populated pool. Once snowbirds arrived in force after Thanksgiving, no doubt the pool would be fully occupied at this time of day.

"You won again," Jenny observed once they were seated. "Congrats."

"Thanks," Joanna said. "Since I was running unopposed except for a nutcase from Kansas Settlement who launched a write-in campaign, winning was pretty much a foregone conclusion."

"No election night celebration?"

"Yes, but only a small one. You have to thank the volunteers, but when it comes to election night parties, there's nothing to top the one where Sage decided to make her initial appearance smack in the middle of it."

"Speaking of my little sister, how was her pizza party?"

"Small but good," Joanna replied. "Last year she wanted to invite her whole class. Thank heaven, this year it was five girls only, Sage included, but I'm afraid the whole thing was a bit of a letdown."

"How come?"

"Because she wants to be a barrel racer just like her big sister, and she was hoping for a horse," Joanna admitted. "She says that since Dennis has Kiddo, she should have a horse of her own, at least one that isn't blind, but Butch and I talked it over and decided eight is still a bit young."

When Jenny turned ten, Kiddo, Jenny's first barrel-racing horse, had been a birthday gift to her from her grandparents, Jim Bob and Eva Lou Brady. Once Maggie, Jenny's new ride, had entered the picture, Kiddo had been passed along to Dennis while Sage was forced to make do with Spot, a blind mare the family had rescued years earlier.

"What if I gave her Maggie?" Jenny asked.

Maggie had been Jenny's mount throughout her college barrel-racing career. After graduating from NAU and knowing she'd be in Denver for a yearlong internship with MMIV, Jenny had passed Maggie along to Equine Helpers, a horse therapy organization in Flagstaff that was located at the same ranch facility where she'd boarded Maggie all four years.

Joanna was taken aback. "You're willing to give her up? Are you sure?"

Jenny nodded. "When Nick discovered that he couldn't handle participating in rodeos and going to vet school at the same time, he did the same thing with Dexter. Dex and Maggie are stablemates at Equine Helpers now, but I'm sure they'd let us take them back. After all, Bisbee is a lot closer to Tucson than Flagstaff is, and if both Dexter and Maggie were at High Lonesome, maybe Nick and I could come down and go riding together sometimes too."

"You're serious then?" Joanna asked.

Jenny nodded. "I can't do it for Sage's birthday, though. I already promised her a late birthday shopping trip in Tucson once I get back home."

"She'll love going shopping with you," Joanna said. "Trying to do that with both Dennis and Sage in tow is like mixing oil and water. It never works. But if you and Nick want Dexter and Maggie to stay with us, I'm sure it will be fine with Butch and me."

"Let's think about Christmas then," Jenny said. "Nick will have some time off then, and he could probably go up to Flag and trailer both horses down to Bisbee."

"You're sure he won't mind?"

"Not at all," Jenny said. "He misses his Dex as much as I miss Maggie."

Their waiter showed up just then. They both ordered filet mignons with baked potatoes and crispy Brussels sprouts, accompanied by single glasses of merlot.

Once they were alone again, Joanna steered the conversation back to Jenny's APOA experience. "How's it been?" she asked.

Jenny paused before she answered. "Not a walk in the park," she said finally.

"Hazing?" Joanna asked.

"Some," Jenny agreed with a nod. "How did you know?"

"Been there, done that," Joanna replied. "When I was here, there were only two women in our class. I had already been elected sheriff, and LeAnn Jessup was an unapologetic lesbian. That made us both fair game."

Jenny frowned. "I seem to remember LeAnn. Wasn't she hurt somehow in all that mess? Whatever happened to her?"

Joanna found it interesting that Jenny had focused on what had happened to LeAnn without mentioning the fact that, as part of "all that mess," Jenny and one of her friends had been locked away in an abandoned bomb shelter while Joanna had engaged in a fatal shootout with their would-be kidnapper. Since Jenny hadn't made reference to that, neither did Joanna.

"At the time I met her, LeAnn was a new hire with the Arizona Department of Public Safety. Eventually she joined the FBI. The last I heard, she was still in DC working as a criminal profiler."

"So you both made it through."

"Yes, we did," Joanna agreed. Then, after a pause, she asked, "What kind of hazing?"

Jennifer sighed and her expression darkened. "There are a couple of other guys from Pima County in the class. They got everybody to call me CJ, short for Calamity Jenn."

"Calamity Jenn?" Joanna repeated. "How come?"

"It's a play on Calamity Jane because of all my years in rodeo, but they also spread the rumor that I was underqualified and only got hired because of my personal connection to Dan Pardee, a close family friend of Sheriff Fellows. They passed that one along to anyone who would listen."

"Sounds somewhat familiar," Joanna said. "Try being here as a trainee when you've already been elected sheriff but you have zero law enforcement experience."

"No fun?" Jenny asked.

"Pretty much, but as far as your being underqualified? I'd guess that, after your year of internship with MMIV, the reality is the exact opposite."

"I learned so much there that it's amazing," Jenny said. "Forensics, collecting and handling evidence, DNA profiling, you name it, but I was also incredibly miserable. I cried my eyes out almost every night. If Nick hadn't talked me down out of my tree time after time, I wouldn't have lasted a month."

Joanna was dumbfounded. "That doesn't sound like you. I've never known you to be miserable for even a single day much less for a whole year. How come? What happened?"

"I was the only Anglo," Jenny answered. "I never knew what it's like to be a minority, but now I do. Everybody else was Indigenous, and I wasn't. Anna Rae Green was great. She couldn't have been nicer. And whenever Dan Pardee was around, he was like a breath of fresh air, but most of the people I interacted with on a daily basis—the lab techs, the clerks, the secretaries? They seemed to resent me and made me feel like an unwelcome interloper."

"Which only goes to show that prejudice works in both directions," Joanna observed. "But you know what? I'm guessing having that kind of experience in your background is going to serve you in good stead as a law enforcement officer, especially when you're dealing with people who've had that same kind of treatment at the hands of people who look like you."

"Maybe," Jenny said, after a moment. "I hope so."

Their food came. The room was filling up with other APOA attendees who were celebrating graduation with their families before the fact rather than after.

"Given all that," Joanna said eventually, "you're probably not thrilled at the idea that I'm tomorrow's guest speaker."

"That's not a problem," Jenny said. "Aside from the guys from Pima County, I probably won't run into any of my other classmates ever again."

"Don't be so sure about that," Joanna told her. "Once you're a full-fledged member of the thin blue line, you'll discover that world is a lot smaller than you think."

After that their conversation moved to less stressful topics—about Nick and Jenny's relatively new apartment on River Road and making tentative plans for the upcoming holidays, which would have to be built around Jenny's schedule. As a newly hired deputy, it was unlikely she'd have much time off when it came to the actual holidays themselves.

Once dinner was over and as they were leaving the dining room, Joanna noticed that on their way, Jenny went to the trouble of introducing her to some of her fellow students while bypassing others.

Back in her room, Joanna called Butch to check in, before turning on the TV set to watch that evening's episodes of *Law and Order*. When it was time to plug her phone into the charger, she did a quick search on Google. Then she added one more item to the outline notes for her speech: Calamity Jane.

JOANNA AWAKENED THE NEXT MORNING WITH A TERRIBLE case of nerves. Over the years, she had delivered countless campaign speeches, so she was no stranger to public speaking. The thing is, for each election, the speeches stressed that year's particular hot button, and once she'd given it a time or two, she'd pretty much had the words memorized. This was different. Graduating from the APOA was the beginning of what might well be a lifetime commitment for some of these trainees, and she wanted her words to be memorable.

Her own APOA graduation certainly had been, but for all the wrong reasons. Two weeks before the end of the session, the class's lead instructor, Dave Thompson, had been murdered, and LeAnn Jessup had been gravely injured, so much so that she'd had to complete her training at a later time. Consequently, what should have been a joyous graduation had been more of a subdued memorial service than anything else.

Joanna was determined this one would be different.

At twenty after nine, Joanna reported to the new APOA campus. The old one had looked like what it was—a former religious facility. The new one resembled a newly built junior college campus. As she pulled into a visitor parking place, Leonard Wilson, a former FBI agent and the facility's new director, rolled up in his motorized wheelchair to greet her.

"Welcome, Sheriff Brady," he said. "I'm guessing this place isn't quite the same as the one you attended."

"I'll say," Joanna said. "It's totally different."

"By the way," he added. "That daughter of yours is one sharp cookie. You must be very proud."

"I am that," she said. "Thank you."

"And thank you for agreeing to be our guest speaker today. Let's get you over to the gym for a quick mic check before the doors open at nine thirty."

Once the sound check was over, Joanna and Wilson remained on the podium as guests began arriving. Those included a collection of police chiefs and sheriffs, including Pima County Sheriff Brian Fellows, who were all in attendance to swear in and pin badges on their newly graduated recruits. When Nick Saunders, his mother, and her new husband turned up and settled in the fifth row back, Joanna sent them a tiny wave.

Finally, at ten o'clock sharp, the cadets themselves filed into the room. All were dressed in the uniforms of their prospective agencies. Once inside, the cadets were seated in the two front rows. Since they were arranged alphabetically, Jennifer Ann Brady was number two in line. That first glimpse of Jenny decked out in her Pima County Sheriff's Department uniform took Joanna's breath away.

The program began with an invocation delivered by the chaplain for Phoenix PD and the recitation of the Pledge of Allegiance. After that, Director Leonard Wilson, serving as master of ceremonies, introduced Joanna, letting the people in the room know that not only was she the sheriff of Cochise County, she was also an APOA alum and the mother of one of the current graduates. Joanna stepped forward with her phone in hand and the Notes page showing. After placing the phone on the lectern in front of her, she began.

"This isn't exactly a homecoming for me, because back when I attended APOA, the campus was in a different location. As far as

I can tell, this facility is a major step up from the old one, but it's not just the location that's different.

"My path here was somewhat different from the one most of you are following. By the time I arrived at the APOA and despite the fact that I had zero law enforcement training in my background, I had already been elected sheriff in Cochise County. At the time of my first husband's untimely death, he was a deputy sheriff running for office against his then boss whose department was later found to have been riddled with corruption. After Andy was shot to death on his way home from work, some of the people in town launched a write-in campaign to have me elected in his stead. Once that happened and my election was certified, the board of supervisors appointed me to serve out the remainder of my predecessor's term without waiting until January when I would normally have been sworn into office.

"Because I'd had no law enforcement prior to the election, it didn't take long for me to mess up. While pursuing a homicide suspect on foot, I made a serious mistake and committed one of law enforcement's ten most fatal errors, the one often referred to as Tombstone Courage, aka failure to call for backup. My case of Tombstone Courage wasn't fatal, but within days of learning that tough lesson, I sent myself to APOA so I could be properly trained.

"By studying the two front rows, I can see that out of a class of fifty recruits, a full dozen of you are female. Congrats on that. When I was here, the total number of women was two. I'm incredibly proud to say that one of today's twelve female graduates happens to be my daughter, Jennifer, known to some of you as Calamity Jenn."

At that point, several grins and knowing nods appeared on faces in the two front rows. "I happen to know a little about hazing," Joanna continued. "I suspect that moniker, a takeoff on Calamity Jane, probably wasn't meant to be a compliment, but in actual fact it is. The real Calamity Jane, a sharpshooting frontier woman who insisted on wearing men's clothing, was born Martha Jane Canary. At age fourteen, after the deaths of both her parents, she single-handedly raised her five younger siblings. And, although she eventually gained fame and fortune while traveling with Wild Bill Hickok's Wild West Show, she was well known throughout her life for her kindness and compassion.

"As for how I happen to know about hazing? Turns out there was a certain amount of that back when I was here too. Not surprisingly, a lot of it was aimed at the two women who had seemingly ventured into no-girls-allowed territory. By the way, LeAnn Jessup, my sole female classmate, started out working for the Arizona Department of Public Safety, but she's spent most of her career with the FBI and is currently living in Washington, DC, where she's one of their criminal profilers.

"But getting back to hazing. I'm assuming you've all been through Shoot/Don't Shoot scenarios, correct?"

That question, too, was answered with knowing nods from everyone in the front two rows and from a number of uniform-wearing members of the general audience as well.

"In my case, on the very first day of class, the director singled me out by calling me up to the front of the room and handing me a revolver—a very heavy one as I recall. I was advised that it was loaded with blanks and then directed to stand in front of a black-and-white TV monitor. I was told that during the course of the upcoming video, I would need to make a decision about whether or not to pull the trigger.

"When the video began, the camera was at chest level on an officer pursuing an armed fleeing offender down a residential street. Suddenly the suspect veered off the sidewalk, through a gate, and up a paved walkway to a front porch where he forced his way inside the residence. Moments after the door to the house slammed shut behind him, it opened again. At that point, both the camera and I were located at the far end of the walkway, but when I caught sight of the weapon in his hand, I realized the gunman was coming back out. Knowing I'd never be able to hit his arm from that distance, I waited with my finger on the trigger, hoping for a body shot, and thank God for that. When the suspect actually stepped out onto the porch, he was holding a baby—a toddler actually—cradled in his left arm. If my revolver had been loaded with real bullets instead of blanks, and if I had pulled the trigger in that moment, the child would have died.

"All these years later, I still have nightmares about that. On those occasions when my dream self makes the wrong decision and the baby dies, I wake up shaking. Over time I've learned to not bother trying to go back to sleep after revisiting that scenario. It doesn't work.

"Unfortunately that situation is one some of you may encounter during the course of your careers in law enforcement—the critical decision to pull the trigger or not pull the trigger, and I pray that if and when one of those incidents comes to pass, each of you will make the right decision.

"In our family, Jennifer is actually third-generation law enforcement. Her grandfather, my father—D.H. Lathrop—served as the sheriff of Cochise County long before I was elected. Andrew Brady, Jenny's late father, was a deputy sheriff in that same jurisdiction, before being killed in the line of duty. Now I'm the sheriff. However, the situation on the ground has changed drastically since my father's day.

"Back then and even at the beginning of my years in office, the Cochise County Jail was populated by short-timers—nonviolent offenders who were incarcerated there for a matter of days or weeks rather than for months or years. But that's not how things are now. Often we're forced to deal with violent offenders who, with no way to be bonded out, have to be held in our facility for extended periods of time while awaiting trial.

"The most dangerous inmate currently housed in the Cochise County Jail, my jail, is a human trafficker who crashed a speeding vehicle loaded with twenty-three undocumented individuals. Nine of the twenty-three perished—five at the scene and four more after being transported by EMS. The offender is now being held without bond while awaiting trial on nine counts of felony vehicular homicide. Having waived his right to a speedy trial, there's no telling how long he'll be there. The problem is, he's also a violent member of the Sinaloa Cartel and poses a constant danger not only to my jail personnel, but also to his fellow inmates.

"Still, human trafficking is only a small part of the problems that currently plague us. We all know about the death and destruction being visited on grieving families all over the country by drug addictions due to the uncountable doses of fentanyl and heroin that are currently pouring into our country. This may not be a traditional war zone, but it's a war zone nonetheless. By raising your hand and swearing to serve and protect in any given jurisdiction in the state of Arizona, you'll also be putting yourself on the front line of that war zone—the thin blue line that is now this country's first line of defense.

"So thank you for being here today. Thank you for stepping up and agreeing to do this necessary, incredibly challenging but also incredibly rewarding job. And today, please accept both my congratulations along with my profound gratitude to each and every one of you. Well done!"

Finished, Joanna picked up her phone and then returned to her chair to a round of enthusiastic applause. After that, Wilson rolled his chair forward. One at a time, he began calling the official representatives of the various agencies to come forward where they individually swore in that jurisdiction's graduates. After each new officer repeated his or her oath of office, shiny new badges were pinned on the chests of their impeccably pressed uniforms.

When Pima County Sheriff Brian Fellows wheeled his own chair up the ramp onto the podium, he and Leonard Wilson exchanged small nods of acknowledgment. Then, taking his place center stage, Sheriff Fellows motioned for Joanna to join him. She stood at attention while Jenny and two other recruits, including a guy named Rory Adcock, were called to the podium to swear their oaths of office. When it came time to pin on her daughter's badge, Joanna's hands trembled so hard that she barely managed to fasten it. Although she did her best to put on a brave front, as she returned to her seat, she found herself wiping away tears. She tried to pretend she'd just gotten a speck of dust in her eye, but she doubted anyone in the room was fooled.

Like many others gathered there that day, Joanna Brady was now the parent of a rookie police officer. Soon her own beloved child's life would be on the line right along with everyone else's.

CHAPTER 3

FERTILE, MINNESOTA
1958–1961

ONCE STEVE AND HIS MOTHER MOVED IN WITH GRAMPS, A miracle happened. From first grade on, Steve was an excellent reader—always in the blue bird reading group rather than red or yellow. When Gramps saw the A+s in reading on Steve's report cards, he didn't seem at all surprised.

"You must take after your grandma Joan," Gramps said. "That woman never had a spare moment when she didn't have her nose buried in a book."

As far as Steve knew, Grandma Lucille never read anything—not even the newspaper. A few months after moving into Gramps's house, when Steve went up to the attic to bring down the Christmas decorations, he discovered a large box filled with books—twenty or so. At dinner that night, after lugging the decorations downstairs, he asked about the books.

"Those belonged to your grandma Joan," Gramps explained. "When Grandma Lucille moved in, she didn't approve of having them in the living room, so she boxed 'em up and stored them in the attic."

"Would it be okay if I brought them down to read them?" Steve asked.

"Sure," Gramps said. "Why not? All they're doing now is sitting around in the attic gathering dust."

Once Steve carried the box downstairs, he found a treasure trove of twenty-six books in all—a dozen Ellery Queens, thirteen Agatha Christies, and a thick one called *The Complete Compendium of Sherlock Holmes*. On the inside cover of each book, Steve found an inscription that said either Merry Christmas or Happy Birthday to Joanie, Love, Ori. Gramps's first name was Orson, and that's what most people called him, including Grandma Lucille, but for Grandma Joan, he'd been Ori, and she'd been Joanie. Reading those inscriptions made Steve feel as though he'd just uncovered a long-hidden family secret.

Of course, Steve read more than just the inscriptions. Using a flashlight under his bedding at night, before Christmas vacation was over, Steve had raced through them all. When school started up again, he did an oral book report on *Murder in the Calais Coach*. Miss Beach, his seventh-grade teacher, gave him an A, but she took Steve aside and quietly explained the correct pronunciation of Hercule Poirot's last name.

With all the books, though, and especially with the Sherlock Holmes stories, Steve concentrated on the details, poring over the tiny mistakes killers made that ended up giving them away and helping them get caught. As someone who had gotten away with murder once, not getting caught was Steve's first priority.

As far as he could tell, most killers were caught because they murdered people they knew—lovers, spouses, family members, or business associates. That meant that, in order to solve the crime, all the investigators had to do was go through the victim's circle of acquaintances to find the murderer. Given that, it didn't take long for Steve to realize that he'd been extremely lucky to get away with taking out Grandma Lucille.

More often than not, the person who found the body and reported it turned out to be the one responsible. He was the one who had called the cops about Grandma Lucille's body, but the fact that he'd been eleven at the time had worked in his favor. No one could imagine that a kid that young could possibly be a cold-blooded killer. The other thing going for Steve was the fact that there were absolutely no witnesses to the crime and no physical evidence, either. If the fishing line had cut into her skin, things might have gone differently, but the string that tripped her had caught on the top of her boot, and no one had ever found the fishing string in the bottom of the burning barrel primarily because no one ever went looking.

While Steve studied the murder textbooks that had come to him by way of Grandma Joan's book box, he continued to listen to his voices. They had all applauded what he'd done in getting rid of Grandma Lucille, but for the time being they seemed to be of the opinion that, although he had started down the path to his destiny at a very young age, for right now he needed to bide his time. So that's exactly what he did—he waited.

IN 1961, WHEN STEVE TURNED SIXTEEN, GRAMPS HANDED his 1956 GMC pickup over to his grandson and bought a new vehicle for himself. For the first time in his life, Steve Roper was free as a bird. He no longer had to depend on his bicycle, his friends, his mother, or Gramps to get around. He could go wherever he wanted completely on his own, and that suited him just fine.

In August of that summer, Steve went to the opening day of the Polk County Fair. He knew it was a hunting expedition, but he wasn't sure what he was looking for. He showed up in the middle of the afternoon and hung out around the midway. While there, he saw a few of the kids he knew from high school, but he didn't really mingle with any of them.

As evening came on and it started to cool off a little, the midway got more and more crowded. Eventually Steve saw what he wanted—a little kid, probably seven or eight, dressed in a Cub Scout uniform. He was standing alone by the merry-go-round, crying his eyes out.

"Is something the matter?" Steve asked.

"I had to go to the bathroom," the kid said. "When I came back everyone was gone—my den leader and everybody. I don't know where they are."

"Come on," Steve said kindly, taking the kid's hand. "Let me help you find them."

"Okay," the little boy agreed, stifling a sob and wiping away his tears.

"What's your name?" Steve asked.

"Brian."

"Do you like cotton candy, Brian?"

The little boy nodded.

"Okay then, let's get some."

At the cotton candy stall, Steve bought two sticks of the gooey stuff, one for Brian and one for himself. As they strolled through the midway side by side, Steve kept an eye out for anyone who looked like a Cub Scout leader and also for anyone he knew. Fortunately he saw neither, and what could be more normal than two people, an older boy and a younger one, walking through a fairground in the semidarkness, both of them eating cotton candy?

"Here's an idea," Steve said, as they neared the place where he'd parked his pickup. "How about if I drop you off at the sheriff's station here in town? You'll be safe there. They'll either take you home or call your mother to come get you."

"Will I be in trouble?" Brian wanted to know.

"Nah," Steve told him. "That's what cops do. They look out for lost kids all the time."

"Okay," Brian said.

In the parking lot, Steve helped Brian climb up into the passenger seat. Once he closed the door, only the very top of Brian's crew cut was visible through the window.

"So, you're a Cub Scout?" Steve asked from behind the wheel.

Brian nodded. "A Wolf," he answered. "Were you in Cub Scouts, too?"

Steve shook his head. "I wanted to but never did. Can I see your pin?"

"Sure," Brian said. It took a moment for him to unfasten it and hand it over.

Steve made as if to examine it, then when passing it back, he dropped it onto the floorboard. Brian started to scramble down to find it.

"Just leave it there," Steve advised. "It'll be easier to find it once we stop."

"Okay," Brian agreed.

Clearly the day at the fair and the stress of being lost had worn Brian out. By the time they were headed north on Fertile's main drag, the boy nodded off, with the remains of his ball of cotton candy stuck to the front of his shirt.

Needless to say, Steve drove past the sheriff's station without slowing down. On the far side of town he turned right and headed northeast toward Arthur Lake. Before turning onto the dirt road nearest the lake, Steve doused the lights. As the car slowed, Brian awakened.

"Where are we?" he asked, looking around.

"It's okay," Steve said. "I just wanted to show you something."

Afraid the boy might bolt, as soon as Steve turned off the engine, he grabbed Brian's wrist. "Come on," he said.

But Brian tried to pull away. "No," he said. "It's dark out there. I don't want to go."

"I said come on," Steve repeated, forcibly dragging the boy across the seat.

"No," Brian wailed. "I don't want to. I want my mommy."

"You can't have your mommy," Steve snarled. "You're stuck with me."

By the time Steve had the squirming kid out of the truck, it was all he could do to hang on to him as he walked the two hundred yards from where he'd parked to the edge of the lake, but somehow he managed. Steve knew Arthur Lake well. It was close enough to Gramps's farm that he'd often gone swimming there alone on hot summer days. On this occasion, he didn't like having to walk into the water fully clothed, but with the kid fighting him tooth and nail, he didn't have a choice.

The lake deepened gradually for the first twenty feet or so before a sharp drop-off. By the time Steve was waist-deep in the water, Brian had a death grip around his neck.

"Please, don't drop me," the kid begged. "Please. I can't swim. I don't know how."

Those words were music to Steve's ears. If Brian knew how to swim, Steve would have had a whole other set of problems, and he would have had to bodily hold the boy underwater. Once far enough into the lake, Steve pried Brian's arms loose from around his neck and then threw him as hard as he could into even deeper water. Brian landed face down with a loud splash. Moments later the boy's pale arm and head emerged from the water.

"Help me," he sputtered. "Please."

But Steve didn't help. He simply stood and watched. Twice more the kid managed to kick his way to the surface, but after that third appearance, he disappeared completely. Steve stood there for another minute or two, making sure it really was finished before turning on his heel and splashing his way back to the truck.

As he walked, Steve was relieved to hear the distant rumble of thunder. That was what he needed. If there were any telltale footprints or tire tracks left on the dirt track that led to the lake, a sudden summer rain squall would erase them completely.

Back at the truck, he searched the footwell until he found the Cub Scout pin. After shoving it into his pocket, he ripped off his pants along with his shoes and socks. If someone came looking, it wouldn't do to have mud from Arthur Lake found in the footwell of his truck.

Back home, he rinsed off his soaked clothing in the metal watering trough by the barn and then tiptoed into the house. His mom and Gramps were in the living room, listening to a major league baseball game on the radio. Gramps was deaf as a post by then, and the volume was turned up full blast. As Steve made his way upstairs, they were completely oblivious.

EIGHT-YEAR-OLD BRIAN OLSON WAS REPORTED MISSING the next day. Everyone from the surrounding area, including Steve and Gramps, participated in the massive search effort that followed. Three days later the boy's body was found floating in Arthur Lake, still wearing his Cub Scout uniform. If anyone noticed that his Wolf pin was missing, no one ever mentioned it, at least not in any of the newspaper articles Steve read about the case. In the immediate aftermath, investigators regarded the boy's stepfather as a person of interest, but eventually he was cleared. After that, the case went cold and stayed that way.

As for Cotton Candy Boy's Wolf pin? That went straight into Steve Roper's cigar box, right along with Grandma Lucille's wedding ring. It became the second item in his collection of treasures.

CHAPTER 4

BISBEE, ARIZONA
Saturday, November 25, 2023

FOR THE FIRST TIME EVER, THANKSGIVING DINNER AT HIGH Lonesome Ranch happened on Saturday rather than Thursday. Jenny was scheduled for graveyard shift the week of the holiday, Thanksgiving Day included, and didn't get off work until eight o'clock in the morning. She had gone home long enough to shower and change clothes, then she and Nick set out from Tucson in a driving rainstorm, arriving at High Lonesome Ranch a little past eleven.

"How was it?" Joanna asked, welcoming them inside. Just walking from the car to the house had left them soaked to the skin.

"I've never driven in rain like that," Nick said, shaking his head.

Joanna was well aware of the weather situation. She had just gotten off the phone with Tom Hadlock, her chief deputy, who had reported that so far deputies had been called out to rescue occupants of three different vehicles stranded in flooded dips between Double Adobe and Elfrida.

"The weather forecasters have been saying for days that a storm out in the Pacific was going to bring an atmospheric river into southeastern Arizona this weekend, and for a change they weren't wrong," Joanna said. "Unfortunately, there are far too many drivers out there who refuse to believe that the words 'Do Not Enter When Flooded' actually apply to them. My department's already been called to several fast-water rescues."

"But everybody's safe?" Jenny asked.

"So far so good," Joanna replied.

Jenny went over to hug Butch, who was standing at the counter putting together the family's traditional Turkey Day fruit salad.

"Smells great," Jenny said, sniffing the air in the kitchen. "What's for dinner?" she asked jokingly.

"The works of course," Butch answered. "I baked pumpkin pies yesterday. The turkey's in the oven and the dinner rolls just came out. We're planning on eating right around four."

"Who all's coming?"

"You and Nick, Jim Bob and Eva Lou, and the four of us. Sage just finished setting the table. You're working graveyard, right? Are you going to want a nap before we eat?"

"How did you guess?"

"Not my first rodeo," Butch replied. "The guest room's all yours. Help yourself."

While Jenny headed for the guest room, Nick wandered into the kitchen and eyed the preparations. "Anything I can do to help?"

"Nope," Butch said, depositing the fruit salad in the fridge. "The potatoes are peeled and ready to boil, and everything else is under control. How about a cup of coffee?"

"Thought you'd never ask," Nick replied, settling his lanky frame on the back bench seat of the breakfast nook. Butch poured a fresh mug of coffee for Nick and refilled the two cups he and Joanna had been using. As he passed her one of the cups, her phone rang.

"Work," she explained over her shoulder as she disappeared into the living room.

Butch carried the remaining two cups over to the table and sat down. "How's school?" he asked.

"It's a lot harder than I expected," Nick answered, "but it's going well. Another year and a half to go."

"That'll go by in a blink," Butch assured him.

"I'm sure it will," Nick replied, "but school's not what I wanted to talk to you about, Mr. Dixon."

"Call me Butch, please, but if this is about bringing Dexter and Maggie down here, not to worry. Joanna and I have already talked that over. We're both completely on board."

"It wasn't about Maggie and Dex," Nick said uneasily. "It's about Jen and me."

Butch shifted in his own seat. "You're not breaking up, are you?"

"Just the opposite," Nick answered nervously. "I know you're not her biological father, but you've been Jen's dad for more than half her life, so I'm asking for her hand in marriage—if it's all right with you, that is."

Butch sputtered momentarily on half a mouthful of coffee, which morphed into a coughing fit.

"You love her, don't you?" he asked once he could speak again.

"Absolutely!" Nick declared.

"Have you asked her yet?"

"Not really, but I have a ring in my pocket, and I'm planning on asking her at dinner today, if you don't mind."

"Bended knee and everything?" Butch asked with a grin.

"That's the idea."

"You've got my approval, but good luck with the bended knee bit," Butch added. "In my experience, these Brady women aren't big on grand gestures."

"What grand gestures?" Joanna asked, returning to the kitchen.

"Nothing much," Butch said quickly. "We were just shooting the breeze, but you look worried. What's up?"

"One of the rain cells parked itself right over San Jose Peak and the headwaters of the San Pedro. The river was already running bank to bank, and we're afraid it's about to get worse. The bridges on Highways 90 and 92 should be fine, but if the water gets too high, on Highway 80 it could damage not only the old bridge in St. David, but also threaten the one that's under construction."

The San Pedro, the only north-flowing river in Arizona, starts at the base of San Jose, just across the border in Mexico, and travels north until it drains into the Gila. Flash floods on the river have been known to come complete with walls of muddy water twelve feet high.

"Are you going to have to go in?" Butch asked.

"Not so far," Joanna replied. "The highway department has observers on the scene. They'll make the call and let us know if we need to post detours."

"Detours," Nick repeated. "Does that mean we won't be able to get back to Tucson the same way we came?"

Joanna nodded. "You may have to go back by way of Sierra Vista. It's a little longer, but, because the roads are better, it takes about the same amount of time."

Dennis shot into the kitchen. "I'm about to turn on *Trains, Planes, and Automobiles*," he announced. "Anybody interested?"

"I'm for that," Nick said, scrambling out of the breakfast nook. "That's one of my faves."

"What's wrong with him?" Joanna asked. "He looked like I'd caught him with one hand in the cookie jar."

"Maybe you did," Butch mumbled under his breath. "But in case you have to go out, I'm going to turn up the heat on that bird and start the potatoes. If I know you, we're better off eating earlier than later."

"Good thinking," Joanna said. "I'll call Jim Bob and Eva Lou and let them know the timeline is changing."

In actual fact, dinner was on the table by three fifteen, a good forty-five minutes early. When it was time for dessert, Nick jumped up and offered to help serve. Jenny's was the last plate he brought to the table, and an engagement ring was front and center, resting in a bed of whipped cream at the very tip of her piece of pumpkin pie.

To Butch's amusement, his future son-in-law really did get down on one knee when he offered Jenny her plate. "Jennifer Ann Brady," he said, "will you marry me?"

For a long moment after she saw it, Jenny simply stared. "Should I eat it or wear it?" she asked finally.

"Wear it by all means," Nick said, "but is that a yes or a no?"

"It's a definite yes," she said.

The joyous celebration that followed, complete with passable coyote yips from both Dennis and Sage, was cut short by another call on Joanna's phone, this one from Dispatch.

Stepping away from the table, Joanna made the sudden switch from wife and mother to cop. "What's up?" she asked. "Is the bridge in St. David okay?"

"The bridge is fine," the dispatcher responded, "but one of the highway workers assigned to clear debris away from under it pulled out a duffel bag. Turns out there's a dead body inside."

"A body?" Joanna repeated.

"Yes," came the answer. "I'm told it's a little kid."

Joanna took a steadying breath. "Okay," she said. "I'm on my way."

"Sorry," she said to the tableful of people who were watching her. "Duty calls."

Before leaving the house, she took her Glock out of the gun safe in the laundry room and belted it in place. Then, glancing outside, she added a slicker and her Stetson. Although she had one of those—regarded as necessary equipment for any self-respecting sheriff of Cochise County—she seldom wore it. Rainy days were the exception because the sturdy felt kept the rain out of her hair and away from her eyes.

Butch followed her out to the garage to kiss her goodbye. "What if the washes are running?" he asked.

There weren't any washes on the highway between Bisbee and St. David. However, there were four major washes on High Lonesome Road between their ranch and Double Adobe Road. The Mule Mountains off to the west marked the back boundary of the ranch itself, and runoff from those could quickly turn those easterly-flowing washes into treacherous rapids.

"I'll be fine," she said, but she wasn't entirely sure.

When Joanna reached the first wash, she actually got out to check. Muddy water was running a little over four inches deep, but with no visible wall of water approaching, she got back into her Interceptor, put it in low, and plowed on, making it through all four washes without pausing again or second-guessing herself.

Once on Highway 80, she took a deep breath and brought her vehicle up to speed as much as the water-soaked pavement allowed. It was still raining, but not nearly as hard as it had been. St. David was fifty minutes plus north of Bisbee. In this weather, she knew it was going to take all of that.

Thinking about what had happened at dinner, she gave Nick Saunders credit for popping the question in front of the whole family. That was something Joanna actually appreciated. Yes, in many ways she'd be losing a daughter once Jenny married, but that generous gesture on Nick's part suggested that, in return, she might end up gaining another son.

With that settled in her mind, Joanna turned her thoughts to what she'd be encountering at the scene. She wasn't sure which of her detectives would be there because Tom Hadlock was now in charge of scheduling. Dispatch had told her that the body in the duffel bag belonged to a child. What child? Whose? As far as she knew no missing children had been reported anywhere in her jurisdiction or even in Arizona, so if this wasn't a currently active case, was it from somewhere else or was it maybe a cold case?

The body had been pulled from the San Pedro. Obviously, the bridge in St. David wasn't the crime scene or even the actual dump site. And since the headwaters of the San Pedro were across the line in Mexico, there was a chance the victim was also from there. Captain Arturo Peña, the man in charge of the Federales unit based in Naco, Sonora, was someone Joanna knew personally. He had attended Bisbee High School as a foreign student and had eventually graduated from the University of Arizona with a degree in criminal justice, but now wasn't the time to call him—not until she knew more about what was going on.

Since the rain was still falling, there was no flash of blue sky as she emerged on the far side of the Mule Mountain Tunnel. The landscape around her was a dingy gray. The usually red rocky cliffs looming over the right-hand side of the highway had turned into cascading waterfalls. Once that water too fed into the Mule Mountain Creek, it would eventually flow into the San Pedro, making things farther downstream that much worse.

Approaching Tombstone, the rain let up a little, so Joanna took the opportunity to call in to Dispatch. "Who all's working the scene in St. David?" she asked.

"Detective Howell is already there. Detective Raymond is ten minutes out. Highway 80 is coned down to one lane on the bridge. Deputies Creighton and Nuñez are directing traffic."

"What about the ME?"

"Dr. Baldwin just arrived. Where are you?"

Kendra Baldwin's home was up Tombstone Canyon in Old Bisbee, so it made sense that she'd be fifteen or twenty minutes ahead of Joanna.

"I'm just passing Tombstone Airport Road," Joanna replied, but glancing out the window, the only evidence of an airport was a dirt runway surrounded by a few metal shacks scattered across a mostly barren landscape. There wasn't a single aircraft in sight. "Let people know I'll be there as soon as I can."

Once she arrived in St. David, due to the traffic backup, Joanna parked on the shoulder of the road, a good half mile from the bridge itself. She nodded in Deputy Nuñez's direction as she walked past. Nearing the river, Joanna was amazed to see pooling water spread across an adjoining field leaving the cattle grazing there wading in three to four inches of standing water.

Prior to the 7.5 Sonoran Earthquake of 1887, the San Pedro had been deep enough that people had been able to use rafts to carry people and goods up and down the river. At that time, the area around what was now the small farming community of St. David had been little more than a malarial swamp. After the quake, however, the river had gone underground. These days there was seldom more than a trickle of water in the riverbed. Today, however, it was filled by a roaring flood that overflowed the riverbanks.

Coming closer, Joanna saw a clutch of people gathered in the middle of the bridge's eastbound lanes where someone was erecting a small metal and canvas canopy. It wasn't until Joanna reached the bridge itself that she was able to see the blue cloth bundle sheltering underneath the temporary structure. Just then a puff of wind blew the distinctive smell of human decomposition into Joanna's nostrils. If this was a cold case, it wasn't nearly cold enough.

Dr. Kendra Baldwin, dressed in a hazmat suit and trailed by both Detectives Howell and Raymond, stepped forward to greet Joanna. "What a way to spend Thanksgiving weekend!" she said.

"I'll say," Joanna agreed. "What have we got?"

"Our victim is a little boy," Kendra answered. "Still has his baby teeth so probably five years. Black hair, so Hispanic maybe, and he appears to be fully clothed."

"Dead for how long?"

"I'd estimate a week at least, but the body hasn't been in the water for nearly that long. I'm guessing someone tried to bury him in the riverbed . . ."

". . . and the floodwaters brought the bag to the surface and carried it here?" Joanna finished.

Kendra nodded.

"Cause of death?"

"No obvious gunshot or stab wounds. We'll have to wait until the autopsy to know for sure, but I'm prepared to call this one a homicide from the get-go. I say we pack him up and get him back to the morgue." With that the ME turned to the two detectives. "This poor kid's been dead for a while, so there's no real rush, and I have out-of-town company. Autopsy Monday morning at nine?"

Detectives Deb Howell and Garth Raymond nodded in unison.

"We'll be there," Deb said.

With most homicide cases, this would be the time to start canvassing the neighborhood, looking for witnesses and information. However, knowing the cows in the field wouldn't have much of anything to say in that regard, there wasn't any point in doing one, so Joanna separated herself from the group and went in search of the crew from the Highway Department. Four guys, using long-handled hooks, were still hauling debris out of the water where it had already formed an eight-foot-tall pile of waterlogged tree branches and junk, which was also stacked in the eastbound lane. Joanna located Bill Snider, the man in charge of the crew, sitting nearby in a pickup, having a smoke, and talking on his radio.

Joanna tapped on the window. "You guys are the ones who found the body?" she asked as soon as he rolled it down.

Snider nodded. "Soon as John Boy zipped open that bag, he barfed his guts out. Stunk like a son of a bitch."

Welcome to my world, Joanna thought.

"How are things looking as far as the bridge is concerned?" she asked.

"We're doing our best to keep the river free of debris so water doesn't dam up against it. The guy who owns that field," he added, pointing toward the wading cattle, "a Mr. Duvall, he came out with a backhoe and dug a diversion ditch. That's taking some of the pressure off the bridge. With the rain finally letting up, the old bridge should be okay, but I'm worried about the freshly poured footings on the new one. Some of those may be goners."

"What about the trash in the middle of the highway?" Joanna asked.

"A dump truck and a front-end loader are coming to haul it away, but that's going to take another hour at least, so I'll need your guys directing traffic until then."

"Fair enough," Joanna said. "I'll let my deputies know."

Back on the bridge, she watched as the body was loaded into the ME's minivan—Kendra's so-called body wagon. Moments later the canopy came down as well. Once the ME drove away, so did the two detectives. Next Joanna consulted with her two deputies, letting them know they'd need to continue directing traffic until the debris could be hauled away. Once that was done, she headed back to her Interceptor, where she discovered she had company.

The vehicle that had been parked directly in front of hers had moved. Joanna quickly recognized the battered RAV4 parked in its place belonged to one of her least favorite people in the world, local newshound Marliss Shackleford.

A few weeks earlier, Marliss and her then boyfriend had had a falling-out. Afterward he had expressed his anger by smashing her car with a baseball bat, without leaving a single panel of the vehicle undamaged. The incident itself had occurred inside the Bisbee city limits, so it hadn't been investigated by the sheriff's department. However, after his arrest, the boyfriend had been unable to post bond, and he was currently one of the inmates contributing to Joanna's overcrowding problem in the Cochise County Jail.

After the incident, the car had been deemed drivable, so while Marliss waited for her turn with a body shop appointment, she was driving a vehicle that appeared to be one short step away from a wrecking yard. A small part of Joanna Brady's soul wasn't sorry that Marliss Shackleford was stuck driving a junker. It was exactly what she deserved.

Previously the woman had been a reporter on the staff of a local newspaper, the *Bisbee Bee*, where her weekly column "Bisbee Buzzings" had often focused on what the columnist perceived as Joanna's many shortcomings in her handling of the Cochise County Sheriff's Department. Once the newspaper had bitten the dust, however, Marliss had reinvented herself by starting a website called Cochise County Courier, featuring her twice-weekly crime column, where she continued to be a royal pain in Joanna's butt. Now the woman herself stood leaning against the hood of Joanna's Interceptor.

"Hello, Sheriff Brady," Marliss said. "Dead kid, right?" she added.

"Active investigation," Joanna muttered through gritted teeth, hoping to put the woman off. "No further comment until after the autopsy, which is scheduled for Monday morning."

"Come on," Marliss wheedled. "I already talked to the poor guy who hauled the duffel bag out of the water and zipped it open. I'll bet he won't do that again. Any idea who the kid is? Where he came from?"

"I said no comment and I meant it," Joanna insisted, bypassing Marliss and heading for the Interceptor's driver's door, but Marliss trailed after her.

"I've been looking online," Marliss continued, placing one hand on the door to keep Joanna from opening it. "I'm not finding any recent reports of missing kids, so where did this one come from?"

"Where he came from is none of your business."

"So it's a boy then?" Marliss crowed. "A missing boy?"

Bodily removing Marliss's hand from the door, Joanna wrenched it open. "Yes," she snapped. "Now get the hell away from my car."

"Any comments about winning the election?" Marliss continued.

"None!" Joanna responded. "No comments at all."

That's when Joanna noticed that Marliss was holding a cell phone in her hand. No doubt it was set to record, and everything Joanna had just said would be front and center on Marliss's next Cochise County Courier crime column post.

So be it, Joanna thought to herself, leaving Marliss standing there watching. *I already won, so do your worst.*

CHAPTER 5

FERTILE, MINNESOTA
Spring 1962

STEVE STARTED HIS JUNIOR YEAR IN HIGH SCHOOL A MONTH after his encounter with Brian Olson in August of 1961. By then the voices of Hoot and King Kong had retired from the field of battle, replaced by ones who were less excitable and somewhat more discreet. His favorite, of course, and by far the smartest of the bunch, was one he called Sherlock. Although Arthur Conan Doyle never said as much, and neither did Steve's personal voice version, Steve suspected that in addition to being a drug addict, there was a good chance that Sherlock Holmes had been queer as a three-dollar bill.

Not that Steve himself was. Early on, he had figured out that he was different from other boys. Most of them were interested in girls. Steve wasn't, and boys who were interested in boys were constant targets for bullying and derision. In actual fact, Steve wasn't interested in boys, either, but he was smart enough to choose the path of least resistance.

He pretended that he liked girls in the same way he had acted sad at Grandma Lucille's funeral. Steve was a fair baseball player for Fertile-Beltrami High School. He didn't do so often, but once he connected with a ball, he could run like the wind. That meant that at school, he hung out with the jocks, whistling and making rude comments about passing girls right along with the rest of them. He smoked and drank and did his fair share of sissy bullying, too. All that served to entrench him as one of the guys, and as a card-carrying member of the in-crowd. It also made him an attractive target for girls.

Of those, Mindy Peterson was by far the most persistent and, ultimately, the most challenging to shake off. She was a cute little blonde, one of the cheerleaders, and a straight-A student. In the spring of their junior year, she was also Steve's date for the prom. That night, however, she was far more interested in making out than she was in dancing, and she was more than a little annoyed when Steve took exception to her idea of their "going all the way."

"You don't have to worry," she pouted when he objected. "My mom got me a prescription. I'm on the pill."

"I said no, and I mean it," Steve had told her. "I'm a virgin, and that's what I want to be on my wedding night." Not that he ever intended to have one of those.

At that point, however, Mindy had gotten out of his car (Gramps's new Buick, really) and flounced off across the parking lot where she caught a ride home with someone else. Word about his refusal spread quickly because, by the next week, guys at school started calling him "Steve, the Verge."

He put up a good front, telling them all in no uncertain terms to go screw themselves, adding that, "I'd a whole lot rather be a virgin than a daddy."

Eventually it became apparent that Mindy had lied to him about her being on the pill. Shortly after the prom, she started dating Wilbur Morton, the Fertile-Beltrami Falcons' lead quarterback. Wilbur was good enough that he probably would have ended up with a full-ride athletic scholarship, but by the time graduation rolled around, Mindy was several months pregnant. They married two weeks after graduation. Steve was already at the University of Minnesota in St. Paul when his mother sent him a clipping of the birth announcement that had shown up in Polk County's weekly newspaper, the *Polk County Register*. As soon as Steve saw the clipping, his heart was flooded with gratitude. *Thank God I dodged that bullet*, he told himself.

But the incident with Mindy still had consequences. In the week following the ill-fated prom, the voices had all chimed in again, because being called "Steve the Verge" pissed them off every bit as much as it did Steve. On Friday, May 25, 1962, a week after it happened, he told his mother that he and some of his buddies were going to spend the weekend fishing at a favorite spot at Detroit Lakes. After packing up his fishing and camping gear, off he went—entirely on his own.

Instead of heading southeast, he took Highway 2 in the opposite direction—northwest. After crossing the state line into North Dakota and driving through Grand Forks, he continued west. Just beyond the entrance to Grand Forks Air Force Base, he spotted a hitchhiker standing on the shoulder of the road. At first he couldn't tell if the person was male or female, but as he pulled over, he was relieved to see an attractive young woman wearing a Levi jacket, jeans, and a pair of worn cowboy boots. Her straight black hair was pulled back in a sleek ponytail, and her tanned skin and prominent cheekbones told him she was most likely Indian.

Steve leaned over and rolled down the passenger window. "Where are you headed?" he asked.

"Devil's Lake," she answered.

"That's on my way," he said. "I'll drop you off. Hop in."

She climbed in, pulling the door shut behind her. Steve noticed she wasn't carrying anything at all—no purse, luggage, or backpack.

"Day trip?" he asked.

She nodded. "It's my grandmother's birthday. I have to be back at work in Grand Forks tomorrow." She sat with her left hand resting on her knee and her right elbow and arm on the armrest.

"Where do you work?"

"I'm a nurse's aide at the hospital."

Steve stole a glance in her direction. She was a little bit of a thing, probably no more than five four, and fairly good looking, except for a pair of very thick glasses. The poor girl had to be extremely nearsighted. That's when he noticed the brightly colored beaded bracelet on her left wrist.

"Nice bracelet," he commented. "Did you make it?"

"My grandmother did," she answered. "She does beadwork."

That was the end of the conversation. Steve knew from previous fishing expeditions with Gramps that the Turtle River, a tributary of the Mississippi, ran west to east a few miles north of Highway 2. Figuring that was as good a place as any for what he had in mind, he immediately began looking for a turnoff. Once he spotted one and began to slow down, his passenger reached for the door handle. Worried she would bail out of the GMC as soon as he slowed enough to make the turn, he reached out and grabbed her left wrist. Struggling against his grip, she seemed to bend over. An instant later he felt a searing pain in his upper right arm.

Much to his astonishment, the little bitch had pulled a switchblade out of her boot and sliced open his arm with the damned thing! Furious, he slammed on the brakes, and the girl shot forward, slamming her forehead on the inside of the windshield hard enough to leave a circular spiderweb of cracks in the glass. Once the truck stopped moving, Steve sat for a shaken moment, watching the blood spurt from the wound in his arm. Then he looked at the girl. Apparently she was out cold, but there was no telling how long she'd stay that way.

Fortunately, there was no visible traffic coming or going in either direction. Steve quickly turned onto the dirt track and headed north. A hundred yards or so later, he stopped again. Hurriedly he grabbed what he needed from the toolbox in the bed of his pickup—a precut length of rope and a roll of duct tape—neither of which ended up being necessary. By the time he returned to the passenger compartment and got a good look at her, he could tell she was still breathing.

Steve knew he needed to get a tourniquet on his arm, but he didn't dare try to do that while still parked on the side of the road. Instead, he drove north, not stopping again until he had reached the relative seclusion of a forested area alongside the river. There he was able to nose the pickup off the shoulder of the road and into a copse of trees. Working with only his left hand, he managed to twist the duct tape into a tourniquet that eventually slowed the bleeding. Of course the arm of his shirt was a blood-soaked mess and so was the cab of his truck.

By then she was starting to come to. Worried about being spotted by a passerby, Steve grabbed her by the neck and squeezed the life out of her, watching for that magic moment when the light went out of her eyes. Once that happened, he hauled the girl out of the truck, hefted her up onto his left shoulder, and headed off. Feeling a bit lightheaded, he made frustratingly slow progress, but eventually he reached the riverbank. Rather than just tossing her into the water at the first available spot, Steve forced himself to keep going. At last, just when he was almost ready to give up, he spotted what he was looking for—a place where a fallen tree had tumbled into the river.

Wading into the shallow water, he attempted to push her body under the log, expecting that being trapped under the tree would help keep her out of sight. Just when he had her almost where he wanted, the body hit a snag of some kind. That's also when he heard the sound of an approaching vehicle. In a blind panic that the driver might pull into the same sheltered spot he had used, Steve gave the girl's face a powerful shove, forcing the back of her head into the soft earth of the grassy riverbank. Then he loped away in such a hurry that he completely forgot about the beaded bracelet. He had intended to take that along with him to add to his cigar box, but by the time he remembered, it was too late. Instead, he kept right on going.

As soon as he got in the truck, the first thing he saw was the white ivory handle of the bloodied switchblade, lying right there in plain sight in the passenger footwell. He grabbed it up, knowing that this time the knife, not the bracelet, would be his trophy. In the future it would also serve as a reminder for him to expect the unexpected.

Only when he was back behind the wheel did he finally remove the tourniquet. Luckily the bleeding had stopped. In Grand Forks, he ventured into a Rexall drugstore where he told the clerk that he'd been in a car accident. Ignoring the clerk's suggestion that Steve should probably stop by the ER for stitches, he bought a package of bandages. He also visited the local JCPenny and replaced his bloodied jeans and shirt, once again claiming that he'd been in a wreck when a deer had smashed into his windshield. When it came time to leave Grand Forks, however, he didn't go the way he had come. Instead he headed straight south to Fargo and then cut over to Detroit Lakes where he set up camp.

Steve's arm hurt like a son of a bitch that night, and he didn't get a wink of sleep. The next morning, he went out early and caught a few fish so he wouldn't come home empty-handed. Before leaving Detroit Lakes, he bought some snacks at a local country store, conveniently leaving the printed receipt in the pocket of his new jeans where his mother was bound to find it.

Somewhere along the way, he stopped off in a secluded spot and used the shovel he kept in the bed of the pickup to attack the windshield, turning the spiderweb of cracks printed on the inside of the glass into a jagged hole from the outside. When he got home, he told Gramps and his mother the same story he'd told everyone else—the one about the deer hitting the windshield.

"Must have been one hell of a buck," Gramps commented upon observing the damage to the truck. "Good thing he jumped over the hood. If you'd hit him head-on, you'd probably be dead, too."

Steve nodded in agreement. "An eight-pointer," he said. "Ended up tearing hell out of my arm."

Opening the door, Gramps studied the bloodied seat. "Looks like you bled like a stuck pig."

"I did," Steve agreed.

"Well, sir," Gramps said after a pause. "Summer's coming on. You can try cleaning that seat till the cows come home, but once the weather heats up, all the blood you can't see is going to stink like crazy."

After that, Gramps walked all the way around the pickup, kicking the tires and examining the spots where rust had eaten through the metal. Finally, he stopped inspecting the vehicle, put his thumbs through the straps on his overalls, and turned back to his grandson.

"Saw a cute little blue-and-white Chevy Bel Air over at the Gus Elkins's dealership this afternoon," he said. "Looks like it might be just the thing for a young man like you to use to drive himself from Fertile here down to St. Paul to go to the university."

Steve's jaw literally dropped. Recently Gramps had sold the farmhouse and the other farms he'd bought after Lucille's death for a surprisingly large amount of money. He still wore his customary overalls, not because he lived on the farm, but because they weren't worn out yet. With some of the proceeds, he'd purchased and remodeled the house in town where he and his daughter and grandson now lived. The house just happened to be within walking distance of the Country Inn, the restaurant where Steve's mother had once waited tables. With Gramps's help, she now owned the joint.

"Wow," Steve said at last. "You mean it? A brand-new Chevy Bel Air?"

"I certainly do," Gramps said. "You've always been a good boy. Now you're a fine young man who'll be going off to college in the fall. I think you've earned it."

"Thanks, Gramps," Steve said. "I don't know what to say."

"Don't say anything at all," Gramps said. "Just keep on doing what you've been doing. Now how about if we go inside and have your mom cook up that batch of fresh fish."

That's what they had for dinner that night. When it was time to go to bed, before Steve Roper laid himself down to sleep, he did his best to clean the blood off the blade of his newly acquired, ivory-handled switchblade. Then he stowed it in his trusty cigar box.

As for the girl whose body he'd dumped in the Turtle River? He never heard word one about her. For people living in western Minnesota, what happened in neighboring North Dakota could just as well have happened in a foreign country. Then there was that other thing. Turtle River Girl was Indian. In a part of the country where people like Gramps were still known to say, "The only good Indian is a dead one," stories about missing or murdered Sioux women didn't get much traction—not with the press and not with law enforcement, either.

For Steve Roper in Fertile, Minnesota, that was all to the good.

Over in Devil's Lake, North Dakota, however, the murder of Amanda Hudson was big news in the *Ramsey County Gazette*:

On Saturday, May 26, the body of Amanda Marie Hudson of Grand Forks, North Dakota, was found in a shallow pool of the Turtle River, twenty miles west of Grand Forks. Investigators from the North Dakota Highway Patrol are treating her death as a homicide.

Miss Hudson, age 21 and a 1959 graduate of Devil's Lake High School, is the daughter of Elmer and Bonnie Hudson of Devil's Lake.

According to a Highway Patrol spokesman, the victim had been dead for approximately twenty-four hours at the time the body was found, and the cause of death was determined to be manual strangulation.

Some blood evidence was located at the scene, but there was no sign of a struggle. The body was fully clothed at the time it was found, and there was no sign of a sexual assault. The North Dakota Highway Patrol is asking for anyone who might have information concerning this incident to please call their local hot line.

After graduating from Devil's Lake High School, Miss Hudson moved to Grand Forks where she was employed as a nurse's aide at Grand Forks General Hospital on a part-time basis while working toward a nursing degree at Grand Forks University.

The eldest of two children, she is survived by her parents, Elmer and Bonnie Hudson, her younger brother, Lucas, and her maternal grandmother, Madeline Running Deer.

Miss Hudson's funeral will be held at 2:00 p.m. on Saturday, June 2, at the Devil's Lake Methodist Church. Burial will follow at Devil's Lake Memorial Cemetery.

The investigation that followed Amanda Hudson's death was cursory at best. No suspicious vehicles had been spotted at the scene, and no suspects were ever identified. Within a matter of months, Turtle River Girl's homicide case went cold and, like Cotton Candy Boy's death in nearby Fertile, Minnesota, it stayed that way.

CHAPTER 6

BISBEE, ARIZONA
Sunday, November 26, 2023

SUNDAY MORNING DAWNED CLEAR AND DRY, AND FOR JO-anna, it really was a day of rest. Their breakfast, featuring Butch's French toast, was almost as celebratory as their Thanksgiving dinner had been. Jenny, with her modest circular cut diamond flashing on her finger, was absolutely aglow. Watching her, Joanna was reminded of how she had felt once she and Butch had become engaged.

Days after that happened, she'd had to renew her driver's license. The photo for that new license was the best one of her that had ever been taken, bar none, including the formal campaign ones she had professionally done over the years. In fact, she still kept that old long-out-of-date license in the bottom of the jewelry box on her dresser.

During breakfast, Jenny and Nick dropped the news that Dex and Maggie would be coming to live at High Lonesome Ranch sometime between Christmas and New Year's, with Dennis in charge of Dex and Sage taking care of Maggie.

Sage was absolutely over the moon. "A real barrel-racing horse, are you kidding?"

"Not kidding," Nick answered.

"Will you give me lessons?" Sage demanded of Jenny.

"When I can," Jenny replied, "but remember, when we come to visit, Nick and I get first dibs on who we ride."

Nick had studying to do that afternoon, so the couple planned to leave for Tucson once everyone else headed out for church. With breakfast over and Nick and Butch in charge of cleanup, Joanna tagged along when Jenny went into the bedroom to pack.

"Things were so busy yesterday that we barely had a chance to talk," Joanna said. "How are things going with your TO?" Joanna knew the name of Jenny's training officer—Deputy Rick Mosley—but that was all.

"Deputy Mosley's old school, but he's okay," Jenny answered. "He may be strict, but he doesn't pull any punches, and I'm learning a lot."

"Good," Joanna said. "Glad to hear it."

"I'm a little worried about being on graveyard right now," Jenny said. "That's when a lot of the bad stuff happens."

Joanna knew that all too well. Midnight to eight was when the bars let out and the drunks hit the roads to commit murder and mayhem. Not only that, coming home to go to sleep when the rest of the world is just waking up is a major disruption to the human body.

"You'll be fine," she said.

"I hope so."

"What about Rory Adcock? Is he still giving you guff with all that Calamity Jenn crap?"

Jenny favored her mother with a searching look. "How did you know he was behind it?" she wanted to know. "I never told you who it was."

"You didn't have to," Joanna replied. "I'm pretty good when it comes to reading faces. He was sitting right next to you at that graduation ceremony. I saw the smirk on his face when I mentioned Calamity Jenn in my talk."

Jenny shook her head. "For some reason, he's been surprisingly quiet."

Not surprising to me, Joanna thought. *Sheriff Brian Fellows probably told him to knock it off.*

"Good," she said aloud. "Let's hope he stays that way."

After church, with Nick and Jenny gone, the house went quiet. Joanna and Butch spent the afternoon watching NFL football. Dinner that night was Thanksgiving dinner revisited. This time there was no engagement ring on anyone's slice of leftover pumpkin pie.

CHAPTER 7

BISBEE, ARIZONA
Monday, November 27, 2023

ON MONDAY MORNING, JOANNA ARRIVED AT WORK A FEW minutes late and a little bleary-eyed. She had spent a good part of the night worrying about Jenny's working the graveyard shift. Obviously nothing out of the ordinary had happened or Joanna would have heard about it by now. She headed straight to Tom Hadlock's office. Her chief deputy was already at his desk.

"How are things?" she asked.

Tom checked his watch. "Everybody's packed and ready to go." His phone rang. He picked it up, listened for a moment, and then said. "Okay, I'll be right there." Standing up he told Joanna, "Gotta go. Chain Gang's waiting in the sally port."

With that he hustled out of his office, and Joanna returned to her own. Chain Gang was Arizona law enforcement's moniker for a network of fifteen-passenger vans that traveled the state, transporting incarcerated individuals from one location to another. Today ten of Joanna's nonviolent long-term inmates would be traveling from the Cochise County Jail to Saguaro Hills, a recently opened but privately operated medium-security penal facility north of Phoenix. Joanna wouldn't have known that was even an option had she not attended Jenny's graduation.

During the reception following the ceremony, Joanna had spotted Sheriff Fellows with his wheelchair parked at a table. She had met him before—and had actually played poker with him at a couple of the statewide Sheriff's Association gatherings, but those events had been strictly professional. Now he was Jenny's boss, so as Joanna had approached his table, she wasn't quite sure how to handle the situation.

"Hey, there, Sheriff Brady," Fellows said when he saw her. "How are things down in Cochise County?"

Joanna set her coffee down on the table. "Let's see," she said. "My jail inmates are on the warpath because the place is jammed to the gills. Turns out I'm short on space for solitary confinement. The only way to get more of that involves doing a major remodel of the jail. The plans are drawn up, but the planning and zoning folks are driving me nuts."

Much to Joanna's surprise, Sheriff Fellows had broken into a burst of hearty laughter. "Tell me about it," he said, "and just you wait. Once you've finished doing battle with planning and zoning, you'll have to deal with building inspectors out the kazoo."

"Sounds like you've been there and done that," Joanna observed.

"Actually I have," Fellows replied with a nod. "Nobody in Pima County ever expected a newly elected sheriff to be someone stuck in a wheelchair. The sheriff's restroom facilities were anything but handicapped friendly. Supposedly it was reserved for my use only, but I couldn't get my wheelchair inside it, much less turn it around. Just because the building inspectors work for the same county I do doesn't mean they gave us any breaks. The bathroom remodel took for damned ever!"

"I'm not alone then?" Joanna asked.

"Hardly," Fellows said, but by then the laughter had gone out of his voice. "About your overcrowding situation, though, have you heard of a place called Saguaro Hills?"

"Never. What is it?"

"A privately operated medium-security facility that just opened north of Phoenix. Right now they've got lots of bed availability and not enough takers."

"So?"

"You know about all those twofer deals at Safeway—buy one get one free?"

Joanna nodded.

"Right now, Saguaro Hills has a similar deal—sort of a grand-opening special. You can send five inmates and only pay for four. You're not the only one dealing with too many inmates and not enough room. I penciled it out. Even after paying to have some of my inmates transported there, with this special deal, the cost's not much more than housing them at home."

Joanna had known instantly that shipping out ten of her inmates would go a long way toward solving the problem. "Thanks," she said. "I'll look into it."

She had started to get to her feet at that point, but Fellows had motioned her back into her chair.

"There wasn't any favoritism, you know," he said. "I didn't hire Jenny because you and I know each other. Believe me, after that year of working for the MMIV, she was miles ahead of all the other applicants. She's top-drawer."

"I did wonder," Joanna admitted, "so thank you for saying that."

"You're welcome," Fellows said, "and don't worry, Sheriff Brady. I'm pretty sure my brand-new Deputy Brady will do just fine."

Settled at her desk, Joanna went to work on her usual Monday morning agenda. Two hours later Detectives Howell and Raymond showed up in her office.

"Autopsy's over?"

Both detectives nodded.

"And?"

"Hyoid bone's broken," Deb answered. "The victim also had a perimortem contusion to the side of his head that might well have rendered him unconscious."

"But the actual cause of death is asphyxia?"

"Yes," Deb replied. "There's no sign of any dental work, so using dental charts to make an identification is a nonstarter. Dr. Baldwin will be hoping for a DNA match, but that's going to take time."

"Any physical evidence?" Joanna asked.

"Some, and not in a good way," Deb told her. "His fingernails had been trimmed down to the quick, so there's no chance of finding DNA under his nails, and Dr. Baldwin found traces of bleach inside his mouth and nose."

"In his mouth?" Joanna repeated in horror. "He was forced to drink bleach?"

"The ME thinks he was bathed in bleach after he was already deceased in an effort to destroy any DNA evidence. His clothing and shoes were also dipped in bleach."

"This sounds like a repeat offender," Joanna observed, "someone who's done this before and is knowledgeable enough to cover his tracks."

Deb nodded. "That's what I'm thinking, too. We took photos of everything—the duffel bag, his clothing, his shoes—before bagging them and bringing them back here. I copied you on all the photos, so they should be in your email. Now we'll have to wait to see what else Casey can find."

Casey Ledford was Joanna's lead crime scene investigator. In hopes of preserving possible evidence, the body had been transported without removing it from the duffel bag.

"Any sign of sexual assault?" Joanna asked.

Deb shook her head. "Not initially," she said.

"Sounds like you've done everything by the book then," Joanna said. "Good work."

"Maybe so," Deb said bleakly, "but without a crime scene or an identity, I don't know where to start."

Joanna thought about that comment for a moment. "I may have an idea on that score," she said finally. "I'll let you know if anything comes of it."

Once Deb and Garth left, Joanna turned to her computer and

opened Deb's email. The autopsy process would be recorded from beginning to end, but Deb's photos provided reference shots that could be printed out and placed directly in the murder book. The first shots were of Kendra removing the body from its duffel-bag wrap. When she pulled the body loose, it was completely clothed with the exception of a single shoe. The missing shoe—a high-topped sneaker that appeared to be two sizes too large for the boy's tiny feet, was found in the bottom of the duffel. After Kendra located the missing shoe, Deb's photo revealed that the shoelace wasn't just untied—it was completely missing.

The empty duffel bag had also been photographed, bagged, and tagged. Next the boy's clothing was removed—a faded blue plaid, long-sleeved flannel shirt, a pair of worn jeans, and a pair of white skivvies. Finally the tiny body was lain out on the morgue's slab. Joanna had some idea of how far decomposition would have progressed by then, and that's when she stopped looking. She didn't need to see any more. At that point she picked up her cell phone and dialed Captain Arturo Peña's cell phone.

"*Buenos días*, Sheriff Brady," he said cheerfully. "*¿Qué tal?*"

"Fine," she answered. "How are things with you?"

"Not bad. How can I be of service?"

"What about lunch?" she asked. "My treat. Daisy's at noon?"

"Make it twelve thirty, and I'm there."

"Okay," she said. "See you then."

The fact that the two officers operating on opposite sides of the border were good friends wasn't necessarily widely known, but with the ongoing contentious nature of border relations between the US and Mexico, their quiet friendship and mutual respect were steps in the right direction.

JOANNA WAS ALREADY SEATED IN A FAR CORNER BOOTH when Arturo arrived at Daisy's. People in town were used to seeing uniformed US Border Patrol personnel there on a daily basis, however they weren't accustomed to uniformed Mexican Federales. Arturo's progress through the room was observed with a good deal of interest and curiosity, but then again, it didn't hurt that the guy was movie star handsome.

"Good to see you," he said, sliding onto the bench seat across from Joanna, "but from the look on your face, I suspect this lunch is more business than pleasure."

"Correct," she said. "We've got a dead kid on our hands—an unidentified four- or five-year-old boy—and he may be one of yours."

"Interesting," he said. "Tell me about it."

"I will," she said. "But let's order first."

Joanna opted for the green corn tamale platter and coffee. Arturo ordered coffee, too, along with the bacon burger. Noting the waitress's raised eyebrow, he gave her a wink and a grin.

"Look," he explained, "I can get green corn tamales in Naco, Sonora, anytime I want. Bacon burgers? Not so much." As the waitress walked away, he turned back to Joanna. "Okay," he added. "What's the deal?"

"Highway Department guys doing flood watch at the bridge on the San Pedro in St. David on Saturday pulled a blue duffel bag out of the water. The body of a little boy was inside. The hyoid bone is broken, so the ME has ruled it a homicide. He's been dead for a while. Our theory is that the killer buried the body in the riverbed, but the floodwaters brought it to the surface. Given the San Pedro's headwaters are in Mexico, I wondered . . ."

"Did he happen to be wearing a blue plaid shirt?" Arturo interrupted.

Joanna was blown away. "As a matter of fact he was."

"Then his name is Xavier Delgado," Arturo told her. "He's four years old, and he's been missing for just over a week."

"Someone filed a missing persons report with you?"

Arturo sighed. "Not exactly," he said. "His mother is nineteen years old—a lady of the street, so to speak, who works from home. Some of the guys in my unit are good customers of hers. Whenever she had 'company,' she'd always send the kid outside to wait. My guys often brought him treats to eat while he was waiting. They're the ones who noticed he's been absent."

Hearing that, Joanna's heart broke a little more. "How could they know to tell you what clothes he was wearing?"

"Easy," Arturo replied. "I'm pretty sure those were the only clothes he had."

"Is there a chance the mother's responsible and that's why she didn't make an official report?"

"I doubt it," Arturo replied. "Her name is Elena Delgado. She came north with a group of migrants and was pregnant when she arrived in Naco. She's been here ever since, fending for herself and the kid and doing what she can to make the best of a bad situation. As far as kids disappearing without a trace? It happens along the border all the time. Human trafficking is a big problem for us. The mother was probably afraid that if she reported him missing, we'd accuse her of trafficking him."

Their food came then. As it was being delivered, Joanna thought about the kind of desperation that would drive a woman into prostitution to support herself and her fatherless child. Making Xavier wait outside while his mother was entertaining her paying visitors sounded bad, but on the other hand, maybe having him witness what was actually happening inside the house would have been worse.

Before walking away, the waitress slapped two separate checks down on the table. Arturo reached for them, but Joanna beat him to it.

"Will my investigators be able to come to your side of the border to interview her?" Joanna asked, slipping both slips of paper under her plate.

"That would be a bit dicey," Arturo said. "How about if you set a time for an interview at your department, and I bring her there myself. Doing that will rattle fewer chains."

"But won't bringing an illegal across the border be a problem?" Joanna objected.

"I can make it work," Arturo replied.

"All right then," Joanna said. "It's a deal. Let's eat."

CHAPTER 8

FERTILE, MINNESOTA
1963

IN MISS HOLT'S HEALTH ED CLASS STEVE'S SENIOR YEAR, everyone was supposed to do a research paper on some member of their immediate family. Since Steve's "immediate family" was composed of exactly two people, he wrote the paper about his mother, Cynthia Hawkins Roper. Part of the process called for actually interviewing the person he was writing about.

During the interview, his mother was thrilled to be able to tell him about her happy childhood, growing up on the family farm with Gramps and Grandma Joan, but Steve noticed that, after the death of her mother, Cynthia tended to gloss over a lot of details. She said very little about having Grandma Lucille as her stepmother, but Steve knew enough about the woman to understand that if Grandma Lucille had been in charge, his mother's teenaged years had been anything but a bed of roses.

No wonder she had taken to Jackson Roper, the first kid who ever asked her out. Details about that relationship were notably absent as well. Steve's mom didn't come right out and admit that neither she nor Jackson had actually graduated from high school. Steve had to track that detail down on his own by checking school records, and she was equally vague about the reasons for their subsequent divorce. However, Steve already knew the basics on that, because Grandma Lucille had spilled those beans to him time and again.

Single mothers weren't exactly in vogue back then, but Cynthia was understandably proud that she had managed to raise her son on her own, and she was equally proud of the fact that, although she had waited tables for years, she was now the sole owner of the restaurant where she had once been employed. In Fertile, Minnesota, that counted as a success story.

In Steve's retelling of the story, he didn't pull any punches. He included the sordid details about his mother being knocked up shortly after her sixteenth birthday. Steve also managed to track down the divorce records in which he discovered that the divorce was granted due to her husband having an adulterous affair with a woman named Verna Slocomb of St. Cloud, Minnesota. Grandma Lucille had always said his father had run away with a godless slut, but until Steve saw the divorce papers, said girlfriend never had an actual name.

Steve didn't show his paper to either Gramps or his mother, but Miss Holt had given him an A+. By then, however, Steve's interest in his father had been piqued. He'd been given a partial scholarship to the University of Minnesota and had already been accepted there. Shortly after high school graduation, he explained to his mother that he wasn't wild about living in a dorm and wanted to go down to St. Paul for a few days to see if he could scout out a possible apartment arrangement.

On that particular trip, however, Steve didn't make it any farther than St. Cloud. Arriving in town in his shiny Bel Air, he stopped off at the first phone booth he saw, grabbed the phone book, and went looking for the name "Slocomb." After finding seven listings for Slocomb, Steve dialed the number for the first one—Amos.

"Hello," a male voice answered.

"Is this Amos Slocomb?"

"Yes, who's this?"

"My name's Steve. I was hoping to locate Verna Slocomb. Do you happen to know her?"

"Of course I knew Verna," Amos said impatiently. "She was my first cousin, my uncle Vernon's daughter."

"Was?" Steve ventured. "Is she . . . deceased?"

"She's dead," Amos said bluntly. "Murdered by that no good bastard husband of hers. He's doing twenty-five to life in the Minnesota Men's Correctional Facility right here in town, and I hope he dies there. I pray that SOB never again sees the light of day. Now who did you say you are again?"

I didn't say, Steve thought, *and I'm not going to*. Aloud he said, "Sorry to bother you." Then he hung up.

After that, he stood in the phone booth for several long minutes, wondering what to do next. Finally, he made up his mind. Since he was already parked at a gas station, he went over and asked the attendant for help. He was told the prison was located on Minnesota Boulevard and was given directions as to how to get there.

STEVE'S FIRST GLIMPSE OF THE MASSIVE EDIFICE MADE OF hand-quarried granite made him think of ancient castles somewhere in Europe. Once there it took lots of talking to worm his way inside, but Stephen Roper had been born with the gift of gab, and he made it work. He came up with a sob story about how his mother had just died, and it wasn't until she was on her deathbed that she had finally told him the truth about his father.

Gradually he worked his way up the chain of command and his patience paid off. With a visitor badge finally slapped on his chest, he was escorted into a grim interview room deep in the bowels of the gloomy structure. He sat there on the far side of a small stainless-steel-topped table for the better part of half an hour, waiting and listening as noisy iron doors slammed shut in the corridor outside. At last the door in front of him opened and a shackled and handcuffed man, accompanied by a guard and wearing a black-and-white-striped uniform, shuffled inside.

Seeing his father for the first time, Steve was stunned. The resemblance between them was striking—the same blondish hair, the same narrow, elongated face, the same piercing blue eyes.

Jackson stopped for a moment and stared back at Steve in his own moment of recognition. Finally his thin face cracked into a grin.

"I'll be damned!" he said. "If it isn't my firstborn son finally come to visit his dear old dad!"

His momentary grin had revealed another similarity. They shared the same crooked teeth. Steve's mother had been told early on that her son needed braces, but in Fertile, Minnesota, in the fifties, only rich kids wore braces, and Cynthia Roper, waiting tables at the Country Inn, was anything but rich. Later, by the time she could have afforded braces, her son wasn't interested.

Jackson eased himself down on a chair opposite Steve. After clicking the prisoner's handcuffs to the metal fastener welded into the tabletop, the guard let himself out of the room, slamming the heavy door behind him.

"To what do I owe the pleasure after all these years?" Jackson wanted to know.

"I just now found out where you were."

"How'd you do that—your mom tell you?"

"I was doing a family history paper for my health ed class," Steve answered. "I found Verna Slocomb's name in the divorce proceedings."

"I'll bet your health ed teacher got a big kick out of finding out your family history included a convicted killer."

"I didn't find out about that until today—until I came to St. Cloud," Steve said. "I talked to Verna's cousin, Amos."

"Amos, the rat fink," Jackson muttered. "Me and him used to be good buddies. At least I thought we were, but he turned against me right along with everybody else. They couldn't get me locked up fast enough. I'm doing flat time. I won't be eligible for parole until I'm fifty-six years old."

"But you did it, didn't you?" Steve insisted. "You really did kill her?"

"Sure, I did."

"How come?"

"Why do you think? Because she was leaving me, that's why!"

But Steve was curious. Thinking about his own experience, he wondered if it was possible that he and his father shared far more than just physical appearance. Maybe Jackson Roper also had interior voices speaking to him and urging him to act.

"You could have just let her go," he countered, "or was there a voice inside you that told you to shoot her instead."

"Like a little birdie talking to me from inside my head? Good grief no! I may be a cold-blooded killer, but I'm sure as hell no nutcase!"

That remark offended Steve Roper to the very core of his being. Just because someone heard voices didn't mean he was crazy. As far as Steve was concerned, that was it. He shoved his chair away from the table, stood up, and made for the door.

"Wait a minute," Jackson objected. "Where are you going? I want to know what's happening with you. Did you graduate from high school? Do you have a girlfriend? Are you planning on going to college?"

"None of your damned business," Steve muttered as he pounded on the door, letting the guard outside know he was ready to leave.

"Will you be back?" Jackson asked.

"No," Steve said.

Steve was still fuming as a second guard escorted him back to the visitors' exit. Physically, he and his father may have looked like they'd been cut from the same cloth, but obviously that wasn't true. Jackson Roper didn't have any stray voices wandering around in his head, and he had a low opinion of people who did. And although they were both stone-cold killers, there was one major difference. Jackson Roper had been caught and thrown in prison while his son was still home free.

Put that in your pipe and smoke it, you son of a bitch, Steve thought as he ripped off his sticky visitor badge and tossed it in the trash.

"Will we be seeing you again?" the smiling clerk at the check-in counter asked as he signed out on her clipboard.

"I don't think so," Steve replied. "This visit was pretty much a one and done."

CHAPTER 9

BISBEE, ARIZONA
Monday, November 27, 2023

BACK AT THE OFFICE, JOANNA STOPPED BY THE BULLPEN to tell Deb Howell and Garth Raymond that their homicide victim most likely had a name, but still no date of birth. Then she called the ME to give her the same news and pass along the information she'd picked up from Arturo.

"Missing for a week," Kendra mused. "That would jibe with my estimated time of death. That suggests that Xavier was murdered close to the time he was taken."

"Any sign of sexual assault?" Joanna asked, dreading the answer.

"Due to the state of decomposition, I couldn't find any indication of that on the body itself, and none on the clothing, either."

"At least the poor kid was spared that," Joanna murmured.

"Indeed," Kendra agreed.

"What about that missing shoelace?" Joanna asked. "Since he was strangled, is it possible that's the murder weapon?"

"I doubt it," Kendra replied. "The hyoid bone was broken in more than one place. That would indicate brute force rather than a garrote."

"But removing a shoelace from a high-topped sneaker isn't an instant process. Why go to the trouble?"

"Trophy, maybe?" Kendra suggested.

"You're suggesting the possibility of a serial killer?" Joanna asked.

"I am," Kendra replied. "A perpetrator smart enough to dip his victim in bleach doesn't sound like an amateur. Since the victim is from Naco, Sonora, you might ask Captain Peña if he can find any similar cases elsewhere in Sonora or even in Mexico at large."

"I will," Joanna answered. "I'll also have Deb and Garth go looking for similar unsolved cases on this side of the border."

"But about those shoes," Kendra began.

"What about them?" Joanna asked.

"They look brand-new as opposed to used. There's almost no wear on the soles, so why would a struggling single mom buy her kid a pair of shoes that are two sizes too big?"

"Maybe someone else bought them," Joanna suggested.

"Maybe so," Kendra agreed. "When I was growing up, each year for my birthday, my dad's mother, who lived out of state, always sent me three pairs of panties that were two sizes too small. Maybe what we have here is someone who erred in the other direction."

That was a nice enough thought, but as Joanna hung up the phone, she doubted that Xavier's new sneakers had come from a distant but loving relative. It was more likely that a vicious killer had used those shoes as opposed to candy or food to lure an unsuspecting child into a vehicle.

Off the phone, she called the bullpen. Garth answered, and she passed this latest bit of information on to him. Then she called Arturo's phone. He didn't answer, so she left him a detailed message. She was off the phone and just turning on her computer when Tom Hadlock appeared in her doorway.

"Chain Gang has arrived at Saguaro Hills, and the transferees are being processed."

"That's a relief," Joanna said. "Sounds as though that went through without a hitch. We've also reassigned beds in the jail. Once we unload one more set of five, we'll be closer to being just overcrowded as opposed to dangerously so.

"Check with Saguaro Hills and see when we can send the next batch. In the meantime, I'll call the contractor's office to see where we are on the permit process."

"Good," Tom replied. "Hearing from you might make a difference. A chief deputy doesn't have nearly the same kind of pull as a sheriff does."

Joanna was about to dial Dave Ruiz's number at the Ruiz Construction Company on her landline phone when her cell vibrated with Jenny's photo showing in caller ID.

"Hey," she answered, "how's it going?"

"When I came home from work, I was worn out, but my body was wide awake," Jenny said. "Going to sleep when the sun is coming up doesn't really work for me. I tossed and turned for a long time, but I finally did get a couple hours of sleep."

"Give yourself a few days," Joanna advised. "How was your shift?"

"Okay," Jenny replied. "A few traffic stops is all. No biggie."

Joanna was all too aware that every traffic stop came with the possibility of going bad and turning fatal, but she didn't say so. No doubt Jenny's instructors at APOA had told her the same thing.

"But there is something I need to talk to you about."

Joanna drew a quick breath. "Okay," she said. "I'm listening."

"Nick and I were talking on the way back to Tucson. We'd like to get married sooner rather than later."

Here it comes, Joanna thought. *History's about to repeat itself. She's about to tell me she's pregnant.*

"And, no, we're not pregnant," Jenny added, as though she had just read her mother's mind. "I have health insurance, and Nick doesn't. The only way I can add him to mine is if we get married, so what would you think if we got married over Christmas? We don't want a big wedding. We can't afford one, and if we do it in Bisbee, the wedding can be at our church up Tombstone Canyon with Marianne officiating. Then, maybe, if you and Dad don't mind, we could have a small reception out at the ranch."

Jenny had spilled out the whole story in a rush of words. When she paused for breath, it took a moment for Joanna to reply. Hearing Jenny refer to Butch Dixon as "Dad" always grabbed Joanna's heart, and the fact that Jenny most likely *wasn't* expecting was cause for nothing short of rejoicing.

"I'll have to talk to him about it," Joanna answered, "but I can't imagine that he'll object."

"You don't mind?" Jenny asked.

"Not at all."

"But please don't talk to Dad about this," Jenny said. "Let me. I'd rather do the asking myself. If he says yes, I'll check with Marianne. I just saw my schedule and know I'll have the Friday and Saturday before Christmas off, so I'll need to see if she's available for either of those."

Not only was the Reverend Marianne Maculyea Joanna's pastor at the Tombstone Canyon United Methodist Church, she'd also been Joanna's best friend since seventh grade on. During the social hour after church on Sunday, Joanna had mentioned to Marianne that Nick and Jenny were engaged, but it hadn't occurred to her that a wedding ceremony this soon might be in the offing. Now, on the phone, Joanna somehow stifled the urge to blurt out that there was no way in hell Jenny and Nick would be able to pull off a church wedding in less than a month.

Instead, she kept her response calm and reassuring. "Okey dokey," she said. "Talk to Dad and see what he has to say."

"But wait," Jenny said. "There's one more thing."

"What's that?"

"Do you still have the outfit you wore when you and Dad got married?"

Years before and just prior to the wedding, someone had set fire to Joanna's house. The blaze had been put out in a timely manner, and the culprit had been apprehended, but her original wedding outfit—a two-piece silk-brocade sheath with a matching full-length jacket—had been reduced to ashes. On that occasion, her mother, Eleanor Lathrop Winfield, had ridden to the rescue by finding a replacement and having it shipped via FedEx. It had arrived just in time for the ceremony.

After the wedding, Joanna had taken the outfit to the dry cleaner's. It hung untouched, still in its clear plastic bag, at the far end of her closet. There had been no other occasion when wearing it would have been appropriate. Nonetheless, she hadn't been able to part with it.

"Of course I still have it," Joanna answered after a momentary pause. "Why?"

"Could I wear it?" Jenny asked. "Please? Not having to buy a dress would save a ton of money."

Jenny's figure wasn't all that different from what Joanna's had been when she and Butch married and before she'd had two more kids, but Jenny was a good four inches taller.

"Of course," Joanna replied. "I'd be thrilled, but won't it be too short?"

"Mom," Jenny replied with a laugh. "We're living in the twenty-first century. No one gives a damn about women's hemlines anymore. So thanks, that takes a huge load off my mind."

"Maybe so," Joanna said, "but you might want to try it on the next time you're in town, just to be sure."

"Will do," Jenny said. "I'm hanging up and calling Dad. Love you."

With that the call ended, but instead of going ahead with her call to the contractor, Joanna simply sat and waited for Butch to get back to her. Five minutes later he did.

"Have you talked to Jenny?" he asked.

"I'm afraid so."

"So you know she and Nick want to get married before Christmas?"

"Yes, I do. What did you tell her?"

"What do you think?" Butch replied. "I said it's a-okay with me. Now the ball's in Marianne's court."

"I'll probably hear from her next," Joanna said, and she wasn't wrong. Bare minutes after the call with Butch ended, Marianne's came through.

"Am I speaking to the mother of the bride?" she asked.

Joanna couldn't help but laugh. "Apparently," she answered.

"And the bride isn't exactly following in her mother's footsteps, either," Marianne added. "Wanting Nick to have health insurance isn't exactly the same as having a bun in the oven."

On that score, Marianne Maculyea knew whereof she spoke. During the early months of Joanna's unexpected pregnancy, aside from Andy, Marianne, her best friend, had been her only confidante.

"In other words, shut my mouth and get with the program?"

"Pretty much," Marianne agreed. "How's that for your comforting pastoral counsel for the day?"

"Just the kick in the butt I needed," Joanna replied. "Did the two of you pick a date?"

"Yup. Two p.m. on Saturday, December twenty-third. I told her we'll need to set up dates in advance of that for some premarital counseling sessions, but I can drive up to Tucson for those instead of having them come here."

"Good enough," Joanna said. "Thanks, Marianne. I'm not at all sure how we'll manage this in less than a month, but one way or another we'll get it done."

CHAPTER 10

ST. PAUL, MINNESOTA
1963–1967

STEVE ROPER WAS SMART BUT LAZY. HE HAD BEEN A GOOD student at Fertile-Beltrami High but he had skated through. Had he applied himself, he could have been valedictorian, but dedicating himself to schoolwork wasn't Steve's thing. He was number seven in his class, and that was fine with him. He wasn't interested in all the unrealistic expectations and stress that came with being *numero uno*.

The guy who came in first, Bill Felton, won a National Merit Scholarship to MIT and headed there determined to become one of the country's top scientists. Steve understood that kind of future would require multiple degrees and years of grueling study followed by more years of laboring forty hours a week to make it to the top of the next heap. Steve Roper had no such ambitions.

His favorite high school teacher, and ironically Bill Felton's, too, was Malcolm Nielson, the guy who taught chemistry and who also happened to be Steve's varsity baseball coach. What Steve noticed most about Coach Nielson was that he was happy. When it came time for school to get out every spring, the coach was almost as giddy about it as his students, and for good reason. During the summers he divided his time between his two favorite pastimes—fishing and golfing. In fact, on the last day of school in 1963—the day before Steve's graduation ceremony—a jubilant Coach Nielson had ridden his brand-new golf cart to school. His house was only two blocks from campus, and local law enforcement had turned a blind eye to his having driven an unlicensed vehicle for two blocks on a city street.

It had been Coach Nielson who, during Steve's junior year, had sat him down and told Steve he had what it took to be the first member of his family to go on to college. Surprisingly enough, Coach Nielson's confidence in Steve helped him have confidence in himself. And so, when it came time to head off to the University of Minnesota, he did so with the plan in mind of becoming a high school teacher. He enrolled with a stated major in English—because English had always been his best subject—and a minor in chemistry—because of Coach Nielson.

He knew in advance that being a teacher wasn't a path to fame or fortune, but he wasn't interested in either one. What he was looking forward to was having three months off every summer to do whatever the hell he wanted. In that regard, golfing and fishing were very low on his list of priorities.

Once in college, in the fall of 1963, he still skated along, getting good grades without really trying. In order to simplify things, for the first time in his life Steve told the voices that he needed them to shut up and go away. Once they were gone, he missed them, but not having to listen to their constant yammering made it easier for him to concentrate. He enjoyed being on campus. He made friends easily in a way that hadn't been possible back home. But part of the reason Steve shut the voices down was out of concern for his own safety. If he targeted one of the coeds on campus, someone who had encountered him at school might recognize him. After all, according to Sherlock, that was the real secret of getting away with it—don't go hunting in your own backyard.

While in St. Paul, Steve dated some—enough to be regarded as available without ever allowing any of those fledgling relationships to become serious. During his junior year, the university's campus was plagued by a series of brutal rapes, and it was several months before the rapist was caught. During that time, upperclassmen were recruited to accompany terrified coeds back and forth between dorms and both their daytime classes and evening activities.

More than once while escorting one sweet young thing or another, Steve was told how much his gallantry was appreciated. He accepted the compliments and thanks with a show of humility, all the while reveling in the irony that these ignorant women were being protected by an actual killer. As for the campus rapist? Steve held the guy in complete contempt. He may have had balls enough to attack young women, but he wasn't man enough to actually murder them. Stephen Roper could have done that in a heartbeat.

Halfway through his senior year, Gramps got sick. That came as a shock. Steve had always thought of Orson Hawkins as indestructible, but stage four stomach cancer was more than he could handle. The last semester of Steve's senior year, in 1967, he made the five-hour trip from the Twin Cities back home to Fertile almost every weekend. At first he visited Gramps at the home in town that he still shared with Steve's mother. Later Steve visited Gramps in the hospital and finally in hospice. Two weeks before graduation, and with the blessing of his professors, he took a pass on finals and went home to attend Gramps's funeral.

This time, sitting in the small Lutheran church, he didn't have to worry about pretending to be sad. In actual fact he was devastated. Once again people stepped forward to say what a wonderful guy Gramps had been, and this time Steve believed it.

At the reception afterward, two important things happened. For one he had run into Coach Nielson. The two of them had stayed in touch during the intervening years, but that day, Malcolm Nielson mentioned that he was retiring at the end of the current school year and that he and his wife were moving to Florida. Then he asked an intriguing question: Would Steve be interested in coming back home to Fertile and stepping into his shoes? If he was, Coach Nielson promised that he would be more than happy to put in a good word for Steve with the local board of education.

Naturally, Steve thanked him profusely, but in that moment teaching at Fertile-Beltrami High School wasn't anywhere near the top of his list as far as what he wanted to do and where he wanted to be. But that's when the other important thing happened—his mother introduced him to her new boyfriend Frederick Chalmers, or as Steve quickly came to call him, Freddy the Freeloader, red hair and all. Gramps had loved Red Skelton and watched him perform every chance he got. Since there had been only a single television set in the house, whenever Gramps watched Red Skelton, everyone else did, too.

"You shouldn't call Frederick that," Steve's mother admonished Steve. "He used to teach art, but he had to stop on account of his high blood pressure. The stress was too much for him. That's why he decided to try his hand at painting for a living."

The whole while Steve was growing up, he had never known his mother to have a serious boyfriend, so this was something new. As soon as Steve met the guy and the two of them shook hands, a chill had passed through Steve's body. In that moment, Sherlock suddenly emerged from hibernation.

Who the hell is this guy? he demanded.

Steve wanted to know the same thing. He was reasonably good at doing small talk, and that paid off in the case of Frederick Chalmers. Steve made it his business to find out everything there was to know about Freddy, mostly as related by Freddy himself. According to him, Frederick Chalmers came from Bismark, North Dakota. After being forced to abandon teaching school due to his health issues, he was now an up-and-coming artist. That was how he and Cindy Roper had met in the first place, when she and some girlfriends had attended an art fair in Fargo where she had purchased one of his paintings and paid big bucks to have it professionally framed.

Steve's mother claimed she loved the painting because of what she called "all its bright pops of color." Steve looked at all those wild colors and saw nothing but a bunch of meaningless doodles, the same kind of crap he himself used to draw in the margins of all his textbooks as a kid back in grade school. He also suspected that Freddy's art might be the kind of thing someone would dash off while under the influence of LSD.

Like any other self-respecting chemistry student of the time, Steve Roper knew all about lysergic acid diethylamide. He never used the stuff himself, but he could certainly have whipped up a batch of LSD had he been called upon to do so. He also recognized the symptoms of drug usage, even if his mother didn't. Steve was pretty sure Freddy was tripped out most of the time, and he quickly made up his mind that he was going to send Freddy packing come hell or high water.

As a result, after Gramps's funeral and before heading back to St. Paul to walk through graduation and pack up his apartment, Steve stopped by the school superintendent's office in Fertile and filled out an application. He also stopped by the high school itself to let Mr. Donner—the same guy who'd been the school's principal throughout Steve's high school career—know that he was interested in the job. Within a matter of days, he knew the position was his for the taking. About the same time, Steve was astonished to learn that, although the bulk of Gramps's estate had been left to his daughter, a sizable bequest in the amount of $50,000 had been left to him.

The day before he was due to head back to St. Paul, he dropped by the house and found Freddy sacked out on the living room couch. Had Grandma Lucille spotted someone sleeping on a sofa with his shoes on, there would've been hell to pay, but Steve didn't say a word. Instead, seeing Freddy's wallet lying on the nearby coffee table, he gingerly picked it up and shuffled through it long enough to locate the driver's license. Then, having memorized the address, he replaced the wallet where he'd found it.

After returning to St. Paul, Steve picked up his diploma, cleaned out his apartment well enough to get his deposit back, and then headed home the long way around—via Bismark, North Dakota. Once there he and Sherlock tracked down the address from Frederick Chalmers's wallet, which led to a seedy boardinghouse in a not-so-nice part of town.

That afternoon, he visited a local pawnshop and bought a pearl-handled derringer pistol, small enough to carry in his pocket. The gun was evidently an antique, made in 1927, so the price was outrageous, but the size was right. And at that point in Steve's life money was no problem.

"You know you only get one shot from this," the clerk cautioned.

"If I ever need to use it," Steve replied, "one shot will be plenty."

"Do you have any ammunition?" the clerk asked as he rang up the sale.

"No," Steve answered, "but I should be able to buy some."

"No need," the helpful clerk said cheerfully. "Have I got a deal for you. After the guy pawned it, I found out it was still loaded. I took the bullet out and put it right here in my cash register for safekeeping. Just for the hell of it, today I'll throw in the bullet for free."

That evening Steve went back to Frederick Chalmers's neighborhood and made a complete canvass of all the local dives, flashing a roll of bills as he did so, and letting folks know that his buddy Fred had mentioned this might be a place to score some coke.

Just before closing time, as he sat in the last of the neighborhood bars sipping on a ginger ale, someone tapped him on the shoulder.

"I hear tell you might be looking to make a deal," a disheveled stranger said. He looked like the kind of bum you'd find living on a sidewalk somewhere.

"That depends on what you have to offer," Steve replied. "I'm looking for the C-word. Do you happen to have some?"

"How much do you want?"

"How about two hundred bucks' worth?"

"Meet me out back in ten," the guy replied before shambling away.

The dealer was good to his word. Minutes later Steve walked away with the goods he needed without having to show his weapon, much less use it.

Back home in Fertile for the summer, Steve was unsurprised to learn that his mother and Freddy were now living together. They had laid claim to Gramps's old room, and the guest room was in the process of being transformed into Freddy's studio.

Steve stayed at the house with the two lovebirds for the next few weeks while he went house hunting himself. That's when he learned Coach Nielson was putting his place on the market. Not only that, it was listed for sale fully furnished. That was too good of a deal to pass up, and Steve jumped on it. With the help of Gramps's generous bequest, he was able to purchase the property in an all-cash deal with some money left over.

Once the sale closed, it was time for Steve to move out of his mother's place completely. During that process, and at a time when both Freddy and Steve's mom were away from the house, Steve donned a pair of gloves and made a thorough search of the master bedroom.

Freddy's chosen hiding place for his stash wasn't exactly inspired. A baggie half full of a white substance Steve assumed to be LSD was concealed on Freddy's side of Gramps's old bed, hidden between the mattress and the box spring. Steve emptied the substance he'd just found into his own baggie, the one loaded with cocaine. After shaking the resulting bag thoroughly to mix the contents, he refilled Freddy's bag with a matching amount of the new concoction and slipped it back into its original hiding place. After that Steve was able to complete his move with no one being the wiser.

But waiting around to see what would happen wasn't easy. At one point, he dropped by the Country Inn ostensibly to have lunch with his mother, but in reality he wanted to know what, if anything, was going on. Not surprisingly, his mother appeared to be totally distracted.

"You look upset," he said to her. "Is something wrong?"

"It's Frederick," she answered. "His blood pressure has shot through the roof."

"Has he seen a doctor?"

She nodded. "They have him on medication, but he's not getting better."

Two weeks later Frederick suffered a massive stroke. He was transported by ambulance to the local hospital but died in the ER before being admitted. Since he was already under a doctor's care, his death was ruled to be natural causes and no autopsy was performed. When no other relatives could be located, a grief-stricken Cynthia Roper had Frederick Chalmers buried in the Hawkins's family plot in Fertile Memorial Cemetery.

During the postfuneral reception, Steve slipped into the bedroom and removed the baggie. He flushed the contents down the toilet. As for the baggie itself and that unused derringer? Knowing he needed something to remember Freddy the Freeloader by, Steve put the derringer in the baggie and added it to his cigar box. Sherlock thought the whole thing was hilarious, and he laughed and laughed.

That was the first time ever that Steve heard any of his voices laughing, but it wouldn't be the last.

CHAPTER 11

BISBEE, ARIZONA
Tuesday, November 28, 2023

JOANNA CAME TO WORK ON TUESDAY MORNING IN SOME- what better shape than she had the day before. For one thing, she'd gotten more sleep. She'd still tossed and turned some, but at least she'd had something to worry about other than having a police officer's daughter working the graveyard shift. Now she had an upcoming wedding to plan. Somehow it was easier to fall asleep while thinking about wedding cakes, flowers, and reception logistics than it was while worrying about murder and mayhem.

Dave Ruiz called half an hour later with the welcome news that the last of the building permits had finally been issued. With that one set of prisoners now being held in Phoenix, the way was finally clear for him to start work on the new solitary confinement part of the jail, and he expected to have a crew on-site bright and early the following morning. Off the phone with him, Joanna spent a good forty-five minutes with Terry Gregovich, zeroing in on exactly how work on the jail would proceed without the construction crew interfering with her prisoners and vice versa.

Shortly after that session ended, a call came in from Captain Peña. "How's it going?" he asked when Joanna answered.

"Fairly well," Joanna answered. "What's up with you?"

"If I were to stop by about two this afternoon with Elena Delgado in tow, would you happen to have an available interview room?"

Joanna had doubted that the boy's mother would agree to come in for an interview, so she was pleasantly surprised. "Absolutely," she said.

"She doesn't speak any English," Arturo added. "Do you want me to translate?"

Joanna thought about that. "I should probably have someone from my team," she said a moment later. "I'll have my chief detective, Lt. Jaime Carbajal, sit in. But is she going to want an attorney present? My people will have to read her a Miranda warning."

"I asked about that," Arturo said. "She says she needs to know for sure if the child is Xavier. That's why she agreed to be interviewed. She doesn't need an attorney, but she'd like me to be present during the interview."

"No problem," Joanna agreed.

"Okay," Arturo said. "See you then."

After consulting with Jaime and letting him know the lay of the land, Joanna made arrangements to have the interview live streamed to the computer in her office. That way she and Detective Raymond would also be privy to everything that was going on.

The rest of the morning passed quickly. With plenty of routine office work to do, Joanna had brought along a sandwich from home and ate lunch at her desk. At ten minutes to two, Arturo appeared in the doorway to her office with a young woman in tow.

Considering Elena Delgado's occupation as a sex worker, Joanna had expected someone rather sexy. Beneath a mane of thick black hair, she was plain as opposed to pretty and a bit on the plump side. She was dressed in a maroon sweatshirt with a fading Corona beer logo affixed to the front. The tears in the legs of her threadbare jeans spoke of long use rather than strategic designer distress.

Over the years, Joanna had picked up enough Spanish to get through the preliminaries. She rose from her desk and stepped forward with her hand extended saying, *"Buenas tardes. Bienvenido. Lamento mucho su pérdida."*

Elena nodded. *"Gracias."*

Joanna was struck by how cold Elena's hand was. Clearly the young woman was careworn and utterly terrified.

"¿No te sentarás?" Joanna asked. "Won't you sit down?"

Elena darted over to one of the two visitors' chairs in front of Joanna's desk, but when she took a chair, she perched on the very front of it as if prepared to flee the room at a moment's notice.

"I'm assuming Captain Peña has told you that on Saturday my officers found the body of a young boy we think may be your son, Xavier."

Arturo translated and Elena nodded.

"You are not under arrest. The purpose of this voluntary interview is to determine if the body we found is that of your son."

Once again a nod followed Arturo's translation.

"Captain Peña will accompany you to the actual interview, one that will be recorded. While there, one of my investigators will read you your rights, but once again, you are not under arrest. Since your presence here is voluntary, you may stop the interview at any time. At some point, my officers will probably ask to swab your cheek in order to obtain a DNA sample. DNA is the only way we'll be able to positively determine the child's identity."

This translation took a bit longer. Elena nodded again, then asked a question of her own in return.

"She wants to know if she can see him," Arturo said.

With her heart aching, Joanna shook her head. "I'm sorry," she said. "The body isn't here. It's at the morgue, but he has been gone too long. No mother should have to see her child the way he looks now."

This time, after Arturo's translation, there was no answering nod. Instead, Elena Delgado lowered her face into her hands and wept uncontrollably, while Arturo patted her shoulder in a vain attempt to comfort her. At last she quieted, raised her head, and blew her nose into a hanky.

"Are you ready?" Joanna asked.

"*Sí.*" Elena said shakily. "*Estoy listo.*"

Joanna led the visitors out of her office and down the corridor to the interview rooms. The door to one of them was open with Lt. Carbajal and Detective Howell already seated inside. Joanna made the introductions and waited for everyone to be seated before she left, closing the door behind her.

Back in her office, Joanna found that the monitor on her desk had been turned around to face the two visitors' chairs where Garth Raymond and Joanna's CSI, Casey Ledford, were already seated.

"It's started," Garth reported, rolling Joanna's chair away from her desk and into the room so she'd be able to see, too. "Jaime just read her rights."

The beginning of the interview was strictly routine, and even though Jaime conducted the interview in English, Joanna was able to follow the answers in Spanish without having to rely on Arturo's translation.

"What is your name?"

Maria Elena Delgado.

"What is your date of birth?"

September 11, 2004.

"Where were you born?"

Mexico City, Mexico.

"What is your son's name?"

Xavier Francisco Delgado.

"What is his date of birth?"

October 14, 2019.

"Who is the boy's father?"

At that point Elena hesitated and turned questioningly to Arturo.

"*Sigue,*" he told her. "*Dígales.*" "Tell them."

Joanna watched as Elena gathered herself by taking a long steadying breath before she spoke again. This time her words came so quickly and softly that Joanna was forced to rely entirely on Arturo's translation.

When I was fourteen, my stepfather sold me to a pimp who put me to work on the streets. I was still a virgin. That meant I was worth more. Later, when I got pregnant, the pimp knocked me out with some drug and sold me to another man who liked women who were pregnant. When I woke up, I didn't know where I was. Someone dropped me off at a house with three other girls, all of them pregnant. They were the ones who told me we were in Guadalajara. A few weeks later, when the first girl gave birth, she disappeared, and so did her baby.

"Do you think the man killed them?" Jaime asked.

Elena shuddered and answered with a nod.

One of the other girls asked him where they went. He said that he got rid of them—that they were his and he could do what he wanted with them.

Hearing Arturo's translation of that, Joanna felt sick to her stomach. This story was almost a carbon copy of one from several years earlier when members of her department had stumbled across a depraved predator named James Ardmore who had been doing something chillingly similar right here in Cochise County to yet another collection of unfortunate young women whom he had held captive, tortured, abused, and finally murdered.

Joanna wasn't the only one who saw the similarity. Raymond turned to her with an anguished look on his face. "Whoa," he said. "That's almost the same thing that happened to Latisha."

Latisha Marcum had been the sole survivor of Ardmore's basement torture chamber, and as a newly hired deputy, Garth had played a key role in rescuing her.

"I wonder what the guy fed her," Garth added. "Ardmore kept his prisoners alive by feeding them dry dog food."

When they turned their attention back to the computer monitor, Jaime was speaking again.

"What happened next?" he asked.

I wanted my baby. No matter if it was a boy or a girl, it was still my baby. If it was a girl, I would have named her Lucia, after my mother, and if it was a boy, I was going to name him Xavier, after my father.

At the house the three of us who were left did everything—cooking, cleaning, housework. One day I was out in the yard hanging the wash when I saw a group of workmen next door. I went over to them and told them that the man in the house was evil—that he was holding us prisoner. Two of the workmen pulled me over the fence—they were very strong—and the man in charge said he would call the police and have the man arrested.

But I didn't wait for the police. I was afraid they wouldn't arrest him—that they would believe the man and not the girls. Or if they did arrest him, they'd let him out, and he'd come find me. So I took off, hitchhiking. I didn't know where I was going. I just knew I had to get far away. I made it as far as a town called San Luis Potosí. That's where I hooked up with a migrant caravan on its way north.

Most of the people in the caravan were nice. They were hoping to go to America to find a better life, and that's what I was hoping for too. Walking all day long every day wasn't easy, especially since I was pregnant, but I did it—for me and for the baby.

Sometimes people gave us rides, but mostly we walked. There were lots more men than women. Some of the men had wives with them but a lot of them didn't, and so . . .

Elena paused for a moment and looked beseechingly at Arturo before leaning over and whispering something into his ear.

He nodded before replying, *"Sí, saben lo que haces."* "Yes, they know what you do."

Resignedly, Elena turned back to Jaime and looked him directly in the eye as she answered.

My stepfather turned me into a prostitute. There were lots of single men in the caravan and very few women. Some of them had plenty of money, and I needed money. Since I'm good at what I do, I made lots of money. I was worried that someone would try to steal it, so I made friends with an old woman—a grandmother. I called her my *Bancos de la Abuela*, my Grandmother Banker. I shared some of the money I earned with her, and she kept mine safe.

At first I thought I would go to Juarez, but along the way, I heard people saying that going to a smaller town might make it easier to sneak across the border. When part of the caravan broke off to come to Naco, I came with them—since Grandmother Banker's family was coming here too.

By then it was almost time for my baby to be born. I decided trying to cross the border right then would be too risky. So I used my money to buy a tiny house, not much more than a shack, but that's where Xavier and I have lived since the day he was born. Grandmother Banker's family managed to make it across the border, but the coyote taking them said she was too old and wouldn't be able to walk fast enough. He refused to take her. Once her family left, she ended up staying with me and helped with the baby. She died of Covid in 2022. I still miss her.

Elena paused her narrative long enough to wipe a tear from her eye, and Joanna could tell that she had come to love the old woman who had befriended and helped her on the difficult journey north.

Detective Howell, who had been silent throughout most of the interview, spoke up, only now Jaime was the one doing the translating.

"When is the last time you saw your son?"

That would be Friday a week ago. Fridays are usually busy for me, and I don't let Xavier stay in the house when I have . . . guests, so I would give him some food and send him outside to play. That night when my company left, Xavier was nowhere to be found. I looked for him for hours but couldn't find him.

"Did you report him missing?" Deb asked.

Elena shook her head.

People like me don't go to the police with our troubles. Policemen are not our friends. I was afraid they would accuse me of doing to Xavier what my stepfather did to me—selling him to traffickers.

They're here, you know, even in Naco. And that's what I suspected when I couldn't find him—that the traffickers had gotten him.

"This was on a weekday," Deb said. "Why wasn't Xavier in school?"

He's only four. He's too young.

"On days when you have company," Deb asked, "do you have any idea what Xavier does when he's out of the house?"

Sometimes he hangs out with kids from the migrant camp. It's right at the end of our street. They're older than he is, but they don't go to school, either.

"Do you recall him ever mentioning any of them by name?"

Elena shook her head.

"As you've no doubt been told," Deb continued after a moment, "we've recently located the body of a young boy who may or may not be your son. I have some photos here. Would you let me know if you recognize anything?"

With that Deb opened the file folder that had been lying in front of her and pulled out two photos, presumably from the ones she had taken during the autopsy.

Elena picked up the first one and examined it closely before dropping it onto the tabletop and bursting into an agonizing howl of anguish. A whole minute passed before Elena was once again capable of speech.

"Is that your son's shirt?" Deb asked.

Elena nodded. "The top button is missing. I noticed it was gone that morning, but I didn't have time to sew it back on."

"What about these?"

As Deb shoved the second photo across the tabletop, Joanna recognized it as a still of the two high-topped sneakers sitting side by side.

Elena looked at those and shook her head. "Those shoes are not my son's!" she declared.

Joanna had thought that the shoes would be the final tipping point in the identification process, but they weren't—not at all.

Clearly Elena Delgado spoke far more English than she had previously let on.

"Do you have a recent photo of your son?" Deb asked.

Elena reached into her pocket and produced a cell phone. After scrolling through it for a moment, she located what she was looking for and passed the phone to the detective.

"I took that last month on his birthday," Elena said.

Deb studied the screen for a moment before asking, "Would you mind sending it to me?"

At that point, Elena looked somewhat mystified. Thankfully, Arturo stepped in.

"I happen to have Sheriff Brady's cell phone number right here," he said, pulling out his own phone. "Why don't I text it to her?"

Moments later Joanna's phone dinged with an arriving message announcement. When she opened it, she saw the image of a little boy smiling impishly up at her from behind what appeared to be a half-eaten snow cone. He was wearing the same blue plaid shirt, only in the photo the top button was still intact. It made Joanna's heart ache to think that the light behind that impish grin had been forever extinguished.

The interview ended shortly thereafter with Deb producing a kit and collecting the necessary cheek swab. After that, Jaime escorted Arturo Peña and Elena Delgado from the room. Of course it would take time for the DNA results to come in, but the people who had observed the interview already knew what the final result would be. Xavier Francisco Delgado, a Mexican national, age four, was definitely their previously unidentified homicide victim.

CHAPTER 12

BISBEE, ARIZONA
Tuesday, November 28, 2023

SHORTLY AFTER THE INTERVIEW ENDED, JOANNA ASSEM-bled her team in the conference room. By then she'd had Kristin make copies of the photo from Elena's phone. After distributing paper copies of Xavier's photo to everyone in attendance, she looked questioningly at the people seated around the table.

"Okay, folks," she said. "What's our next move?"

"I'll get a copy of the photo to Dr. Baldwin," Deb said, "but I want this cheek swab in the hands of the Department of Public Safety's DNA lab in Tucson sooner than later."

Garth raised his hand. "The fastest way to make that happen is to hand deliver it. I'll be glad to drive it up there."

"Good," Joanna said. "You do that, and tell them we want a rush on it."

"Right," Deb observed dryly, "but just in case you didn't catch the news, it was a bang-bang, shoot-'em-up weekend in and around Tucson with a couple of lethal shootings and two fast-water fatalities. We're from out of town. That means we'll have to take a number and get in line."

Joanna knew from experience that no matter where you lived, DNA requests from small-town jurisdictions were generally slow in coming.

"Okay then," she said. "We'll have the DNA results when we have them. What else?"

"From what the mother said," Deb replied, "it's possible the kids from the migrant camp are among the last people to see Xavier alive. We need to interview them, but given they're in Mexico, and we're not, that's going to be complicated."

"You're right," Jaime said, "but how about this? Instead of sending uniformed officers across the border, what if Deb and I head down to Naco in plainclothes? Maybe we could talk to them, with Detective Howell asking the questions and me doing the translating. We'll show them Xavier's picture and tell them we're looking for a little lost boy without mentioning we're cops."

"I'll check with Arturo, but that sounds good," Joanna agreed. "My guess is you're more likely to get answers that way than if you go around flashing badges and looking tough. Anything else?"

Casey raised her hand. "Our killer clipped off Xavier's fingernails down to the quick, so the victim must have inflicted some physical damage on his killer in the course of the murder. The killer also went so far as to dip his victim in bleach. That tells me our perpetrator is most likely a repeat offender who has done this before, so I'll start doing a computer search looking for similar unsolved cases—murdered children where the killer has gone to great lengths to make sure no usable DNA has been left behind."

Joanna nodded. "Good thinking," she said. "I'll see if Arturo can do the same on his side of the border. Anything else?"

With no further comments forthcoming, the meeting broke up. Joanna headed for her office only to find Marliss Shackleford lying in wait, parked on a chair in the waiting room next to Kristin's desk.

"Do you have a minute?" Marliss asked.

Joanna took a deep breath. As far as local press coverage was concerned these days, Marliss's website was the only game in town. There was no sense in pissing her off.

"Of course," Joanna replied. "Come in."

Marliss didn't waste any time getting down to business. "Are you making any progress in identifying the little kid the Highway Department pulled out of the San Pedro River in St. David on Saturday?"

"We're working on it," Joanna said. "We have a tentative ID, but we're currently awaiting DNA results for a final determination. Once we have that, we'll let you know."

Marliss wasn't happy with Joanna's reply. "I'm hearing rumors that the victim might be a kid from across the line in Mexico rather than someone from here in the States."

"No comment," Joanna said.

Saying those words to Marliss Shackleford and leaving her frustrated was one of the few perks of Joanna's job. She was not allowed to discuss active investigations with anyone outside law enforcement, and there was nothing she enjoyed more than being able to say so to some nosy reporter, this one in particular.

"So no suspects? No persons of interest?"

"Marliss," Joanna said with growing impatience, "the investigation is ongoing. That's all I'm going to tell you."

"Then why were you seen having lunch in Daisy's yesterday with Captain Arturo Peña, a member of the Federales unit based in Naco, Sonora?"

That was one of the hazards of being a cop in a small town where everyone knows everyone else along with a good deal about everyone else's business.

"Captain Peña and I are friends of long standing," Joanna answered. "We may be on different sides of an international border, but we run law enforcement agencies in the same general area and have many of the same concerns. The fact that the two of us meet from time to time to discuss those mutual concerns shouldn't come as a surprise to anyone."

"So more than forty-eight hours into what's likely to be a homicide investigation, you and your people have absolutely nothing, and you're sticking to no comment?"

"That's the general idea," Joanna said with a dismissive smile.

At that point Marliss rose to her feet and stormed from the room.

Good riddance, Joanna thought. *And don't let the door hit your butt on the way out!*

At home that night, dining on what Butch assured her were the last of the Thanksgiving leftovers, she related the story to him.

"You shouldn't torment the poor woman," Butch chided gently. "She's just doing her job."

"And I'm doing mine," Joanna replied. "The sooner she figures that out, the better."

CHAPTER 13

1967 on

STEVE ROPER'S FIRST YEAR OF TEACHING SCHOOL AT Fertile-Beltrami High wasn't as easy as he thought it would be. Andrew Donner may have been the principal of a small-town high school, but he was no pushover, and he required lesson plans from each of his teachers every Monday morning, no exceptions. As a beginning teacher, Steve's lesson plans underwent extra scrutiny. He was scrupulous about doing them, but once again, the voices in his head provided some invaluable advice—cheat!

Both his chemistry classes and his English ones used the same textbooks year after year, so that first year, when he did his lesson planning, he did so with a sheet of carbon paper placed under every page. That meant that every year, all he had to do was copy what he had written the first time around. He did the same thing for years thereafter, and Mr. Donner never caught on.

Steve's classes were made up of juniors and seniors—kids who were only five or six years younger than he was. Since many of them were also jackasses, he was afraid they'd end up eating him alive. He decided that the best way to handle the situation was to nip it in the bud and strike terror into the hearts of his students on the first day of school. That strategy worked like a charm. By starting out fierce and staying that way, the troublesome students he heard other teachers complaining about in the teachers' lounge weren't a problem for him.

On the first day of school each year, he marched into the room, slammed his books on his desk, and then delivered the same speech to every class. It was something that could have come straight out of Grandma Lucille's playbook.

"Hello, I am Mr. Roper. For your information, I am not 'Hey, Teach,' and I'm not 'Hey, you,' either. You will address me as Mr. Roper or Sir. You are all upperclassmen. At this point, some of you may be under the mistaken impression that you're smart and that you know it all. I'm here to tell you that you know NOTHING! I expect you to come to my class with your minds open and your mouths shut. If I assign homework, I expect it to be done and turned in on time. All homework will be graded, and F's for incomplete homework will count every bit as much as F's on tests.

"I'm not here to win any popularity contests. In fact, I expect the opposite outcome, but I promise you this. You may walk away from this school hating my guts, but you'll be a hell of a lot smarter than you are today."

End of speech. If Mr. Donner had ever learned that Mr. Roper used a curse word in class on the first day of school each year, he would have had been appalled, but none of Steve's students dared spill the beans. Besides, when subsequent standardized testing showed a distinct upswing for students in Mr. Roper's classes, no one had cause for complaint.

By 1969 the Vietnam War was in full swing. Toward the end of that school year, Steve's draft number came up. He was a killer, true, but he killed people for the fun of it and because he liked doing so. The idea of having to kill someone because he'd been ordered to do so by someone else didn't have the same appeal. However, with no reason to request a deferment, Steve Roper went to his physical fully expecting to be called up. That's when the doctor discovered that he had a previously undiagnosed heart murmur, one that made him

4F—unfit for military service. Needless to say, his personal Greek chorus of voices was thrilled with that news, and so was Steve.

That summer of 1970 he rewarded himself with a road trip to New York City. He timed his travel so he'd be in time for Coney Island's historic fireworks display on the Fourth of July. He suspected, rightfully so, that parents with their eyes focused on the sky would be far less vigilant than they should have been. In this instance he spotted a little blond girl, probably five or so, sound asleep on a nearby park bench. When he picked her up and carried her away, she snuggled comfortably into his chest without even stirring.

By the time the fireworks display ended, Steve was miles away with his prize safely stowed in the trunk of his brand-new Camaro. He drove well into New Jersey before stopping the car in the middle of a bridge on a sparsely traveled highway. He had never heard of the Rahway River before, but that's what the sign on the bridge said it was.

He knew the little girl had been awake during part of the drive because he had heard her crying, but by the time he opened the trunk she was asleep again. Then Steve donned his gloves and did what had to be done. The abject terror on her face as he squeezed the life out of her and the magic moment when the light disappeared from her eyes were all the reward he needed. Then he tossed her lifeless body over the rail and into the water below, but not before removing one of the red, white, and blue barrettes she had worn in her hair.

Steve never knew Coney Island Girl's name. Once her parents realized she was missing, all hell must have broken loose, and the story was probably all over the news, but Steve never heard a peep about it. By the time the sun came up the next morning, he was well on his way home—out of New Jersey and a long way across Pennsylvania. He made it home to Fertile without any complications.

That one successful excursion was enough to shut his voices up for the remainder of the summer, and that was fine with him. He'd made a good job of it and was ready to take it easy.

The fact that a little girl named Deborah Miller had gone missing during the Fourth of July Fireworks display on Coney Island was indeed big news in New York City. The Miller family, Deborah and her parents, Donald and Charlotte Miller of Boston, Massachusetts, had been in NYC visiting relatives over the Fourth of July weekend. After Deborah's disappearance, her anguished parents were on every news channel and in every newspaper begging for her safe return. Weeks later, a fisherman in New Jersey found the fully clothed but badly decomposed body of a young girl along the banks of the Rahway River. She was identified by comparing the clothing found on the remains with photos taken of Deborah earlier that day on various rides in Coney Island.

No suspects in her homicide were ever identified.

CHAPTER 14

BISBEE, ARIZONA
Wednesday, November 29, 2023

JOANNA WAS ON HER WAY TO WORK WEDNESDAY MORNING when a call came in from Jenny.

"Hey," Joanna said. "If you're off shift, shouldn't you be sleeping?"

"I'm headed to bed shortly," Jenny answered, "but I wanted to give you a heads-up. I'm pretty sure one of my traffic stops from last night will end up on the news."

Joanna's heart went to her throat. As far as putting cops in danger, domestic violence calls come in first, but ordinary traffic stops run a close second, and middle-of-the-night traffic stops can be the worst.

"What happened?"

"Rick and I were patrolling Highway 86 between the Tucson city limits and the reservation boundary west of Three Points. About one thirty in the morning, we were headed back toward town when this Toyota Tundra Dual Cab pickup came barreling off Valencia Road and turned left in front of us without stopping or even slowing down at the stop sign. As the vehicle roared past us heading westbound, I could see it was a female driver, and it's a miracle she didn't hit us. I pulled a U-ie, lit up my lights, and went after her. She was all over the road, but finally, three or four miles later, she pulled over.

"I got out of my unit and approached the vehicle on the driver's side. Because she'd taken so long to pull over, Rick got out, too, and approached from the passenger side. When I got there, the window was still rolled up, but I could see the woman inside was staring straight ahead and sipping away on a can of Coors. I tapped on the window, and finally she rolled it down.

"'What seems to be the problem, Officer?' she wanted to know."

"Drinking and driving for one thing," Joanna put in.

"'License and registration,' I told her," Jenny continued.

"'Don't need 'em,'" she said. "'This is a free country, and I'm a sovereign citizen.'"

Joanna sighed. She'd heard all the sovereign citizen crap herself on occasion, always coming from people who claimed that the laws of the land didn't apply to them. "Not that same old BS," she said aloud.

"Yup," Jenny agreed. "Same old same old. I told her I needed her to turn off the engine and step out of the vehicle. And what did she say to that? 'No dice. It's cold as hell out there, and I'm not wearing a coat. If you want me out of this car, honey bun, you're going to have to make me, and I don't think you can.'"

Joanna's stomach tightened. "Wait, was she armed?"

"No, she wasn't," Jenny replied, "not exactly, but she weighed a good four hundred pounds. Even with the seat all the way back in the Tundra, her body was up against the steering wheel so tight that I don't know how she managed to steer. Anyway, by then, Rick was coming around the vehicle to assist me, but at that point, the woman places the beer can in her cup holder, puts the car in gear, hits the gas, and takes off like a shot.

"Naturally Rick and I hopped into our vehicle and went after her. Since she was fleeing and most likely prepared to resist as well, he got on the radio asking for backup. A couple of miles later, almost at Three Points, she veered into the left-hand lane again before slamming into a bridge abutment hard enough for the airbags to deploy. When we got to her, she was bleeding some, but she didn't seem to be badly injured. The pickup, however, was totaled. It was such a mess that when we tried to open the doors, they were all jammed. At that point, the driver couldn't have gotten out of the Tundra even if she'd wanted to."

By then Joanna had pulled into her parking place at the Justice Center, but she made no effort to exit her vehicle. She needed to hear the rest of the story.

Jenny continued. "With the wreckage partially blocking the left lane, we had to slow traffic enough so other unsuspecting drivers wouldn't smash into it. With our backup still ten minutes out, I positioned my patrol car in front of the wreckage with all lights flashing and then put on a reflective vest so I could direct traffic around that while Rick radioed in to Dispatch, letting them know that we needed EMS, somebody with the jaws of life, and a tow truck.

"As luck would have it, the first eastbound vehicle that came along happened to be a KOLD camera crew returning from covering a contentious school board meeting over in Ajo. As far as they were concerned, lucking into a car wreck was a big improvement over what had gone on during the meeting, so they set up shop and started filming.

"Eventually our backup showed up, and so did the jaws of life, but guess what? The woman *still* refused to exit her vehicle. In the end it took four officers and three EMS to drag her out. Then, when they tried to load her into the back of a patrol car, she wouldn't get into that, either. She sat down on the pavement saying, 'Are you nuts? My tits won't even fit in that thing.'

"Unfortunately she was right about not fitting. They ended up transporting her by ambulance to the Pima County Jail. By then the guy running the camera was laughing his head off. He thought it was screamingly funny. As for the rest of us? Not so much!"

For someone not directly involved, Joanna could see that the cameraman wasn't wrong—the situation really was funny, but she fought back her own urge to laugh.

"Did she actually resist?" she asked.

"Not really, but she didn't have to," Jenny replied. "She just sat there and wouldn't move. She also refused to take a Breathalyzer, so she's booked into jail on suspicion of DUI."

"Well," Joanna said, "that's one for the books."

"Isn't it just," Jenny agreed, "but if it hits the news, I'm pretty sure they'll cut the line about her tits. I can laugh about it now, but last night it was no laughing matter."

"It could have been worse," Joanna said. "I'm grateful that you're safe and glad no one was hurt. Now try to get some sleep while I go to work. After last night, your shift tonight is bound to be better."

Once inside, Joanna passed through her office and stuck her head into the reception room. "Sorry I'm late," she told Kristin. "Anything I should know about?"

"Actually there is. You'd best get over to the jail. One of the inmates found out where the work crew had squirreled away their lunches and made off with them. The workers are threatening to go on strike."

"On my way," Joanna said. "Get on the phone to Daisy's and tell them my department will be putting in an emergency take-out order to replace those missing lunches as soon as I figure out what everybody wants."

As she headed for the jail, it occurred to her that depending on where you stood, the case of missing lunches was probably almost as funny as dealing with a four-hundred-pound drunk, but this time the laughter shoe was on the other foot.

Offering to buy replacement lunches fixed things and quelled what had threatened to turn into a pitched battle between the workers and her inmates. Figuring out what everyone wanted and making sure it was ordered properly wasn't easy, but eventually Joanna managed, promising the food would be there by the time the workers were ready for their lunch break. It was also determined that, for as long as the work crew was on-site, all their foodstuffs would be stored in a locked cabinet in the jail commander's office where they would be safe not only from thieving inmates, but also from Mojo, the jail's resident K-9.

Back in her office, Joanna gave Kristin her departmental credit card and sent her into town to place the order and fetch the food. Then she settled in to work at her desk. When she'd first appointed Tom Hadlock as her chief deputy, it had been something of a bumpy ride, but now that he'd settled into the position, he was truly her right-hand man and had relieved her of much of the routine office work that had once been the bane of her existence. There was still plenty of that, but these days it was doable rather than overwhelming.

Again, she had brought lunch from home—a peanut butter and jelly sandwich rather than turkey—which she ate at her desk. Joanna was relieved to learn that Elena's cheek swab was now in the hands of the Department of Public Safety. The DNA results would arrive when they arrived and not a moment sooner.

A little before two, Deb Howell and Jaime Carbajal showed up. "How did the interviews go?" Joanna asked.

"Not very productive," Deb replied. "We weren't wearing uniforms, but the kids knew we were cops, and they live under a strict policy of loose lips sink ships. None of them had seen anything or heard anything. As for the kid in the photograph? They all claimed they'd never seen him before."

"Which, since they all live on the same street, probably isn't true," Joanna put in.

"Exactly," Deb agreed. "Arturo says he'll keep asking around. He may have better luck getting through to someone in that bunch than we did. According to him, the Federales have an anonymous tip line that covers all Sonora, so maybe someone will make that call."

"Let's hope," Joanna said. "Marliss Shackleford is all over my case because we haven't solved it already when, in actual fact, we don't have so much as a single lead."

"Marliss Shackleford is a pain in the butt," Deb said. Obviously Detective Howell, like her boss, had already had a few unpleasant run-ins of her own with the incredibly annoying reporter.

Joanna laughed aloud at that. "She certainly is, but please don't say so in public."

CHAPTER 15

FERTILE, MINNESOTA
1972

FIVE YEARS IN, STEPHEN ROPER'S CAREER IN TEACHING was going swimmingly. He no longer had to deliver his opening day speech each fall because his reputation preceded him. By the time students entered his classrooms, they were already terrified. At first people wondered a bit about his bachelor existence, and occasionally a newly arrived female teacher would make a play for him, but he quickly made it clear that he wasn't interested. Why would he be lonely? After all, his voices were always with him.

After several years of driving east for his summer excursions, he turned his attention in the other direction. In early June of 1972, he treated himself to a brand-new Camaro in anticipation of his upcoming road trip. He had been tempted to buy a flashy red one, but those were too noticeable, so he settled for deep blue instead. With the latest issue of the *Rand McNally Road Atlas* in hand, he headed out, crossing over into North Dakota at Grand Forks and heading due south.

Stretches of interstate were being constructed here and there along the way, but Steve stuck to less traveled roadways, staying at modestly priced, family-owned motels in smaller towns—Milbank and Yankton in South Dakota, Norfolk and Hebron in Nebraska, before crossing into Kansas. After an overnight stay in Salina, he headed off on a diagonal route across the state that landed him in Liberal for that night's stay. A quick trip across bits of the panhandles of both Oklahoma and Texas found him in New Mexico. His first glimpses of vast desert landscapes with blue-tinged mountain ranges off in the distance were so awe-inspiring that, despite being a lifelong Minnesotan, Steve Roper unaccountably felt right at home.

He had heard people talk about "dry heat," but only then did he finally understand it. After tolerating the Midwest's humid and muggy summers, June in New Mexico was pure bliss. He spent his first night in Tucumcari and his second in Lordsburg. The next day, deciding he'd give Phoenix a try, he headed into Arizona for the first time, traveling west on US Highway 70.

Along the way he'd kept an eye out for suitable victims, but so far nothing had caught his eye. Finally, somewhere between Safford and Globe and just past a tiny burg called Bylas, the stars aligned with the muttering voices in his head to offer up exactly what he wanted—a dark-haired young woman wearing a sky-blue squaw dress who was walking westward on the shoulder of the road.

He slowed the vehicle enough to put it in reverse and came to a stop next to her. "Need a lift?" he asked, rolling down the window.

Nodding demurely, she reached for the door handle, opened the door, and stepped inside. Once the car started moving again, she sat huddled next to the door in total silence. Glancing in her direction, Steve noticed she wore an ornate silver and turquoise necklace with what looked like a horseshoe front and center.

"Nice necklace," he observed.

The girl touched the horseshoe with one hand and murmured a quiet thank you.

After that she fell silent once more. Steve didn't say anything, either, mostly because he didn't want to alarm her—at least not until it was too late.

Several miles later he said, "Where are you headed?"

"Globe," she answered. As far as small talk went, that was it.

Steve Roper was a serial killer whose preferred deadly weapons were his hands. He'd figured that strategy out early on. Bullets or shell casings left at a crime scene could be traced. He still had the switchblade he'd taken from the Turtle River bitch and the one-bullet derringer he'd purchased in advance of his Freddy the Freeloader drug purchase, but those were back home in Minnesota, still hidden in his cigar box.

As for the cigar box itself? That was locked away in the safe he'd had installed in the far back corner of his basement, concealed behind a mountain of boxes. But even if he'd had the switchblade with him, he wouldn't have used it. Knives were messy. Ditto for instruments that caused blunt-force trauma. Strangling worked best for him. For one thing, it made for a clean kill. It was also up close and personal.

When it came to disposing of the corpses, his first choice was always dumping his victims into bodies of water. That way, any physical evidence would most likely be washed away. At that moment no bodies of water were in evidence. US Highway 70 seemed to be traveling parallel with something called the Gila River, but the several culverts he'd crossed, ones that presumably held washes that would eventually feed into the river, were bone dry, leading him to believe that the riverbed itself was also probably dry as dust.

But then, just past a tiny place called Peridot, barely more than a wide spot in the road, he saw a sign indicating that the next intersection was with something called Coolidge Dam Road. If there was a dam, didn't that mean that water of some kind had to be out there somewhere? If so, Steve intended to find it.

The Camaro was almost on top of the intersection when he slammed on the brakes and spun the steering wheel sharply to the left. His unsuspecting passenger's body slammed against the car door while her head bounced off the passenger window. Momentarily dazed, it took her a few seconds to recover. Meanwhile Steve, having regained control of the vehicle, floor-boarded it. By then the girl had come to enough to realize she was in danger. Screaming in alarm, she grabbed the door handle as if determined to throw herself out of the moving vehicle. Before she could do so, he seized her left wrist and held it in an iron-clad grip.

She fought for all she was worth, forcing Steve to stop the vehicle in order to gain control. While he was occupied with that, she somehow managed to lean over far enough to bite the hell out of the back of his hand. The wound instantly spurted blood. At that point, he dragged her across the bench seat where he was able to pin her body against his by clamping his right arm around her throat. Then, using only his left hand to steer, he once again set the Camaro in motion. Luckily there were no other vehicles nearby to bear witness to what had just occurred.

She struggled against him, trying to loosen the pressure on her neck, but it was no use. Eventually she went limp, but in case she was only playing dead and trying to trick him, Steve maintained the pressure on her throat. He wanted to be sure the bitch was really dead before loosening his grip.

Several miles later Steve finally caught sight of a body of water he later learned was the San Carlos Reservoir. On the way, he encountered only two oncoming vehicles. If anyone had noticed the couple snuggled together in that speeding blue Camaro, they probably assumed it to be a pair of carefree young lovers on their way to a secluded spot near the water for an afternoon make-out session.

The girl was deceased long before Steve arrived at the shoreline. Some cars were parked here and there, but not many and not enough to be worrisome, and Steve managed to locate a sufficiently secluded spot. Even though his hand was bleeding like crazy, the first thing he did was yank off the girl's necklace and stuff that into his pocket. Then, knowing the bright blue dress would be easy to spot, he took the time to undress her. After unhooking her bra, he wrapped that around the wound on his hand to stem the bleeding. Once he had stowed her clothing under the Camaro's spare tire, he carried her into the murky water, let go of her, and watched the body sink to the bottom.

Heading back to the highway, Steve's hand hurt like hell! *Damned Indians*, he thought, staring at the bloodstains marring the page of his road atlas, which was still open to the map of New Mexico. *How come those savages fight back so hard?*

He had planned to stop at the first available car wash to remove the telltale dust from his vehicle, but once he left Reservoir Girl behind, he realized that Globe was too close to the scene and so was the next burg over, a town called Superior, so he headed for Apache Junction and Mesa.

By the time he reached Apache Junction, the bleeding had stopped. He pulled into the parking lot of the first pharmacy he saw. Before going inside, he went around to the trunk of the car where he stuffed the blood-soaked bra in with the dead girl's other clothing. Then he rewrapped his damaged hand in a clean handkerchief that he took from his luggage.

Inside the store, he collected a bottle of peroxide—Grandma Lucille's preferred first aid treatment—along with a stock of gauze and tape.

"What happened to your hand?" the concerned pharmacist asked while ringing up Steve's purchases.

"Neighbor's dog bit me," he said.

"Any chance he's rabid?"

"No, the guy who owned him claimed he'd had his rabies shots, but I can promise you this, that dog sure as hell won't be biting anyone else."

"You take care now," the pharmacist added as Steve walked away. "Whatever you do, don't let that thing get infected."

After leaving the drugstore, Steve treated his injured hand and wrapped it properly before tracking down a do-it-yourself car wash. By then he was beyond exhausted. He located a nearby motel, checked in, and showered, all the while managing to keep his bandaged hand out of the water. After that he went straight to bed without even bothering to go looking for something to eat.

His hand was still aching once he got into bed. Lying there, he couldn't help regretting that he hadn't been able to watch the light go out of the little bitch's eyes, but at least he had her necklace. That counted for something.

CHAPTER 16

MESA, ARIZONA
June 1972–1976

STEVE'S THROBBING HAND KEPT HIM AWAKE MUCH OF THE night. When he awakened the next morning, it was already after ten. He cleaned the wound on his hand, dosed it with more peroxide, and applied a new bandage. By then it was dangerously close to his designated checkout time of eleven a.m.

Stepping out of his room into the parking lot, it felt as if he'd walked into an oven. People might claim it was "only a dry heat," but this kind of scorching was ridiculous. When he stopped by the office to let them know he was leaving, he asked the desk clerk if there were any decent restaurants nearby.

"There's a Bob's Big Boy just up the street," she said. "Will that do?"

"As long as their air-conditioning works."

Steve located the restaurant, managed to park in a small patch of shade, and bought a newspaper from a machine on his way inside. Thankfully the AC in the restaurant worked just fine.

"How hot is it out there?" he asked his waitress when she came to take his order.

"It's a hundred and six right now," she answered, "but it's supposed to get up to a hundred eleven by later today."

In other words, Steve thought, *I'm not sticking around Mesa or Phoenix for a minute longer than necessary.*

Once Steve opened the newspaper, he went looking for the weather map of Arizona. Studying it, he was astonished to see the wide disparity in temperatures throughout the state. While Phoenix was predicted to top out at 111 degrees that day, Tucson, a hundred miles to the south, was expecting 101, while Bisbee, another hundred miles south of Tucson, would clock in at only 92. North of Phoenix, a place called Sedona was set to hit 90, while Flagstaff wasn't expected to exceed 85.

Before departing the restaurant, Steve made up his mind that Flagstaff was his next destination. Using directions from his waitress, Steve made his way to the Black Canyon Freeway. In addition to providing directions, the waitress had also explained that Flag, as she called it, was only a hundred fifty miles or so from Mesa, and that the road was "pretty good." Pretty good meant that part of it was four lanes with controlled access, but a lot of it wasn't. For one thing, long swaths of what was destined to be Interstate 17 were still under construction. For another, most of those hundred and fifty miles were entirely uphill. On this ridiculously hot Friday, even though it was only late morning, it seemed as though everyone in Phoenix was determined to get out of Dodge and head for the mountains.

Trucks passing other trucks didn't necessarily get the hell out of the way in a hurry, so for much of the time, traffic slowed to a crawl. Not only that, the shoulder of the road was dotted with overheated stalled vehicles with their hoods open and their radiators steaming. Luckily, Steve's Camaro managed the steep grades with no hitches and no overheating.

Once in Flagstaff, Steve had a hell of a time finding a place to stay. By two o'clock in the afternoon, No Vacancy signs were everywhere. He finally ended up in a scuzzy downtown hotel that reminded him of that old Roger Miller song about "no phone, no pool, no pets." It wasn't especially clean, either, but even without air-conditioning in the room, with the window open and a slight breeze, it was tolerable.

Whenever Steve was on the road, he made it a point to call his mother on Saturday morning, because now he was all she had. After her divorce from Jackson Roper, she had never remarried. As far as she was concerned, Frederick Chalmers had been the love of her life, and she had never gotten over losing him.

These days she wasn't in the best of health, either. Decades of standing on her feet, first waiting tables and later managing the restaurant, had taken their toll. Her legs were a mess of varicose veins, and she'd worn compression stockings for years. In the last six months or so, things had gotten so bad that she'd finally been forced to sell the restaurant. As the only game in town, the Country Inn had been a going concern, and she'd gotten good money for it. The proceeds from the sale combined with living mortgage-free in the house Gramps had bought after liquidating his properties meant she was in good financial shape, but her lifelong dreams of traveling the world in retirement were now on hold.

After breakfast the next day, Steve rounded up a fistful of change and located the nearest payphone. Once he placed the call, he was surprised when it was answered not by his mother, but by Becky Thompson, his mother's next-door neighbor.

"Oh, Stephen," she said. "I'm so glad you called. Your mother asked me to wait here at the house this morning in case you did."

"Mom's not home?" he asked. "Where is she?"

"In the hospital in Bemidji. They took her there by ambulance the day before yesterday. She told me you were traveling and that she had no way to reach you."

"Took her in by ambulance?" Steve repeated. "How come? What's wrong?"

"She has a DDT," Becky said breathlessly.

"You mean a DVT?" Steve asked. "A deep vein thrombosis."

"I suppose that's it," Becky agreed. "I never can keep all those letters straight. They're giving her blood thinners to try to dissolve it, but if they can't, there's a chance it might break loose and go to her lungs."

Steve was aware of the likely outcome from that.

"Are you planning on going to the hospital today?" he asked.

"Yes," Becky answered. "I'm heading there as soon as we get off the phone."

"Does she have a phone in her room?"

"Not in the ICU."

Steve took a breath. "Okay," he said. "I'm in Arizona right now. I don't know how long it'll take me to get home, but I'll head that way as soon as I check out of my hotel. Tell her I'll be in touch with the hospital and see if I can call while I'm in transit."

"Do you need the number of the hospital?"

"No," he said. "I'll be able to get it from information."

He was underway within the hour. After consulting the bloodstained page of his atlas, he decided to head straight east from Flagstaff and turn north at Albuquerque. As he crossed the state line into New Mexico, Steve Roper knew one thing for sure. Arizona was the place where he wanted to be. Not Phoenix for sure and probably not Tucson, either. He'd want to live somewhere cooler, but he would be back. What he didn't know at the time was that it would take several years before that could happen.

UNLIKE HIS OUTGOING TRIP, THE RETURN DRIVE WASN'T leisurely. He arrived back in Fertile exhausted after two and a half days of forced-march driving. His mother was out of intensive care by then, but she was still in the hospital. While being treated for the DVT, her doctors had discovered a spot on her breast and they were now treating her for breast cancer—starting with a double mastectomy.

Once in the privacy of his own home, Steve went down to his basement, opened the safe, and made two additions to his cigar box—the turquoise necklace, a squash blossom necklace as he later learned, and the bloodied map of New Mexico which he'd torn from his *Road Atlas* and folded into a square small enough to fit inside the box.

Fortunately the wound on the back of Steve's hand didn't become infected, but the scar tissue it left behind began to look exactly like what it was—a bite mark. Eventually he made up a story about spending a couple of days volunteering at an Arts and Crafts fair in Taos, New Mexico, where one of the artists had accidentally dropped an overheated piece of metal on the back of his hand.

Cynthia Hawkins Roper survived the blood clot but died of breast cancer four years later in the spring of 1976. And who cared for her all that time? Her son, that's who. Steve wasn't an empathetic individual and didn't take naturally to caregiving, but he forced himself to do it—not because he necessarily cared about his mother, but because the appearance of being a good and loving son made for an excellent disguise. Around Fertile his unwavering caregiving made him look downright heroic.

While handling his mother's affairs, Steve discovered that Gramps had been a canny investor and had left his daughter with plenty of money, which probably wouldn't have been the case had Freddy the Freeloader managed to lay his hands on it. Thanks to Steve's timely intervention, that hadn't happened. In actual fact, Cynthia Roper could have retired years earlier if she'd wanted. Since she hadn't, everything that was left over—the remains of Gramps's estate and the proceeds from selling the Country Inn and the house—would come straight to Steve.

That's when the voices in his head tuned up and started suggesting that maybe he should speed up his mother's passing, but he told them absolutely not in no uncertain terms. Reading Arthur Conan Doyle and Agatha Christie had taught him one thing for sure—killers get caught because they murder people they know or else they target victims where the killers themselves have something to gain financially. Caring for his mother for those four years was tedious as hell, but making sure his mother died of indisputably natural causes was the price Steve Roper had to pay for him to be able to go on killing people he actually wanted to kill.

At his mother's funeral, when people told him what a wonderful person he was to have looked after her so lovingly, he nodded and smiled and told them thank you very much. At the cemetery, he saw to it that her grave site was just where she wanted it to be—right next to Fred Chalmers's. But when he got home that evening, after everything was said and done, he settled down in his easy chair, closed his eyes, and told the voices aloud what they really wanted to hear.

"It's finally over," he said, "and good riddance."

CHAPTER 17

BISBEE, ARIZONA
Thursday, November 30, 2023

JOANNA ARRIVED AT HER OFFICE THE NEXT MORNING TO the noisy but welcome sound of jackhammers. That meant Dave Ruiz's crew was cutting through the jail's concrete floor to create trenches to install plumbing in the redesigned solitary unit.

She dropped her purse on her desk and then peeked into the reception area. "Any trouble in lunch land this morning?" she asked.

Kristin laughed. "So far so good," she said.

"Okay, then," Joanna replied.

At her desk she busied herself with writing the report she would need to present to the Board of Supervisors at their Friday morning meeting. No doubt they would require a full update from her on the construction process and the seemingly unnecessary expense of the prisoner transfer, to say nothing of the credit card charge covering the lost-lunch fiasco. As soon as Marliss Shackleford caught wind of that, Joanna knew she'd be only too happy to spread the word near and far.

Joanna was deep into the process when a call came in from Arturo Peña. "Good morning," she said.

"What are you up to?" he asked.

"My job," she replied. "And no, it's not solving crimes. I'm dealing with endless paperwork. Why do you ask?"

"Because I'd like you to come for a visit today, and not in my office—at my house."

Joanna was puzzled. "Why?" she asked. "What's going on?"

"A possible informant has come forward, but she doesn't want to come to my office, and since she's a migrant who can't be caught on the wrong side of the border, I can't exactly bring her to yours."

"What time?"

"Say two o'clock?"

"Two it is," she said. "Give me the address, so I can key it into my GPS."

Arturo gave her the address before adding, "One more thing—well, two."

"What?"

"No uniform and no official vehicle."

"In other words, your informant doesn't want anyone to know she's talking to the cops."

"*Exactamente*," Arturo said. "See you at two."

At noontime, Joanna went home to change clothes. She hadn't planned on disturbing Butch because she knew he was hard at work on his next manuscript. Nevertheless, he emerged from the den as soon as she stepped into the house.

"Did I somehow forget that you were coming home for lunch?" he asked, following her into the bedroom.

"You didn't forget because I'm not home for lunch," Joanna told him. "I'm coming here to change into civilian clothes and to trade my Interceptor for the Enclave."

"How come?"

"I need to pay a visit to Naco, Sonora, this afternoon. Arturo Peña has a potential informant in the Xavier Delgado case, and she's not someone who can cross the international border without going to jail and jeopardizing any chance of her being allowed to enter the US illegally."

"So a migrant then?"

"Evidently."

"But you will be home for dinner."

"That's the plan."

"Okay, then," Butch said. "Good luck, but I'm going back to work. I need to make some forward progress before the kids get home from school."

AT FIVE TO TWO, JOANNA CLEARED THE BORDER AND drove to the Peña residence, a modest home on Calle 5 de Mayo, right on the edge of town. Arturo answered the door when she rang the bell.

"Come in," he said. "She's already here."

He led Joanna into the living room where a dark-haired middle-aged woman wearing jeans and a leather jacket sat on a sofa.

"This is Señora Aña Mendoza," he said, indicating the woman, "and this is Sheriff Joanna Brady."

Joanna was taken aback when Arturo made the introductions in English, but Aña didn't seem surprised, so Joanna responded in English as well. "Glad to meet you," she said.

"I'm glad to meet you, too, Sheriff Brady," Aña replied. "Before my father was murdered, he taught English at the Universidad Americana in Managua. He also taught me. He was a good teacher with the wrong politics. For people like that, Managua can be a dangerous place. After he was murdered, I was afraid I would be next, so I applied for refugee status in the US, but rather than stay in Managua, I came here to wait. I don't actually live at the camp. I have the means to rent a room, so I do, but at the camp, although no one pays me to do it, I try to teach the kids to speak English, and when I'm there I hear things. The kids trust me. That's why no one must know that I have spoken to you."

"In other words," Joanna said, "you wish to be a confidential informant."

"Correct," Aña said. "Confidential. So what do you know about an organization called Hands Across the Border?"

Joanna thought about that. "It's my understanding that it's a charitable organization that provides assistance to migrants waiting to cross the border into the US."

Aña nodded and smiled. "That's right, and there are chapters in towns all along the border. They provide necessities wherever possible—food, clothing, blankets, that sort of thing."

"I believe there's a chapter in Bisbee," Joanna added.

"That is also correct," Aña said. "A couple of years ago one of their members bought an old food truck and converted it into a traveling storefront. It's called *La Tienda Gratuita*—The Free Store. It comes across the border every other Friday. Usually the driver brings sack lunches, but mostly he brings things people have donated. Secondhand clothing is better than no clothing."

Joanna nodded.

"The man who drives the Free Store truck is a man named Mr. Roper. The kids call him Señor Santa Claus."

"Mr. Roper," Joanna repeated thoughtfully. As far as she knew, the only person by that name living in the area was Stephen Roper—a long-retired teacher from Bisbee High School. He'd actually been Joanna's English teacher during her senior year at BHS.

"Stephen Roper?" she asked in disbelief.

"Correct," Arturo put in. "I checked with the border guards. They told me he's the Free Store guy."

"Yesterday, after the detectives came to talk to some of the kids, I overheard two of them talking. According to them, the last time Mr. Roper was here, the kids from the camp went to collect their lunches and see what else he had to offer. Because Xavier was too young to go to school, when that was in session, he'd get lonely and tag along with older kids from the camp. They call him *El Pequeña Plaga*, the Little Pest.

"When they went to the Free Store, Xavier tagged along. For some reason, Mr. Roper had a fresh supply of shoes, all kinds of shoes in lots of different sizes that he'd gotten because a shoe store in the States was going out of business. Most of the kids walked away with new shoes. They said Xavier was still there when they left, and the last time they saw him, he was talking to Señor Santa Claus about a certain pair of shoes, ones he really liked."

Joanna's heart skipped a beat. "Did they say what kind of shoes?"

"Yes, *zapatillas de caña alta*," Aña said, momentarily slipping back into her native Spanish. "High-topped sneakers."

A layer of goose bumps flashed across Joanna's body. Before his retirement in the early 2000s, Stephen Roper had been a teacher at Bisbee High School for decades. He was not only a well-respected member of the community, he was also someone Joanna Brady knew personally. Just because he may have been one of the last people to see Xavier Delgado alive didn't mean he had killed the boy, but it also didn't mean he hadn't. Still, the idea that Xavier had been looking at a pair of high-topped sneakers the last time the kids from the migrant camp saw him was striking. The detail about the high-topped sneakers was a holdback, something no one outside Joanna's investigation team knew anything about.

Trusting her face not to betray her roiling emotions, Joanna spoke again. "This has been very helpful, and we'll certainly look into it."

"If you end up arresting him, will the boys be required to testify in court?" Aña asked.

"They might be," Joanna said. "I can't say for sure."

Of course, given the boys' migrant status, she wondered, would having them testify even be possible? Would the county prosecutor's office be able to negotiate a peace treaty with the feds that would enable the boys and maybe the rest of their families to cross the border legally? Answering those questions was a battle for another day.

"Please don't let them know that I told you," Aña begged.

"Believe me, we won't," Joanna assured her. "You've given us something very valuable, Señora Mendoza, and something we didn't have before—an actual named suspect. But until we can verify his involvement in this case with something more solid than what you've told us so far, we won't even approach him."

"Thank you."

"No, thank *you*," Joanna insisted. "Thank you not only for the information you've just provided, but also for doing what you're doing—teaching kids who are not only desperately in need of someone who can teach them, but also for being someone they can trust."

Aña stood up then. "I'll be going then," she said with a smile. "Thank you for meeting with me. I hope this helps. Anyone who would murder an innocent boy like that is a monster."

"He certainly is," Joanna agreed, "and if Mr. Roper turns out to be the killer, then he's been hiding in plain sight for decades."

Arturo showed Aña out and then came back into the living room. "Well," he said, "what do you think?"

"I think she may have just handed us our guy," Joanna replied, then she took several minutes to clue him in about the high-topped sneakers.

"What are you going to do now?" Arturo asked.

"I'm going to go back to my office and put people to work finding out everything there is to know about Stephen Roper and Hands Across the Border."

"You're not going to go interview him?"

"Nope," Joanna replied, "not yet. I don't want him to have any idea that we've made a possible connection between him and Xavier Delgado's death until I'm damned good and ready. When I do get around to paying him a call, I'm hoping I'll do so with an arrest warrant in hand."

"If there's anything more I can do to help, please let me know," Arturo said.

"You and Aña have already helped immeasurably," Joanna told him. "Before meeting Aña, my investigators had nothing at all to go on. Now we do, and the faster we can get the killer behind bars, the better."

AS SOON AS JOANNA CLEARED CUSTOMS AND WHILE STILL in Naco, Arizona, she dialed Casey Ledford's number.

"I believe I've got a person of interest for you in the Xavier Delgado homicide," Joanna said, once the call was answered.

"Really?" Casey replied. "Who is it?"

"Stephen Roper."

"Did you just say Stephen Roper?" Casey repeated after a moment of stunned silence. "You've got to be kidding! The same Mr. Roper who used to teach chemistry at Bisbee High?"

"The very one," Joanna replied.

"But he's who got me interested in chemistry in the first place," Casey objected. "He's the reason I became a CSI."

"Be that as it may," Joanna said, "it's possible that he's also our killer. For right now, don't say a word about this to anyone outside your lab. I'm going to call a team meeting tomorrow morning first thing to discuss this lead, and I'll want all hands on deck. In the meantime, I want you and Dave Hollicker to track down everything there is to know about Mr. Stephen Roper and about a charitable group called Hands Across the Border. If you end up having to work all night, fine. I'm authorizing the OT."

"Okay, boss," Casey replied. "Not to worry. Once I clue Dave in, we'll be on it."

Joanna's next call was to Kristin, giving her the list of people she expected to be in the conference room for a mandatory meeting at ten o'clock the following morning and asking her to notify them of same.

"Wait," Kristin objected. "Isn't ten a.m. the same time you're due at the Board of Supervisors meeting?"

Joanna instantly realized Kristin was right. With the issues that currently needed to be presented to the board, Sheriff Brady herself had to be on hand. This wasn't an appearance that could be delegated to her chief deputy.

"You're right," Joanna agreed with a sigh. "Make the meeting time 2 p.m."

"Do you want me to tell them what it's about?" Kristin asked.

"No," Joanna said decisively. "Just tell them it's mandatory, no exceptions."

After ending the call, however, Joanna could see the bright side of changing the meeting time. It would give her CSIs that much more time to see what information they could dig up on Stephen Roper.

CHAPTER 18

FERTILE, MINNESOTA
1975–1976

EVEN AS STEVE HAD HEADED HOME TO MINNESOTA IN 1972 to care for his ailing mother, he had already decided that one way or the other, Arizona was the place for him. Over the course of the next several years, while being her caregiver, there wasn't much he could do about it. Not only that but also to the dismay of his voices, he'd had to forgo his summertime adventures.

The public library in Fertile carried a few daily newspapers for their patrons to read—*The Wall Street Journal*, *The New York Times*, and the dailies from Minneapolis/St. Paul—but other than posting the expected high and low temperatures for Phoenix on any given day, they offered very little Arizona-specific weather information. Wanting to know more, Steve began to subscribe to several Arizona papers, ones from locations in which he might be interested—Pinetop, Sedona, Bisbee, Prescott, and Flagstaff. The weather information he gleaned from those gave him a much clearer idea of where he might want to settle and where he wouldn't.

For instance, he was astonished to discover that Flagstaff, at an elevation of 6,800 feet, could often have as much as seven feet of snow over the course of the winter. He immediately took that city off his list. One of the reasons he was leaving Minnesota was to get away from cold weather, not to be buried in seven-foot snowdrifts in sunny Arizona. Because of their high temperatures, Tucson and Phoenix were never on his radar in the first place.

Steve read his newspapers in the evenings, often in those later months, while seated at his mother's bedside. "What's going on with you?" she had asked him once. "You never used to be interested in newspapers."

Fortunately, she was more interested in what was on television at the time and hadn't tumbled to the fact that the papers he was reading were all from out of state.

"Just trying to keep up with current events," he told her.

The other person in town who noticed his new interest in newspapers was Walt Whipple, the postmaster. Because there were often too many papers to fit in his P.O. box, Steve would have to go up to the service window to collect them.

"You thinking about moving to Arizona?" Walt inquired one day as he handed over Steve's latest batch of mail.

Fortunately, Steve already had a plausible answer lined up and ready to deploy. "I've been having some trouble with my back lately," he explained. "The doc told me it's early stages of rheumatoid arthritis and that I might need to consider moving to a high, dry climate, so that's what I'm doing."

"Sorry to hear that," Walt said. "Your mother would be lost without you."

"Yes, she would," Steve agreed. "That's why I'm only considering it at the moment. I haven't mentioned a word about it to her or anyone else, and I'd appreciate it if you didn't, either."

"Absolutely," Walt replied. "My lips are sealed."

By the spring of 1976, Cynthia Hawkins's medical situation had worsened to the point that Steve knew it was time to make his move. After reading the *Bisbee Bee*, he learned that a number of local teachers, unhappy with the current superintendent of schools as well as the school board, were pulling up stakes and leaving town. Shortly after reading the article, Steve placed a long-distance call to the superintendent's office, asking if there were any teacher openings expected for the upcoming year.

Eager to reassure parents and students alike that there would be no educational disruptions, the superintendent wanted to fill those previously unanticipated vacancies as soon as possible. He allowed as how there were indeed several openings, and having someone who could teach both English and chemistry was just what the doctor ordered.

A job application from the Bisbee School District and addressed to Steve Roper arrived by mail four days later, along with his latest supply of Arizona-based newspapers. Fortunately that day's mail all fit in the P.O. box, so Steve didn't have to pick it up from the window and deal with Walt Whipple's nosiness.

At that point, Steve was finally forced to come clean about his intentions with Mr. Donner because he needed a reference from his current principal as part of the job application. By then, however, his mother's death was imminent, and she never had any reason to suspect he was leaving. She died two days after the job application arrived. Two weeks after her funeral, Steve received a special delivery letter containing both the job offer and a contract in need of signing.

He did so and sent it back by return mail. Then, after writing a formal letter of resignation to the Fertile School Board, Steve was left with a month and a half to close up his life in Minnesota. By the first of May, he had informed all his students he was leaving. By the end of May he had unloaded his mother's house and goods and sorted out her final affairs. Years earlier, he had bought Coach Nielson's house fully furnished, and he sold it the same way, with much of the Nielsons' original but now well-used furniture still in place.

Having decided that when he left town for good he'd only be taking whatever fit in his car, Steve went to visit Gus Elkins's car dealership one last time. This time he passed on a Camaro in favor of an Impala. Camaros were for younger hotshot types. It was time for

Steve Roper to graduate into respectable middle age, and his new Chevy Impala filled that bill perfectly. Flush with his inheritance, he was able to pay cash. Unsurprisingly, Gus Elkins was very sorry to see him go.

When it came time to pack up and leave, the first item Steve loaded into the trunk was the large suitcase holding his work clothing—the suits, ties, and dress shirts that teachers were expected to wear—as well as his most prized possession, Gramps's cigar box.

Steve left Fertile bright and early on the morning of June 5, 1976. He felt no regret as he put his hometown in his shiny new rearview mirror. In actual fact, he felt lighter than air. He was giddy at the idea of being off on a brand-new adventure, and the voices in his head, awakening from years of enforced slumber, felt exactly the same way.

CHAPTER 19

BISBEE, ARIZONA
Friday, December 1, 2023

ON HER WAY TO THE BOARD OF SUPERVISORS MEETING the next morning, Joanna checked in with Tom Hadlock to make sure everything with the construction team was on track. Fortunately, it was.

"What's up with the big meeting this afternoon?" he asked. "Is something going on that I should know about?"

"There is, and you'll know about it when everybody else does," Joanna told him, "and that includes me, by the way. Just be there."

The Board of Supervisors meeting kicked off promptly at ten at the Cochise County Complex on Melody Lane south of Huachuca Terraces. As per usual, it was both boring and interminable. Since Joanna's spot on the agenda was at the very end, she had to sit through all of it. Admittedly, she let her mind wander. Today was already December first. Jenny's wedding was only twenty-two short days away, but other than settling on a date and a dress, as far as Joanna knew, no other arrangements were in place.

Then, once she tired of stewing about wedding issues, Joanna's thoughts meandered over to the homicide investigation. She was tempted to send Casey a text asking for a preview of what would be coming in this afternoon's meeting, but in the end, she didn't. She'd do just as she expected Tom Hadlock to do and find out the details at the same time everyone else did.

As the minutes ticked by, though, she couldn't help but worry that she might be making a huge error. Steve Roper had been part of the Bisbee community for decades. It was likely the whole town would be in an uproar if they heard so much as a hint that he was being investigated in conjunction with Xavier Delgado's homicide. Of course people already *were* in an uproar about that. Even though the Department of Public Safety had not yet provided the final DNA results giving them a positive identification on their victim, Marliss Shackleford had somehow gotten wind of the boy's name and had posted it on her website.

Damn her hide anyway, Joanna thought. *Where the hell is she getting her information?*

"Sheriff Brady," Claire Newmark said. "Hello, are you there?"

The sharp summons yanked Joanna out of her reverie. Claire was president of the Board of Supervisors, and the impatience in her voice suggested this wasn't the first time she'd spoken. "Do you or do you not have a report for us this morning?"

"Sorry," Joanna said, quickly rising to her feet. Walking up to where the board members were seated, Joanna handed out printed copies of the report she had written the day before. Then she sat down again, allowing the board members time to read through the information.

Once they had done so, a discussion followed. Naturally they voiced concerns about the added expense of rehousing prisoners and asked questions about the time it would take to complete the remodel now that it was finally underway. Joanna bit back the urge to tell them that most of the delays had been due to stalling from the county's planning and zoning department and that the project's completion date would be entirely dependent on when the building department got around to signing off on inspections.

Once Joanna's grilling was over and the meeting let out, she headed for Daisy's. Each Friday, as an antidote to her usually challenging meetings with the Board of Supervisors, she and Reverend Marianne Maculyea got together for lunch. Marianne had her own set of problems, mostly due to testy meetings with the church council, exacerbated over challenges created by ever-rising costs along with an ever-shrinking church membership. Their weekly luncheons gave both women a private place to vent their frustrations.

They'd been friends for so long that they could read each other's mood at a moment's notice. "Why the long face?" Marianne asked as Joanna slipped into their customary booth.

"The usual," Joanna said. "The supervisors are all in a twitter because the jail remodeling project is taking so long. The problem is, most of the delays are coming from red-tape issues with county-run departments."

"What about that awful homicide?" Marianne asked. "Are you making any headway on that?"

As the department's official chaplain, it came as no surprise that Marianne knew a good deal about the Xavier Delgado case. In fact, it would have been odd if she hadn't. In addition, Marianne was the only civilian with whom Joanna was free to actually discuss active investigations. Still, with regard to the Stephen Roper situation, she held herself to the same no-comment standard she had required of her CSIs.

"Maybe," she said. "We have some suspicions, but that's all, nothing concrete as far as physical evidence is concerned and zip when it comes to probable cause."

"All right then," Marianne said, "let me give you some good news. I'll be going to Tucson tomorrow for a three o'clock appointment with Jenny and Nick. That meeting will take the first of the premarital counseling sessions off the list. There's not much time to squeeze in all three."

On that much happier note, they ordered their respective lunches. By the time Joanna showed up at the Justice Center an hour later, she was feeling a whole lot better than she had when she'd left the county administration complex after the board meeting.

When Joanna entered the conference room at five minutes to two, she glanced around the room. Since all the invitees were already in attendance, there was no reason to wait around for the appointed start time. Closing the door behind her, she made her way to the head of the table. Usually she would have taken a seat there. This time, she remained standing.

"First off, I want everyone in the room to turn off their devices—no iPhones and no tablets." She paused, waiting while people complied before continuing. "I'm sure you're all wondering why you've been summoned to a mandatory meeting with no advance hint as to what it was about. Here's the deal.

"Yesterday, Captain Arturo Peña, the commander of the Federales unit posted to Naco, Sonora, called me to say that a possible informant had come forward with information about the homicide victim found floating in the San Pedro River on Saturday afternoon. It turns out the informant is a woman who teaches English to the children at the local migrant camp. She overheard two of her kids talking about a young boy who had followed some older ones when they had gone to visit what they call 'The Free Store' on Friday morning.

"The Free Store in question isn't a store at all. It's a refurbished food truck, owned and operated by a local member of an organization called Hands Across the Border. Every two weeks it crosses into Mexico at the Naco point of entry on Friday mornings, bringing food, clothing, and other necessities for the people living in the camp. Earlier in the investigation, Detectives Howell and Carbajal had visited the camp, showing the kids a photo of Xavier Delgado, the boy we believe to be our murder victim.

"At the time they were interviewed by Deb and Jaime, they all claimed ignorance, but the informant overheard two of them talking, saying that the boy in the picture had followed them to the Free Store and was still inside the truck talking to the proprietor when they left. That's the last time any of the kids saw Xavier alive. According to them, while in the truck Xavier had been particularly interested in a pair of high-topped sneakers. As you may or may not be aware, a pair of high-topped sneakers were found with Xavier's body during the ME's autopsy.

"After speaking to the informant, Captain Peña was later able to consult with border crossing personnel to confirm the identity of the driver of the truck, but here's the problem. That individual happens to be a longtime resident of this area. He's also someone with whom many of us have interacted over the years.

"I've asked Casey Ledford and Dave Hollicker to gather whatever information they can on the individual in question, and I'll be turning the meeting over to them in a moment so they can give us their report, but before I do, I want to offer a word of caution. Not one word about our person of interest is to be mentioned or discussed with individuals not currently in this room. That includes family members as well as personnel inside this department. Evidence Dr. Baldwin discovered in the course of the autopsy—the fact that the body had been dipped in a bleach solution and the fact that Xavier's fingernails had been cut down to the quick—suggest that our perpetrator is knowledgeable about crime scene evidence and is likely to be a repeat offender. At this point I don't believe the person in question has any idea that we've made a connection between him and our victim. Until we have more solid information to go on, I want it to stay that way, understood?"

She sent a searching look around the table, focusing on each face in turn and waiting until that person nodded in agreement before moving on.

"You may be wondering why I'm so concerned about a possible leak from someone inside the department. That's simple. It's because it appears to me we have one. At this point, although we've yet to receive DNA confirmation from the Department of Public Safety giving us a positive identification on our victim, Marliss Shackleford has already posted Xavier Delgado's name. I'm here to promise you this: If I learn that our suspect's name has been disclosed to anyone outside this room without my personal approval, and if it ends up surfacing in the media, local or otherwise, I will track down the source of that leak, and whoever it is will be terminated on the spot. It won't matter who you are or how long you've worked here, your ass will be grass. Is that understood?"

Joanna prided herself on running her department with a light touch, but the idea that one of her employees might be Marliss's tipster absolutely infuriated her, and she wanted people to know that any leaks about the current investigation would not be tolerated. Finished with her diatribe, she paused long enough to see another round of nods of assent from everyone in the room. Once she had them, she turned to the rolling whiteboard stationed behind her and moved it front and center. Then, using an erasable marker, she printed the suspect's name on the board in all capital letters: STEPHEN ROPER.

Gasps of recognition and disbelief came from several of the people gathered around the conference table, but Joanna didn't allow time for any discussion. That would come later. Instead, she turned to her two CSIs who were seated next to each other to her right.

"All right, Casey," she said. "You and Dave have the floor. It's all yours."

Casey stood up. "I happen to be someone who knew Mr. Roper well. He was my high school chemistry teacher, and that class was the first step in my becoming a CSI. I've always been grateful to the man and idolized him. I suspect I'm not the only person in this room who encountered him as a teacher, so deep down, I'm hoping all this is wrong. Unfortunately, we live and work in a small community. We don't get to choose the people we have to investigate, so here goes.

"Stephen Roper was born in Fertile, Minnesota, on June 24, 1945. He's the son of Cynthia Hawkins Roper and Jackson Clyde Roper. The couple divorced shortly after Stephen was born. He was raised by a single mom. Cynthia never remarried. Jackson later went to prison for murdering his second wife. He died of Covid in 2022 while still incarcerated at the Minnesota Men's Correctional Facility in St. Cloud.

"Stephen Roper graduated from Fertile-Beltrami High School before attending the University of Minnesota in St. Paul. After graduating with a teaching degree, he went back home and taught at his old high school for a number of years. In 1976, he applied for a teaching position here in Bisbee and worked here until his retirement in 2002. He's a member in good standing of the Faith Lutheran Church in Warren. He's also a member of a loosely organized charitable organization called Hands Across the Border.

"After arriving in the Bisbee area, he purchased a property on what is now Country Club Drive north of Naco, Arizona, where he has resided ever since. Four years ago Mr. Roper acquired a junker food truck that he had refurbished into the vehicle known as 'The Free Store,' which Sheriff Brady mentioned in her previous remarks. The vehicle is owned and operated by him. For a number of years he regularly drove the vehicle back and forth across the border. A couple of years ago, following a health crisis—purportedly a cancer diagnosis—he was no longer able to carry out those duties, but relatively recently—over the last six months or so—he's been able to resume his volunteer work.

"During his teaching career and even after his retirement, Mr. Roper has been a part-time Bisbee resident, staying in town during the school year and then traveling during the summer months. He was on one of those trips when he came across the food truck and had it transported back here to be refurbed into what it is now."

"So even after he retired from teaching, he still continued to travel during the summers," Garth remarked. "Any idea where he went?"

At that point Tom Hadlock raised his hand. "Minnesota," he said. "I remember him telling us once that he spent every summer going back home to help out on the family farm."

"Good to know," Casey said, making a note of that on a piece of paper before continuing, "but other than that we have no idea about where he went during his travels.

"As far as we can tell, Mr. Roper never married nor does he have any children. In searching law enforcement databases, we've found no record of any criminal history, not even so much as a traffic ticket. One would think that if he were a repeat offender of some kind, there would be some record of his fingerprints in AFIS or of his DNA in CODIS. So far we've found nothing. It's possible that he participated in previous crimes that remain unsolved. In that case, unknown prints and an unknown DNA profile might still be on file somewhere, but without our having samples from him, there's no way to tell."

"Asking him to voluntarily submit samples now would put him on notice that he's currently under suspicion," Joanna observed.

"Exactly," Casey added. "And, at the moment, we're nowhere near having enough probable cause to require him to do so. Given his proximity to Mexico, if Roper becomes aware that we're investigating him, it would be easy for him to flee the country. I'm sure that's one of the reasons Sheriff Brady is so concerned about the possibility of a leak.

"While I was researching Mr. Roper, Dave was busy doing a deep dive into Hands Across the Border. There are chapters of HATB in many communities—mostly small towns—located along the US/Mexico border. As far as we can tell, it's made up mostly of goodhearted people who, although not well off themselves, are committed to helping those less fortunate than they are. So far we've found no other instances where the organization has been involved in any kind of criminal or suspicious behavior. Thank you."

With that, Casey sank back onto her chair, and Joanna rose to her feet. "Any questions?" she asked.

Detective Howell was the first to respond. "Having reports of Xavier Delgado being seen in Mr. Roper's Free Store, possibly expressing an interest in a pair of high-topped sneakers, may seem like flimsy circumstantial evidence, but here's the rest of the story. When the ME removed Xavier Delgado's body from the duffel bag, he was wearing a single high-topped sneaker, one that was at least two sizes too large for him. Its mate was found loose in the bag with the shoelace missing. That may be why the shoe fell off in the first place—because someone had removed the shoelace."

"Thank you, Deb," Joanna said. "As the mother of a kid who still loves his high-topped Keds, I can tell you that lacing and unlacing those are a pain in the neck. I can assure you that I've never once bought shoes that were two sizes too large, with the expectation that Dennis would grow into them. But a kid four or five years old? If he saw a pair of shoes that he wanted, he wouldn't be looking at the sizes. He'd be looking at the shoes. As for our killer? If this guy really is a repeat offender, he might be using the shoelace as a trophy."

A moment of complete silence followed.

"What are the next steps then?" Jaime Carbajal asked after a moment. "Most of the time in a case like this, we'd be out on the streets talking to friends and neighbors of the suspect to see if they'd noticed anything out of the ordinary, but again we can't do that without letting Roper know we're onto him. Not only that, his residence on Country Club Drive is so isolated that putting him under any kind of surveillance isn't feasible."

Garth Raymond raised his hand. "What about trash DNA?" he asked.

"Good suggestion," Casey said. "I'll check with Waste Management. If he has an account with them, I'll find out what day it's collected."

"When's Roper's next scheduled visit to the migrant camp?" Jaime asked.

"According to Captain Peña, it'll be next Friday, a week from today," Joanna told them. "Arturo assures me that while Roper is in Sonora, his guys will have eyes on him."

"Between now and then we have to sit on our hands waiting to see if he grabs another kid?" Tom Hadlock asked. "That sucks!"

"I agree," Joanna said. "It does suck."

But Tom was on a roll. "What time does the Free Store truck come back across the border?"

"Early to midafternoon," Casey answered.

"That means this must have happened in broad daylight with plenty of people coming and going," Tom continued. "How the hell did he smuggle the kid across the border without anyone noticing? If somebody had tried to grab me when I was that age, I would have screamed bloody murder."

"Maybe Xavier went willingly because he was bribed with something he wanted—like the shoes, for instance," Deb suggested. "Or maybe he was incapacitated."

"According to Dr. Baldwin, he had a perimortem contusion that might have rendered him unconscious."

The room went quiet once more. "Anything else?" Joanna asked, but when she examined the somber faces gathered around the table, no one answered.

"Okay," she said. "This is where we are. Until we know for sure that Stephen Roper is our suspect, he remains a person of interest. It's possible that another informant may come forward with additional information, so keep your eyes open and ears to the ground. Who knows? We might get lucky, because luck is what it's going to take to get justice for Xavier Delgado and his grieving mother—luck and a whole lot of hard work."

Joanna Brady was the last person to leave the conference room. Before she exited, she made sure that every vestige of Stephen Roper's name had been erased from the whiteboard. When it came to possible leakers, there was nothing to say the culprit couldn't be a janitor as opposed to one of her officers, and she didn't want to take any chances.

CHAPTER 20

BISBEE, ARIZONA
June and July 1976

FOUR DAYS AFTER LEAVING MINNESOTA, STEVE ROPER arrived in Bisbee, Arizona, and checked into a motel called the San Jose Lodge. When he asked the clerk about the establishment's name, she pointed out through the glass door to where a distant, solitary mountain peak rose up majestically out of an otherwise flat desert landscape.

"That's San Jose Peak," she told him. "It's in Old Mexico."

Never having heard the term before, Steve was puzzled. "Old Mexico?" he repeated.

The clerk gave him an exasperated look. "This is Arizona," she explained. "New Mexico is just to the east of us, and Old Mexico is to the south. That's what we call them around here, old and new."

"Okay," Steve said. "I'll try to remember that."

His room was a long way from deluxe, with questionable carpeting and a worn, flowered bedspread. There was an air-conditioning unit under the window, but dry heat or not, the outside temperature was still somewhere in the mid-nineties. Since the room faced due west, the laboring AC barely made a dent in the hot, still air.

Prior to leaving home, Steve had placed a long-distance call to Bisbee, asking Information for the number of a local real estate office. As a result of that call, he'd been in touch with a company and had both the name and address of a prospective agent, one Linda Mulligan. Since he had no idea how to get to the real estate office in question, he went back to the registration office to ask the desk clerk.

"That's easy," she said. "Their office is in the lobby of the old Lyric Theater." Then she gave him a small one-page map, pointing out where he was and showing him how to get to what she called "Upper Bisbee."

Because he had come to town on Highway 80 via Lordsburg and Rodeo, New Mexico, Steve had approached Bisbee from the east, through terrain that had been relatively flat. Now he backtracked far enough to reach a grassy traffic circle, went two-thirds of the way around that, and then drove uphill past what appeared to be the back side of a run-down business district. The local map indicated that neighborhood was called Lowell. Then he traversed a long flat curve of roadway that appeared to have been carved out of the gray-green innards of a mountain. According to the map, it was an open-pit mine called Lavender Pit. After that the twisting road began climbing again, eventually bringing him into the midst of some steep, red shale mountains dotted with low-growing shrubs. There he entered another business district, this one designated as Upper Bisbee.

The clerk at the hotel had helpfully drawn an X on the map to indicate the exact location of the real estate office. The marquee overhead indicated the building had once held a movie theater, but now it advertised the name of the real estate company rather than promoting some current offering from Hollywood.

Inside, Steve found a series of four desks scattered around what had once been the theater's lobby. A middle-aged blond-haired woman was seated at one, which, to Steve's way of thinking, had most likely been the location of a long-gone popcorn machine.

"May I help you?" the woman asked.

"I'm looking for someone named Linda Mulligan."

"You've come to the right place then," she said with a smile. "I'm Linda. What can I do for you?"

"I'm Stephen Roper," he answered.

From that moment on, that's who he was—who he became. Steve Roper was someone who came from Fertile, Minnesota, and who lived in the past. Stephen Roper was the new guy, the one who would live and thrive in Bisbee.

"Oh, my goodness," she said. "We've talked on the phone, but I'm so glad to meet you in person. I understand you're one of the new teachers at the high school, and I've put together a list of available properties that should be within your price range. When would you like to take a look at them?"

"I've just now driven into town, and I'm a little road weary," he said.

"How about tomorrow then, say one o'clock in the afternoon."

"Sounds perfect. Is there anywhere to get a decent meal around here?"

Linda gestured to her right. "When you go outside, turn to your right, go past Brewery Gulch and then up Howell Avenue. The Copper Queen Hotel is just up the hill on your right. You can't go wrong there. The dining room probably isn't open right now, but the bar will be, and you'll be able to order food there."

"All right," he said. "I will, and see you tomorrow."

His meal at the hotel was early, but it wasn't half bad, and by the time he got back to San Jose Lodge, his room was blessedly cool. After a long shower, he went to bed and slept like a rock.

THE NEXT SEVERAL DAYS WERE TAKEN UP WITH HOUSE hunting. Linda showed Stephen several places in town as well as one that was pretty much out in the boonies. The last one wasn't in Bisbee itself, but a mile or two south of the city limits and just north of a tiny town called Naco that sat directly on the US/Mexico border. The property, located on an unnamed dirt road, was a three-acre parcel due north of a golf course. Having a golf course that close by would have been great for Coach Nielson, but it was of no particular interest to Stephen.

The frame, two-bedroom house wasn't all that great. It was about the same age and size as the one he'd owned in Fertile. It had linoleum floors, which weren't his first choice, and there was considerable evidence of termite damage to the exterior of the structure. But Stephen wasn't all that fussy about the house itself. He had never been one to entertain, and he didn't see that changing. His favorite part of the place was a stand-alone garage that included a spacious workshop. That was a big improvement. In Fertile he'd always had to park on the street. Not only that, the price was right. The house had been listed for months with no takers in sight. When Stephen made a lowball, all-cash offer, the sellers leaped at it.

Wanting to be moved in and settled before school started, Stephen turned to Linda, his only real acquaintance in town. She helped him locate a contractor who was willing to fix the termite damage and update the kitchen and bathroom, along with ripping out all the linoleum and installing new flooring. The contractor assured him that the entire job could be completed by the second week in August, which was two weeks before Stephen was scheduled to report for work.

Linda then took him to a local furniture store called Whitehead's where the in-store designer helped him pick out furniture that would be put aside and available for delivery the moment the house was ready for occupancy.

With that all under control, and more than tired of living in his room at the San Jose Lodge, Stephen decided it was time to treat himself to a road trip. He told the desk clerk that since he couldn't move into the house until the contractor finished, he was going to take a drive around Arizona and see what there was to see.

"You mean you aren't going to stay for the Fourth of July?" she asked incredulously. "It's going to be a really big deal this year because of the bicentennial. There'll be coaster races, a parade, the B-Hill climb, and fireworks, as long as the rain doesn't drown them out."

"Rain?" Stephen repeated in disbelief. "What rain? I've been here for days and haven't seen a drop."

"Not to worry," she said. "Rainy season is coming. It usually starts right in the middle of the Fourth of July fireworks."

"Sorry," Stephen told her. "I think I'll pass. I want to spend some time getting acquainted with Arizona—maybe drop by the Grand Canyon and the Painted Forest. After that maybe I'll pop over to California and spend some time on the beach."

"Have fun," she said. "I wish I could go with you."

No you don't, Stephen thought. *Having you along wouldn't be a good idea for either one of us.*

The long dormant voices in his head were absolutely overjoyed with the possibility of taking a trip and could hardly wait to hit the road. Stephen didn't blame them. He was more than ready, too, but first he needed to tend to a couple pieces of business.

One important issue was the distinct scar on the back of his hand. Over the years it had faded some, but it hadn't gone away entirely, and that offended him. It always reminded him of "Reservoir Girl." The real problem with the scar, however, was that people—even complete strangers—noticed it and asked about it. If you're someone who wants to blend in, having any kind of distinguishing mark is a bad idea, so Stephen decided to hide it.

He went to a nearby drugstore and purchased a box of surgical gloves that he stored in the Impala's glove box, making up his mind that he would wear gloves the entire time he was on the road—in the car and out of it. And if anyone happened to ask him about them? He'd explain that he had a terrible case of eczema and that he was wearing gloves on doctors' orders. Nobody ever questioned those.

The other problem with the scar was that it reminded him of the serious miscalculation he'd made when picking up Reservoir Girl. Getting someone into his vehicle wasn't difficult. The real issue was one of control. If he was still driving when his would-be victims suddenly figured out something wasn't right and tried to bail, he needed to have some way to secure them until he was able to bring the car to a safe stop in a suitably secluded location.

Stephen had studied chemistry, all right, but he was also a problem solver, and he soon came up with a logical solution—chloroform, which also happened to be readily available. He didn't have to purchase anything from some chemical supply company, because the necessary ingredients for that were readily available at every corner store—acetone and bleach. Mixing a batch of chloroform up at home wasn't exactly rocket science, either. All you needed to do was make sure you mixed the ingredients in the right proportions.

Once Stephen landed on chloroform as the answer, his next issue was figuring out a way to deploy it. If he was driving, the stuff needed to be readily accessible, preferably under the driver's seat. That way, between the time a would-be passenger reached for the door handle and before he or she could settle into the passenger seat, he'd be able to have a chloroform-soaked cloth in his hand and ready to slap across his victim's nose and mouth.

Eventually, while prowling the home goods section of the Western Auto Hardware Store in Upper Bisbee he found just the thing—a two-piece, air-tight plastic container that resembled Tupperware and was designed to hold a single sandwich. With the lid closed properly nothing could leak out, and any piece of cloth left inside with a half-inch or so of his homemade chloroform mixture would remain ready for action for as long as necessary—for days on end if need be.

Once the real estate deal closed, Stephen was finally able to move most of his belongings into the garage and lock them away for safekeeping until the house itself was ready for occupancy. Then, using the tiny bathroom in his motel room as a lab, he mixed up his first batch of chloroform. After putting half an inch of that in the bottom of his sandwich container, he dropped a neatly folded handkerchief into the mix. Once the lid was tightly affixed, he slipped the covered container under the Impala's driver's seat, making sure it was within easy reach.

When packing for his road trip, Stephen used the smallest piece of luggage he owned, but tucked in with his shaving kit, extra shoes, and clothing was a pint-size Mason jar holding the remains of that initial batch of chloroform. That way, if he ended up needing a refill somewhere along the way, there'd be no need to mix up more.

On the morning of Saturday, July 3, 1976, Stephen, feeling fully prepared for all contingencies, was ready to head out. Yes, he would miss Bisbee's Fourth of July celebration, but he was sure there'd be plenty of fun in store for him elsewhere.

He had lied to the desk clerk earlier when he'd told her about wanting to see the Grand Canyon. Screw the Grand Canyon. What Stephen really wanted to do was to spend time exploring the beaches along the California coastline. Several years had passed between his encounter with Reservoir Girl on what he now knew to be the San Carlos Apache Reservation, but he suspected that his best bet for a happy hunting ground would be some kind of Indian country. After studying his new *Rand McNally*, he landed on the Papago Reservation. It was due west of Tucson, but it occurred to Stephen that a jog along Highway 86 through the reservation wasn't that far out of the way to his first planned destination, San Diego.

After donning a pair of gloves, he got underway. At noontime, he stopped at a busy truck stop on the outskirts of Tucson. He hoped that a possible victim might present herself there, but that didn't happen. After lunch, on his way back to the car, he noticed a towering mountain of thunderclouds rising up over the horizon to the south, so maybe the desk clerk was right, and rain really would show up in time to wash out Bisbee's Fourth of July fireworks.

Once back in his Impala, he followed the freeway signs that took him first onto southbound I-19 and immediately thereafter onto Ajo Way and Highway 86. Shortly after passing the Tucson city limits, the road narrowed to only two lanes peppered with one deep dip after another. Two things struck him about that particular stretch of highway—the scarcity of traffic and the fact that there weren't many residences along it, either.

Ten or so miles later, Stephen was sure he was going to come up empty, but then, a mile after passing something called the Three Points Trading Post, he hit the jackpot when he spotted a lone hitchhiker—an old man in raggedy clothing—standing on the shoulder of the road with his thumb extended. A lousy bum wasn't exactly what Stephen had had in mind, but sometimes you had to take what was offered. With no approaching traffic visible in either direction, the old guy was just too good to pass up, and the gleeful voices in Stephen's head chattered in enthusiastic agreement.

Stephen pulled over and stopped, dragging the sandwich container out from under the seat and placing it in his lap while he waited for his passenger to jog up to the car door and climb in. It was hard to tell how old he was. His deeply wrinkled bronze skin suggested he was somewhere between sixty and eighty. When he removed a grimy Stetson to wipe the sweat from his forehead onto an equally grimy shirtsleeve, his hair was gunmetal gray. And the guy stank to high heaven in an almost lethal combination of old shoes, sweat, woodsmoke, and booze, with the emphasis on the latter.

"Where to?" Stephen asked.

The guy pulled a pint of clear booze out from under his shirt, took a long swig of whatever it was—vodka most likely—and gestured vaguely toward the west. "Sells," he said. "That way."

Less than a mile or so ahead, Stephen saw a sign indicating a side road leading off to the right and switched on his turn signal.

"Need to take a leak," he explained.

"Fine with me," the old guy muttered, downing another mouthful of booze.

Half a mile in on a narrow dirt road, another one came into view, this one turning off to the left. A hand-painted sign at the intersection announced the presence of a shooting range, and not an upscale one by any means. Beyond that, the road they were following got much worse, turning into a rugged dirt track far more appropriate for a four-wheel-drive Jeep than a sedan. A hundred yards or so beyond the shooting range turnoff, they came to a place where a wide, sandy wash crossed the road. Worried that the Impala might get stuck, Stephen stopped just short of the edge.

When he got out of the car, he didn't bother bringing along the sandwich box. The guy was so drunk that using chloroform wasn't even necessary. Stephen simply opened the passenger door, hauled him out onto the ground, and strangled him then and there, right next to his idling car.

After the deed was done, Stephen stood staring down at his victim. Although the guy was probably dirt poor, the threadbare belt that strung through the loops of his aging Levi's was fastened with what appeared to be a solid silver buckle with some sort of maze design carved into it. Realizing this would be a good way to remember him, Stephen retrieved a pocketknife from his shaving kit and used that to collect the belt buckle for his cigar box. Then he dragged the body of Maze Man into the wash.

Pulling that much dead weight through hot, deep sand wasn't easy. After no more than twenty yards, Stephen gave up. He dropped the load in the sand and left Maze Man lying there on his back with his sightless eyes staring up at the sun. Back in the Impala, Stephen discovered that the road was too narrow for him to turn around, forcing him to drive in reverse until he reached the turnoff to the shooting range. Fortunately, he didn't encounter another soul, coming or going.

Both exhausted and jubilant, Stephen got back on Highway 86, speeding along in air-conditioned comfort. Less than four hours into his road trip, he already had what he wanted. After that long forced hiatus, he wasn't done, either. Three days later, in downtown LA, he picked off an older model prostitute plying her wares outside a sleazy strip joint. After yanking off one of her dangly pierced earrings, he hoisted her into a nearby dumpster. He called her Alley Girl, although using the term girl was something of a misnomer.

On Monday, July 7, 1976, the decomposing body of a white female was found in a garbage dumpster at a construction site in downtown LA. She was fully clothed. Her ears were pierced. One earring was present while the other had been torn from her earlobe. Her manner of death was ruled to be homicide; cause of death was asphyxia due to manual strangulation. The victim was never identified. The case remained unsolved.

Meanwhile, hundreds of miles away from Arizona, Stephen Roper was totally unaware that summer monsoon season hadn't bothered waiting around for Bisbee's Fourth of July fireworks celebration before making an appearance. On the afternoon of July third, a powerful storm had marched up from Baja California, drenching the Sonoran Desert with almost four inches of pounding rain in a matter of hours and turning bone-dry washes and riverbeds into raging floods. That included the offshoot of Brawley Wash where Stephen had left Maze Man.

Two days later and forty miles away, a body was spotted washed up on the banks of the Santa Cruz River in Pinal County. The victim was eventually identified as fifty-four-year-old Richard Romero of Sells, Arizona, last seen alive around noon on Saturday, July third, at the Three Points Trading Post, in Three Points, Arizona.

At first authorities thought Mr. Romero to be the victim of an accidental drowning; however, when his autopsy revealed a broken hyoid bone, the cause of death was ruled to be asphyxia due to manual strangulation and the manner of death homicide. It was assumed that Mr. Romero had been murdered somewhere near Three Points and the body subsequently dumped into Brawley Wash, which, filled with floodwater from a fierce monsoon, eventually carried it into the Santa Cruz.

While removing the victim's clothing, the coroner noted that the victim's belt had been cut to remove whatever belt buckle he'd been wearing, one later described by Mr. Romero's grieving relatives as the Man in the Maze. The homicide was briefly investigated by detectives from both Pima and Pinal counties and by Law and Order officers from the Tribal Police in Sells, but the case quickly went cold for all of them.

As for Stephen Roper? Those two deaths in one week were enough to satisfy his bloodlust for a while and to silence his yammering voices as well. Although he wore gloves the whole time, the remainder of his trip was uneventful. When he got back to Bisbee, three weeks later, he spent some time gathering up the household goods that he'd need once the house was ready—linens, dishes, pots and pans—storing all those in the garage until the contractor was done with the finishing touches on the house, which happened a week before the beginning of teacher orientation.

By the first day of school at Bisbee High, Stephen Roper was ready to be Mr. Roper again, and he began, as he always did, by scaring the piddle out of his new students with his standard first-day-of-school, my-way-or-the-highway speech. That one worked every time.

CHAPTER 21

BISBEE, ARIZONA
Sunday, December 3, 2023

CHIEF DEPUTY TOM HADLOCK WAS OFF THAT WEEKEND, SO Joanna was on call. Unbelievably, nothing happened, at least not at work. Joanna was looking forward to having some relaxing downtime. Then Jenny called between breakfast and church asking if it would be possible for her to stop by for a while that afternoon to discuss wedding plans.

"Absolutely," Joanna said. "That way we'll at least be able to get a start on things."

After church, Sage, a perpetual tomboy who had zero interest in wedding planning, opted to spend the afternoon in town playing video games with a friend. Dennis had invited Jeffy Daniels, Jeff and Marianne's son and Dennis's best friend, to spend the afternoon taking Kiddo and Spot on a leisurely horseback ride up High Lonesome Road. As for Butch? He bailed, too, saying he was just getting to the crashing climax of his book and needed to stay focused. As soon as Sunday lunch was over, he retreated to his den.

Happy to have something to think about other than the Xavier Delgado homicide, Joanna turned her attention to the wedding. During her years as sheriff, she had learned that the best way to mow through a complicated group of tasks was to make a list of them and check them off once completed. To that end, between lunchtime and Jenny's ETA, Joanna used her iPad to create what she hoped would be a comprehensive list of what needed to be accomplished in that initial planning session.

Jenny arrived at half past two. As soon as greetings were out of the way, Joanna wanted to get down to business. "Shall we start with the dress?" she asked, leading the way to the master bedroom.

"Sounds good to me," Jenny said with a shrug.

Joanna had already removed the wedding outfit from the dry cleaner's plastic wrapper and laid it out on the bed. Once Jenny slipped into the sheath, it fit perfectly. Years earlier when Joanna had worn the dress, the hemlines of both the dress and the matching full-length satin jacket had fallen just below her knees. On Jenny they landed an inch or two above. Naturally Jenny hadn't thought to bring along a pair of heels for trying on the dress, so what she saw in the mirror probably wasn't the most flattering. Even so, she seemed pleased with the result.

"It's perfect, Mom," she said. "And don't worry about the shoes. I'll be able to find a pair online with no trouble."

"What about a nice hat or veil?" Joanna asked.

"Nope," Jenny said. "Neither one. Don't need 'em."

"Do you want to take the dress home with you so you can show it to Nick?"

"Not on your life. He's not supposed to see it before the wedding, and this is where I'll be wearing it. I'm happy with putting it back in your closet where it belongs."

Leaving the bedroom they settled at the dining room table where Joanna placed her iPad front and center.

"I suppose you made a list?" Jenny asked. Joanna's propensity for list-making came as no surprise to her daughter.

"Of course."

"I'm assuming the dress was number one?"

Joanna laughed. "Yes, it was. Next up is invitations. Those need to be printed and in the mail by the end of next week at the very latest."

"OMG, Mom!" Jenny exclaimed, rolling her eyes in exasperation. "You do know that it's 2023. Nick and I won't be mailing out printed invitations. We'll be sending them via email. We found one we both like on a greeting card website, and you can order thank-you notes that match the invitations. We have a list, and we're planning on sending the invites out either later tonight or tomorrow."

"Okey dokey," Joanna said, realizing she'd just been put in her generational place, and deservedly so.

"What's next?" Jenny asked.

"Who all's in the wedding party?"

"Nick's best man will be his older brother, Gavin. Cassie will be my matron of honor, and Leah will be the flower girl. Dennis and Jeffy will be the ushers, and Sage will be in charge of the guest book."

Cassie Parks had been Jenny's closest friend all through school. Now married to Leonard Dupnik, a Bisbee firefighter, she had a five-year-old daughter named Leah and was expecting her second child, a boy, due in early March.

"That's it?" Joanna asked.

"That's it."

"What about flowers then?"

"Marianne and I talked about those yesterday," Jenny said. "It'll be Christmastime, so the church will be full of poinsettias. That means we won't really need flowers to decorate the church. The colors will be red and white—red and white roses for my bouquet and red boutonnieres for all the guys. Also red and white rose corsages for you and Nick's mom. Since there's no longer a flower shop in Bisbee, I'll order those from one in Sierra Vista. They'll have to be picked up, but I'm sure we'll be able to manage that."

"Cake?" Joanna asked.

"Cassie's mom volunteered."

"How many people?" That was the last item on Joanna's list.

"Twenty-five to thirty tops. This isn't a big wedding, Mom. We're only inviting relatives and good friends. And, no, we're not inviting

Butch's folks. I think we all had more than enough of his mom the last time they were here."

Joanna agreed wholeheartedly, and she was sure Butch would be on the same page. Butch's dad, Donald Dixon, was all right, but his mother, Margaret, was a holy terror.

"What about food for the reception here at the house afterward?"

Jenny laughed. "I'm leaving that up to Butch. I prefer Mexican food of some kind, but I'm pretty sure he'll be able to figure it out."

Amazed, Joanna turned off her iPad. Every single item on her list had been handled, and Joanna couldn't help but admire her daughter's commonsense, get-it-done attitude. With her at the helm, not only was planning a wedding in under a month's time doable, it was already in the bag.

Jenny left for Tucson around five. Half an hour later Butch emerged from his study.

"Where's Jenny?" he asked.

"On her way back to Tucson."

"Already? How did the wedding planning go?"

"It's done."

"Done?" Butch echoed in astonishment. "That fast?"

"Signed, sealed, and delivered," Joanna replied.

"Amazing," he said. "I thought it was going to be a huge ordeal."

"So did I," Joanna agreed.

"Did she mention how many people and what kind of food she wants for the reception?"

"The number will be right around thirty," Joanna answered. "As for food choices? She's hoping for Mexican, but a final decision on food is up to the FOB."

"The what?" Butch asked with a puzzled frown.

"That means you, buddy boy," Joanna told him. "You're the father of the bride."

CHAPTER 22

BISBEE, ARIZONA
Monday, December 4, 2023

THE NEXT MORNING, JOANNA HAD BEEN IN HER OFFICE for only a few minutes when a call came in from the ME.

"Good morning, Kendra," she said. "How's it going?"

"The DNA results landed in my inbox this morning," she said. "It's a match. Our victim is definitely Elena Delgado's son, Xavier."

Joanna had never doubted that would be the finding. Still, hearing the confirmation hurt.

"Will you be handling the next-of-kin notification?" Kendra asked.

Joanna thought about that for a moment. On the one hand, since the body had been found in Cochise County, notifying the family was her department's responsibility. In this instance, however, it seemed that having Arturo do the honors would be more appropriate. For one thing Elena already knew the man, and receiving the news directly from him in her native language might be less difficult for all concerned.

"Captain Peña is in charge of the Federales unit in Naco, Sonora," she said. "I know he's acquainted with the victim's mother. I'll ask him. I'm pretty sure he'll be willing to do it."

"Okay," Kendra said, "just as long as it gets handled."

"Once it's done," Joanna added, "I'll schedule the news conference."

"Good-o," Kendra said.

When Arturo heard about the DNA results, he wasn't any more surprised than Joanna had been. As for the notification?

"Of course, I'll do it," he agreed, "but I'm not looking forward to it. I know she's expecting it, but still . . ."

"Yes," Joanna said, "it'll be tough, but it'll be better if the news comes from someone she actually knows. Thanks in advance. The next thing I need to do is hold a press conference."

"That won't be any more fun than doing the notification."

Joanna laughed. "You've got that right."

She was about to hang up but Arturo stopped her. "One more thing," he said. "I had a brainstorm overnight. How about this? Stephen Roper has crossed the border countless times."

"So?" Joanna asked.

"People who cross the border on a regular basis like that are known to all the border guards and are mostly waved through checkpoints with no questions asked. Right now he has no idea that he's under any kind of suspicion, right?"

"As far as I know," Joanna replied. "I warned my people that if any word about his being a person of interest gets out to the public, I'll fire the leaker on the spot. Why do you ask?"

"I have a lot of pull with the border guards," Arturo continued. "Just like everybody else around here, they're up in arms about what happened to Xavier. So what if I told them that next Friday they should pull Roper and his Free Store truck aside for an extensive search? They can tell him that it's routine—that on orders from headquarters they've now been directed to pull aside and search every fifteenth or twentieth vehicle, and his is it. Who knows what'll happen? They might come up empty, but then again they might not."

"But won't he be suspicious?" Joanna asked.

"I doubt it. They'll tell him they're looking for drugs, weapons, or cash. Besides, he won't be anywhere near the vehicle during the search itself—drivers have to sit in a waiting room inside the station while the search takes place. I'll tell the guards involved to report their findings directly to me, but regardless of what they find, they should leave it where it is and allow Roper to go on his merry way once they're done."

This seemed like a novel but very tempting idea. Joanna's people would need a search warrant in hand to go through Roper's vehicle. Border guards don't need warrants. Searching vehicles for contraband is their job.

"Let me think about this," she said. "I'll be back in touch."

Off the phone with Arturo, Joanna headed for Casey Ledford's lab. On the way she stopped by Kristin's desk.

"We've got a positive ID on our homicide victim," she said. "Please send out a mass mailing to our media contacts, letting them know I'll be holding a press conference this afternoon at four."

"Will do," Kristin said.

Joanna found Casey and Dave Hollicker with their noses deep in their computer monitors. "What are you up to?" she asked.

"We're still doing our deep dive into Stephen Roper. He has an email address, but that's it. As far as we can tell, he has no social media presence. If we could look at his computer or phone, those might tell a different story, but, as you know, we'll need warrants."

"What if there was a way to search his Free Store truck without needing a warrant?" Joanna asked.

"I'm all ears," Casey said.

"So am I," Dave added.

Joanna told them about Arturo's suggestion of having the Mexican border guards do an extensive search of the vehicle. By the time she was finished, Casey was nodding her head.

"You know, Dave and I were just talking about that," she said. "Specifically, about what we discussed in our meeting yesterday about how Roper managed to smuggle Xavier across the border. We're assuming that he'd been knocked unconscious. But he might also have been drugged. Something like horse tranquilizer would have worked, but that would require the use of a hypodermic of some kind. If I were a little kid and someone tried to poke me with a needle, I'd raise all kinds of hell, but a drug that could be dissolved in a soda would work, too."

"Like a date rape drug maybe?" Joanna asked.

Casey nodded. "Some of those can also be inhaled in powdered form, but so can chloroform, too. That's readily available since you can make it at home with ordinary household ingredients.

"So if the border guards' search happened to turn up something suspicious in liquid or powder form, and if they could collect a sample and give it to me, I have a whole library of test kits here in the lab that will identify the substance."

"In other words, you think this is a good idea?" Joanna asked.

"I do."

At that point, Dave spoke up, adding in his two cents. "Do the border guards have body cams?"

Joanna shrugged. "I don't know. Maybe. Why?"

"Because if they do, and if the search came up with any kind of damning evidence, we'll need to have an incontrovertible record of the whole thing to hold up in court."

With that, Joanna reached for her phone and put the call on speaker.

"Back so soon?" Arturo asked when he answered.

"I'm in the lab talking to my CSIs. They're on board with the whole idea of doing that vehicle search, but they're wondering if the border guards are equipped with body cams."

"I'm not sure, but I'll find out," Arturo vowed. "If they don't have them right now, I'll figure out a way for them to have body cams by Friday."

"Okay then," Joanna said. "Let's say it's a go."

"But will it work?" Dave Hollicker asked, horning in on the conversation.

"Will what work?" Joanna demanded.

"Will evidence obtained that way be admissible in a court of law?" Dave insisted. "If not, we might be shooting ourselves in the foot."

Joanna felt as though Dave had just dumped a bucket of ice water on what had seemed like such a promising idea, but maybe the man had a point.

"That was Dave Hollicker, one of my CSIs," Joanna explained to Arturo, "and he could be right. Don't put anything in motion until I check with the county attorney."

"Okay," Arturo said. He, too, sounded deflated. "Let me know what you find out."

Ten minutes later, after a quick phone call to the county attorney's office, Joanna was on her way to Old Bisbee. As always when pulling into the parking lot on Quality Hill, she found herself thinking about her dad. Back when D.H. Lathrop had been sheriff, his office and the jail, too, had been located right across the street in the basement of the old courthouse. Things were a lot different now.

Cochise County's longtime prosecutor, Arlee Jones, had passed away from a heart attack the previous summer. Arlee had been absolutely old school and a misogynist to boot, a guy who had taken a dim view of females in law enforcement. He and Joanna had been at loggerheads for much of the time she'd been sheriff. After his passing, the assistant county attorney, Craig Witherspoon, had been appointed to fill out Arlee's term of office and had been elected in his own right weeks earlier at the same time Joanna had won reelection.

Joanna hadn't had that many dealings with the new guy, but since Craig was a good forty years younger than Arlee and a couple years younger than Joanna herself, she was hopeful they'd have a somewhat better working relationship, and she drove there with a hopeful heart.

Some of the differences between the two men were apparent the moment Joanna stepped inside Craig Witherspoon's office. Arlee's walls had been decorated with ego-boosting framed diplomas and countless awards. Craig's walls displayed a collection of family photos, including his wife, a young kid in a Little League uniform, and an adorable little girl decked out as a ballerina.

Arlee had always treated Joanna as some kind of interloper. Craig greeted her warmly. "I guess mutual congratulations are in order, Sheriff Brady. Welcome to your fourth term."

"Congrats to you, too," she said. "I'm looking forward to working together."

"Speaking of which, is this about the dead kid found in the San Pedro?" he asked.

Joanna nodded. "Yes, it is."

"What's the deal?"

Joanna spent the next ten minutes laying out the background of the Xavier Delgado case. Craig knew about it, of course, because the assistant county attorney had been at the recovery scene in St. David that miserable Saturday afternoon along with everyone else, but he was unfamiliar with the current state of the investigation. He listened attentively, with his index fingers steepled in front of him, but before Joanna even finished her pitch, he was already shaking his head.

"Sorry," he said, "but it's never going to work. In this instance we would have officials from both sides of the border conspiring to effect a warrantless search, and that would be regarded as a violation of Mr. Roper's constitutional rights. In addition, any evidence that came in as a result of that illegal search, including evidence found later during the execution of any subsequent search warrants, would be considered fruits of the poisonous tree and also be deemed inadmissible."

Joanna had thought that at last they'd be making some actual headway in the case, but she did her best to hide her disappointment.

"Well," she said lamely, "it seemed like a good idea at the time."

"I'm sure it did," Craig agreed. "Your job is to catch the guy. Mine is to make sure we can prove he did it in a court of law."

"I understand completely," she said. "I want to prove it, too."

"What else have you got?" Craig asked.

"Not much," she admitted. "There's a possibility that our guy might be a repeat offender, but so far Roper's got no criminal history."

"So no prints or DNA on file?" Craig asked.

Joanna nodded. "None at all. We're hoping to collect some trash DNA to see if we can connect him to any unidentified profiles in CODIS, but otherwise we're coming up empty."

"Look," Craig said, "I happen to agree with you that there's a good chance Roper's our guy, and I want him off the streets every bit as much as you do, but suspicions don't carry the day. We have to be able to prove it. So remember that old story about the tortoise and the hare—slow and steady wins the race."

Driving back to the Justice Center, Joanna was still disappointed, but she was also grateful. Thanks to Dave Hollicker, she hadn't made a legal blunder that might have allowed a child killer to walk free.

Joanna made two calls on her way back to the Justice Center. The first was to Arturo, telling him sorry, but the whole deal was off. The second was to Casey Ledford.

"Tell Dave he was one hundred percent correct, and that I'm sending him a big thank-you," Joanna told her. "That whole warrantless search thing sounded like a good idea, but whatever evidence was found would have been thrown out as a violation of his constitutional rights, so I guess we're getting nowhere fast."

"Not entirely," Casey told her. "I just got word that Stephen Roper does indeed have a Waste Management account. His garbage pickup is scheduled for Wednesday morning."

"So tomorrow night you'll have someone there to grab his trash the moment he hauls it out to the street?"

"Absolutely," Casey replied. "My wiseass partner has already volunteered to do the job."

At four that afternoon, Joanna went to the conference room for her previously scheduled press conference. It wasn't well attended.

None of the Tucson papers or TV stations bothered to send reporters or camera crews for a dead body in a flooded river sixty miles away. Roy Huggins, a reporter from the *Sierra Vista Daily*, was on hand, however, and so was Marliss Shackleford. They were it.

Joanna's comments were brief and to the point. "DNA results from the State Department of Public Safety have now confirmed the identity of the homicide victim found in the San Pedro River in St. David on Saturday afternoon. His name is Xavier Francisco Delgado, born in Naco, Sonora, on October 14, 2019. His mother's name is Elena Maria Delgado, also of Naco, Sonora.

"The ME's autopsy has ruled that the cause of death is asphyxia and his manner of death is homicide. Detectives from the Cochise County Sheriff's Department are investigating. That's all I have to say at this time."

Before Joanna could make an exit, Marliss's hand shot into the air. "How did the victim end up in the river?" she asked. "Did he just wash up from Mexico, or was he placed in the riverbed somewhere on this side of the border? Do you know where any of this happened?"

"We have yet to identify an actual crime scene," Joanna replied.

"So you don't actually know if he was murdered in Mexico or the US?"

"As I said, we have not established where the death occurred."

"I understand his mother is . . . well, let's just say on the colorful side and might have friends or associates who aren't exactly on the up and up. Is it possible that she or one of her several boyfriends might be involved in Xavier's death?"

Obviously Marliss had been nosing around enough to know exactly how Elena Delgado earned her living.

"At this point everyone's a suspect," Joanna said, even though that wasn't true. As far as she was concerned, Elena had been ruled out as the perpetrator almost immediately.

"In other words," Marliss said, "you and your people have made zero progress."

"And I have no further comment at this time," Joanna said. "Have a good day."

With that, she turned on her heel and left the room. It was a good thing, too. If Marliss had asked one more question, Joanna might well have bitten her head off.

CHAPTER 23

BISBEE, ARIZONA
1977

HAVING GROWN UP IN A SMALL TOWN, STEPHEN SETTLED into life in Bisbee with no difficulty. Initially he was regarded as a "good catch" as far as single males were concerned, and people from both church and the school district tried to fix him up with available women. He made it plain to his would-be dates that he just wasn't interested. Eventually, when people started listening to that new radio program called *A Prairie Home Companion*, he was jokingly passed off as one of Garrison Keillor's "Norwegian bachelor farmers." That seemed to do the trick, and people finally got the message.

From the beginning Stephen maintained that he stood with one foot in Bisbee, Arizona, and one in Fertile, Minnesota, claiming that during the summers he would need to head home to help with the upkeep of the family farm. Eventually people got used to that idea, too, teasing him about his being less of a local and more of a snowbird. It didn't matter what they called him, as long as they didn't hassle him about being gone.

Of course the family farm story was entirely fictional. After leaving Fertile, he never once returned to his hometown for a visit, but claiming to go there gave him good cover. While people imagined he was in Minnesota staying with family or friends, he was actually on the road, doing his thing. And how could he afford all that traveling on a teacher's salary? He couldn't have, not on his own. But the truth is he had plenty of money.

The lady tellers at the First National Bank branch in Bisbee's Bakerville neighborhood were the only people in town who really knew how much he was worth, but between the money his mother had left him and the continuing stream of investment income from Gramps's holdings, Stephen's financial situation was just fine and dandy, thank you very much.

For his travels Stephen favored the blue highways he found in the most recent edition of the *Rand McNally Road Atlas*. He ordered the new edition every April so it would be in his hands by the middle of May. Those less traveled roadways led him to places where law enforcement was thin on the ground, making it easier for him to get away with murder.

His 1977 road trip netted him two kills. One was a teenager riding a bicycle on a farm road a few miles outside Fulton, Missouri, just before noon on a Saturday morning in June. He sideswiped her bike, knocking her to the ground. She was easy to overpower and didn't put up much of a fight. When Stephen was done and went looking for a trophy, there was nothing to be found—no jewelry or barrettes—so he settled for one of her shoelaces. He called her Farm Girl. Afterward, he threw both her body and her bicycle into a nearby reservoir. Then, driving sedately, and without ever traveling through Fulton itself, he left both the scene and the area. By the time Lucianne Highsmith's worried mother called the Callaway County Sheriff's Department at four o'clock that afternoon to report her daughter missing, Stephen had already checked into a hotel room in Springfield, Illinois, four hours away. The body was found days later. No suspects in Lucianne's homicide were ever identified.

After that, with the voices quieted for a while, Stephen took a few things off his bucket list. He drove up to Chicago and took in a Cubs game, then he traveled along the Great Lakes, including the

Upper Peninsula in Michigan, and, finally, went east to Niagara Falls. He drove at a leisurely pace. After all he had the whole summer to spend. Eventually he made his way to New York City. No, he did not revisit Coney Island, but he stayed in town long enough to take in a couple Broadway shows—*Jesus Christ Superstar* and *Man of La Mancha*.

Then he headed west again. Tired of being on the road, he made it as far as Gunnison, Colorado, where he rented a cabin on the Gunnison River and spent a relaxing month fishing (fishing always reminded him of the good times he had spent with Gramps) and reading through the shelfful of paperback books—mostly mysteries and westerns—that had been left behind by previous guests.

It was verging on the middle of August when it came time for him to head home. He made his leisurely way down to the Four Corners area. Just north of Shiprock, New Mexico, he picked up a hitchhiker—a boy, this time, most likely a Navajo, who was wearing a bright red bandanna. The kid turned out to be wiry and tough. For that one Stephen needed his chloroform. Once the boy was dead, Stephen removed the bandanna. For trophy purposes that worked fine, and Stephen decided to call this one Bandanna Boy.

After dumping the body in the San Juan River, Stephen drove away. He spent that night in Flagstaff. It was August, yes, but it was also a weekday, so he was able to find a decent room with little difficulty. The day after that, he was back home in Bisbee, Arizona, ready to start his second year of teaching at Bisbee High School.

CHAPTER 24

BISBEE, ARIZONA
Tuesday, December 5, 2023

WHEN JOANNA BRADY SHOWED UP AT WORK ON TUESDAY morning, things were blessedly quiet. For one thing, trenching was over and that annoying jackhammer racket was a thing of the past. Also, according to Dave Ruiz, the plumbing and electrical rough-ins had been installed and were awaiting a visit from the building inspector, who might or might not arrive today.

As far as the jail commander was concerned, things were doing okay, but Terry Gregovich was wondering how soon Joanna could manage the transfer of five more prisoners. She told him she'd look into it.

Detective Raymond had left word that he was taking the day off because he'd be doing Operation Garbage Can that night, which, with any kind of luck, would include a late-night trip to Tucson to deliver a load of possible DNA evidence to the Department of Public Safety (DPS) crime lab.

Joanna was just settling into her computer to look at the upcoming scheduling sheet when Detective Howell entered her office.

"Hey, Deb," Joanna said. "What's up?"

"I just now got off the phone after having a very interesting conversation with Detective Kurt Dawson of the Polk County Sheriff's Department in Crookston, Minnesota."

"Wait," Joanna said. "I thought we weren't going to make any inquiries concerning Stephen Roper until we knew more about what we're up against."

"We're not making inquiries here," Deb responded, "but I figured it couldn't hurt to ask a few questions in his hometown. For one thing, we know that even though he was retired, Roper was still taking summers off the same way he did back when Tom Hadlock was in high school. I thought that was worth checking out, so I called the motels in Fertile—both of them. They don't have any record of anyone by that name ever staying there, not since they switched over from paper records to computerized ones."

"What about an Airbnb?" Joanna asked.

"No such animal."

"I learned there's no one by the name of Roper living in the area, so I checked his mother's maiden name, Hawkins. Came up with zilch there, too. Then I thought, what the hell? Why not try calling the local sheriff's office and see if anyone there can tell me something? That's where I got lucky. Turns out, back in high school the mother of one of their detectives, Detective Kurt Dawson, used to work in the restaurant owned by Stephen Roper's mother. The two women were evidently good friends.

"He told me a lot of the same stuff we heard from Casey in the briefing, but he added in a few more details. Remember Tom Hadlock told us Roper claimed that he went back home every summer to work on the family farm?"

Joanna nodded.

"Turns out that's a bunch of bull. The family farm in question belonged to Stephen Roper's grandfather, Orson Hawkins, who owned several farming properties in the area. Apparently he unloaded all of them at a healthy profit and moved into a house in Fertile with his daughter and grandson while Stephen was in high school."

"So no family farm to worry about," Joanna put in.

"Exactly," Deb said. "According to Detective Dawson, as far as he knew, in the mid-seventies, after Stephen's mother passed away, he sold off everything, quit his teaching job, and left town."

"And never came back?" Joanna asked.

"I asked Detective Dawson that very question, so he called his mom while I was still on the line. That's what she said, too—that she didn't think he ever came back."

"If he lies about one thing . . ." Joanna began.

"What else is he lying about?" Deb finished.

Joanna paused for a moment thinking about what she'd just heard. "So supposing Roper really is a serial child predator. With three months a year free to do whatever he damned well pleases, how much damage could he do?"

"A lot, unfortunately," Deb replied, "because he'd have the whole country as his playground, and it's likely he's been doing it for decades."

"What about closer to home?" Joanna asked. "Do we have any matching unsolved cases from around our neck of the woods?"

"Nope," Deb said. "Not that I could find."

"Even so," Joanna Brady declared, "the buck stops here! One way or another, we're going to put that son of a bitch away for good."

Deb left Joanna's office a few minutes later, leaving her to consider what she had just said. If Stephen Roper really was a serial predator, then there was a good chance that his unidentified DNA profile really was sitting around in an evidence locker somewhere after being found at the scene of some long-unsolved homicide.

Suddenly Detective Raymond's "Operation Garbage Can" had just risen to an entirely different level of importance. It was possible that by obtaining Stephen Roper's DNA profile and getting it uploaded into CODIS, not only might it help solve Xavier Delgado's homicide, it might also provide answers to any number of other cases all over the country.

At that point, Joanna Brady did something she seldom did in her office—she sat at her desk, closed her eyes, and folded her hands in prayer.

"Please, Lord, help us in this investigation, not only for the sake of Elena and Xavier Delgado, but also for any other families out there whose loved ones Stephen Roper may have harmed. You know the names of those families, even if we don't. Help us find them, so we can bring them some measure of justice and peace. In Jesus's name, Amen."

Then Joanna got up out of her chair, left her office, and went in search of Casey Ledford to huddle with her to discuss if this new information from Deb had opened up any new lines of investigation.

CHAPTER 25

BISBEE, ARIZONA
1977–2022

THE LATE SEVENTIES AND EARLY EIGHTIES WERE STEPHEN Roper's golden years. During fall, winter, and spring he taught school. During the summers he hunted wherever the hell he damned well pleased. He tried going to Florida once. That was a mistake. Even in Bisbee, summers could be hot, but in Florida, with all that humidity, they were downright brutal.

Stephen liked sticking to places where the climate was moderate. Summertime in the Pacific Northwest was good for that. He grabbed a six-year-old girl from the Rose Festival in Portland one year and a seven-year-old girl from Seattle's Seafair hydro races a few years later. He was always astonished by how oblivious some parents could be. With kids, shoelaces made for good trophies. They didn't take up much room in his cigar box, and he differentiated between boys and girls by marking the ones belonging to boys with blue ink. He wasn't happy when shoe manufacturers started dropping shoelaces in favor of Velcro.

In terms of best bets for victims, hitchhikers came in second after little kids. On hot summer days, once one of those tired and thirsty travelers settled into Stephen's air-conditioned vehicle—he had graduated to driving Oldsmobile Cutlasses by then—they often dozed off, which gave him the opportunity to do what needed to be done.

On his jaunts, he never followed any set pattern, sticking to secondary roads and staying in small towns. He bought a decent camera and used that as part of his camouflage. If people noticed him stopped at a spot on some isolated roadway, the presence of that camera allowed him to explain that he'd heard that a rare bird of some kind had been seen in the area, and he was hoping to catch it on film.

As far as work was concerned, he was fine. When the mines in Bisbee closed down, it looked for a while as though the community was destined to become a ghost town. As families with young children left town to find work elsewhere, attendance in the school system dropped like a rock. For a time, Stephen worried that he'd end up being laid off. That didn't happen. Quite a few of the teachers left town right along with the miners, providing enough natural attrition that actual layoffs weren't necessary. Besides, with the ability to teach science—both chemistry and biology—along with English, he was regarded as a real asset.

When Phelps Dodge liquidated their holdings of company-owned housing at bargain-basement prices, an influx of new people came to town—artists and craftsman—who were looked down on by older residents who dubbed them "hippies." Having that dividing line in town worked just fine for Stephen because he didn't fit in on either side.

By the mid-eighties and early nineties, however, Stephen's hunting expeditions became more challenging. For one thing, most people stopped hitchhiking. For another, parents seemed to be far more attentive. After that he had to settle for a steady diet of prostitutes. It was easy to get them into his vehicle, but, once there, they were often difficult to handle. That's when his homemade chloroform came in handy. Even with prostitutes, he still took trophies, but often, since the women were almost interchangeable, he simply put an X on the folded and bloodied *Rand McNally* New Mexico road map he still kept in his cigar box. So far his collection of Xs numbered twenty-three.

When Stephen started out on his Killing Journey, as he liked to think of it, each law enforcement jurisdiction had kept its own collection of fingerprints, and that was it. Somebody could commit crimes in towns only miles apart without anyone being the wiser. But then people started talking about creating something called AFIS—the Automated Fingerprint Identification System. That meant that fingerprints collected from one crime scene or one jailed prisoner could be connected to prints from any other jurisdiction in the country. That would have been a lot more worrisome to Stephen if he hadn't been disposing of bodies in water all along. Not only that, thanks to Reservoir Girl's bite mark, he'd been wearing gloves at his crime scenes for years.

Then in 1994, along came the O.J. Simpson trial. If that wasn't a shock to Stephen's system! At first DNA had seemed too slow and cumbersome to pose a threat to him, but over time, with the advent of CODIS—the Combined DNA Index System—it became more serious. CODIS made it possible to compare a DNA profile gained from one crime scene to DNA profiles from anywhere else. Despite the fact that Stephen had never raped any of his victims, the idea that he might have left behind a single hair at one of his crime scenes was utterly terrifying. But years after the advent of CODIS, when no one came knocking at his door, he began to breathe a little easier.

The next blow to his Killing Journey came with the advent of surveillance cameras. At first they were only on businesses, but still that made him have to think twice about picking up a prostitute even in some filthy back alley or on a city street. These days it seemed like everybody and his uncle had one of those Ring doorbell video systems. That made him grateful that, after retiring from teaching in 2002, and much to the dismay of the voices, he had pulled the plug on his hobby as well, quitting both pursuits cold turkey. The voices begged him to change his mind, but he was adamant, telling them that continuing was just too damned risky.

He still went on trips during the summers, choosing to go somewhere cool, where he often rented cheap cabins and actually fished for a change. He told people in Bisbee that his brother had finally sold the family farm, so he no longer had to help with that. Sometimes he visited his old haunts, driving by his former crime scenes just for the hell of it, but he never stopped or lingered.

Now, as opposed to being an actual participant in the world of crime, Stephen used his computer keyboard to become an online student of all things forensic. His new hobby allowed him to follow the careers of his brothers-in-arms. Surprisingly enough, there were serial killers everywhere. He cheered when they succeeded in baffling the cops and sympathized when they were apprehended. Sympathized, yes, but he also followed every detail of their subsequent trials and convictions.

He wanted to know how they had screwed up. Sometimes they killed people not only in too close proximity to each other but also in close proximity to the killer himself. Sometimes they were stupid and couldn't resist raping their victims either before or after murdering them, leaving behind all kinds of damning DNA evidence.

But the 2018 arrest of the Golden State killer brought Stephen up short. With DNA from an unknown perpetrator, authorities were able to figure out who he was by using something called forensic genealogy. Turned out one of the killer's distant relatives had put his DNA profile into one of those public family history databases. Using a partial DNA match, cops had created a family tree and found the guy in short order.

For Stephen, that was another heart-stopping moment. He knew that Gramps had been an only child, but he didn't know about Grandma Joanie. As for his father's side of the family? He had no idea about them, not a clue. But as long as they didn't have Stephen's DNA, even if he did have a busybody second or third cousin somewhere who was into family genealogy, the cops still wouldn't be able to touch him.

That was about the time he hooked up with Hands Across the Border, mostly because he was bored but also because having access to all kinds of undocumented immigrants might be a good source of potential victims in case he decided to take up where he'd left off.

He found a food truck, had it remodeled, and started driving the Free Store back and forth across the border. Some of his neighbors didn't approve of people who helped migrants, but there were lots of people who did. A Tucson TV station ended up sending a reporter and camera crew down to Bisbee to interview the guy people in the area were starting to call Señor Santa Claus.

Stephen was just beginning to relish his newfound good-guy status when the pandemic hit. When everything shut down, so did the Free Store. During the pandemic, as far as health care was concerned, Covid seemed to be the only game in town. Minor issues were placed on a back burner. When Stephen started noticing that the skin on his chest was getting a little scaly, he didn't go rushing off to see a doctor. He treated the condition himself by trying a number of different moisturizers, but they didn't seem to make any difference. Neither did changing his laundry soap. Even after the lockdown started easing up, when everybody else went racing off to see their GPs, Stephen avoided the crowd and put off making an appointment a little longer.

In the spring of 2022 when Stephen finally went in for his first "annual" physical in three years, he was floored when, after a biopsy, the doctor told him he had breast cancer.

"Breast cancer," Stephen repeated in dismay. "I thought only women get breast cancer."

"Not true," Dr. Manuel Guerrero told him. "Is there a history of breast cancer in your family?"

Stephen nodded. "Both my mother and grandmother died of breast cancer."

Dr. Guerrero shook his head. "That's a definite risk factor, then," he said. "It's too bad you didn't come see me sooner."

The doctor pulled a pad of paper out of his desk drawer. After pausing long enough to look up something on his computer, he began to write, talking as he did so. "I'm going to refer you to Dr. Andrew Fillmore at the Mayo Clinic in Phoenix. He's an oncologist who specializes in breast cancer in males. He's also up to speed on all the most recent treatment options."

Stephen took the proffered paper, but he did so with the sinking sensation that someone had just handed him his own death warrant.

CHAPTER 26

BISBEE, ARIZONA
Wednesday, December 6, 2023

"**ANY WORD ON OPERATION GARBAGE CAN?**" **BUTCH ASKED** as he handed Joanna her coffee cup on Wednesday morning.

"Not so far," she said.

As a consequence, once at the Justice Center, Joanna made a beeline for the bullpen, the room dedicated to her investigation team. When she arrived, Detective Raymond was nowhere to be seen.

"How'd Operation Garbage Can go?" she asked Detective Howell.

"All right," Deb replied, "but it turns out Stephen Roper is a night owl. He didn't turn off his TV and go to bed until after one, so Garth wasn't able to stage his raid until close to two. He came away with one bag of trash and one of recycling, but it took until seven this morning for him to drive to Tucson, make the drop-off, and then make it back to Elfrida. He sent me a text saying he was home, and I told him to take the rest of the day off."

"Deservedly so," Joanna said. "How long do you think it'll take for the DPS crime lab to come up with a DNA profile?"

"Days if we're lucky," Deb replied. "Weeks if we're not."

"Then I guess we have to take an old, cold tater and wait," Joanna said.

Her next stop was the chief deputy's office. "Anything major happen overnight?" she asked.

"Not much," Tom Hadlock said. "Two DUIs, one DV, and a couple of speeding citations. That's about it."

"No drop-offs from our friends at the Border Patrol?"

"Not today for a change," he told her.

"How about the jail?"

"No problems there," he said, "and as far as construction goes, I just checked in with Mr. Ruiz. The rough-ins for electrical and plumbing passed their inspections late yesterday afternoon. As we speak, Dave's crew is in the process of unloading the concrete blocks for the walls. Those should start going up later today."

"Sounds like everybody's making good progress then. Good on you."

But things didn't seem so sunny once she arrived at her own office and found Marliss Shackleford waiting for her.

"Any progress on the Xavier Delgado case?" Marliss wanted to know.

"Nothing I can share," Joanna told her. "When we're ready to do updates, you'll be the first to know."

"I understand Jennifer is getting married at the end of this month," Marliss said. "Is it possible that issues with planning a hurry-up wedding are interfering with your duties as sheriff? Considering your own history, maybe you're having a hard time keeping your eye on the ball."

Marliss had clearly gotten wind of Jenny's impending wedding and assumed that, due to the short time frame, the bride was already expecting. Joanna had never made a secret of the fact that she'd been pregnant at the time she and Andy had tied the knot, but Marliss's snide insinuation that Joanna's history was about to repeat itself with Jenny was a step too far. Most of the time, Joanna was able to keep her temper in line, but this was not one of them.

"My daughter's personal life is none of your damned business!" she fired off. "Now get the hell out of here before I have you thrown out." Then she marched into her own office, slamming the door shut behind her.

An hour later, she was still fuming and regretting her angry outburst when Kristin tapped on her door and warily poked her head inside.

"Have you had a chance to cool off?" Kristin asked.

"A little," Joanna said. "Why?"

"I've got a call for you from Anna Rae Green in Denver, Colorado. She says she's with the MMIV."

Joanna started to point out that Anna Rae Green wasn't just *with* the Missing and Murdered Indigenous Victims Task Force. She was the agency's director in chief, but she let that pass. Knowing Jenny had used Anna Rae as a reference on her job application, Joanna assumed the woman was calling to see how things were going with Jenny's new job at the Pima County Sheriff's Department.

"Thanks," she said, reaching for her phone.

"Sheriff Brady here, Anna Rae. Good to hear from you. If you're calling about Jenny, Pima County Deputy Jennifer Ann Brady seems to be doing just fine, thanks in large measure to you."

"I'm delighted to hear that, and I'm not the least bit surprised," Anna Rae said, "but that's not why I'm calling. I wanted to know more about our match."

Joanna was mystified. "Match?" she repeated. "What match?"

"Oh, I'm so sorry," Anna Rae said quickly. "The notification came in to us here in Denver a little while ago. I thought for sure the DPS lab in Tucson would have let you know as well."

Joanna was astonished. "Wait," she said. "Are you talking about the trash evidence we delivered to them earlier this morning? They've already created a DNA profile and have a match? How's that even possible?"

"Who said anything about DNA?" Anna Rae asked in return. "The hit came in on AFIS. The DPS crime lab found a partial palm print on a soda can your detective pulled out of a suspect's trash. Turns out it's a match to a partial palm print from one of our cold cases—the 1962 murder of Amanda Marie Hudson, a Lakota from Devil's Lake, North Dakota. What can you tell me about our suspect?"

For a moment, Joanna was too stunned to reply. Before she could, Kristin reappeared. "There's a call for you from the DPS lab in Tucson. Do you want me to keep them on hold or will you call them back?"

"Hang on," Joanna said to Anna Rae. Then to Kristin she said, "Transfer the DPS call over to Deb Howell."

As Kristin retreated, Joanna turned her attention back to Anna Rae. "That was the DPS lab calling. I turned them over to the lead detective on our case. The suspect is a guy named Stephen Roper. He's a longtime resident of Bisbee, Arizona—a retired schoolteacher with no priors that we could find. He was actually my English teacher when I was a senior in high school.

"He came on our radar recently after the body of a four-year-old boy from Naco, Sonora, Mexico—Xavier Delgado—was found floating in a duffel bag in the San Pedro River on this side of the border. The autopsy showed Xavier died of manual strangulation. Our suspect participates in a charity that uses a remodeled food truck to deliver food and other necessities to migrants stuck in Sonora waiting to cross the border. According to one of our sources, Xavier visited the food truck the day he went missing, making Roper possibly one of the last people to have seen him alive."

"Have you taken him into custody?" Anna Rae asked.

"Are you kidding? We haven't even talked to him," Joanna replied. "At this point I don't believe he has any idea that he's under suspicion. Some of the details in the case make us suspect he might be a repeat offender. For one thing, the victim's body had been dipped in a bleach solution, and his fingernails had been cut off down to the quick."

"To destroy possible DNA?" Anna Rae asked.

"Exactly," Joanna agreed. "That's why I was hoping for a possible DNA match to evidence from somebody else's cold case, but I never even considered a match might come through AFIS. If you don't mind, I'd like to bring the lead detective on our case into this conversation so we're all on the same page."

"Fine with me," Anna Rae said.

"Okay," Joanna said. "Hang on while I call her." Joanna was in the process of buzzing Kristin to have her summon Deb when the detective herself appeared in the doorway.

"Have you heard?" she demanded.

Joanna nodded. "Just now," she said. "I have Anna Rae Green of the MMIV on the line. Turns out the match is to one of her Indigenous cases. I'm going to put her on speaker so she can brief us both at the same time."

As Deb took a seat, Joanna pushed the speaker button. "All right, Anna Rae," she said. "Go ahead. Detective Howell is here now. We're all ears."

CHAPTER 27

BISBEE, ARIZONA
Wednesday, December 6, 2023

"AS YOU MAY OR MAY NOT KNOW," ANNA RAE GREEN began, "most of MMIV's cases come to us by way of other law enforcement agencies. Amanda Hudson's case came to us through a relative—her younger brother, Luke Running Deer. Amanda's mother never recovered from losing her daughter and passed away several years after Amanda's death of cirrhosis of the liver. Luke was sixteen when Amanda graduated from high school. He wasn't on the best of terms with his parents. He went to live with his maternal grandmother, Madeline Running Deer, about the time his sister left home to go to college. Once Luke became an adult, he ended up taking his grandmother's last name.

"After graduating from high school, he did a hitch in the army before going back to school and earning a B.A. in business. He's now a retired CPA living in Rapid City, South Dakota. Recently MMIV's South Dakota field agent, Nadia Grayson, was able to close the long cold cases of two young girls, sisters from Pine Ridge, who were kidnapped and murdered in 1992. As a result of those cases, Nadia did several local television interviews, one of which Luke saw.

"When his grandmother died in the early nineties, he was the one who handled her final affairs and prepared her home for sale. In the process of clearing out the house, Luke came across an envelope addressed to his mother from the Grand Forks County Coroner's Office. It contained Amanda's personal effects—a pair of glasses, a beaded, deerskin-backed bracelet Madeline Running Deer had made for Amanda on the occasion of her sixteenth birthday, and a whetstone."

"A whetstone but no knife?" Joanna asked.

"Correct. All three items were still sealed in glassine evidence bags from the coroner's office, but the one that held the glasses contained a film of fingerprint dust. Over the years, Luke had forgotten all about those items, but seeing Nadia Grayson's interview brought them back to mind and prompted Luke to go down to his basement and dig out the envelope."

"Which he took to the MMIV field agent?" Joanna asked.

"Exactly," Anna Rae replied. "Once Luke recounted his sister's story and showed Nadia the bags, she went nuts. The presence of the fingerprint dust suggested to her that, at some point, someone had tried to lift prints from the glasses. She immediately contacted Philip Dark Moon, her North Dakota counterpart, and put him on the case.

"Philip went through his records and saw that Amanda Hudson's case wasn't among the ones that had been forwarded to him from the North Dakota Highway Patrol when we sent out our request for cases involving Indigenous victims. When he finally found the case file, he discovered Amanda Hudson's Lakota origins hadn't been noted. On her birth certificate, she was listed as Caucasian.

"According to the file, she was reported missing on Friday, May 25, 1962, when she failed to show up for her grandmother's birthday celebration in Devil's Lake. Her body was found the next day by a family looking for a picnic spot along the Turtle River west of Grand Forks. She was found fully clothed lying in the river, with her head pushed up against the riverbank. The man who found the body was initially considered a person of interest, but he was soon cleared. No other suspects were ever identified. Surprisingly enough, the Highway Patrol's file contained no prints of any kind.

"Philip Dark Moon's next stop was in Grand Forks. What was once the coroner's office is now the Grand Forks County Medical Examiner's Office. When the coroner performed the autopsy in 1962, he noticed what appeared to be a handprint on the front of Amanda's glasses. He dusted the glasses for prints. In the early nineties, when the coroner was replaced by an ME who was a forward-thinking kind of guy, he went through his files, looking for any unsolved cases, and uploaded any existing prints from those to AFIS. That palm print from Amanda's glasses has been sitting in AFIS for more than thirty years."

"But why a palm print?" Deb Howell asked.

"The crime scene photos show that Amanda was partly in the water and partly out of it, with the back of her head shoved into a slightly raised section of riverbank," Anna Rae answered. "The theory is that while her killer was trying to dispose of the body, he may have been interrupted. Concerned about getting caught, he must have put his hand across her face and shoved the back of her head into the bank, in hopes of keeping her out of sight while he took off, probably in a hell of a hurry."

"Which explains the partial print on the glasses," Joanna said. "When was this again?"

"May 26, 1962."

Joanna turned to Deb. "How old was Stephen Roper in 1962?"

Deb consulted her notes. "Sixteen in May of that year," she answered.

"He killed her while he was still in high school," Joanna murmured, "and he's gotten away with it all this time? I hate to think what else he's been doing in the meantime."

"That makes two of us," Anna Rae replied.

"What was Amanda's manner of death again?" Deb asked.

"Manual strangulation."

"Same with our victim, Xavier Delgado," Deb offered, "only he's a four-year-old kid. How old was Amanda Hudson?"

"Twenty-one," Anna Rae answered.

"Any sign of sexual assault?"

"No, and she was fully clothed when she was found."

"Ditto with us," Deb offered. "Xavier was fully clothed, and there was no sign of sexual assault. His body was also dumped in a river, except the San Pedro didn't have any water in it at the time. When a flash flood came through, the body, which had been loaded into a canvas duffel bag, floated downstream where it was caught in debris stuck under a bridge."

"Any DNA on the bag or the body?" Anna Rae asked.

"Nope," Deb answered.

"What about the bag?" Anna Rae asked. "Anything identifiable there?"

"Casey, our lead CSI, says it came from Target, but there's no telling which store," Deb replied. "The one in Sierra Vista is closest, but there are several locations in Tucson as well. The bag could have been purchased at any one of them, so we'll be looking into that. As soon as I get off the phone, I'm planning on driving out to Sierra Vista to check with the store manager there."

"How close are you to having probable cause for an arrest?" Ana Rae asked.

"Not nearly as close as we'd like to be," Deb replied.

"That's why we don't want to do anything to spook him before we're ready to take him into custody," Joanna put in.

"All right," Anna Rae said thoughtfully, "we have two homicides, committed sixty years apart, with the same cause of death—manual strangulation, no sexual assault, and similar disposal sites. To me, those three commonalities count as a signature, so it's possible it's the same perpetrator. Assuming the killer has been doing this all along, there have to be other unsolved cases out there. I'll put some of my people to work looking for comparable cases."

Joanna knew that Casey Ledford had already started working on that idea, but there could be little doubt the MMIV had a lot more resources on that score than the Cochise County Sheriff's Department.

"Unsolved cases with Indigenous victims or otherwise?" she asked.

"Both," Anna Rae replied. "If our killer doesn't discriminate as far as his victims are concerned, neither should we."

CHAPTER 28

PHOENIX, ARIZONA
2022

BEING REFERRED TO DR. FILLMORE AT THE MAYO CLINIC was one thing. Getting in to see him was quite another. Stephen had to take a number and get in line. His first actual doctor's visit didn't happen until late spring of 2022. First he underwent a whole series of scans—chest x-rays, CT scans, PET scans, and bone scans. A biopsy determined that his cancer had spread to some lymph nodes but had not yet metastasized to other parts of his body.

At first he drove back and forth from Bisbee to Phoenix for the tests—four hours each way. When Stephen's lumpectomy was finally scheduled, and knowing he'd be doing both chemo and radiation therapy after the surgery, he broke down and booked a room at the nearest Residence Inn, which offered an in-house restaurant as well as shuttle service back and forth to the hospital campus.

That was the beginning of what Stephen Roper regarded as his six-month stay in hell—aka Phoenix. From April through September it was ungodly hot. The chemo made him sick as a dog. The food in the restaurant was probably fine, but it mostly didn't stay down. He lost thirty pounds in the blink of an eye. The postsurgery physical therapy sessions to improve movement of his shoulder and upper arm were painful, and the radiation treatments weren't exactly fun, either.

Naturally he lost all his hair. The only consolation concerning that was due to the fact that many of the hotel's other guests were in the same boat, but some were in even worse shape and stuck in wheelchairs. At least Stephen could walk on his own.

The voices had remained blessedly quiet for years, but they started tuning up again during his stay in Phoenix. By the time his chemo treatments ended, they were going full force, even though he kept telling them to shut the hell up. What made them think he could go hunting when he couldn't even drive? As for having the strength to strangle someone with his bare hands when he was weak as a kitten? No way in hell was that going to happen!

By the beginning of October 2022, he was finally well enough to drive himself back to Bisbee. When he got there, the long drive had worn him out. He didn't bother driving into the garage. Instead, he parked in front of the house and left his luggage in the car, but oh, did Bisbee's cool mountain air feel good on his skin!

Stephen had expected the house to be a stuffy mess, but it wasn't. One of the ladies from church who had checked on him regularly had learned that he was about to be released. She had gone to his house, located his spare key under a flowerpot in the front yard, and had then organized a cleanup crew. They had come through like a whirlwind, mopping and dusting. They had also left the fridge stocked with a supply of milk, butter, fruits and vegetables, while the freezer had dozens of premade, heat-and-serve meals for one. The night of his homecoming, however, he was too tired to eat. Even though it was only five o'clock in the afternoon, he went into the bedroom, fell across the bed fully clothed, and slept until morning.

Stephen forced himself to unload the car the next day because he needed to access the meds he'd left in his luggage locked in the trunk of his five-year-old Mercedes S550. Then slowly, one tiny step at a time, he began rebuilding his life. He found a local physical therapist who picked up where the ones from the Mayo Clinic had left off. Gradually, he regained both strength and movement in his right arm and shoulder.

On Christmas Eve 2022, when the rest of the world was focused on peace on earth and goodwill to men, Stephen finally had enough strength to open the trapdoor in his bathroom that allowed him to go down into the crawl space and access the safe he'd had installed there.

While other people were busy wrapping gifts or hanging stockings, Stephen Roper sat alone in his living room, savoring the gift he was giving himself—revisiting the contents of his cigar box, one precious memento at a time.

After all, if this was a night when people were supposed to count their blessings, why shouldn't he?

CHAPTER 29

SIERRA VISTA, ARIZONA
Wednesday, December 6, 2023

BY NOON, A STILL WEARY DETECTIVE GARTH RAYMOND showed up at the Justice Center. He hadn't been able to fall asleep at home and decided he might as well come to work. Consequently, when Detective Howell set off for Sierra Vista that afternoon, Garth was riding shotgun. On the way Deb brought him up to date with everything that had come to light that morning.

"Wow," he said when she finished. "Sounds like my garbage raid really paid off!"

"It sure as hell did," Deb agreed.

Once in Target, they located the manager, one Mr. Hobart, introduced themselves, and then told him what they needed. They had come armed with a copy of the information on the tag in the duffel bag that had been hauled out of the San Pedro.

After some dinking around on his computer, Mr. Hobart said, "Oh, yes, that's our five-star duffel—a very popular item. According to this, we started out with five bags in this dye lot. We still have some in other colors, but the blue ones are completely sold out."

"Can you tell when they were sold?"

"Unfortunately I can't. For that I'd need to see actual receipts."

"Thank you, Mr. Hobart," Deb told him. "You've been very helpful."

He beamed at her. "You're quite welcome," he said.

"But he wasn't helpful," Garth objected once they left the store.

"I think he was," Deb returned. "The fact that all the blue ones are gone suggests to me that one person may have scored the whole batch."

"If we could subpoena Roper's bank records, we could find out if it was him," Garth muttered, "but without that, we're stuck."

"Maybe not," Deb said. "I think someone needs to make another trip south of the border."

"How come?"

"To find out if any of the migrant kids have ever seen Señor Santa Claus using a blue duffel bag."

When they got back to the Justice Center, they dropped by Joanna's office to make that suggestion.

"I'll check with Captain Peña and see what he says," Joanna agreed.

Once she had Arturo on the phone, she laid out everything that they'd learned over the course of the day. She could tell he was as excited as she was, but when she suggested sending Jaime and Deb back down for another visit with the migrant kids, he drew the line.

"At this point Roper still has no idea he's under suspicion, correct?"

"As far as I know," Joanna replied.

"If you want to keep him in the dark, sending your officers back down here is a mistake. The Free Store is due to be here again this coming Friday, right?"

"Correct."

"Let me talk to Señora Mendoza to see if she can learn anything more from the kids without giving away the farm. She usually holds her classes with the migrant kids during the mornings. I'll be in touch with her tonight and let her know it would be helpful to know if any of them have seen any sign of one of those blue duffel bags."

Off the phone with Peña, Joanna made her way to the bullpen. "I told Arturo what's happened. He thinks we're better off working with our informant rather than sending anyone across the line, but good work," she told Garth and Deb. "We still don't have probable cause, but thanks to you, we've at least got some lines of inquiry to follow up on. That's a hell of a lot more than we had before."

CHAPTER 30

BISBEE, ARIZONA
Spring 2023

BY THE SPRING OF 2023, STEPHEN FINALLY STARTED FEEL-ing like his old self again. He had regained most of the weight he'd lost. He began wearing bright pink cancer-survivor T-shirts and became a one-man evangelist, letting people know that, when it comes to breast cancer, men can have it too. Once his postchemo hair grew in, it was terribly thin. Rather than resorting to a combover, he began wearing hats.

While undergoing treatment, he'd watched a lot of PGA golf, and since Bryson DeChambeau was his favorite pro golfer, Stephen bought himself several Bryson DeChambeau–style golf hats in every available color. On Fridays, though, the golf hat stayed home in favor of his red-and-white Santa Hat. That clashed with his pink T-shirt, but since the migrant kids didn't seem to give a rat's ass about his mismatched wardrobe, neither did Stephen.

By the end of April 2023 he was ready to resume operating the Free Store, which, in his absence, had been managed by other Hands Across the Border volunteers. During that time, one of the group's Bisbee volunteers had begun providing fifty or so homemade sack lunches for him to distribute each time he went across the border. That meant that before driving to Naco, he had to stop by her house and pick them up.

Unfortunately the lady's idea of transporting her bagged lunches consisted of a never-ending collection of plastic grocery bags to say nothing of multiple trips. Looking for a more suitable arrangement, while on a routine shopping trip to Sierra Vista, Stephen happened across Target's collection of duffel bags. *Why not use one of those?* he thought.

The bags came in several colors. Since blue was Stephen's favorite color, he chose a blue one, leaving four more still on the shelf. Then, thinking about how much other fetching and carrying was involved in stocking the Free Store on a daily basis, he decided, *What the hell? Why not take them all?*

That's just what he did.

CHAPTER 31

BISBEE, ARIZONA
Thursday, December 7, 2023

ON THURSDAY MORNING, JOANNA HAD BARELY SETTLED down at her desk when a call came in from Anna Rae Green. "We've got two more possibles," she said.

"Two?" Joanna asked. "Really?"

"Really," Anna Rae replied. "The first one happens to be back in Dan Pardee's patch. A girl named Inez Johnson disappeared from Bylas, Arizona, in June of 1972."

"Oh, no," Joanna said. "Not another girl from the San Carlos!"

"I'm afraid so," Anna Rae said. "She left home planning on hitchhiking from Bylas to Globe to visit friends but never arrived. Two days after she was reported missing to tribal police, her body was found floating in the San Carlos Reservoir. She was found naked, although there was no sign of sexual assault. Her clothing was never located nor was the turquoise and silver squash blossom necklace she reportedly was wearing at the time she disappeared."

"Cause of death?"

"Manual strangulation."

"Those are our common denominators," Joanna observed. "Manual strangulation, no sexual assault, and disposal in a body of water."

"Correct," Anna Rae said, "and here's a case from 1977. This one was a fifteen-year-old boy named Michael Young from Shiprock,

New Mexico. After hanging out with a group of friends, he left to go home but never arrived. His body was found in the San Juan River two days after his mother reported him missing. Manual strangulation, no sexual assault, and his signature red bandanna was missing. So with both these cases we have something missing. What about your victim?"

"A shoelace was missing from his Keds," Joanna answered.

"It sounds as though Mr. Roper likes to keep trophies."

"Yes, it does," Joanna agreed. "Was anything missing from Amanda Hudson's body?"

"Not that I know of," Anna Rae said, "but I'll have Philip Dark Moon get in touch with her brother and see if he knows of anything that should have been there that wasn't."

"Yes, do that," Joanna agreed, "but what time of year did these cases happen?"

"Inez disappeared in June of 1972. Michael disappeared in mid-August of 1977."

"Our understanding is that Roper traveled primarily during the summers, supposedly going back and forth between Minnesota and Arizona, which, it turns out, wasn't true. We have it on good authority that once he quit his teaching job there he never returned," Joanna supplied. "But mid-August would coincide with his needing to be back in Bisbee in time for the start of school the first of September. It's sounding more and more like he's our guy."

"I wholeheartedly agree," Anna Rae said, "and the palm print gives us a connection to Amanda Hudson, but I don't yet see how we're going to connect him to these other cases."

Suddenly, a light bulb exploded inside Joanna's head. If Roper had targeted victims from small communities all over the country, there were probably lots of jurisdictions like hers—ones with limited resources—who had an aging, still unsolved cold case on their books, one that continued to haunt the guys who had investigated it without ever being able to resolve it. If you're a homicide cop, those are the ones that never go away.

"Wait a minute," she said excitedly. "What do we do when we have an unidentified suspect on the loose?"

"Send out a BOLO, of course," Anna Rae replied, but then she quickly understood where Joanna was going. "You're saying that, instead of telling other jurisdictions to be on the lookout for a suspect, we send out one for possible victims?"

"Exactly," Joanna said, "victims of unsolved murders with the same commonalities we've already established."

"What a great idea," Anna Rae said.

"Yes," Joanna said, "but that's not something a small-town sheriff from Podunk, Arizona, can pull off."

"Not to worry," Anna Rae replied. "Leave that to me. Somebody from the FBI would be able to do that in a blink. I may not have enough influence to make it happen on my own, but my boss sure as hell does. She just happens to be the secretary of the interior. Since your case is primary, I'll have her tell them that information on any hits is to be forwarded directly to you."

"Sounds like it pays to have friends in high places," Joanna observed.

Anna Rae Green laughed. "Sometimes," she said, "but a lot of the time it can be a pain in the ass."

JOANNA WAS HOME AND WAS JUST SITTING DOWN TO dinner that night when Arturo called. Not wanting the kids to hear anything about the ongoing case, she went into the other room to answer.

"What's going on?" she asked.

"Aña just left," he told her.

"And?"

"I'm not sure how much this helps, but when Señor Santa Claus delivers sack lunches, he does so out of a blue bag. Not a red one or a green one, but a blue one."

"Interesting," Joanna said. "According to Detective Howell, the Target in Sierra Vista had recently sold five of those. So if the one with the lunches turns out to be the same dye lot and item number as the one holding Xavier Delgado, that could be the link we need. The thing is, I still don't believe we have enough evidence to go for a search warrant."

"When he's down here tomorrow," Arturo said, "I'll have people keeping an eye on him. If he tries to make a run for it, we'll grab him."

"Good," Joanna said. "Appreciate it."

Back at the table, Butch gave her a questioning look.

"Just work," she said. "No biggie."

It was a biggie, actually, but for now that was all the kids needed to hear about it. Once the case showed up on Marliss's website, however, the news would be all over town, and Joanna would probably have some serious explaining to do as far as Sage and Dennis were concerned.

CHAPTER 32

BISBEE, ARIZONA
Friday, December 8, 2023

STEPHEN ROPER AWAKENED THAT FRIDAY MORNING FEEL- ing groggy and out of sorts. It had been the longest and worst two weeks of his life. Usually one of his kills was followed by a period of euphoria. Not this time. Instead he'd been living in a nightmare.

For one thing, he'd really overdone it as far as his gimpy shoulder was concerned. Even with pain pills, it kept him awake night after night, but so did worry. For the first time ever, Stephen Roper was afraid of getting caught.

That day in the Free Store when most of the voices had been yelling at him to take the kid, there had been one dissenter—Sherlock. "Don't do it," he had warned. "He's too close to you. You'll get caught." But had Stephen paid any attention? He had not. He'd grabbed the kid anyway. When Xavier had let out a yelp of alarm and fought back—Stephen had resorted to banging his head against the edge of the counter hard enough to knock him out.

By rights, Stephen should have killed him then and there, on the floor of the food truck, but he hadn't dared. He knew from experience that manual strangulation takes time, and he was afraid one of the Free Store's regular customers might come wandering inside. Instead, Stephen had secured Xavier with duct tape—binding his arms and legs and slapping more of the tape over his mouth—

before folding the still unconscious boy into a plastic tote and hiding that behind the counter long enough for him to close up shop and head for the border.

He'd been approaching the crossing when he realized the backs of both hands were bleeding. In the course of that brief but fierce struggle, the one in which Stephen had reinjured his shoulder, the little bastard had somehow managed to scratch the hell out of the backs of Stephen's hands. Before reaching the guard shack, he quickly shifted his grip from the sides of the steering wheel to the bottom so the damage wouldn't be visible.

The guards on the Mexican side sent him through with their customary smile and wave. The guard on the American side wanted to chat.

"So Señor Santa is leaving early today?" he asked, as Stephen rolled down the window.

"I'm a little under the weather," Stephen told him.

"Take care then," the guard told him. "Feel better."

Stephen had barely driven away from the crossing when the kid came to and began kicking the hell out of the inside of the tote, rocking it back and forth and sending it shooting out from behind the counter. It was all Stephen could do to keep driving. It was only a matter of a few minutes from the crossing to his place on Country Club Drive, but with the kid raising hell, it had seemed to take forever. Once the truck was parked next to his house, Stephen had pounced on the tote, ripped off the lid, and put the damned kid out of his misery right then and there, but instead of feeling a sense of triumph, Stephen Roper was experiencing something he'd never encountered before—outright terror!

He had broken one of his cardinal rules—he'd murdered someone literally in his own yard. He'd gotten away with doing that once long ago with Grandma Lucille. In that instance the cops had turned up and taken the body away. This time getting rid of the body would be Stephen's problem, and it was a big one.

For one thing, he hadn't been wearing gloves, so his DNA would be all over Xavier's body. He knew that bleach was the only way to get rid of DNA, and he happened to have a gallon and a half of that already on hand. At least he wouldn't have to go on a late-night shopping trip to Safeway and end up being caught on video picking up an emergency supply.

He'd had to wait until dark before he could bring the kid inside. Initially he tried using the tote, but with his shoulder on fire, that was a nonstarter, so he had stuffed the boy's body into the sack lunch duffel bag, making the body far easier for him to handle. Now wearing gloves, Stephen set about cleaning up his mess. By the time he'd finished bathing the kid, trimming his fingernails, and redressing him, he'd decided that the only sensible way to get rid of the body was to bury it somewhere far away from his place on Country Club Drive.

In its natural state, dirt in the Sonoran Desert is usually the same consistency as hardened concrete. From that standpoint, digging a grave in the softer sand of a dry wash or riverbed seemed like a plan, and the San Pedro River, just a few miles to the west on Highway 92, was as good a place as any. Stephen was confident that his all-wheel-drive Mercedes would be up to the challenge of getting him there.

It was close to midnight before Stephen had the body along with a pick and shovel loaded into the trunk of the Mercedes. Deciding he needed to unload the plastic tote as well, he took the added precaution of carrying it inside to examine it in the light—and a good thing, too. Sure enough, there were small smears of blood showing on the inside of the tote—no doubt from Stephen's damaged hands. He scrubbed that in the remaining bleach solution that was still in his bathtub. Then the tote went into the Mercedes's back seat. As for the duct tape he'd used to secure the kid? That went into a ziplock bag under the driver's seat.

Stephen had been beyond exhausted when he finally went to bed that night. Even so, he hadn't slept a wink. Four hours later he staggered out of bed, dressed, and headed for the San Pedro, bringing along his old camera equipment to provide cover, something that proved to be unnecessary because he never saw a soul.

Unfortunately, just because the sand in the riverbed wasn't hard-packed didn't make it easier to dig. For every shovelful he dug out, half that much slipped back into the hole as the sides kept collapsing. It took over an hour for him to hollow out a trench deep enough to cover the kid's body without leaving behind a telltale, child-size mound. Then, rather than heading home, he drove west through Sierra Vista and then on to Tucson where he dropped the apparently clean tote off at a Goodwill donation center. Then, after downing a Subway sandwich, he stuffed the ziplock holding the incriminating duct tape inside the bag the sandwich had come in and placed that in a trash can located just inside the restaurant's front door.

Feeling he'd done all he could to cover his tracks, Stephen went home. Knowing the scratch marks were all too visible, the first person he called was Shirley, his friend from church, telling her that he'd just tested positive for Covid, so he for sure wouldn't be in his regular pew this Sunday and, depending on how things went, maybe not the following one, either.

"Would you like me to come by and drop off some food?" Shirley had asked solicitously.

"No, thanks," he told her quickly. "Don't bother. I've got everything I need."

After that, he had settled in to wait. He'd watched the news compulsively—the lead stories, anyway—waiting to hear that a child had been reported missing in Naco, Sonora, but the Tucson stations maintained radio silence on that score. Had Stephen bothered to stay tuned for the "upcoming" weather reports, saying that a fierce storm was bearing down on southern Arizona, he might not have been so surprised by the pummeling rain that hit the area over Thanksgiving weekend.

Once the body showed up, his life got infinitely worse. The Tucson stations still weren't running with the story, but Marliss Shackleford was. She was the one who identified the dead child pulled from the San Pedro as Xavier Delgado before anyone else did. And Marliss's coverage was also how Stephen learned that Joanna Brady's Sheriff's Department was in charge of the investigation.

Stephen remembered her from a senior English class at Bisbee High School, back when she was still Joanna Lathrop. As he recalled, she'd done all right in class and probably ended up with either an A- or B+. (The Bisbee School District had still been doing letter grades at the time.) But obviously Joanna hadn't exactly been focused on schoolwork since she'd managed to get herself knocked up that year and hadn't been allowed to walk through graduation.

She'd ended up becoming sheriff by a fluke when her first husband, a candidate for sheriff, had been murdered, and she'd been elected by write-in voters. When she had won, Stephen had been appalled. How could someone with no law enforcement experience whatsoever be elected to the office of sheriff? He had thought her winning that first election to be a fluke, but she'd been elected to three subsequent terms, and he had voted against her every time.

He assumed that, if she was running the investigation, it would end up being a ham-fisted, amateurish effort—too bad for her, good for him. Having followed Marliss Shackleford's many takedowns of Sheriff Brady's job performance over the years, Stephen was sure he wasn't the only person in Cochise County who felt that way—even if they were always outvoted.

As his days of self-imposed solitary confinement wore on, Stephen found himself feeling more and more anxious. He may have had a pretend case of Covid, but his loss of appetite was real enough. He barely ate or slept, either, and not only because his shoulder was bothering him. Although the other voices were alarmingly absent, waking or sleeping, Sherlock's voice was a constant presence, jeering at him for being so stupid, for making such a mess of things, and for thinking that he could somehow skate around this disaster and still get away with it.

By Thursday of the second week, however, evidence of Xavier Delgado's scratches had all but disappeared. So on this Friday morning, a still sleep-deprived Stephen Roper forced himself out of bed and got dressed, donning one of his bright pink shirts and his customary red-and-white hat. Today would be Señor Santa Claus's first visit since Xavier Delgado's murder, and Stephen was determined to put on a good face. The last thing he did before leaving home was pause long enough to check Marliss's website. Had there been any new developments, she would surely have mentioned them, but there was nothing.

On that happy note, he went outside, fired up his truck, and headed off on his rounds, starting with the sandwich lady's house. Señor Santa Claus left home convinced that, in spite of everything, this would be just another ordinary day at the Free Store.

CHAPTER 33

BISBEE, ARIZONA
Friday, December 8, 2023

ON FRIDAY MORNING, WHEN JOANNA STAGGERED OUT OF bed and into the bathroom to shower, she'd had less than four hours of sleep. She had lain awake for hours, with her mind running a mile a minute. This was fast turning into the biggest case of her law enforcement career, but how the hell was she going to pull it off? In her years as sheriff, she had never felt the weight of that office as much as she did right now because this case involved so many people and carried so much heartbreak. How was it possible that Stephen Roper had spent decades masquerading as a normal human being while he was actually a murderous monster? And how could she and her department make sure that his reign of terror ended here and now without anyone else being hurt?

By the time she got to the kitchen, Sage and Dennis had already left to catch the school bus.

"I didn't sleep very well last night," she admitted as Butch handed her a cup of coffee.

"Oh really?" he returned. "Just so you know, neither did I. You tossed and turned so much that I was tempted to go sleep on the couch."

"Sorry," she murmured.

"Was it the case?"

Joanna nodded. The evening before and well out of the kids' earshot, Joanna had told Butch everything that was going on, so at least he knew what she was up against.

"One way or another, the whole thing is going to come to a head today," she told him. "Since Stephen Roper is someone who puts zero value on human life, I'm worried someone besides him will end up being hurt."

"You may be worried about everyone else," Butch said. "I'm worried about you."

He offered to cook breakfast for her, but she declined. "I'll stick to coffee and toast," she said. "I'm not sure anything else would stay down."

Finally, as she headed out the door, and just when it seemed things couldn't get any worse, they did. In the garage, the right front tire on her Interceptor was flat as a pancake. Where she had managed to pick up that offending roofing nail was anybody's guess. Naturally, Butch dropped everything and came out to change the tire for her, but by the time she left the house, she should already have been at the office. Then, when she reached the Justice Center, she had to drop the Interceptor off at the motor pool garage to have the flat fixed.

The shortest way to her office from the garage was through the public entrance, one she seldom used. One wall of the lobby was decorated with black-and-white photographs of Cochise County's current and previous sheriffs. With a single exception, the others were male. In their official portraitlike photos, they all wore white Stetsons, and their facial expressions varied from serious to somber. Joanna's photograph, on the other hand, and one her mother had begged her to change, featured a towheaded little girl with her hair in braids. She was wearing a Brownie uniform, beaming a toothless ear-to-ear grin, and dragging a wagon loaded with Girl Scout cookies.

Most of the time when Joanna saw that photo, standing in stark contrast to all the serious ones, she found it amusing. That Friday morning it wasn't funny. *Today that little girl is up against a deadly killer,* Joanna thought to herself. *Having a load of Thin Mints along for the ride isn't going to do a bit of good.*

Entering the building through the public entrance meant Joanna had to pass Kristin's desk to reach her own. As she stepped into that secondary waiting room, Joanna was well aware that she was more than forty minutes late. Kristin had a phone to her ear. When she caught sight of Joanna, she gave her boss a scathing look and held up her hand in a traffic-stop gesture while saying into the phone, "She's here now. If you don't mind holding, Sheriff Brady will be right with you." After pressing the hold button, she slammed the receiver back into its cradle.

"Who is it?" Joanna asked.

Instead of answering, Kristin went on the offensive. "What the hell did you do?" she demanded, holding up a handful of yellow message slips and passing them along to Joanna. "The phone has been ringing off the hook, and nobody's bothering to go through the switchboard. Everyone in the universe seems to have your direct number."

Joanna glanced at the topmost message. That call had come from someone named Ed Cox, in Fulton, Missouri. "Who's this?" Joanna asked.

"Beats me," Kristin replied tartly. "I guess you'll have to call him back to find out."

"And who's on hold?"

"His name is Dan Hogan. I hadn't gotten around to writing down his details when you came in. You'll have to talk to him yourself if you want to find out."

Once seated at her desk, Joanna paused long enough to put her purse in the bottom drawer before picking up the telephone receiver. "Sheriff Joanna Brady here," she said. "To whom am I speaking?"

"Glad to meet you, Sheriff Brady. My name's Daniel Hogan, but most people call me Dan. I'm a retired sheriff from Polk County, Minnesota. I started out there as a deputy, ran the investigations team for a while, and then served three terms as sheriff. Polk County's pretty much off the beaten path. Not many homicides happen here, and the ones that do are usually cut-and-dried and end up being solved in short order. But we've got one unsolved on the books that happened just after I moved to investigations—a little kid named Brian Olson who disappeared from the Polk County Fair on August 19, 1961. His body was found three days later, floating in Arthur Lake. He'd been strangled."

Joanna was taken aback to realize that the detective assigned to the case remembered the exact date of the crime more than sixty years later. And hearing him mention the commonalities with the cases Joanna already knew about was enough to take her breath away. A moment passed before she could respond. "Was he fully clothed?" she asked.

"Yes, he was still dressed in his Cub Scout uniform. Paulette Hansen, his den mother, had taken her troop of boys to the fair. Somehow Brian got separated from the group and simply vanished. Poor Paulette never got over it. She blamed herself for his death. When she committed suicide a number of years later, she left a note that was primarily a letter of apology to Brian's folks.

"The thing is, as lead detective on that case, I never got over it, either. Even now that I'm retired, I make it a point to drop by the department each year on the first day of the fair to take a look at the file, although my eyes are getting so bad I don't know how much longer I'll be able to keep that up. Anyway, I'm enough of a pest about it that, as soon as your BOLO came in last night, Elmer Pollock, the current sheriff, gave me a call. He also gave me your phone number."

"Was anything missing from the body?" Joanna asked.

"Yes," Hogan replied without hesitation. "As a matter of fact, his Wolf pin. It was brand-new. His den leader, Mrs. Hansen, had just awarded it to him a week or so before he disappeared. It was one of those little clasp things that you have to squeeze like hell to get it on or off. So who's your guy, Sheriff Brady, and to your knowledge has he ever been anywhere near Fertile, Minnesota?"

"His name is Stephen Roper," Joanna answered quietly. "I believe he was born in Fertile."

There was a sharp intake of breath on the other end of the line, followed by a fit of coughing, as though someone had swallowed wrong. "Not him," Dan Hogan croaked at last, once he could speak again. "Are you frigging kidding me?"

"Wait," Joanna said. "You actually knew him?"

"Hell yes, I knew him," Dan replied. "I knew the moment I laid eyes on that kid that there was something wrong with him. I tried to tell the detectives on the case that I thought he had something to do with it, but I was a newbie deputy at the time, and no one gave my opinion the time of day."

Joanna was confused. "What case?" she asked. "I thought you just told me you were the lead detective."

"Not Brian Olson's death, Stephen Roper's grandmother's—his step-grandmother, actually. Lucille Johansen Hawkins was Orson Hawkins's second wife. Fell down the front steps of her house and busted open her head on a concrete walkway. Steve, that's what we all called him back then, was the one who called it in, and I was the first officer to arrive on the scene. There was just something off about him. When he ran into the house to call for help, he splashed right through her blood and left a trail of bloody footprints from the front door to the wall phone in the kitchen. Most kids wouldn't have stepped in a pool of blood like that for all the tea in China."

"So his grandmother was murdered?" Joanna asked.

"I thought so, but Henry Fransen, the detective on the case, along with a lot of other people thought Orson Hawkins, Lucille's husband and Steve's grandfather, had knocked her off in order to lay hands on her life insurance. Lucille's daddy, Mitch Johansen, was the insurance agent here in town. When his three daughters were born he bought a $100,000 twenty-pay life policy on each of them. Two of the daughters took off for parts unknown as soon as they turned eighteen. Lucille hung around.

"She was an odd duck. All she wanted to be was a farmer. She wore work boots and overalls when most of the other women in town wouldn't have set foot out of the house in a pair of pants. When she and Orson got hitched, a few rumors flew here and there that he had married her for her money, and once she was dead, that sprinkle of rumors turned into a downpour. After all, back then, $100,000 wasn't something to sneeze at. But Orson had an airtight alibi for the whole day she died. Eventually the coroner ruled her death as accidental, and that was it."

Joanna was listening, but she was also thinking of her list of possible similarities. "Was anything missing from Lucille's body?" she asked when Dan Hogan paused to take a breath.

"You damned well better bet there was," he replied heatedly. "Her gold band wedding ring. When Orson Hawkins found out it was missing, he came down to the sheriff's office and raised all kinds of hell. Came right out and accused me of taking it off her finger before the ambulance ever got there, but I didn't, I swear. I never even saw the damned thing."

Joanna took a breath as well. "I believe, Mr. Hogan," she said at last, "after all these years it may be time to change Lucille's manner of death from accidental to homicide. You've just described Stephen Roper's signature. He kills his victims and then takes something from them. He stole Lucille's wedding ring the same way he took Brian Olson's Wolf pin."

"Really?" Dan asked, as though he still couldn't quite believe what he was hearing.

"Really."

"But he couldn't have been more than ten or eleven at the time. That's why Detective Fransen laughed at me when I suggested Steve might have had something to do it. 'Impossible,' he told me. 'Why, Steve's nothing but a snot-nosed kid.'"

"He may well have been a snot-nosed kid," Joanna agreed, "but I'm willing to bet he was also a snot-nosed killer."

"But how did he do it?"

"Who knows," Joanna replied. "The only way we'll ever find out for sure is if he gives us a full confession, and I'm not counting on that. In the meantime, if you could get back in touch with your current sheriff . . ." She paused, embarrassed that the name had fallen out of her head.

"Sheriff Pollock," Dan Hogan supplied. "Claude Pollock."

"Thank you. If you'd get back to Sheriff Pollock and ask him to send me whatever he can copy from those two files, I'll be incredibly grateful. I'm pretty sure our email and/or fax information is on the BOLO."

"Ya, sure, you betcha," Dan Hogan said. "I'll be on it like flies on crap the minute we're off the phone."

When the call ended, Joanna retrieved her purse, grabbed up the fistful of missed call messages, and headed for Kristin's desk. The secretary tried to add three more messages to Joanna's mix on her way past, but Joanna shook her head.

"Take all these straight to the bullpen," Joanna told her, handing over the others. "Every one of them needs to be returned ASAP. They're about cases that may or may not be related to Xavier Delgado's homicide. I want the investigations team returning those calls, but I'm also going to need boots on the ground—lots of them. Call in all the deputies. If they're off duty or if it's somebody's day off? Too bad. Call them in anyway. Tell them to drop what they're doing and get their butts to Bisbee."

"Where are you going?" Kristin asked.

"To have a chat with the county attorney."

"When will you be back?"

"No idea."

Joanna left the building the same way she'd entered, only this time she didn't give the little girl with her wagonload of Girl Scout Cookies a second glance, because the older version of that little girl was on a mission now, and Stephen Roper was about to go down.

CHAPTER 34

BISBEE, ARIZONA
Friday, December 8, 2023

BEING SHERIFF DID HAVE ITS PERKS. EVEN THOUGH JO-anna had dropped off her Interceptor less than half an hour earlier, the spare tire had been replaced with a new one while the old one was being repaired.

Once in the car, and just to be sure she wasn't going on a fool's errand, Joanna called the county attorney's office to be sure Craig Witherspoon was actually in his office that morning. "Please tell him Sheriff Brady is on her way to see him on an urgent matter." Once that call was finished, she dialed Anna Rae Green.

"Did it work?" Anna Rae asked once she realized who was on the phone.

"Are you kidding?" Joanna said. "Our phones are ringing like crazy. I just talked with a former sheriff from Polk County, Minnesota. After speaking to him, I'm pretty sure Roper was responsible for the death of a little kid who disappeared from the Polk County Fair in Fertile, Minnesota, on August 19, 1961."

"Wait," Anna Rae said. "Isn't Fertile Stephen Roper's hometown?"

"Yes, it is."

"And how old was he?"

"He would have been sixteen," Joanna answered, "but here's the kicker. The guy I spoke to, Dan Hogan, was also the first officer to arrive on the scene years earlier when Stephen called for help after his grandmother, Lucille Hawkins, fell off the front steps of her home, cracked her head open, and died on the spot. Her death was ruled to be accidental, but Hogan always suspected Stephen of having had something to do with it. I happen to agree with that assessment, by the way."

"How come?" Anna Rae asked.

"When Orson Hawkins went to collect his wife's personal effects, her wedding ring was missing."

"So there's a good chance Roper started down this road when he was what?"

"Eleven years old," Joanna answered.

"Geez!" Anna Rae muttered. "How can I help?"

"I'm on my way to the county attorney's office right now to see if he thinks we have enough probable cause to go for a search warrant," Joanna told her. "I'm not holding my breath on that score, so I'm wondering if you can get one issued for Amanda Hudson's murder in North Dakota. We know Roper keeps trophies, and they're bound to be somewhere inside his residence, but we've got to gain access to his place and find them before he gets wind that we're onto him and destroys them."

"I'll get in touch with Philip right away and see what he can do," Anna Rae promised. "Good luck with your prosecutor."

"Thanks," Joanna said. "I'll need it."

Once again it took several minutes to drive to the county attorney's office, and again Craig Witherspoon greeted Joanna with a smile. "Back so soon?" he asked. "What happened with your trash DNA?" he asked.

"Nothing yet," Joanna replied. "As far as I know they've yet to develop a DNA profile, but we got a hit off AFIS."

"AFIS?" Witherspoon repeated in disbelief. "You actually found a fingerprint in the Delgado case?"

"Not a fingerprint, a palm print," Joanna answered. "And it's not from our case, either. It's from somebody else's."

Fortunately, along the way, she'd been making iPad notes of names, dates, and places. After consulting them for a moment, she continued. "The palm print was found at the crime scene in the murder of one Amanda Marie Hudson somewhere near the Turtle River in North Dakota on May 26, 1962."

"Are you serious?" Craig asked. "You've got a crime scene palm print from a case that's more than sixty years old?"

Joanna nodded and then quickly filled him in on the background.

During the telling, Craig's fingers were steepled again. That meant he was thinking, so Joanna continued. "I've also just gotten off the phone with a guy named Dan Hogan, the former sheriff of Polk County in Minnesota. He was the lead investigator in the 1961 homicide death of a boy named Brian Olson. At age eight, he disappeared from the Polk County Fair in Fertile, Minnesota, which happens to be Stephen Roper's hometown. Stephen would have been sixteen at the time and still living at home. In addition . . ."

"Stop, stop, stop," Craig said. "You've convinced me. Do you have evidence of the AFIS match to the North Dakota case?"

"Yes, the official match came in from the DPS crime lab in Tucson yesterday morning. Since Amanda Hudson was half Lakota, Anna Rae Green of the federal Missing and Murdered Indigenous Victims Task Force was able to get the FBI to send out a BOLO for unsolved homicides with striking similarities to ours. That's how the call from Dan Hogan came in to me."

"Well," Craig said, "whoever came up with that BOLO idea is pretty damned smart."

Joanna could have taken full credit, but she didn't. She was more interested in getting the job done than she was in accumulating bragging rights.

"If there's an arrest warrant, the authorities in North Dakota will need to come up with that," Craig Witherspoon continued, "but I believe you have enough probable cause to justify a search warrant here. Once your people get it written up, have them take it to Judge Askins. I'll call and give him a heads-up that the request is coming his way. Let's get this bastard off the streets before he has a chance to hurt anyone else."

CHAPTER 35

BISBEE, ARIZONA
Friday, December 8, 2023

AS JOANNA HURRIED BACK TO HER CAR, SHE PLANNED TO call into the office and get that warrant in progress, but her cell phone rang before she had a chance. With a Rapid City, South Dakota, number showing in caller ID, Joanna figured it had to be one of two people—Nadia Grayson, MMIV's field agent for South Dakota, or Luke Running Deer, Amanda Hudson's brother. It turned out to be the latter.

"You don't know me," he began once she answered, "but Anna Rae Green gave me your number."

Joanna already understood that no matter how long ago a loved one might have died from homicidal violence, the pain of that loss never goes away. The fact that Luke Running Deer had called Joanna within minutes of hearing from Anna Rae only served to underscore that belief.

"I know who you are, Mr. Running Deer," Joanna interrupted before he could complete his self-introduction. "You're Amanda Hudson's younger brother."

"Yes," he said quietly. "Yes, I am."

Not was, Joanna thought. *Still am.*

"Anna Rae asked if there was anything missing from Amanda's personal effects when they were returned to us," Luke continued.

"The thing is, I wasn't on the best of terms with my parents when all this happened. Neither was Amanda, for that matter, so I didn't even know which of Mandy's personal effects came back until years later when I cleaned out my grandmother's house. That's when I realized the knife was missing, but by then so much time had passed and nothing seemed to be happening in her case. I tried mentioning it to someone at the Highway Patrol, but he wasn't particularly interested."

As soon as she heard about a missing knife, Joanna instantly recalled Anna Rae saying that a whetstone had been found among Amanda's possessions. She'd also said something about Amanda being estranged from her parents at the time of her death.

"There were issues between you two kids and your folks?" she asked.

Luke sighed. "As a young woman, our mother, Bonnie Running Deer, was drop-dead gorgeous. On the other hand, our father, Elmer Hudson, wasn't anything to write home about. He was also a jerk and a bigot. Grandma Running Deer called him *wasicu*."

"A what?" Joanna asked.

Luke chuckled. "That's a derogatory Lakota term for Caucasians—on a par with calling Hispanics wetbacks, only worse. Somehow, when Elmer married our mother, it never occurred to him that their kids would end up looking like Indians instead of looking like him. There was still a lot of anti–Native American prejudice back in those days, so when our father filled in the information on our birth certificates, he failed to mention Amanda and I were half Lakota. He checked the Caucasian box and that was it. As an adult, I had to jump through all kinds of hoops to regain my tribal identity."

"That goes a long way in explaining why, when MMIV was asking for unsolved murders involving Indigenous people, your sister's case was missed."

"That's what Nadia Grayson told me, too."

"Was your father abusive?"

"Of course he was," Luke responded. "To Amanda and me and to our mother too. Amanda left home a week after she graduated from high school. She went to Grand Forks, got a job as a nurse's aide in the hospital, and started taking night courses so she could become an RN. I left home about the same time she did, but since I was two years younger, I only got as far as Grandma Running Deer's house. I lived with her until I graduated from high school. After that, I joined the army. I was through basic training and stationed at Fort Ord in California when Amanda was murdered. I came home on leave for her funeral.

"After that, things went downhill for my mother real fast. She'd always been a drinker, but it got a lot worse. Once Mom was diagnosed with cirrhosis, my father packed up her and all her stuff and dumped her off at Grandma's house, which is where I finally found the unopened envelope from the coroner's office after both my mother and grandmother passed away."

While listening to this long family saga, Joanna had been dying to ask about the knife. Realizing this was a story Luke had needed to tell for a very long time, she managed to keep her mouth shut, but when he finally paused for a breath, she had her opening.

"You mentioned a knife?" Joanna prodded.

"Oh, yes, the knife," Luke said. "I was sixteen when Amanda left home to go live in Grand Forks. For someone living in Devil's Lake, Grand Forks was the big city, and I worried about her. She didn't have a car—couldn't afford one. I was afraid someone might come after her when she was walking home from work or school, and I just happened to have a switchblade. I wasn't supposed to have one, but I did, so I gave it to her for protection.

"Amanda wasn't the kind of girl who carried a purse, but she always wore boots, so I gave her the knife, along with a little deerskin holster so she could slip the knife inside one of her boots and carry it there."

"As a concealed weapon?" Joanna asked.

"Yes," Luke allowed. "I suppose it was."

"Was the holster included in Amanda's personal effects?"

"No," Luke said. "Only the glasses, the bracelet, and the whetstone."

"What about her clothing or her boots?"

"As far as I know, none of those were returned."

"Tell me about the knife."

"It had an ivory handle and a four-and-a-half-inch blade," Luke replied. "I also gave her the whetstone so she could keep the knife sharp. As soon as I saw the whetstone in the envelope, I realized the knife was missing. I tried contacting the North Dakota Highway Patrol to tell them about it, but, as I said, Amanda's death was a cold case, and no one gave a damn."

"Maybe they didn't, but I do," Joanna declared. "We're reasonably sure our killer takes trophies. If we can find him, your description of that knife may be a key piece of physical evidence linking him to your sister's murder."

"Do you think you'll be able to nail him for it, even after all this time?" Luke asked.

"I hope so," Joanna said. "I'm working on it, and so are lots of other people."

"And you'll let me know what happens?"

"Absolutely," Joanna replied. "I promise."

CHAPTER 36

BISBEE, ARIZONA
Friday, December 8, 2023

BY THE TIME THE CONVERSATION WITH LUKE RUNNING Deer ended, Joanna was pulling into her parking place at the Justice Center. She was glad she'd heard the man out. For decades he'd needed to tell his story to someone who was actually listening, but now Joanna's head was on fire with everything that had to be done.

As soon as the outside door to her office closed behind her, Kristin showed up. "Everyone's in the conference room."

"Good," she said. "Tell them I'm coming, but first I need to make a call." *To say nothing of gather my thoughts*, she told herself as she dialed Anna Rae's number.

Once the call was answered, Joanna quickly recounted both her meeting with Craig Witherspoon as well as her long conversation with Luke in which he'd told her about the missing knife, ending by saying, "We'll handle the search warrant on this end if you can come up with an arrest warrant."

"Will do," Anna Rae said. "I'll get Philip Dark Moon on this right away. Assuming he's able to get one, I'll have it sent to your department so you can take Roper into custody."

"Good deal," Joanna said.

The call ended then, but for a minute or so after she was off the phone, Joanna remained seated at her desk, giving herself time to do some strategic thinking. Having warrants in hand would be great, but her main concern was Stephen Roper. Not only did she need to figure out how to keep track of his whereabouts until those warrants could be issued, but also how to handle him once he realized law enforcement was closing in. Would he come quietly, make a run for it, or put up a fight? Knowing she had to be prepared for all contingencies, Joanna squared her shoulders and headed for the conference room where she found the place already jammed. The previous conference room meeting had been limited to her top officers and the investigation team. This one included everyone. Her deputies had shown up without any idea as to why they were being summoned, and now they needed an explanation. Looking around the room, however, Joanna couldn't help but wonder if Marliss Shackleford's source was sitting there along with the rest of her team.

Before speaking to everyone else, Joanna addressed her chief CSI. "Casey, do you happen to have your iPad with you?"

The question was strictly rhetorical since Casey was never without her tablet, but she obligingly held it in the air.

"In a few minutes, I'm going to need a Google map of Bisbee and its surroundings up on this screen," Joanna said, pulling it down. "Can you do that?"

"Yes, ma'am," Casey said.

"All right then," Joanna said, turning back to the others. "First off, thank you for showing up even though you were given no specific reason for doing so. Here's the deal. I'm sure you're all aware that we've been investigating the death of a child, Xavier Delgado, of Naco, Sonora, whose body, stuffed in a duffel bag, was found in flood debris in the San Pedro last Saturday. We've since learned that Xavier is most likely the latest victim of a serial killer who has been living and working in Bisbee for decades."

"Did she just say serial killer?" The question came from someone in the far corner of the room who turned out to be Deputy Sunny Sloan.

Sunny's husband, Dan, was the only one of Joanna's officers ever to die in the line of duty. At the time of his death, Sunny had been pregnant with their only child. Knowing all too well what it was like to be a widowed single mother, Joanna had eventually offered Sunny a job working as a civilian clerk in the department's public office. She had done that for a number of years before becoming a deputy. For the past several, she'd served as a sworn officer.

"Yes, Sunny," Joanna replied. "I said serial killer. I've just come from a meeting with the county attorney. With his blessing, as soon as Deb Howell can prepare the documents, she'll be going to Judge Norman Askins requesting a search warrant on the home of our suspect, a Mr. Stephen Roper."

That news was met with gasps of shocked surprise. "The guy who used to teach chemistry at Bisbee High?" someone asked.

"The very one," Joanna answered. "The same one who, since his retirement, has built a good-guy reputation around here by playing Señor Santa Claus for a charity called Hands Across the Border while delivering food and other necessities to impoverished migrants stuck in Naco, Sonora. Two weeks ago today, on the day Xavier disappeared, we have eyewitnesses who place the boy inside Mr. Roper's refurbished food truck eyeing a pair of high-topped sneakers in the hours before he disappeared.

"During the course of the autopsy, Dr. Baldwin discovered details that made her suspect the killer might be a repeat offender. That suggested the possibility that an unidentified DNA profile from a previously unsolved crime might have been uploaded to CODIS. Without enough probable cause to initiate a search warrant requiring his DNA, on Tuesday Detective Raymond staged a middle-of-the night trash raid at Mr. Roper's residence, the contents of which he delivered to the DPS crime lab in Tucson. As far as I know, they have not yet developed a DNA profile, but using AFIS, they found a match to an unsolved homicide that occurred in North Dakota in 1962.

"The victim in that case, Amanda Hudson, was Lakota. As a result, her case falls under the purview of MMIV—the Missing and Murdered Indigenous Victims Task Force, a federal agency operating all over the country. I believe that MMIV's field officer for North Dakota, Philip Dark Moon, is currently seeking an arrest warrant on Stephen Roper, which, once forwarded to us, we should be able to execute.

"At this time, we also believe that not only is Mr. Roper a suspect in both the Delgado case as well as in Ms. Hudson's, but that he may be connected to several more as well. That's why we've kept our investigation so close to the vest. We didn't want him to have any idea that we had him in our sights until we had enough probable cause to search his residence if not actually arrest him.

"My hope is that he can be taken into custody without incident. But as my dad used to say, 'Hope for the best, but plan for the worst.' That's why you're all here. On the off chance that Mr. Roper decides to either resist or make a run for it, you're here to stop him.

"Casey, could we have that map now please. First let's focus in on the area just north of the golf course in Naco."

While Casey brought up the map, Joanna located a pointer. "Okay," she said, pointing, "this dirt road leading off to the right from Naco Highway is Country Club Drive. There are five or six residences on the street. Mr. Roper's is the last one on the right. At the moment he's most likely still in Naco, Sonora, operating what's called the Free Store, which he does every other Friday. He usually crosses back into Arizona between two thirty and three. With any kind of luck he'll do the same thing today and simply go back home. Before he arrives, I want to have surveillance set up on Country Club Drive so we'll know if he takes off again.

"As I said, he's currently in Naco, Sonora. While there, Captain Arturo Peña of the local Federales contingent assures me that he has officers keeping an eye on him. In the event that he decides to head south and tries to flee into the interior of Mexico, the Mexican authorities will intercept him.

"My guess, though, is that if he's going to make a run for it, he'll do so on this side of the border. From his residence, there are essentially four ways for him to get out of Dodge—westbound on Highway 92 toward Sierra Vista, westbound on Highway 80 toward Tombstone, eastbound on Highway 80 toward Douglas, or eastbound on Border Road toward Paul's Spur and eventually to eastbound Highway 80. I want units with stop sticks located at strategic points on all those routes.

"Sunny, you're to handle Border Road. Just beyond the overpass in Bisbee Junction, there's a cattle guard followed immediately by a sharp left turn. If you set up there, just beyond the cattle guard, he won't be able to see you until he comes over the overpass and is right on top of you."

Sunny nodded. "Will do," she said.

"Deputy Creighton?"

Bill Creighton raised his hand. "Where do you want me?"

"You'll be stationed just inside the entrance to the Justice Center to stop him if he heads east on Highway 80. And Terry?"

The jail commander had responded to Joanna's summons along with everyone else, and he quickly raised his hand.

"If and when we know Roper's on the move," Joanna continued, "I want you and Mojo to leave the jail for just long enough to provide backup for Deputy Creighton."

"No problem," Terry Gregovich said. "Will do."

"Deputy Frosco?"

Deputy Richard Frosco was a Bisbee native but a relative newcomer to Joanna's department.

"Yes, ma'am," he said.

"I want you set up on Highway 80 north of the tunnel at the intersection of Highway 80 and Old Divide Road."

"Got it," he said.

"Deputy Nuñez," she said turning to Manuel Nuñez.

"Yes, ma'am."

"I want you to set up on the far side of Willson Road on Highway 92. That's the only backdoor route out of Naco that intersects with 92."

"Okay," he said.

"All of you stay tuned to your radios, but remember there's to be no mention of Roper's name over the airways. He's only 'our subject.' People listen in on scanners, and I don't want him alerted to what's going on. If and when he leaves his residence, as soon as we determine what vehicle he's in and which route he's taking, we'll let you know. If he isn't coming your way, pack up, leave your assigned post, and head for wherever he's going. All of you go on ahead now. I want you in position and set up ASAP."

Hoping one of the departing deputies wasn't her leaker, Joanna waited until they were gone before turning to Detective Carbajal. "From the moment Roper crosses the border, I want him under surveillance. Jaime, you know the Naco area better than anyone else here. That's your part of this operation. If he leaves Naco and goes to his residence, let us know. If he heads somewhere else, let us know that, too. As soon as Garth and Deb have the search warrant in hand, they'll be situated somewhere on Country Club Drive, but I want you parked along the Naco Highway. That way, if and when Roper leaves his residence, you'll be able to tell us which way he's going."

"Got it," Jaime replied. "Want me to go now?"

Joanna nodded. "Yes, please," she said, "on the off chance Roper decides to leave Naco, Sonora, earlier than usual."

Once Jaime did so, Joanna turned back to the people still in the room. "Garth and Deb, you're with me back in the bullpen. We need to discuss the contents of that search warrant. As for the rest of you? I want you to hang out here until something happens. You'll be on standby until we know where you're needed, either to assist with executing the search warrant or, if we end up with an arrest warrant, in handling the takedown, whichever comes first. Who does what will depend on the situation on the ground. I want all of you here ready to gear up and deploy at a moment's notice. Is everybody clear on that?"

She waited for answering nods. "Okay," she said. "Thank you. Let's get this guy, but be safe."

With that she headed for the bullpen with Garth and Deb on her heels. Deb sat down in front of her computer, opened it to a standard Search Warrant form, and began filling in the details.

"What are we asking for?" she wanted to know.

"The usual," Joanna said. "We want to search his electronics, his residence, any out buildings, and any and all vehicles. In addition, we're specifically looking for a shoelace with traces of bleach on it, an ivory-handled switchblade knife, a gold wedding band, and a Cub Scout Wolf pin."

"Whose knife and whose ring?" Deb asked with a frown.

"The switchblade belonged to Amanda Hudson. It was missing when the Grand Forks Coroner's Office returned her personal effects to the family."

"And the wedding ring?"

"That belonged to a woman named Lucille Hawkins, Stephen Roper's step-grandmother who died after a fall at her home in 1956 when Stephen was eleven. He was the one who called it in. The deputy who responded to the scene always thought Stephen had something to do with it, but her death was ruled to be accidental."

"Her wedding ring went missing from the crime scene?" Deb asked.

"It certainly did," Joanna replied, "and guess who was accused of stealing it?"

"The deputy?" Garth asked.

Joanna nodded. "And you'd better believe he's still pissed about that."

Minutes later, Garth and Deb took the warrant in search of Judge Askins, leaving Joanna alone in the bullpen. She stood there for a moment thinking about what to do next, but there wasn't really a choice. She had a new fistful of missed phone calls to return, and it was time she got started.

CHAPTER 37

BISBEE, ARIZONA
Friday, December 8, 2023

BACK IN HER OFFICE, HOWEVER, BEFORE RETURNING ANY of those missed calls, Joanna picked up her phone and dialed Alvin Bernard, Bisbee's longtime chief of police.

"Hey, Joanna," he said cordially once he answered. "How are things going?"

"A little complicated at the moment," she told him. "That's why I'm calling. Do you happen to know a guy named Stephen Roper?"

"Sure," he answered. "Señor Santa Claus from Hands Across the Border. He's spoken to our Rotary Club a couple of times. How come? Has something bad happened to him?"

"No," Joanna replied. "Something bad has happened to several other people, and we believe Stephen Roper may be the one responsible."

There was a short pause. "What do you mean?" Alvin asked finally.

"You know about Xavier Delgado, right?"

"Sure," Alvin replied. "The dead kid found in the San Pedro a week or so ago. What about him?"

"I hate to burst your bubble, Alvin, but Stephen Roper is our prime suspect in that case. As of this morning, we also have physical evidence linking him to a homicide that occurred in North Dakota, in 1962."

"You've got to be kidding," Alvin said. "He seems like such a nice guy."

"Appearances can be deceiving," Joanna replied. "I believe your Mr. Nice Guy is actually a serial killer, a wolf in sheep's clothing, and we're hoping to take him into custody later this afternoon. That's why I'm calling—we may need your help."

Chief Bernard took a moment to gather himself. "Okay," he said finally. "What can we do?"

"First off," Joanna said, "don't reveal the suspect's name to anyone. Refer to him as our subject. So far we don't believe he knows that he's under suspicion, and we want to keep it that way."

"Not to worry," Alvin said. "My lips are sealed, so what's the deal?"

Over the next several minutes, she brought him into the picture on everything that had transpired, including the precautions she'd taken to prevent Roper's escape should he attempt to flee.

"Two of his four possible escape routes bring him right through the City of Bisbee," Alvin observed when she finished.

"Not just through Bisbee," she said. "One way or another, he's going to have to go around the Traffic Circle. My first choice is to take him into custody at his home on Country Club Drive north of Naco. But if he takes off and comes your way, the Traffic Circle might be a good place to make the arrest. That would be a far less dangerous place to take him into custody than in some populated business or residential area, but we'll need to block all the entrances and exits."

"What about Lowell School?" Alvin asked. "That's directly across the drainage ditch from the Traffic Circle."

Joanna was well aware of the location of Lowell School. That's where Dennis was attending sixth grade. As for the drainage ditch in question? It often carried the mineral rich runoff from Lavender Pit just north of Lowell to the mile-long tailings dump that ran alongside Highway 80 on the far side of the Traffic Circle.

Joanna glanced at her watch. The morning had vanished. It was already closing in on noon.

"I suggest you call the superintendent of schools and advise him that Lowell needs an immediate early dismissal today due to expected police activity. Let him know that, if he delays, he might end up having to put the school on lockdown, and that would be a whole lot worse. If you give him a choice, he'll most likely go for an early dismissal. That'll cause less backlash than a lockdown."

"Okay," Alvin said. "You're right. Bob Dobbs is bound to opt for an early dismissal, but how soon it can happen will depend on how soon the buses can get there. For argument's sake, if Roper . . ." He paused momentarily before continuing, "If the subject ends up coming our way, how much notice will we have?"

"He lives on Country Club Drive, just north of the golf course in Naco," Joanna answered. "If he leaves there heading northbound, there's a fifty/fifty chance that he'll be coming your way. At that point you'll maybe have six or seven minutes of warning."

"If he's coming by way of Highway 92, he'll have no way of knowing the circle is blocked off until he's almost inside it," Alvin replied. "The fire department is right next door. I'll talk to the chief and see how fast he can deploy fire trucks to function as temporary roadblocks."

"By the way, make sure you keep every bit of this off the air. As I said, there are people in town who are listening in on everything we say on police scanners."

"People?" Alvin asked. "Or one person in particular whose initials happen to be MS."

"Exactly," Joanna said. "And thank you, Alvin. I really appreciate the help."

Once that call ended, next up was one to Butch. "FYI," she said. "There's a good chance that Lowell school will have an early dismissal today due to possible police activity."

"Which you're not going to discuss in any detail."

"No, I'm not," Joanna said.

"But you're going to take him into custody?"

"I sure as hell hope so."

"Good luck then," he said, "and be safe."

"Thank you," she said. "I will."

Then taking the first missed call message off the top of the stack, she picked it up and dialed a number in what the message said was Fulton, Missouri.

"Sheriff Ed Cox," a deep male voice answered.

"And this is Sheriff Joanna Brady from Cochise County, Arizona."

"Ah, yes," he said. "The BOLO. I talked to someone about that earlier, Deborah something."

"Yes," Joanna said. "That would be Detective Howell. We've been really busy around here today, so she didn't have a chance to tell me what the two of you discussed. I hope you don't mind going over it again."

"Callaway County's a pretty peaceable kind of place," Sheriff Cox allowed. "Not many murders happen around here, and Lucianne Highsmith's from 1977 is our only unsolved. I wasn't even born yet, but here are the high points. Lucianne went missing while riding her bike from her folks' place to a friend's farm a couple miles up the road. When she didn't turn up at the friend's place or return home, her mother reported her missing. The sheriff's department initiated a ground search. Both her body and the bike were found four days later in a nearby reservoir a few miles away from where she would have been riding. The details match up with your BOLO—manual strangulation, disposal in a body of water, and something missing."

"What was missing?"

"When they retrieved the body, she was wearing only one shoe. The sheriff sent in a dive crew, they found both her bike and the missing shoe. The shoelace was MIA."

"A shoelace," Joanna uttered aloud.

"Does that mean something to you?" Sheriff Cox asked.

"I'm afraid it does," Joanna replied. Then she spent the next ten minutes giving Sheriff Cox the details of their current investigations—both Xavier Delgado's and Amanda Hudson's.

"Whoa there, Nelly," Cox responded. "You're saying you've got a current serial killer who's been active since the seventies?"

"Since the fifties, actually," Joanna said. "But tell me about Lucianne's relatives. Are any of them still around?"

"Her folks both passed years ago. I believe she has a sister, somewhere. I've been trying to locate her ever since your detective called. So far no luck, but we'll keep after it."

"Please let me know if you find her," Joanna said.

"Yes, ma'am," Sheriff Cox said. "Sure will."

Call waiting buzzed just then. Excusing herself from Sheriff Cox, the new caller turned out to be Chief Bernard. "You called it," he said. "Early dismissal it is. The buses will be there by 1:30."

"That's good news," Joanna said.

"And Chief Flowers says that as long as there aren't any fires, he can have six trucks in position within five minutes of being notified. They'll block the four entrances and exits to Highway 80, and the ones to Bisbee Road. Once Roper enters the Traffic Circle, my units will close ranks behind him. That should leave the bastard literally running in circles."

"Let's hope," Joanna said.

"Whenever you know he's on the move, I'll be responsible for bringing in the fire department," Chief Bernard added.

"Good to know," Joanna said. "Appreciate it."

She glanced at her watch. The time was 12:45. It would be another forty-five minutes before the school buses would show up for early dismissal—the longest forty-five minutes of her life.

CHAPTER 38

NACO, SONORA
Friday, December 8, 2023

IT WAS A TOUGH DAY AT THE FREE STORE. STEPHEN HAD been unduly nervous that morning as he approached the border crossing, but the guards on both sides waved him through the same way they usually did, with no indication that anything was amiss, and nothing seemed out of the ordinary during the course of the day. Even though he'd been exceptionally busy, he'd still tried to pay attention to what was going on outside. A new contingent of migrants had arrived overnight, and they needed everything. By one in the afternoon, not only were all the sack lunches gone, the shelves were virtually bare. With nothing more to distribute, at 1:15, he closed up shop and headed home.

He crossed the border without incident, but when he drove up to the house a few minutes later, a vehicle he didn't recognize, and not a cop car, either, was parked in his driveway in the very spot where he needed to park the truck. Alarmed and irritated by having an unexpected visitor, he stopped on the shoulder and got out, determined to send the interloper packing. As he exited his vehicle, however, so did the female driver of what he could now see was a beat-up RAV4. At first he thought the woman was a total stranger, but as he got closer he recognized her, mostly because of her smile.

He had seen Marliss Shackleford's smiling headshot every time he logged on to her website.

"Mr. Roper?" she said, holding out her hand. "My name is Marliss Shackleford. I hope you don't mind my dropping in unannounced like this, but I was wondering if I could speak to you for a few minutes."

Stephen was stunned and terrified, too. What the hell was she doing here? Hoping to mask his inner turmoil, he stifled the urge to order her off his property.

"Sure," he said as cordially as he could manage, "but do you mind pulling your car out of the driveway? That's where I park my truck."

"Of course," she agreed. "No problem."

While she moved the RAV4 back out to the street, Stephen parked the truck in its accustomed spot. Then, standing on the front porch, he struck what he hoped was a casual pose while he waited for her to finish.

"I was hoping you'd be home about now, and I trust you don't mind my waiting around," Marliss said as she came back up the driveway.

"Not at all," he replied. "By the way, I read your stuff. You do a good job of keeping up with the local scene."

Her face brightened. "Really? Thanks for saying that. I'm always happy to meet one of my followers."

"What's on your mind?" Stephen asked.

"I'm doing a piece on the Xavier Delgado case, and I understand you were one of the last people to see him alive. I was wondering if I could talk to you about that?"

The very last thing Stephen Roper needed right then was to have his name splashed all over Marliss's website in connection to Xavier Delgado. This was a catastrophe, but he needed some time to figure out how to deal with it. To that end, when he responded, he forced his face to remain noncommittal.

"Of course," he said, hoping he sounded unconcerned. "That whole thing is a nightmare. I don't mind speaking to you about it, but here's the thing, and please don't think me rude, but I'm a man of a certain age. I've just done a four-hour shift at my Free Store down in Naco, Sonora, so before we sit down to talk, I'll have to excuse myself to use the facilities."

Stephen Roper wasn't someone who entertained often. The furnishings in his home were still the same ones he had purchased all those years earlier when he'd first come to town. They'd been fine back then, but he was sure that, through Marliss Shackleford's eyes, they looked threadbare and old-fashioned.

Ushering her inside, his mind was racing. From following Marliss's posts, he suspected she had anonymous sources inside various law enforcement agencies in the area. If she was here asking questions, someone had put him on her radar. That meant he was most likely on somebody else's radar, too. So what the hell was he going to do about her?

Unsurprisingly, at that point the voices chimed in. "Get rid of her. Get rid of her." That made sense, but before doing so, he needed to know more about what she knew.

Once Marliss took a seat, Stephen headed for the bathroom, all right, but not to relieve himself. Shoving aside the bath mat that covered the trapdoor in the floor, he climbed down into the crawl space far enough to open the safe and retrieve the items he kept there, starting with his precious cigar box. If things got ugly, he might very well need a weapon, so he opened the lid, removed his one-bullet derringer, and shoved that into his pocket. He also picked up a few just-in-case zip ties and pocketed them, too. Then he emptied out the safe.

Years earlier, on the outside chance that this day might come, Stephen had contacted a bank in the Cayman Islands and created an account he'd be able to access should he ever need to. He'd also set aside a large amount of cash that would make it possible for him to disappear. With the money and the cigar box stowed in one of the lunch lady's spare grocery bags, he climbed back out of the crawl space, closed the trapdoor, and replaced the bath mat. Next he flushed the toilet and ran water in the sink long enough to wash his hands.

He returned to the living room by way of the kitchen where he left the loaded grocery bag on the kitchen counter. Then, back in the living room he settled on the sofa, facing his guest who sat with a computer open on her lap and her fingers resting on the keyboard.

"Okay," Stephen said. "What do you want to know?"

"Has anyone from the sheriff's department spoken to you about the case?"

"Not yet," he answered. "I haven't heard a word from them."

As soon as he said that, he realized what a blunder he'd made. He'd taken the fact that he hadn't been interviewed as a sign that he wasn't under suspicion when, in fact, the exact opposite was probably true. He and the migrant kids had been among the last people to see Xavier alive, so by all rights they should all have been questioned and so should he. Had investigators spoken to the kids? Stephen had no way of knowing, and neither did the voices in his head who were continuing to shout their alarm.

"But you did see him that day," Marliss insisted.

"Of course I did," Stephen answered, trying to listen to her over the voices' racket, "although I never knew his name. He was younger than the other kids, but he was always there when it came time for me to hand out lunches."

"Which you've been doing for some time."

"Not that long," he replied. "The sack lunches are a fairly new addition, but, other than the months while I was dealing with a cancer diagnosis, I've been operating what they call the Free Store for Hands Across the Border for the past several years. In all that time, I've never known anything like this to happen."

"Don't you think it odd that detectives haven't spoken to you even though you should clearly be a person of interest in this case?" Marliss asked.

Stephen had already arrived at that same conclusion, but how had she? Obviously she'd gained access to some aspect of the investigation and knew he was under suspicion. Now she was here to get the goods on him. At that point, Stephen's only option was to make sure his unwelcome visitor didn't leave the house alive. That meant he needed to put Marliss at ease and get the two of them on the same page. In a moment of inspiration, he knew how to make that happen.

"Odd?" he repeated with a forced chuckle. "Yes, but surprising? No. With Joanna Brady running the show, that's hardly unexpected. She's never been the sharpest knife in the drawer, and how someone that inept can keep being reelected time after time is more than I can understand."

"Isn't that the truth," Marliss agreed.

"Did you know I had her for senior English back in high school?" he added for good measure. "She didn't strike me as all that bright back then, either. So how do you think the investigation is progressing?" Stephen continued, deftly turning the tables. Now he was the one asking questions.

"Well," Marliss said with a shrug. "It looks to me as though she and her whole department are in over their heads."

By then the woman had visibly relaxed, but to take care of her once and for all, Stephen knew he would need some assistance. A half-full pint jar of leftover chloroform had sat unopened in his fridge for years on end. Would it still work after all this time? He didn't see any reason why not.

"Say," he said aloud. "I'm feeling parched and need a little something to wet my whistle. I'm going to have a soda. Diet Coke's all I have on hand. Would you care for one?"

"No, thanks," she said. "I'm fine."

You may think you're fine, Stephen thought to himself, *but you're not fine at all!*

CHAPTER 39

BISBEE, ARIZONA
Friday, December 8, 2023

RATHER THAN WATCH THE MINUTES TICK BY AT AN AGO-nizingly slow speed, Joanna turned to the next missed-call slip. On this one the name was Marvin Begay and the area code indicated a northern Arizona location, so it wasn't difficult to expect that this was about Michael Young from Shiprock.

When Joanna dialed the number, her call was answered by a recording. "You have reached the Navajo Nation Division of Public Safety. Press 1 for Criminal Investigations; Press 2 for Internal Affairs; Press 3 for Department of Corrections; Press 4 for Navajo Fire and Rescue; Press 5 for EMS."

Taking a wild guess, Joanna pressed number 1. Criminal investigations seemed likely to be the one she needed. After the call went through, she sat on hold for a good three minutes before a human came on the line.

"Criminal Investigations."

"I'd like to speak to Marvin Begay."

"May I ask who's calling and what this is about?"

"My name's Sheriff Joanna Brady from Cochise County. He called my office earlier this morning in regards to a BOLO that was sent out last night."

"One moment, please."

Joanna expected to spend another three or four minutes on hold. Instead, the call was picked up almost immediately. "Marvin Begay here."

"This is Sheriff Brady . . ." she began.

"Yes," Marvin said impatiently. "One of my staff brought your BOLO to my attention earlier this morning, and the specifications seemed to match one of our cold cases. I spoke briefly to one of your investigators, but she wasn't very forthcoming. What can you tell me?"

Joanna spent the next several minutes hitting the high spots of the investigation into Stephen Roper's long history while Marvin Begay listened in dead silence.

"And you think you'll be able to take him into custody today?" he asked when she finished.

"We're hoping for an arrest warrant on the Amanda Hudson murder from North Dakota. Once we have that in hand, we'll be able to take him into custody on their behalf."

Marvin sighed. "I only wish my dad was still alive," he said.

That was not a response Joanna expected.

"I beg your pardon?" she said.

"As kids, my father and Michael Young were best friends," he said. "The year Michael was murdered, all the boys in his class wore red bandannas to school every day as a reminder that his killer was still on the loose. My father was in the hospital and on his last legs when I took this job, but that's the first thing he said to me. 'Maybe now you'll finally be able to figure out who killed Michael.' He never got over losing his friend."

"I'm sure he didn't," Joanna said quietly. "People never do, but if you don't mind my asking, what exactly is your job, Mr. Begay?"

"I'm the chief of police for the Navajo Nation," he said. "Unfortunately, Michael Young's death is only one of our unsolved cases."

"Arresting Stephen Roper may take one of those off your list," Joanna said. "And believe me, once we have him in custody, I'll be sure to let you know."

"Thanks," Marvin Begay said. "Appreciate it, but you probably only have my office number. Here's my cell phone number. I want to hear from you the moment that happens, no matter the time, day or night."

"You will," she said, adding his cell phone number to his missed-call message. "You have my word on that."

By the end of that second phone call, Joanna's watch read 1:25. That meant early dismissal at Lowell School should be close to underway. She was beginning to wonder why she hadn't heard from her detectives when Deb called.

"We've got the warrant," she announced.

"Good," Joanna said. "What took so long?"

"That's an interesting story," Deb replied. "We were told Judge Askins was having lunch at the Copper Queen, but when we went there, he was nowhere to be found. We finally went back up to the courthouse to wait, and that's where we were when he and his secretary returned from something that didn't appear to be an innocent lunch. I doubt Mrs. Askins has any idea about what's going on."

"Oops," Joanna said. "That's definitely none of our business! Where are you now?"

"On our way to Roper's residence. We just left Don Luis and started down Naco Highway. Jaime told us that on the far side of Roper's house and just before Country Club Drive dead-ends, there's a little pullout where local teenagers go to make out, drink, or both. He suggested we duck into that. That way our vehicle will be out of sight when Roper arrives home. Fortunately there's a pair of binoculars in the glove box, so we should be able to see him without his seeing us. You do want us to wait until he's home before we execute the search, correct?"

"Absolutely," Joanna said. "I've got officers standing by here who, along with the CSI team, will be able to come assist with that whenever you're ready."

Just then she heard Garth's voice muttering something in the background. Deb responded first with, "Are you sure?" followed by a heartfelt, "Crap!"

"What's the matter?" Joanna demanded in alarm. "What's going on?"

"We just drove past Roper's place," Deb replied. "The food truck's not there, but you'll never guess who's parked in his driveway—Marliss Shackleford!"

Joanna's heart fell. "What the hell is she doing there?"

"No idea. We just turned into the pullout. Do you want us to go back and tell her to get lost?"

Garth spoke again, saying something indecipherable. "Really?" Deb asked.

"What?" Joanna asked.

"It's too late to send her packing. Roper's truck is just now turning onto Country Club."

Joanna could barely believe what she was hearing. There was no way her department could initiate a search warrant with an innocent civilian on the premises.

"Okay," she said. "Everybody's on standby here. Let us know the moment Marliss is out of the way, so we can send backup."

"Will do," Deb said, "but what on earth is Marliss doing there?"

"I don't know," Joanna replied. "But I can tell you this, I'm sure as hell going to be gunning for that leaker!"

As soon as the call with Deb ended, Joanna got up and stalked out of her office.

"Where are you going?" Kristin asked as she marched past.

"Dispatch," Joanna asked. "All hell is about to break loose. I may not be able to be *where* the action is, but I'm sure as hell going to be *running it*!"

CHAPTER 40

NACO, ARIZONA
Friday, December 8, 2023

WITH A CHLOROFORM-SOAKED DISH TOWEL IN HAND, STE-phen left the kitchen and approached Marliss from behind, catching her totally unawares. Once the chloroform did its job, he zip-tied both her arms and legs and tied a gag around her mouth. Much as the voices would have liked him to strangle her on the spot, he didn't. There wasn't time.

His first thought was to put Marliss in the back of his car and then dump the body someplace else, but he knew instantly that was a nonstarter. Remembering how difficult it had been to move Xavier Delgado's much smaller body, Stephen knew that his gimpy arm and shoulder would never stand up to carrying a full-grown woman. But getting rid of her was paramount, and since it seemed likely no one knew she was here, and since he had no intention of ever coming back, leaving her here in the house seemed like his best option.

With that in mind, he dragged her into the bathroom and opened the trapdoor. The distance from there to the floor of the crawl space was probably a seven-foot drop. If half that distance had been enough to do in Grandma Lucille, twice the height should be more than enough to get the job done.

Before shoving her headfirst into the hole, Stephen went through her pockets. That's when he found her car keys. He immediately realized that taking her car made more sense than using his own. After all, Sheriff Brady's crew would be looking for his vehicle, but he doubted anyone would be looking for Marliss Shackleford's RAV4.

With Marliss's key fob stowed in his pocket, he gave his victim a shove and then listened for the dull thud as she landed on the concrete slab below. The voices were ecstatic about that, but Stephen ignored them. If he was going to make the best of this very bad bargain, it was essential that he remain totally calm and completely focused.

With that in mind, Stephen hurried into his bedroom to pack. As he stuffed his shaving kit and medications into his suitcase, he worried about those. Getting refills might be an issue, but he'd tackle that problem farther down the road. The contents he'd already retrieved from the safe—the bag of money and the cigar box—went on the bottom layer of his suitcase. The clothing he grabbed was mostly casual stuff—slacks and golf shirts. None of the pink cancer survivor T-shirts made the cut, and neither did any of his golf hats. At the first opportunity, he planned to shave off the rest of his hair and be completely bald.

Twenty minutes after dropping Marliss to what he supposed was an instant death he brought his loaded suitcase into the living room. That's when he spotted her belongings. Her purse still sat beside the easy chair exactly where she'd left it. Her laptop had fallen to the floor in the course of their brief struggle.

He still had one last duffel sitting unused in the coat closet next to the front door. He tore that out of its plastic wrapper and then stuffed the wrapper into the duffel bag along with the laptop and purse. Then he took a final look around the room. Nothing was in disarray. There were no knocked-over pieces of furniture or broken knickknacks to indicate that a struggle had occurred in the room.

Gathering up his two pieces of luggage, Stephen headed out. On the porch, he paused long enough to close and lock the door. He had lived here for the better part of fifty years, but he felt no particular sadness about leaving this place behind, just as he'd had no regrets about leaving Fertile all those years earlier. To prove it, once the door was locked, he literally threw the key away, tossing it into the thicket of prickly pear that was part of his xeriscaped front yard.

Then, as casually as if he were going away on a weekend outing, Stephen Roper walked over to Marliss's RAV4 and loaded his luggage. After adjusting the seat and mirrors, he started the engine, pulled a U-ie, and drove away without a backward glance. The battered SUV wasn't much of a drive compared to his Mercedes sedan, but beggars can't be choosers.

CHAPTER 41

BISBEE, ARIZONA
Friday, December 8, 2023

SHERIFF BRADY COUNTED ON HER DISPATCHERS TO BE THE heart of her department, but she generally spent very little time in that room, so when she showed up, Tica Romero was surprised to see her.

"What's going on?" Tica asked, removing her headphones.

"All hell is about to break loose, and I'll need to be able to hear everything that's going on. Can you make that happen?"

Tica nodded as her fingers clicked on her keyboard. "What's up? It's been really quiet out there."

Joanna had asked her people to maintain radio silence, and they had obliged. She was starting to give Tica a briefing, when Garth Raymond's voice came through the computer's speaker. "We've got movement," he shouted. "Our subject just left his residence, heading east on Country Club Drive in Marliss Shackleford's RAV4."

"Can I talk to Garth?" Joanna asked.

Nodding, Tica plugged a handheld microphone into her computer and handed the mic to Joanna.

"Is Marliss with him?" Joanna asked.

"No, he left the residence alone, but he was carrying two pieces of luggage."

Alone, Joanna thought. *That's not good news. And if Marliss had a police scanner, it probably wasn't in her RAV4.*

"Jaime," she said aloud. "Are you hearing this?"

"Yes."

"Where are you?"

"Parked just south of Green Brush Draw. I'll be able to see him when he pulls out of Country Club Drive onto Naco Highway."

"Everybody else, listen up," Joanna said. "Wait for Jaime to clue us in on his direction before you make a move."

With the microphone still in her left hand, Joanna used her right to extract her cell phone. Chief Alvin Bernard's name and number were at the top of her recent calls list. She punched that.

He answered before the first ring ended. "Is it a go?" he asked.

"It is," Joanna replied. "Shut her down. He's driving a banged-up white RAV4."

Jaime spoke again. "He's headed northbound on Naco Highway."

Chief Bernard came back on the line. "I gave the word to Chief Flowers. He's moving his fire trucks into position to block all Traffic Circle entrances and exits except for the entrance from Highway 92."

"Good-o," Joanna said. "All units, be aware that the Bisbee Fire Department is deploying trucks to block entrances and exits to the Traffic Circle. If he takes Highway 92 eastbound at Don Luis, once he's inside the Traffic Circle, Bisbee PD will block that entrance and exit, too, so he won't be able to get back out."

Tica was still sitting in front of her monitor, looking up at her boss in dismay. "If you're running Dispatch, what am I supposed to do?"

"Go to the conference room. Tell the people there to put on their body armor and mount up. The Arrest Team should head for the Traffic Circle and the Search Warrant Team should head for Stephen Roper's residence on Country Club Drive in Naco. There's going to be a hell of a traffic jam in town in just a few minutes. Tell the Search Warrant crew to drive to Naco via Bisbee Junction."

Tica stood up to do as she'd been told, but she paused for a moment. "Stephen Roper? The guy who used to teach at Bisbee High School?"

"The very one," Joanna said grimly.

Just then Jaime Carbajal spoke again. "Okay, everybody. The subject just turned right on Highway 92 in Don Luis."

"Are you still following him?" Joanna asked.

"Yes, I am," Jaime answered, "but far enough back that I doubt he can make out this is a cop car."

"Stay behind him long enough to make sure he doesn't turn off on School Terrace Road. That's his last possible exit. If he drives past that, we've got him," Joanna said. Then, after taking a breath, she added. "Deputy Nuñez?"

"I'm here," he said.

"Leave your post and follow Jaime toward the Traffic Circle to provide backup."

"Will do," he responded.

Deb Howell's voice was next. "We're at the residence. No one is answering the door."

"Then break it down," Joanna ordered. "Marliss Shackleford is still inside, and something bad may have happened to her."

Tica returned. "They're on the way," she said.

"Good," Joanna said. "Thanks."

Another minute or two passed. Joanna tried to not hold her breath, but she could feel her heart pounding in her chest.

"Just passing School Terrace Road," Jaime said. "He didn't turn off."

"Did you hear that?" Joanna said into her phone to Chief Bernard.

"Sure did," he answered. "We've got him."

"All units," Joanna said into the mic. "Trap is sprung. All units head for the Traffic Circle."

CHAPTER 42

NACO, ARIZONA
Friday, December 8, 2023

AS GARTH AND DEB PULLED UP TO STEPHEN ROPER'S RES-idence, they donned their vests and activated their body cams. Garth was the one who did "the knock," while shouting, "Open up! Police! We have a search warrant!" They waited a beat. When nothing happened, he shouted again.

Then he turned to his partner. "Break it down?" he asked.

"Be my guest," Deb said.

It took three solid hits from Garth's shoulder before the door gave way. They entered with weapons drawn and cleared the house. It was empty.

"So where did she go?" Deb asked. "The garage maybe?"

"No," Garth said. "She's got to be here inside someplace. I wonder if there's a crawl space."

It took several minutes but finally he located the trapdoor hidden under the mat on the bathroom floor. From above he could see a ladder leading down into the darkness. As he began to climb down, his hand touched a chain that, when pulled, illuminated the space's only overhead light bulb. That's when he saw her. Marliss lay sprawled on the concrete floor with her bound lower legs still entangled in the ladder.

"I found her," he shouted back up to Deb. "It looks like she's badly hurt. Call EMS. And once you call for an ambulance, call Sheriff Brady, too. She's going to want to be here."

Kneeling on the floor beside the injured woman, Garth sliced through the zip tie binding her hands in order to check for a pulse. "She's still alive," he called back up to Deb. "I've got a pulse."

Next he cut through the zip tie on her feet. Afraid to move them, he left her lower legs in the same ungainly position before removing the gag covering her mouth. As he did so, her eyes fluttered open.

"Where am I?" she asked faintly. "What happened?"

"You've had a bad fall," Garth told her. "We've called for an ambulance." Even as he said the words, he wondered if, with all the traffic disruptions happening in town, an ambulance would make it there in time.

"Why can't I feel my hands and feet?" Marliss asked.

Garth didn't want to say what was likely the ugly truth. "Help is coming," he assured her. "Hang in there. I'm going to go upstairs for a second."

Deb was sitting on the edge of the bathtub waiting when Garth's head popped back up through the trapdoor. "How bad is it?"

"Bad," Garth replied. "She can't feel her hands or legs."

Deb put her hand over her mouth and took a deep breath. "Okay," she said. "I'll go down and talk to her. You get on the horn to Sheriff Brady and let her know what's going on. No telling how long before an ambulance can get here. Be there to flag them in."

"Will do," Garth said. "On my way."

Detective Howell took a deep, steadying breath. Ernie Carpenter, the long-retired cop who had been her mentor, had taken a mere deputy and turned her into a capable homicide investigator. This was a crime scene—either murder or attempted murder—and this was possibly the last chance anyone would have to question the only eyewitness—the victim. Steeling herself for the task ahead, and with her body camera running, Deb lowered herself through the trapdoor and climbed down the ladder.

Marliss lay supine on the floor, her eyes open and blinking. She was still alive.

"Hey, Marliss," Deb said. "Remember me? Detective Howell. My partner's outside waiting to flag down the ambulance. Can you tell me what happened?"

"We were talking," Marliss said.

"Who's we?" Deb asked.

"Stephen Roper and I. He went to the kitchen to get a soda. When he came back, he walked up behind me and put a wet, evil-smelling cloth over my mouth. I don't remember anything after that until I woke up just now. How bad is it?"

"Pretty bad," Deb replied. "We don't dare try to move you until EMS gets here."

"It's my back, isn't it," Marliss said. "That's why I can't feel my arms or legs."

Neck most likely, Deb thought but didn't say.

"And I'm cold," Marliss went on. "Terribly cold. Can you find a blanket?"

Deb started up the ladder. Her head emerged through the trapdoor just as Garth reentered the bathroom.

"She's cold," Deb said. "Find some blankets. I'll wait here."

Garth darted out of the bathroom and returned a moment later with a duvet and several blankets. "I called Sheriff Brady. She's on her way, and she's talking with the hospital."

"And Roper?"

"He's stuck at the Traffic Circle just the way he's supposed to be, but it's turned into a standoff. He's armed with a weapon and threatening to shoot himself."

"Couldn't happen to a nicer guy," Deb muttered under her breath as she grabbed the armload of bedding and clambered back down the ladder.

After covering Marliss with a layer of blankets, Deb settled down on the floor next to the injured woman and took her hand.

"Is the ambulance coming?" Marliss asked.

"On its way," Deb answered. "It'll be here soon. Why did you come here today?"

"I heard a rumor that they were looking into Stephen Roper. I wanted to check it out."

"A rumor?" Deb asked. "Who told you?"

"My cleaning lady. Her sister's husband is a border guard in Naco, Sonora. She said he told her that people were asking questions about Señor Santa Claus, and I just couldn't believe it."

Marliss's eyes closed. For a moment Deb thought she was gone, but then they fluttered open again.

"I'm really cold," Marliss murmured. "Could you please bring me a blanket."

"Of course," Deb said, wiping a tear from her eye because the blankets were already there.

Marliss turned her head slightly to the left. "I know you," she said. "You're Detective Howell."

Deb nodded. "Yes, I am."

"Have you been here long?"

"For a while," Deb answered. "Are you in any pain?"

Marliss frowned. "No," she said. "Nothing hurts, but I'm scared. Would you mind holding my hand?"

"Of course," Deb said, squeezing the hand she was already holding and biting back the sob that was rising in her throat.

"Please don't leave me," Marliss added.

"Don't worry," Deb whispered. "I won't."

CHAPTER 43

BISBEE, ARIZONA
Friday, December 8, 2023

WITH HER CELL PHONE IN ONE HAND AND A MICROPHONE in the other, Joanna Brady stood behind Tica Romero's chair in Dispatch with absolutely no idea of what she should do. A little over a mile away, serial killer Stephen Roper had fallen into the trap she had devised and was now driving in mad circles around what appeared to be a mini-racetrack, with all entrances and exits blocked by fire trucks and police vehicles. After literally decades of his getting away with one murder after another, her department was about to take him into custody. That arrest should be the crowning glory of her career.

But some nine miles away, just outside Naco, Joanna's archenemy, Marliss Shackleford, had been gravely injured by that same serial killer who had fled this latest crime scene in the victim's own vehicle. According to Garth, Marliss was in desperate need of medical attention, but with fire department personnel, including EMS responders tied up in Joanna's Traffic Circle blockade, there was no telling how long it would be before medical assistance could arrive. By rights, Joanna should be at that scene, too, but she couldn't do both.

"Can you connect me to the ER at the Copper Queen Hospital?" Joanna asked Tica.

With a few clicks on her keyboard, the call was made. "Copper Queen Hospital ER. How can I help you?" a voice asked.

"This is Sheriff Joanna Brady. There's been a serious incident down by Naco. I need to speak to the doctor in charge."

"One moment."

Seconds later someone else came on the phone. "Dr. Ybarra here," he said. "What seems to be the problem?"

"This is Sheriff Brady. There's been a serious incident at a home on Country Club Drive north of Naco where a woman was dropped headfirst into a crawl space. She's on the floor. Two of my detectives are with her, but she has no feeling in her arms or legs. My people have called for an ambulance, but there's a big tie-up at the Traffic Circle, so there's no telling when EMS will be able to get there."

"I've heard about the traffic problem," Dr. Ybarra said, "but I could get around that by using School Terrace Road. What's the address?"

Joanna gave it to him. Then, when the call ended and having done everything she could for Marliss Shackleford, Joanna buckled on her body armor, fired up her Interceptor, and headed for the Traffic Circle.

By the time Joanna arrived, Chief Deputy Hadlock had things pretty well in hand. He'd had some of the blockading fire trucks move aside enough for several police vehicles to squeeze through. They had created enough of a pinch point that Roper could no longer get past, forcing him to come to a stop at the eastbound Highway 80 exit where Joanna's body-armor-clad arrest team was congregated.

"Hands on your head and step out of the vehicle," someone shouted over a bullhorn as Joanna made her way toward the front of the crowd.

For a moment, nothing happened inside Marliss Shackleford's battered RAV4, but then someone else called out the chilling warning, "Gun!"

Ducking for cover, Joanna could see the small handgun Stephen Roper was holding next to his ear. She was determined the confrontation wouldn't end that way. The last thing she wanted was for Roper to get away with killing himself without ever being called to account for his unspeakable crimes. Spotting the guy with the bullhorn, Joanna made her way over to him and tapped him on the shoulder.

"May I?" she asked pointing at the bullhorn.

He handed it over without a word. "Mr. Roper," Joanna shouted into it. "Sheriff Brady here. As you can see, you're surrounded. There's no getting away. My officers are here to take you into custody without you or anyone else being injured."

"Screw you, Joanna Lathrop," he shouted back. "You're doing no such thing."

After that he seemed to struggle with the weapon for a moment. Everyone at the scene, including Joanna, held their respective breaths, waiting for the report of a gunshot—one that never came. After a moment, Roper seemed to examine the gun before holding it up to his ear a second time. In that instant, people realized the gun wasn't firing, and officers swarmed the car. Within seconds, Roper had been dragged out of the vehicle and placed facedown on the ground while handcuffs snapped shut around his wrists.

"What are you arresting me for, bitch?" he demanded of Joanna once he was back on his feet. "For the murder of that little kid?"

Joanna was well aware that all they had on the Xavier Delgado case so far was a search warrant, and the arrest warrant in the Amanda Hudson case had not yet materialized.

"No," she said. "I'm arresting you on suspicion of the attempted murder of Marliss Shackleford."

Roper hadn't been expecting that, so for Joanna, the shocked expression on his smug face was worth the price of admission.

Once he was in the back of a squad car, Joanna broke away from the group and made her way around the circle, using the Interceptor's lights and siren to clear snarled traffic out of her way. When she arrived at Stephen Roper's residence on Country Club Drive, an ambulance from Sierra Vista was parked outside. They had been summoned to serve as backup and had made it as far as Miracle Valley when the emergency EMS call came in.

Walking toward the house, Joanna spotted Garth and Deb sitting on a porch swing off to one side of the front door. Garth's arm was around Deb's shoulder in a comforting manner, and she was clearly crying.

Joanna walked up to them. "She didn't make it then?"

Garth shook his head.

With her own tears welling, Joanna turned on her heel and returned the way she'd come, finally sinking down on the porch steps. She and Marliss had been at each other's throats for years, but she'd never once wished harm would come to her. Joanna sat there for several long minutes, trying to get her emotions under control. Then a man wearing scrubs sat down beside her.

"Good to see you again, Sheriff Brady," he said. "Not under these circumstances, of course."

Joanna looked at him. He was a heftily built Hispanic man in his forties, with a bit of gray hair showing around his temples.

"I'm sorry," she said. "Do I know you?"

"I'm Nacio," he said. "Ignacio Salazar Ybarra, remember me? The Douglas Bulldog quarterback who fell in love with the head cheerleader from Bisbee High?"

The story came back to her in a flash—Ignacio Ybarra and Bree O'Brien. Their story had been a southern Arizona version of Romeo and Juliet. He had been a talented football player from Bisbee's longtime athletic rival, Douglas High School. He had been seriously injured in the final football game of his life at Bisbee's Warren Ballpark. Brianna, Bisbee's "it" girl—the one voted most likely to succeed—had been standing close enough to the action to hear the bone in his leg shatter, and over time the two of them had bonded over that horrific incident.

Ignacio was Hispanic; Bree was Anglo. He came from an impoverished background. Her family was well-to-do, and neither set of parents had approved of their teenaged romance. While on an ill-fated camping trip to Skeleton Canyon, Bree had been murdered, and her family had been quick to point the finger at Ignacio. Eventually Joanna's investigation had revealed Nacio to be blameless. In her last conversation with Bree's grieving father, Joanna remembered David O'Brien saying that he planned to use the funds he had originally intended to use to send Bree to college to pay for Ignacio's schooling instead.

Sitting on Stephen Roper's front porch, awash in guilt that she hadn't somehow prevented this awful tragedy, Joanna learned for the first time that David O'Brien had been good to his word.

"So you did become a doctor then?" she asked.

He nodded. "Bree's dad paid my way through college and medical school both. He became like a second dad to me and an extra grandfather to my kids. They called him Pops. Last year, when he passed away, he left Green Brush Ranch to me.

"Sonja, my wife, is also a physician—a surgeon. We met in med school. We were living and working in LA when we found out about inheriting the ranch. I had been wanting to get out of the city and come back to Arizona for years. Her family immigrated to the US from Mexico when she was three, and the idea of living close to the border appealed to her, too. We both hired on at the Copper Queen Hospital, but we've only been here a short while. We got here just in time for the start of school last September."

For Joanna, Nacio's uplifting story of good overcoming evil was like spotting a lifeboat in a sea of despair. It gave her the strength to ask the next question.

"So what happened here? The last I heard from my detectives, Marliss was talking to them but couldn't feel either her arms or legs. Now she's dead?"

Nacio—Dr. Ybarra, Joanna reminded herself—nodded. "We won't know for sure until Dr. Baldwin performs the autopsy, but my best guess is that a fall from that height shattered at least one and maybe more of the vertebrae in her neck. When EMS attempted to load her onto a board, a bone fragment must have penetrated her medulla oblongata. When that happens, there's nothing to be done, and maybe that's a blessing," he added. "She most likely would have been destined to live out her life as a quadriplegic. That's a kind of hell I wouldn't wish on my worst enemy."

I wouldn't, either, Joanna thought, *but could I have prevented it?*

Just then, Dr. Kendra Baldwin herself pulled up in her "body wagon." She greeted Nacio with a handshake and Joanna with a nod. "Sorry for the delay," she said. "There's some big tie-up at the Traffic Circle, and it took forever to get through."

"My fault," Joanna said, "but I'm pretty sure we have Xavier Delgado's killer in custody." She took a breath before adding, "And now he's Marliss Shackleford's killer, too."

Kendra appeared shocked, but so did Ignacio Ybarra. "Marliss, too?" she asked.

"Wait," Nacio interjected. "You're talking about the little boy who disappeared from the migrant camp in Naco, Sonora?"

"Yes, to both," Joanna replied. "The guy we've taken into custody at the Traffic Circle is one Stephen Roper. He's lived in Bisbee for decades. We have reason to believe he's also a prolific serial killer."

"You're talking about the guy with all the pink T-shirts, Señor Santa Claus, who operates the Free Store?" Dr. Ybarra asked.

Joanna nodded. "The very one," she said.

"But I thought he was a good guy," Ignacio said.

"So did everybody else," she said sadly, "including Marliss Shackleford."

CHAPTER 44

BISBEE, ARIZONA
Friday, December 8, 2023

BY THE TIME JOANNA GOT BACK TO THE JUSTICE CENTER, she wasn't surprised to see the parking lot teeming with TV vans and carloads of reporters. A dead kid from Mexico hadn't been enough to bring them out of the woodwork, but the death of an erstwhile reporter and the simultaneous arrest of a pillar of the community was enough for the piranhas to show up.

Kristin must have had her ear to the ground for the sound of Joanna's private door opening and closing. She showed up holding a handful of additional missed-call slips while Joanna was still putting her purse away.

"Glad everyone's okay," Kristin said. She was talking about members of the department, but something in the expression on Joanna's face must have given her pause. "Except for Marliss, that is," she added. "What happened to her is terrible."

"Yes," Joanna agreed with a nod. "It certainly is. Now, what's happened here while I've been gone?"

"It's been pretty hectic," Kristin said. "I've been checking your office email. The arrest warrant from North Dakota came in just a little while ago, but with Roper already under arrest, I guess you don't really need it."

"I'll be happy to serve it all the same," Joanna said grimly. "And I have a feeling the North Dakota Highway Patrol isn't the only law enforcement agency that's going to want a piece of him. What else?"

"Garth and Deb were able to locate Marliss's next of kin, her mother—Dianne Borison—in San Diego. Officers from San Diego PD will be doing the notification."

"And?" Joanna prodded.

"Dave Hollicker is in charge of the CSI examination of the crime scene in Naco. Casey is going through items that were removed from Mr. Roper's vehicle."

"Like what?" Joanna asked.

"She mentioned something about a blue duffel bag and a cigar box, but I don't know any details. You have several more calls from the BOLO. Those are here in your stack of missed calls. And Tom Hadlock wants to know if, with all those reporters outside, you want to hold the press conference or should he?"

"I'll talk to him," she said.

She walked to his office next door and entered without knocking.

"Tough day," he said. It was a statement, not a question.

She sank into a nearby chair. "I'll say," she said.

"And Marliss is really dead?"

Joanna nodded.

"Sorry," he said.

"Me, too," she said, "but I'll handle the press conference. Please schedule it for 6 p.m. Can you notify the usual suspects?"

"Will do," Tom said, "but most of them are already here. Anything else?"

"Nope," Joanna said. "That'll do it."

With that, Joanna returned to her office to call Butch and let him know she wouldn't be home in time for dinner.

"Did you get him?" Butch asked as soon as he answered her call.

"We did," Joanna answered. "He's behind bars."

"That's great!" Butch exclaimed. "And Dennis was delighted to get out of school early, but you sound a little off. What's wrong?"

Joanna loved the fact that he could see into her soul even when they were miles apart. She spent the next several minutes telling him about everything that had happened, including her encounter with Ignacio Ybarra.

"We were just dating at the time," Butch said, "but I remember that case. It affected you almost as much as this one has."

Joanna thought about that for a moment before agreeing with him. "You may be right about that."

"And I'm right about this, too," Butch added. "After today, you're going to need some comfort food, so as of now I'm making green chili casserole. It'll be warm in the oven regardless of what time you get home."

"Thank you," she said. "Love you."

"Love you back."

After leaving her office, Joanna's first stop was the bullpen. Detective Howell was there. Detective Raymond wasn't. "Where's Garth?" she asked.

"On his way to Tucson to deliver Roper's phone and computer to the DPS crime lab," Deb replied. "They have the technical resources to crack them. We don't."

"Good plan," Joanna said. "What else?"

Instead of answering, Deb burst into tears. "It was awful," she said, once her crying jag quieted enough that she could speak. "Marliss told me she was scared and asked if I'd hold her hand. The thing is, I was already holding her hand, and she couldn't tell. Then medics showed up and the next instant she was gone. I didn't even like the woman. She could be a real pain in the ass sometimes, but still . . . We had the search warrant. We should have just gone in instead of waiting for her to leave. Maybe we could have stopped it."

"What happened to Marliss isn't your fault," Joanna said. "If anybody's at fault, it's me, because I'm the one who ordered you and Garth to wait until she left before executing the warrant. But right now, we both have to focus on our jobs. Where do we stand?"

Deb took a deep breath. "Roper's lawyered up, so we can't talk to him," she said.

"No surprise there," Joanna remarked.

"In fact," Deb added, "the attorney himself called me just a little while ago—a Mr. Ralph Whitmer of Los Angeles, California."

"A lawyer from out of state?" Joanna asked.

"Make that a big-time defense attorney from out of state," Deb replied. "I just googled him. In the last few years he's gotten three different killers off on insanity pleas, and from what I'm seeing online, he charges big bucks to do so. According to him, he'll be flying into Sierra Vista Municipal Airport by private jet tomorrow morning so he can confer with his client."

"Where's Roper going to get that kind of money?"

"Ask Casey. While she was searching the contents of Roper's car she evidently found bundles of cash in a bag inside his suitcase."

"Casey's my next stop," Joanna said. "Anything else?"

"I'm in the process of writing up what went down at Roper's residence today. We have it on our body cams, but Tom said that since a death was involved, Garth and I should provide written statements as well."

"Probably a good idea," Joanna said, "but when you finish doing that, go home and get some rest, and tell Garth to do the same. Today's been rough and tomorrow's not going to be any easier. Whether or not we can interview Stephen Roper, that's the day we'll finally begin unraveling the life and times of a serial killer, starting with obtaining a search warrant for his banking and credit card records. I'm going to need all my detectives at the top of their game."

"We will be," Deb assured her, "every single one of us."

Joanna's next stop was the lab where a glove-clad Casey Ledford was hunched over her desk, using a pair of tweezers to pull apart what appeared to be a tangled web of shoelaces. At some point they had probably all been white, but now most of them were a grubby shade of gray.

"You found his trophy case?" Joanna asked.

"Sure did," Casey replied, nodding in the direction of the old cigar box at her elbow. "There it is."

"And that's all that was in it, a bunch of shoelaces?"

Just then, Casey managed to extract one of the laces, an especially white one, from the tangle. Once the lace was loose, she held it up to her nose and sniffed. "Try this," she said.

Following suit, Joanna got a whiff of something familiar. "Bleach?" she asked.

Casey nodded. "I doubt the others got the bleach treatment, so this one is probably Xavier's."

"What else?" Joanna asked.

"Everything's bagged and tagged," Casey said, turning her attention back to the remaining tangle of shoelaces. "It's all over there on the counter."

Joanna walked over to the stainless steel counter where a collection of sealed evidence bags was laid out in neat rows. The first one that caught her eye held a turquoise squash blossom necklace. Seeing it, Joanna took a breath. "This necklace belonged to Inez Johnson," she said aloud, "a girl from Bylas, Arizona, on the San Carlos."

Casey's chair was shoved back. A moment later she was standing next to Joanna.

"I swabbed that," Casey said. "I found some particles of dried blood on the turquoise under some of the silver prongs, but how on earth do you already know the name of the victim?"

"From the BOLO Anna Rae Green had sent out last night, asking for information on unsolved homicides with certain commonalities. The response has been amazing. Calls have been coming in all day long." She picked up a bag containing a red bandanna. "This belonged to Michael Young, a young Navajo who was murdered near Shiprock, New Mexico. And this ivory-handled switchblade? That's from Amanda Hudson, a Lakota girl from Grand Forks, North Dakota."

"I'm planning on swabbing that, too," Casey said, "but I'll have to take it apart first. The blade looks clean, but just like the necklace, there's a good chance I'll find dried blood on the inside hinge."

That's when Joanna spotted the gold wedding band. "I'm guessing that belonged to Stephen Roper's step-grandmother, Lucille Hawkins. Earlier today I spoke to Dan Hogan, a former sheriff from Polk County, Minnesota, where Roper grew up. Dan was a relatively new deputy when he responded to an emergency call to a family farm where Lucille was reported to have fallen off her front steps. Her death was ruled accidental, but the deputy who eventually became sheriff always thought the kid who called it in was somehow involved."

"And that kid just happened to be Stephen Roper?"

"Yup," Joanna replied. "You've got it."

"How old was he at the time?"

"Eleven," Joanna said.

"That young?" Casey groaned.

Joanna nodded.

"I don't know if this is any help," Casey added, "but there's an engraving inside the ring. It looks like the initials LJ and OH with a heart between them."

"That fits," Joanna said. "I'm pretty sure Dan Hogan told me Roper's grandfather's name was Orson Hawkins, and I think Lucille's maiden name started with a J."

One by one she examined the remaining bags. There were several barrettes, and a number of earrings, four different class rings, a glow-in-the-dark cross pendant like the one Joanna had received as a kid after attending Daily Vacation Bible School, and a piece of what looked like yellow plastic tape. *A tiny piece of crime scene tape?* Joanna wondered. There was also a folded-up map of New Mexico, evidently torn from an old-fashioned *Rand McNally Atlas*. A number of X's showed in the margins. When Joanna started to count them, Casey stopped her.

"Don't bother," she said. "I already did. There are twenty-three."

The next item Joanna spotted was a tiny pearl-handled pistol, also in a sealed evidence bag, sitting off to one side, away from the others.

"Is that what he used to try to kill himself?" she asked.

Casey nodded. "It's an antique—a single-round derringer pistol with a serial number that indicates it was manufactured by Remington in 1927. The weapon may have been fired at some time in the past, but I'm pretty sure it was never cleaned. There was a live bullet inside, but the works were so gummed up with a century's worth of dirt and grime that it's no wonder it didn't fire."

Next to the pistol was another evidence bag, which initially appeared to be empty. Examining it closely, however, Joanna realized that a second plastic bag held what looked like a plain old sandwich bag, the kind that predated Ziploc ones. The second bag appeared to contain a thin film of whitish powder.

"What's with the sandwich bag?" Joanna asked.

"Interesting question," Casey replied. "The powdery residue inside it turns out to be a combination of LSD and cocaine. The same powder turned up on the exterior of the pistol. I'm guessing that, for some reason, the gun was stored inside the bag. No idea why."

"And what about money?" Joanna asked. "Deb mentioned something about finding some money in his vehicle."

"Not just *some* money," Casey replied. "A lot of money! A cool hundred and fifty thousand bucks, all of it in hundreds, was in a bag in his suitcase along with the trophy case. And no, I didn't count all the bills. I counted the bills in one bundle and then I counted the bundles. I already locked the money in the evidence room."

"How many shoelaces?" Joanna asked.

"I won't know the exact number until I finish picking them apart."

"And then there's a blue duffel bag somewhere?" Joanna asked.

"There certainly is," Casey said, pointing to another counter. "It's over there. I didn't do much more than glance at it. Marliss Shackleford's purse and presumably her computer were the only things inside, but about the bag itself, and just so you know, the dye lot listed on the label is the same as the one we found on the bag that was fished out of the San Pedro with Xavier Delgado's body in it."

Joanna glanced at the clock. Caught up in examining the evidence, she had lost track of time. "Oops," she said. "I'm fifteen minutes late for my own press conference, but I'm pretty sure nobody's leaving until I show up. Are you going to call it a day soon?"

Casey shook her head. "Not until every single shoelace from that frigging cigar box is properly bagged and tagged."

Joanna went to the press conference then. In the course of it, she didn't reveal Stephen Roper's name because he had not yet been officially charged. She referred to him only as a "longtime Bisbee resident." She allowed as how the investigation into Xavier Delgado's death had led detectives to believe that the suspect in that case might possibly be a serial killer. She also mentioned that earlier in the afternoon, when investigators had gone to the suspect's home to execute a search warrant, they had found his most recent victim, another Bisbee resident whose name was also being withheld pending notification of next of kin.

The reporters weren't happy with only a bare-bones outline of what would most likely turn out to be a bombshell story, but that was all Sheriff Joanna Brady was prepared to give them. Her audience was still grumbling about that as she left the room, but she had more important things on her mind. She had promised several people that she would keep them apprised of the progress of the investigation, and she intended to do just that.

One call went to Dan Hogan, the former sheriff of Polk County, who had recognized Stephen Roper for what he was, even as an eleven-year-old kid. Joanna told him that her CSIs had found a wedding band that might well be Lucille Hawkins's missing wedding ring. Another call went to Luke Running Deer, telling him that an ivory-handled switchblade presumed to be Amanda's had been located and her likely killer was in custody.

Luke was floored. "You really caught him then?" he asked in disbelief. "After all these years?"

"Yes, we did," Joanna replied. "What tripped him up was evidence found at your sister's crime scene."

"So Amanda helped you catch him?"

"She certainly did," Joanna replied. "A girl from Devil's Lake helped bring down a monster."

Joanna's next call was to Marvin Begay at his home, telling him about finding Michael Young's red bandanna. She also left a message on Sheriff Ed Cox's answering machine in Fulton, Missouri, letting him know that several sneaker shoelaces had been found to be in Stephen Roper's possession, one of which might well belong to Lucianne Highsmith.

After that a totally drained Sheriff Brady went home where she downed not one, but two helpings of Butch's still-warm green chili casserole. Over that, bit by bit, she told him the story of her day—all of it, with no holdbacks. He listened gravely, nodding as she went but saying very little. The last things she mentioned were the heartbreaking phone calls she'd made before heading home.

"That's it?" Butch asked finally.

She nodded.

"What a hell of a day!"

Joanna nodded again.

"You did good work, though," he added. "You caught the bastard. He's sleeping behind bars tonight."

"But Marliss is dead," Joanna retorted, "and it's my fault! If I hadn't told Garth and Deb to wait for her to leave Roper's place before executing that warrant . . ."

"Marliss put herself in that position," Butch countered. "And your not sending the detectives in with a search warrant while an innocent civilian was present was not only the right thing to do, it was also the responsible thing to do. For all you know, there's a good chance that Marliss could have been pushed into that crawl space long before Garth and Deb arrived on the scene. If that were the case, no telling how long it would have taken to find her."

"You're saying that no matter what I did or didn't do, she probably would have died anyway?"

"That's exactly what I'm saying," Butch replied, taking Joanna's hand in his. "Do you have any idea why she went there in the first place?"

"Because of her cleaning lady," Joanna answered. "She told Deb that the cleaning lady's brother-in-law mentioned that people were looking at Señor Santa Claus in regard to the Delgado homicide."

"So Marliss's informant wasn't from inside your department after all."

"No, he wasn't," Joanna agreed.

"The thing you need to remember, Joey, is that Marliss Shackleford sealed her own fate the moment she stepped inside Stephen Roper's front door."

Joanna thought about that for a moment before responding. "Thank you for that," she said. "Maybe now I'll be able to sleep."

CHAPTER 45

BISBEE, ARIZONA
Saturday, December 9, 2023

JOANNA WAS SOUND ASLEEP SEVERAL HOURS LATER WHEN her cell phone jarred her awake at 4:15 a.m. Groaning, Butch turned over and pulled a pillow over his head, while Joanna, knowing this was work, padded into the bathroom and shut the door to take the call.

"Sheriff Brady," she said.

"Burt Peterson," the caller said. "Sorry to disturb you."

Burt was the graveyard jail supervisor.

"No problem," she said. "What's up?"

"Stephen Roper is raising all kinds of hell," Burt replied. "He's demanding to speak to you right now."

"In the middle of the night?" Joanna objected. "Can't this wait until morning?"

"He says not. He claims he's willing to give a full confession, but only to you, only if you bring his cigar box along—whatever that means, and only if it happens before his lawyer shows up in town sometime later on this morning."

"Why me?" Joanna asked. "Why not the detectives?"

"No idea," Burt said. "I'm just passing along what he said, but if he's willing to give you a confession, I thought you'd want to talk to him."

"You're absolutely right," Joanna replied. "I do. Put him in an interview room, cuff him to the table, and let him sit there and stew in his own juices until I get there. I'm on my way."

But she wasn't on her way, not really. Instead, she took her own sweet time, showering before getting dressed, blow-drying her hair, and doing her makeup. She was pretty sure this was going to be an adversarial situation, and she wanted to be at her best. When she finally left the bathroom, she was relieved to see that Butch had managed to fall back asleep.

Once at the department, it took a while for her to locate the contents of the cigar box. The evidence bags were no longer on display on the counter in the lab. Finally, after checking the entry log to the evidence room, Joanna realized Casey had loaded the cigar box and all its bagged contents into a banker's box and left it all stored in the evidence room, safely under lock and key.

With the banker's box in hand, she headed for the interview room, where the guard who had accompanied the prisoner from his cell stood waiting patiently just outside the door. Once she arrived, however, Joanna didn't immediately enter. Instead, she stood for several moments, peering into the room through the two-way mirror and sizing up her opponent.

It had been decades since she had encountered Stephen Roper up close and personal. He appeared to be a perfectly harmless, elderly gentleman. His narrow, angular face was even narrower than she remembered. He'd once had a full head of blondish hair. What little was left of that had turned white rather than silver, but his blue eyes were still as piercing as ever. Despite his currently difficult circumstances, however, Roper seemed totally at ease. He leaned back in his chair as far as his cuffed arm allowed and sat with his legs stretched out full length beneath the stainless steel table.

Finished with her examination, Joanna turned to the guard. "Is the video camera turned on?" she asked.

"Yes, ma'am," he replied. "I activated it as soon as I got him cuffed to the table, and I'll be here to let you out whenever you're ready to leave. All you have to do is knock on the door."

Once the door opened, Roper straightened into an upright posture, grinning as he did so. "Why lookie here," he said. "If it isn't little Joanna Lathrop, all grown up now and wearing a badge."

So that's how you want to play this, Joanna thought. *You're the teacher and I'm the lowly student? Not on your life! You're a damned serial killer, you asshole, and this isn't my first rodeo.*

"Hello to you, too, Mr. Roper," she said, setting the box down on the floor on her side of the table, well out of reach of his long legs. Then she took her own seat, one directly facing his.

"I understand you asked to see me."

"I did, but where's my cigar box?"

"The cigar box is right here," she said, nodding toward the banker's box, "and so's everything that was in it, which happens to be quite a haul. There's enough evidence in there to put you in prison for the remainder of your miserable life. But since you specifically asked to see me, and since you've already invoked your rights and hired an attorney, I'm going to have to read you the Miranda warning again, just to ascertain that you're willing to speak to me at this time without your attorney being present."

"I already told you . . ." Roper began.

"Sorry," she said. "Regardless of what you said, rules are rules. If you're willing to give me a confession, I want to be sure that it'll hold up in court. You have the right to remain silent . . ."

As she read through the familiar phrases, Roper recited them along with her from memory, as though they were doing a responsive reading in church.

"Satisfied?" he sneered when they finished.

"Completely," she said, "so how do you want to do this, and where do you want to start?"

"We could pretend we're playing strip poker," he suggested. "You know, you show me yours, and I'll show you mine."

"So I show you something from the box, and you tell me what happened?"

"I suppose," he said with an indifferent shrug. "You're the dealer. You call it."

"Chronological order then?" Joanna asked.

"I suppose."

Roper's casual responses led her to believe that he had no idea how much she knew, but thanks to the BOLO and Dan Hogan's phone call, she knew a hell of a lot more than he thought. She dug through the box until she located the bag that contained Lucille Hawkins's wedding band. Holding it in her hand, she considered what to do next. What she really wanted to do was put the ring down on the table just beyond Roper's reach so he wouldn't be able to touch it. But then she thought about why he'd collected all those trinkets in the first place. No doubt he'd done so in order to remember and savor each of those individual crimes. Maybe now that he was prepared to talk, allowing him to handle his treasured touchstones one last time might help him recall details that would otherwise be forgotten.

"How about we start with first things first?" she asked, putting the bag with the ring in it down on the table before deliberately pushing it over to him. She fully expected Roper to pick it up and study it. Instead, he drew away from it as if it were a coiled rattler. But when he raised his eyes to look at Joanna, she saw an expression on his face that she wasn't expecting—a look of complete astonishment. Lucille Hawkins's death had been declared an accident for close to seventy years. No one had ever hinted it might have been a murder, but his involuntary response to seeing it made her realize that he was dismayed to learn that someone as insignificant as Joanna Lathrop Brady had unearthed one of his most closely guarded secrets.

"Well?" Joanna prompted, as the silence between them lengthened. "You had her ring in the cigar box along with everything else, so are you going to tell me what happened to her or not?"

Another long pause followed before he answered. "She was a hateful bitch," he snarled at last. "She bossed me around every chance she got."

"She was also your grandmother," Joanna observed. "You were eleven years old and probably needed bossing."

"She wasn't my real grandmother," Roper retorted. "She was only my step-grandmother, and she treated me like shit."

"So you killed her?"

Roper's response was an unconcerned shrug.

"How?"

"She fell off the front steps," he answered. "It was an accident. I found her lying there and took her ring, then I called the cops."

Joanna picked up the evidence bag, tossed it into the banker's box, and then made as if to put the lid back on the box.

"Wait," Roper objected. "What are you doing?"

"I'm leaving."

"Why?"

"Because I came to hear a confession—a complete confession," Joanna told him. "I didn't show up at this ungodly hour of the morning to sit here and listen to a bunch of lies, so either tell me exactly how Lucille Hawkins fell off those steps, or I'm out of here."

"I tripped her," he said.

"How?"

"I strung some fishing line between the top posts of the banisters on the front steps, then I told her that a raccoon had gotten to her cat and she needed to come quick. She rushed out in such a hurry that she never saw the string. She tripped over it, and down she went, just like that." He slammed the palm of his free hand on the tabletop for emphasis.

"Didn't the string cut into her legs?" Joanna asked. "Why didn't the autopsy mention that?"

"She always wore boots, and not ladies' fashion boots, either, but clunky men's work boots. She stomped around town in those looking like a clown straight out of a circus. The other kids made fun of her and teased me about it."

"So you decided to murder her."

"I guess," he said.

Good enough, Joanna thought. *Confession number one.*

She paused long enough to consult her iPad and review the notes she'd made during her conversation with Dan Hogan. Then she dug through the evidence bags until she located the one containing Brian Olson's Cub Scout Wolf pin. Looking at that put a lump in Joanna's throat. Her own son, Dennis, had started out in Cubs and had earned a Wolf pin, too, although when he'd been old enough to join the Boy Scouts, he'd opted for 4-H instead.

"What about this?" Joanna asked, holding up the bag. "By my count, this should be number two."

This time she was gratified when Roper actually shifted uncomfortably in his chair before answering.

"It belonged to a kid," he said.

"Yes," she agreed, "a boy named Brian Olson who disappeared from the Polk County Fair in Fertile, Minnesota, your hometown, in 1961. You were sixteen years old at the time. His body was found a few days later in Arthur Lake. I don't know the actual location of the farm where you used to live, but I'm willing to bet it wasn't far from where Brian's body was found."

Joanna paused and waited. "So?" she prodded finally.

"So what?" Roper asked.

"Did you murder Brian Olson?"

"I guess," he answered.

"Did you or didn't you?"

"Did," he said. "I did it. I found out his name later because it was all over the news in Fertile, but I always called him Cotton Candy Boy. He had to take a leak and got separated from the people he was with. So I bought him some cotton candy and offered to take him to the sheriff's department so they could help him get home."

"Instead you drowned him."

Roper shrugged. "He didn't know how to swim."

Joanna was so filled with revulsion that she almost couldn't proceed with the interview, but quitting wasn't an option. This time when her hand emerged from the box, she was holding the knife.

"That little bitch," Roper muttered. "Who knew she had a switchblade hidden in her damned boot? She cut the hell out of my arm. Bled like crazy!"

"So when we test the dried blood found on the hinge inside the knife, is some of it going to come back to you?" Joanna asked.

"Probably," Roper said.

"Do you even know her name?"

"Who cares about her name? I called her Turtle River Girl, because that's where I left her," he said, "in the Turtle River."

"Unfortunately for you," Joanna said, "she wasn't quite in the river, but her name was Amanda Hudson and she came from Devil's Lake. She was twenty-one years old when you murdered her, but she's also the reason we're here today. When you shoved her head into the riverbank, you left your palm print on her glasses."

Once again Joanna was gratified to see that Stephen Roper seemed astonished.

"I always wore gloves," he blurted.

"Not that time," Joanna responded, "and not when you drink Diet Coke, either. Ever hear about Trash DNA? This time we're talking about a trash palm print, one we lifted from a soda can found in your trash. When we ran it through AFIS, it matched one found on Amanda's glasses. It had been sitting in AFIS for decades, just waiting to take you down."

"Crap!" Roper said.

And that's how it went, in a marathon that started at 5 a.m. and lasted for the next three and a half hours. When Joanna brought out Michael Young's evidence bag, Roper referred to him as Bandanna Boy. When she produced the one holding Inez Johnson's squash blossom necklace, Roper reflexively covered the back of his handcuffed hand with the free one.

"I called her Reservoir Girl," he said. "She bit me."

"Bit you?" Joanna echoed.

"Damn right, she bit the hell out of the back of my hand," he said. "The scar's still there."

Joanna wanted to say, *Good for her,* but not wanting to break the flow she refrained.

Roper acknowledged that the earrings and bits of jewelry and the class rings, too, most likely belonged to prostitutes, but he couldn't recall where they were from or when he'd killed them. He also allowed as how the X's in the margins of the *Rand McNally* highway map in one of the bags belonged to unnamed prostitutes, ones who weren't wearing jewelry. Ditto for the bags containing individual shoelaces. He acknowledged those belonged to kids and most of them elicited zero reaction, but not the last one.

"And this," she said, laying out the one she suspected was from the most recent killing in front of him, "is no doubt the one missing from Xavier Delgado's high-topped sneaker. It looks like the end of the shoelace has been dipped in ink. How come?"

"So I could tell the boys from the girls," Roper replied with an indifferent shrug. "Boys' laces got dipped. Girls' didn't."

"But he's where you screwed up, isn't he?"

Roper said nothing.

"I have to give you credit," Joanna allowed. "There are several reasons you got away with this for so long. For starters, no one believed that an eleven-year-old was capable of murder when you killed Lucille Hawkins. And leaving your victims in water of some kind usually took care of most physical evidence. So did wearing gloves. With the sole exception of the palm print in North Dakota, you usually left nothing behind.

"In addition your victims were almost always unknown to you. Stranger-on-stranger homicides are the most difficult ones to solve. The problem is, you knew Xavier Delgado, if not by name, at least by sight. And here's the proof—the missing shoelace from Xavier's high-topped sneakers, the very ones the kids from the migrant camp said he was admiring the last time they saw him."

"All right," he agreed sullenly. "The voices got to me."

"Excuse me?" Joanna asked.

"You know, the voices inside my head. They were screaming for blood and I gave in and let them have it. I never should have."

"Voices?" Joanna repeated.

"That's what I said, isn't it?" Roper asked irritably.

"Are the voices the reason you were shopping for an attorney who specializes in insanity pleas?"

"Probably."

"So why are you confessing to me, then?" she asked.

"Because I didn't want to go through all that hoopla. I'm a private kind of person."

"Is that why you killed Marliss Shackleford? Was she intruding on your privacy?"

"She's the one who let me know you were on to me," he admitted finally. "With her out of the way, I thought I might still be able to get away."

"Well," Joanna remarked as she began gathering the evidence bags and loading them back into the box. "You were certainly wrong about that, so what are you planning on telling your attorney when he gets here?"

"What do you think I'm going to tell him?" Roper snarled. "I'm going to say, 'You're fired.'"

CHAPTER 46

BISBEE, ARIZONA
Saturday, December 9, 2023

WHEN JOANNA LEFT THE INTERVIEW ROOM, SHE WANTED nothing more than to go home and take a shower. After spending three and a half hours locked in a room reeking of evil personified, she felt completely depleted. She was stunned by the callous disregard Stephen Roper had exhibited toward his victims. His chilling lack of empathy combined with his mentioning having voices inside his head might be indicative of mental illness of some kind, but as far as she was concerned, even if Stephen Roper was crazy as a bedbug, that didn't give him a get-out-of-jail-free card, not on her watch.

It wasn't yet nine o'clock in the morning, but she felt exhausted. She was tempted to go home and crawl back into bed, but that wasn't an option. Instead she returned the banker's box to its proper location in the evidence room and headed for her office.

Since it was Saturday, the place was relatively deserted. Feeling the need to get away from Roper's all-encompassing darkness, she walked past Kristin's empty desk and through her own office without even pausing. Letting herself out through her private entrance, she spent the next half hour pacing the parking lot under a bright blue sky while breathing in the brisk December air. Eventually she began to feel better.

Listening to the gut-wrenching confession had cleared six homicides, including one that had never been regarded as a homicide in the first place. But all those other evidence bags in the banker's box meant that there was still more work to do—starting with that stack of as-yet-unreturned calls. Rolling up her mental shirtsleeves, she prepared to make that first phone call, but one from Butch came in first.

"Where'd you go at o-dark-thirty?" he asked. "Who's dead?"

That was what middle-of-the-night phone calls usually meant in Joanna's life—a homicide had most likely occurred or maybe a serious-injury automobile accident.

"Roper was demanding to see me because he wanted to confess."

"Confess?" Butch repeated. "I thought you said he had an attorney coming."

"He did and probably still does, but he changed his mind about talking. It was a three-and-a-half-hour ordeal of sitting with someone who, to my way of thinking, is the devil himself. He talked about murdering people as casually as you might mention running into someone at the store, and he did so without a shred of remorse. I've met a few killers in my time, but Stephen Roper is an absolute monster."

"Are you okay?"

"I am now. Well, better, maybe. I took myself outside for a walk. Now I'm back in the office. By my count, that meeting with him cleared six cases, but there are still more unsolved ones than there are solved."

"So you'll be working today?"

"Seems like."

"Me, too," he said.

Off the phone, Joanna reached for the stack of messages. The topmost one was from Robert Moody, the sheriff of Elko County, Nevada. He had given Kristin both a work number and a cell phone number. Since this was Saturday, Joanna tried that one first.

"Sheriff Moody," he answered.

"This is Sheriff Joanna Brady returning your call. I'm sorry I couldn't get back to you sooner," she added, "but yesterday was a pretty hectic day around here."

"No problem," Moody said. "That happens. About your BOLO, though. We've got a cold case from 1981 that fits your criteria—manual strangulation, no sign of sexual assault, disposal in a body of water, and something missing from the deceased."

"Tell me," Joanna urged.

"Name was Janice Jensen. Her daddy, Arthur Jensen, was sheriff at the time she disappeared. She was eighteen years old. She had just graduated from high school and was working nights at the bowling alley here in town before heading off to the University of Nevada in Las Vegas in the fall. The family lived on a ranch a ways out of town. When her parents woke up in the morning and discovered she hadn't come home, they went looking. Found her car broken down on the highway a couple miles from home. There was no sign of a struggle in the car. She just vanished. A week later her body was found dumped in a dry creek bed about thirty miles from here."

"You seem to know a lot about it," Joanna observed. "Were you part of the original investigation?"

"Me?" Sheriff Moody replied with a laugh. "Hell no, I was only in kindergarten at the time, but since her daddy was sheriff, you'd better believe this case is still open. When your BOLO came through, our cold case guy was all over it. We both spent all day yesterday reading through the file."

"So what was missing?"

"A class ring—not hers, her boyfriend's. Janice and Kenneth Norris were high school sweethearts and had been going steady for years. They wore each other's rings on chains around their necks sort of as promise rings. Kenny was questioned at the time, but he was going to summer school in Vegas, so he had an airtight alibi and was immediately ruled out. No other suspects were ever identified. We have three other unsolved homicides on the books, but, because of her daddy, Janice's is the one that hurts the most."

Joanna thought about the collection of class rings she'd seen earlier in the banker's box, but she didn't want to say anything out of line that might raise unwarranted hopes.

"Excuse me, Sheriff Moody," Joanna said. "Something's just come up. Can I call you back?"

"Sure."

Joanna made tracks back to the evidence room and rifled through the banker's box until she located the rings. Three of them were small and most likely belonged to girls, but one was much larger. Joanna tried peering at it through the intervening plastic. She could make out that there were letters engraved in gold mounted in the middle of a square-shaped blue stone. More letters were engraved on either side of the stone but it was impossible to decipher any of them. Finally, Joanna resorted to using the flashlight on her iPhone to make them more readable. The letters EHS were the ones in the center of the stone. As for the others? The one on the left was a K, and the one on the right was an N.

Joanna was still in the evidence room holding the bag when she called Sheriff Moody back.

"Hello again," he said.

"I'm standing in our evidence room here in Bisbee, Arizona, and I'm holding what I believe to be Kenneth Norris's class ring in my hand. The letters EHS are on the middle of the stone, and the initials K and N are on either side of the stone."

"You're frigging kidding me!" Moody exclaimed.

"I'm not," Joanna told him. "We've arrested a man named Stephen Roper, someone we believe to be a prolific serial killer. Yesterday, when we took him into custody, we found what's apparently his trophy case. The ring I'm holding in my hand is one of four class rings found in his collection."

"Who is this guy?" Moody asked.

"Someone who's lived here in town for decades. He taught during the school year while spending the summers prowling the country for potential victims. What time of year did Janice Jensen die?"

"June 16, 1981."

"So that would fit our guy's time frame."

"And he was a schoolteacher?" Moody confirmed.

"Believe it or not, I was in his English class my senior year in high school."

"Ouch," Moody said, "but you're sure it's him?"

"Early this morning he gave me a full confession to six different homicides in five different locations. He's being held in my jail, but he won't be officially charged until Monday. I can promise you this, though, with that many cases pending, he's not going to be released on bond any time soon."

"So I can go tell Ida?"

"Who's Ida?"

"Janice's mother. Her father passed away ten years ago. Ida lives in an assisted living facility right here in town, but she calls our department every year on June sixteenth to ask if we have any leads. She's going to be overjoyed, and so will Kenny, Janice's boyfriend. Once he graduated from school, he came back home and established a law practice here. He's married and has a couple of kids, but I know from talking to Ida that he still stays in touch with her. Can I give them your number?"

"Of course," Joanna said. "They're welcome to call me, but I probably won't have anything more to add to what you already know until sometime next week."

"Sheriff Brady?" Joanna heard her name being broadcast over the intercom. "Please report to the front lobby."

"Sorry, I have to go now," Joanna told Moody.

"I'm sure you do," he replied, "but believe me, Sheriff Brady, you have our community's heartfelt gratitude."

Being able to finally supply answers to a mother who had been grieving the loss of her child for more than forty years put a bit of a spring back in Joanna's step as she left the evidence room and headed for the lobby. Since it wasn't open to the public on weekends, Joanna was surprised to be summoned there. As soon as she stepped through the door, she saw a guy wearing a suit that had probably set him back several thousand dollars. He was staring at the photo of the little girl with her wagonload of Girl Scout cookies. She knew immediately he had to be Stephen Roper's once-and-now-most-likely-former attorney, Ralph Whitmer.

"Good morning," she said. "I'm Sheriff Brady. May I help you?"

"Is that you?" he asked, jerking his head in the direction of the photograph.

"A long time ago," she answered.

"Did it ever occur to you that, if you were planning on becoming a sheriff, maybe you should have been studying up on the United States Constitution as opposed to hawking Girl Scout cookies?"

Joanna bristled at his condescension, but she kept her voice steady. "By that I'm assuming you're referring to a person's right to remain silent and to have an attorney present during the course of police questioning?"

"Exactly."

"I'm well aware of both of those, Mr. Whitmer," she said. "Now, if you'll be so kind as to join me in my office, there's something I'd like you to see." She led him into her office and asked him to be seated in one of the visitors' chairs on the far side of her desk.

Body cams had been a long time coming to her department, but once they were there, Joanna had made it her business to learn how to access individual files so she'd be able to play them back and make her own assessment about whatever had gone on. When someone was threatening a lawsuit claiming police brutality, it was really helpful to be able to know for certain if the accusation had any merit.

She had no difficulty locating Burt Peterson's footage from the night before and queuing it up to a 4:30 a.m. time frame. She found the point where Burt's motion-activated camera came online as he left the jail's administration office. At that point, she turned her desktop's monitor around so it faced the other way. By the time she was seated next to Whitmer, Burt's body cam indicated he was walking down a corridor with barred cells on either side. In the background someone could be heard yelling indecipherable words and banging on the bars of a cell.

"What are you showing me?" Whitmer asked, although the answer should have been obvious.

"This is footage taken in my jail early this morning. Just be patient."

Burt came to a stop in front of a particular cell. "What seems to be the problem, Mr. Roper?" he asked.

At that point the banging and yelling ceased. "I already told you. I want to see Sheriff Brady, and I want to see her now."

"Sheriff Brady isn't here at the moment. When she comes in, I'll be sure to let her know that you're anxious to speak to her."

"Anxious, my ass!" Roper exclaimed. "You get that bitch on the phone and tell her that I'm willing to give her a full confession right now, but only to her, only if she brings my cigar box, and only if it happens before my asshole attorney shows up in town later today."

"All right," Burt said. "Let me see what I can do."

Joanna turned to Whitmer. "Does that sound like a forced confession to you?" she asked.

Whitmer said nothing, so Joanna rose from her chair and returned to her keyboard on the far side of her desk. "If you'd like, I can also access the footage of my interview with him during which he confessed to six different homicides. Where, as you'll be able to see, I begin by repeating his Miranda warning. Would you like me to start there?"

"Screw it!" Whitmer muttered, rising to his feet. "I'm done here."

"Yes, you certainly are," Joanna agreed with a smile. "I trust you can find your way out."

CHAPTER 47

BISBEE, ARIZONA
Saturday, December 9, 2023

SETTLED AT HER DESK, JOANNA WAS REACHING FOR HER phone to call Anna Rae Green when it rang. "Sheriff Brady," she answered.

"Craig Witherspoon here. I hear you've been busy, and apparently you didn't need that arrest warrant. I understand Stephen Roper is in custody, so if I'm going to be in court for an arraignment hearing bright and early on Monday morning, I'm going to need to do some catching up, and not just on the cases here in Cochise County. I'll need some insight into all those other cases as well."

"You're right," Joanna said. "A lot has happened, and some of those other cases aren't just suspected. They may not yet be proved, but they're confirmed."

"What do you mean 'confirmed'?" Craig asked.

She quickly brought him up-to-date as far as Roper's confession was concerned as well as the fact that he had most likely fired his defense attorney.

"All right," Craig said when she finished. "I'm going to need to talk to all your investigators to see where we are. After that, I intend to watch every minute of that interview."

"How soon will you be here," Joanna asked.

"Twenty minutes to half an hour."

"Okay, I'll put everybody on notice."

As she set down the phone, Joanna heard Tom Hadlock's voice, coming from the office next to hers. She went to his door and poked her head inside, waiting while he finished a phone call. Clearly he was finalizing arrangements for shipping the next batch of jail inmates to Saguaro Hills. With everything else going on, that detail had completely slipped her mind.

"When do they leave?" she asked when Tom ended the call.

"Bright and early Monday morning," he said. "I was making sure we've got the Chain Gang in place. How are things with you?"

"You mean other than the fact Stephen Roper called me in and gave me a full confession earlier this morning?"

"Really?" Tom asked with a frown. "I thought he lawyered up."

"So did I," Joanna replied, "but he evidently changed his mind. So here's what I need. The county attorney is on his way. He wants to touch bases with all the investigators, then he'll view the interview. Is everybody here?"

"Yes, ma'am," Tom replied, "all present and accounted for and with their noses to the grindstone."

"Tell them I want everyone in the conference room half an hour from now, ready to give the county attorney a complete briefing on our progress."

"Will do," Tom said.

With that, Joanna went back to her office and dialed Anna Rae Green's home number.

"Hey," she said. "What's going on?"

"A lot," Joanna told her. "Roper's in custody."

"Thank God," Anna Rae murmured. "On the arrest warrant from North Dakota? Philip Dark Moon told me they were sending it."

"I know it's here, but we didn't actually need it," Joanna said. "Stephen Roper is locked up on suspicion of committing two separate homicides, including our original one, the little kid from Mexico."

"Who's number two?" Anna Rae asked.

"A local reporter made the mistake of stopping by his place to ask if he was aware that he was under investigation. While attempting to flee, he shoved her through a trapdoor into his crawl space and broke her neck."

"Yikes," Anna Rae said.

"But that's not why I'm calling. Roper raised all kinds of hell last night, demanding that I come in so he could give me a complete confession."

"And did he?"

"He certainly did—for the next three and a half hours. In the process he cleared six separate cases, three of which happen to be MMIV-related."

Joanna went on to give Anna Rae a detailed description of what had gone on.

"Do you think he was deliberately targeting Indigenous victims," Anna Rae asked when Joanna finished, "or were they simply crimes of opportunity?"

"It's too soon to tell," Joanna replied. "From the number of items we found in what we believe to be his trophy case, those six cases barely scratch the surface. We're going to need to identify a lot more victims. We might even consider sending out a second BOLO."

"All right," Anna Rae said. "I'll let Philip and Nadia know what's going on. Does someone need to call Luke Running Deer?"

"Nope," Joanna answered. "I already let him know."

Off the phone, she sat there and considered her next step. With Craig due in a little over twenty minutes, she decided there was probably enough time for her to make one more phone call. Having made that decision, she reached for her stack of missed-call messages.

She plucked the topmost message off the pile—Sheriff Augie Nesbitt, Lauderdale County, Tennessee. The only number listed was for work. Since it was Saturday, Joanna wasn't at all surprised when it was answered by voicemail, but she didn't bother leaving a message. Searching the department's website, she finally located a non-emergency number that was answered by a human being.

"I'm Sheriff Joanna Brady from Bisbee, Arizona," she announced. "Yesterday Sheriff Nesbitt responded to a BOLO we sent out concerning a serial killer. I just tried calling him, but since it's Saturday, he's not answering. Can you help me?"

"I can't give out his number," came the reply, "but if you'll give me yours, I'll pass it along."

Joanna's first instinct was to immediately dial the next number, but she decided to give it five minutes. In case Nesbitt did call back, she didn't want to have to hang up on someone else in order to take his call, and that strategy paid off. Nesbitt called back in three minutes flat.

"Sheriff Brady?" he asked. "Nesbitt here. What's going on?"

"We have a suspected serial killer in custody in our jail."

"The guy from the BOLO?"

"Yes," Joanna said. "So do you have a case that might match up?"

"We do," Nesbitt said, "but it's from so long ago that I doubt there's a connection."

"Humor me," Joanna said. "Tell me about it."

"Happened right here in Ripley back in 1986. A seven-year-old Black kid named Jimmy Gibson disappeared from the Tomato Festival."

"What time of year?" Joanna asked.

"Summer—July 13, 1986," he answered. "I don't know that off the top of my head. I pulled the file and went through it."

Crimes committed in the summer, Joanna thought. *That's another commonality.*

"What happened?" she asked aloud.

"Jimmy's mother, Gail, was a recently divorced single mom. She came to the festival to perform with a gospel choir. She left Jimmy sitting alone in the audience and told him to stay there, but when the performance was over, he was gone. Days later his body washed up on the banks of Forked Deer Island in the Mississippi. The body was so decomposed it had to be identified by dental records. He'd had his first-ever cavity filled only the week before."

"Gail immediately pointed the finger at her ex-husband, John. The two of them were involved in a fierce custody battle. He was really the only suspect, and he didn't have an alibi. According to him, he was home alone, watching TV. But there was no physical evidence to tie him to the scene. He was never arrested or charged, but as far as the town was concerned, he did it. When he committed suicide five years ago, that pretty much clinched his guilt as far as public opinion was concerned."

"What was missing?" Joanna asked.

"Gail was First Baptist all the way, and Jimmy had just attended Daily Vacation Bible School. All the kids who had perfect attendance at that got a cross."

Joanna's heart skipped a beat. "A glow-in-the-dark cross by any chance?"

"How the hell did you know that?" Nesbitt demanded.

"Because I've got one of those in an evidence bag here at my office right this minute," Joanna answered. "Jimmy Gibson's father didn't kill him."

"Who did?"

"The guy in my jail," Joanna told him. "His name is Stephen Roper. Last night he confessed to six murders. This morning I confirmed one more. Jimmy Gibson makes eight."

"Poor Gail," Nesbitt said. "She's remarried, but she still lives here in town. As soon as we get off the phone, I'll go tell her. She'll be relieved to finally have some answers, but it'll be hard on her to have to reopen this can of worms. Can't help but feel sorry for the poor woman."

The call ended. Sitting there alone in her office, Joanna felt sorry for Gail Gibson, too, but she felt even sorrier for Jimmy's dad. After years of being hounded and blamed for something he hadn't done, the man had eventually committed suicide. But in Joanna's heart, although Stephen Roper would never be charged in John Gibson's death, she knew without a doubt that he was responsible.

CHAPTER 48

BISBEE, ARIZONA
Saturday, December 9, 2023

WHEN JOANNA WALKED INTO THE CONFERENCE ROOM AT ten a.m. sharp, she found a full house. Everyone was already assembled, including Craig Witherspoon. Joanna caught Deb's eye. "Autopsy done?" she asked.

Deb nodded.

"Okay," Joanna said. "Good to know." Then she turned to the group. "Good morning, everybody. Thanks for being here. I have a feeling this is going to be another long day. The county attorney is here today to be updated on the progress of our investigation in preparation for Stephen Roper's charging hearing on Monday morning.

"First and foremost, I want to thank you all for the hard work you've done so far, and it's paying off. Last night, Mr. Roper changed his mind about lawyering up and summoned me to the jail where he gave me a full confession to six separate homicides. Due to Casey's hard work on examining items in what we consider to be the killer's trophy case—we have physical evidence to back up every one of those. As of this morning, I've been able to connect two more unsolved homicides to Mr. Roper, again due to contents of his trophy collection combined with the BOLO we sent out two days ago. But based on the number of items in our evidence room, there are a lot more unidentified victims out there, and it's our job to find them.

"But first things first," she added. "Detective Howell, what can you tell us about Marliss Shackleford's autopsy?"

It turns out that Kendra Baldwin had confirmed Dr. Ybarra's initial assessment of the situation. When the EMTs had attempted to move Marliss away from the foot of the ladder, pieces of shattered vertebrae had shifted in her upper neck and pierced her medulla oblongata, resulting in an inability to breathe. In addition, Deb reported that she and Garth were in the process of creating search warrant requests to examine Roper's electronic devices along with his banking records. They were also requesting warrants to examine Marliss Shackleford's electronic devices.

Dave Hollicker reported that his crime scene examination of Roper's residence had turned up a glass jar on a kitchen counter that contained remnants of chloroform. He had also located a chloroform-soaked dish towel in the plastic bag lining the killer's kitchen garbage can.

"He may have been intent on getting away," Joanna commented, "but at that point he was no longer making any effort to cover his tracks." Then she turned to Casey.

"What about you?"

Casey Ledford reported that, by the time she'd finished untangling all the shoelaces, she had fifteen in all—six of them dipped in blue ink.

"Roper explained that when I spoke to him last night," Joanna said. "Blue ink indicates the victim was a boy. The ones without ink are girls, so six and nine, respectively. How many evidence bags in all?"

"Seventy-six," Casey answered.

"And did you happen to count the number of X's on that *Rand McNally* road map?"

"I did," Casey said. "There are twenty-three. Why?"

"Mr. Roper indicated to me that each X was for a prostitute who didn't have a suitable trophy item available."

"Twenty-three plus seventy-six?" Craig demanded, speaking aloud for the first time. "That makes a total of ninety-nine victims. Are you kidding me?"

"And Marliss Shackleford makes an even one hundred," Joanna put in. "As I said, we still have a lot of unidentified victims."

"I've got a lead on some of them," Casey said, "the four class rings. Last night when I was looking online at a class ring manufacturer, I stumbled across a Facebook page that uses crowdsourcing techniques to reunite lost-and-found class rings with their original owners. I went ahead and joined the group, saying that I had four class rings that might or might not be connected to a serial killer, and they expressed a real interest in helping."

"The owner of one of those rings was already identified this morning, by Sheriff Moody of the Elko County Sheriff's Department."

"Which one?" Casey asked.

"The one with the initials EHS engraved on it. EHS stands for Elko High School in Elko, Nevada. The ring was owned by a kid named Kenneth Norris, but he wasn't wearing it at the time it disappeared. His eighteen-year-old girlfriend, Janice Jensen, was. She disappeared on her way home from a nighttime bowling alley job on June 16, 1981. Her father was the sheriff of Elko County at the time of his daughter's death. He's now deceased, but Janice's mother is still alive, and once Sheriff Moody got off the phone with me, he was heading out to let her know that, after forty-plus years, her daughter's killer has most likely finally been identified and taken into custody.

"So that's where we are, folks. We've identified nine of what appears to be at least a hundred different victims. I still have a few original BOLO callbacks to make. Anyone else have any of those?"

Deb raised her hand. "Garth and I have a couple."

"Give them to me, and I'll make myself useful by handling those. The rest of you have plenty of work to do, but for now my major focus—and I want it to be yours, too—is to bring answers to ninety-something still-grieving families."

"Should we send out a second BOLO?" Deb suggested.

"Maybe," Joanna replied, "but first try crowdsourcing those class rings. They've all been swabbed for prints and DNA, right?"

Casey nodded. "I swabbed each item before putting it in a bag."

"Who's our best photographer?" Joanna asked.

Dave Hollicker raised his hand. "I am," he said.

"All right. Start by photographing the other class rings so Casey can send those out to her crowdsourcing crew. Come to think of it, take individual photos of each separate piece of evidence. Maybe we can include those in our BOLO as well. So back to the salt mines, people. Let's solve ourselves a whole bunch of unsolved homicides."

CHAPTER 49

BISBEE, ARIZONA
Saturday, December 9, 2023

LEAVING THE CONFERENCE ROOM, JOANNA HEADED BACK to her office, weary to the bone. When her phone rang with a call from Dispatch, her first thought was, *Oh, no. What now?*

"Sheriff Brady," she answered. "What's up?"

"I've got someone on the line named June Martin," Tica explained. "She called in on our 911 line asking to speak to you. She's a cold case detective with Seattle PD, calling with regard to your BOLO."

Joanna went on full alert. "Put her through," she said.

"I've been off work all week with a family emergency," June explained, "so I didn't see the BOLO until today, but I may have a match for you. Lisa Daniels, age seven, disappeared from Seattle's SeaFair Hydro Races in August of 1983. Her mother, Josie, was . . . let's just say a bit of a wild thing. The father was never in the picture. Josie was attending the races with a new boyfriend when she lost track of her daughter. The girl was found hours later floating face down in Lake Washington. Initially she was thought to be a drowning victim, but an autopsy revealed her cause of death to be asphyxia due to manual strangulation."

"What was missing?" Joanna asked.

"That's what was so odd," Detective Martin said. "She was found fully clothed, including both shoes, but one shoelace was missing."

For Joanna Brady another piece of the puzzle snapped into place. Roper had used summer festivals or crowded activities of some kind—times when the parents might be preoccupied with something else—to snatch their children.

"I checked," Detective Martin said. "Cochise County is in Arizona, and that's a long way from Seattle. Do you have a possible connection?"

Knowing another of Stephen Roper's white shoelaces now had a name, Joanna told the whole story.

"In other words, you have the guy in custody," Detective Martin said, "but there's no way to prove it."

"There might be," Joanna said. "Let me call you back."

Leaving her desk, Joanna made her way to the jail where she asked for Stephen Roper to be brought to an interview room.

"Is this round two?" he asked once he was seated and cuffed to the table.

"Maybe," she said. Once again, she read him his Miranda warning.

"Do we have to go through this every single time?"

"Yes, we do," Joanna replied.

"What do you want to know now?"

"Did you ever snatch a little girl from the SeaFair Hydro Races in Seattle?"

"Sure," he said. "That was sometime in the eighties. I called her Hydro Girl."

Just like that, a second shoelace in the collection of Stephen Roper evidence bags had a name.

Joanna then proceeded to have Roper identify the Elko High School class ring taken from Janice Jensen and Jimmy Gibson's glow-in-the-dark cross. As she was on her way out of the interview room, she turned back to Roper and said, "By the way. I ran into your so-called attorney. He was an arrogant asshole."

"I noticed," Roper replied. "He gave me all kinds of hell for talking to you, and when I told him he was fired, I thought he'd blow a gasket. He told me he'd be billing me for the cost of his private jet flight from LA to Sierra Vista. I told him good luck with that. He said he'd see me in court. I was still laughing when he walked out the door."

Back in her office, Joanna called Detective Martin back to give her the news.

Detective Martin was astonished. "He admitted to it just like that?"

"Just like that," Joanna repeated. "He promised me a full confession, and it seems as though he's a man of his word as far as that is concerned. Is Lisa's mother still alive?"

"No," Detective Martin replied. "She died of a drug overdose in 1985, two years after Lisa's death. Josie's mother, Darlene, used to call periodically to ask if anything was happening on the case. The last call from her that's noted in the file was in 2019. By then she was getting up there. I wouldn't be surprised if Covid got her. But I'll check to see if there are any other relatives."

"Thank you," Joanna said.

Her next returned call was to Gunnar Hanson, the chief of police in Cannon Beach, Oregon. He wasn't in, either, but in Cannon Beach, once Joanna explained who she was and why she was calling, whoever answered the phone was happy to pass along the chief's cell phone number.

When she called him, he immediately explained, "We're a small jurisdiction, with only one unsolved homicide on our books. As soon as I saw your BOLO, I wondered if maybe there was a connection, so I dug up the file just in case. Calvin Dobbs, from Beaverton, was nine years old in 1982 when he snuck out of his Cannon Beach hotel room while his parents were taking a nap. When they woke up and found him gone, the only other thing that was missing was his brand-new Star Wars kite. Later that day, his wrecked kite was found in a dumpster close to the beach. We still have the kite stored in our evidence locker. As for Calvin's body? It was found a few miles south of here two days later. His death was ruled a homicide—

manual strangulation. So that all jibes with your BOLO. The problem is, you said something should be missing, and as far as we could tell, everything was there."

"Tell me about the kite," Joanna said.

"I took a look at it at the same time I retrieved the file," Chief Hanson said. "It featured a picture of Yoda and had a bright yellow tail."

Remembering the piece of yellow plastic ribbon in the evidence bag, Joanna said, "Can I call you back?"

"Sure."

For the third time that day, she headed for the interview room. Stephen Roper was already seated when she got there.

"Another Miranda warning, I suppose?" he asked.

"Yes, indeed," she told him.

"What is it this time?" he asked when she finished.

"Cannon Beach, Oregon," Joanna said. It was a statement, not a question.

"Oh, right," Roper said. "I remember now, Kite Boy. I had forgotten about him. How are you doing this, by the way?"

"By tracing your trophies," she said. "By looking for unsolved homicides where items are missing."

Roper considered that for a moment and then shook his head. "Pretty smart," he said. "Maybe I should have given you an A, after all, instead of that B+."

"Maybe you should have," Joanna agreed.

She hurried back to her office and called Hanson back. "I just spoke to Stephen Roper, the man we currently have in custody and who's already confessed to being a serial killer. All I had to do was mention Cannon Beach, and he remembered Calvin. Called him Kite Boy, but it turns out you're wrong. There was something missing. We have a piece of bright yellow plastic ribbon inside one of our evidence bags. I'm betting if we run it through a spectrometer, it'll match up to the ribbon on the tail of that kite."

"I can't believe you've solved it after all this time," Hanson murmured.

"I can't, either," Joanna agreed. "Are you still in touch with his parents?"

"There's nothing here in the file," he answered, "but I'll do my best to track them down."

"Thank you," she said. "Please do."

CHAPTER 50

BISBEE, ARIZONA
Saturday, December 9, 2023

JOANNA BRADY HAD ALWAYS BEEN A THREE-MEAL-A-DAY-type girl. It was now after three p.m. She had been at work since five in the morning without so much as a cup of coffee or a bite of food. She had a terrible headache, probably due to caffeine deprivation, and she was beyond exhausted. Yes, four more homicide victims had been identified, and she called both the lab and the bullpen to pass along those bits of good news, but by then she was done.

Going to Tom Hadlock's office, she tapped on his doorframe. "Sorry to be a party pooper," she said, "but I've got to go home."

"Don't blame you a bit," Tom said. "And, if you'll pardon my saying so, you look like hell."

"Gee, thanks," she said, but that little exchange actually made her smile. There was a time not too long ago when Tom would never have cracked a joke in her presence, to say nothing of saying one to her face.

She was in her Interceptor and on the highway for her ten-minute commute back to the High Lonesome when her cell phone rang. Her first instinct was to ignore it, but then she saw Anna Rae Green was the caller.

"We've identified four more victims," Joanna said into the phone without bothering to say hello. "Not only did we identify them, so did Stephen Roper. The BOLO is working. I think we need to send out another."

"I don't," Anna Rae replied.

Joanna was taken aback. The results from the first one had been nothing short of astounding. "Why not?" she asked finally.

"You don't need a BOLO. You need a press conference."

Joanna thought about one of the recent press conferences she'd held, specifically the one with only two attendees, one of whom had been Marliss Shackleford.

"I don't see how that's going to help," she said.

"How many people are in your press distribution list?" Anna Rae asked.

"Thirty total, maybe," Joanna said. "It's mostly locals, but it includes news outlets in Tucson and Phoenix, although Phoenix hardly ever shows. Why?"

"You need a BIG press conference," Anna Rae insisted. "You have victims from all over the country, and you need to attract reporters from all over the country. You write up the release, and I'll send it to our distribution list. Believe me, that's national and it includes every network known to man, including Telemundo."

"But what do I say?" Joanna asked.

"Some of Stephen Roper's treasures were his victims' treasures too. Those missing items might not mean anything to the cops involved, but they'll mean something to grieving families if they ever have a chance to hear about them. And what about the commonalities?" Anna Rae asked. "Manual strangulation, no sexual assault, fully clothed, disposed of in bodies of water, and something missing. Anything else?"

"Yes," Joanna said. "I've identified more since I talked to you. Roper went hunting for victims during the summers, so a summer timeline is important. Also, he liked to target special occasions—

festivals, fairs, that kind of thing—in small jurisdictions with limited law enforcement capability."

"Okay," Anna Rae said. "As I said, write it up. If you hit a wall, you've got a husband who's a writer. Get him to help you. Let people know that Roper has murdered people all over the country, and see what happens. Cops care, yes, but families care more. Send it to me tonight if possible, so I can get it out first thing in the morning. Mention that the charging hearing will be on Monday, correct?"

"Correct," Joanna agreed.

"Then set the press conference for late in the afternoon," Anna Rae added. "That'll give people from the East Coast a chance to get there."

"How many people do you think will show?"

"Several hundred, unless I miss my guess," Anna Rae said. "So be sure you have a venue that's big enough."

Joanna thought about possible venues in town. The high school auditorium would probably work, but given the fact that Roper had taught at the high school for decades, asking to use it didn't seem feasible.

"We'll probably use the parking lot at my department," she said after thinking it over.

"In December?" Anna Rae asked.

Joanna laughed. "December in Arizona is a lot different from December in Denver, but about that press release. One of my CSIs is taking photos of all Roper's trophies. Should I include those?"

"Nope," Anna Rae replied. "Make it short and sweet. Mention that photos will be available upon request at the press conference. That should up the attendance."

By then Joanna was already turning onto High Lonesome Road. At the house, the kids were nowhere to be seen, and the door to Butch's den was closed. Knowing he was working, Joanna let him be. Instead she made a pot of coffee, dished up a bowl of Cheerios, and then settled into the breakfast nook with her laptop at the ready.

Writing a press release was a lot like writing an essay, and the last time she'd been assigned to do one of those had been in Stephen Roper's class all those years ago. She seemed to remember that he'd given her a C+ on that one. *This one,* she decided, *is going to be an A+.*

On Monday, December 11, 2023, a suspect in two separate homicides will be arraigned in Cochise County's Superior Court. While investigating those crimes, detectives from the Cochise County Sheriff's Department found evidence suggesting that the suspect in question is most likely a prolific serial killer.

Starting in the fifties this individual left a trail of slaughtered victims, many of them children, all over the country—in Washington, Oregon, Arizona, New Mexico, Nevada, North Dakota, Missouri, Minnesota, and Tennessee.

Homicide investigators are in possession of a trophy box that indicates he may be responsible for close to a hundred murders. Only a few have been resolved. The grieving loved ones of the others need answers.

We are asking for jurisdictions from all over the country to open their cold case files and search for crimes with these commonalities: a summer time frame; a victim who vanished from crowds during a festival or celebration of some kind—a county fair or community event; cause of death was manual strangulation; the body showed no signs of sexual assault; remains were found fully clothed and dumped in a body of water; and finally something belonging to the victim was missing from the remains.

Right now, the key to solving many of those long-unsolved crimes may depend on items that were found in our suspect's trophy case. We've already gained clarity on several cases by connecting trophy case items to the deceased. We expect to have the remaining items available and on display in time for our press conference, which will be held on Monday afternoon, December 11, 2023, at 4:30 p.m. The address is 205 N. Judd Drive Mile Post 345, Highway 80, Bisbee, AZ 85603.

If you are unable to attend but have any questions, please feel free to contact me or my department.

Joanna was reading back through it when Butch emerged from his den, empty coffee cup in hand. "I didn't know you were here," he said. "When did you get home, and what are you doing?"

"A writing assignment," she answered. "Anna Rae thinks we need to do a press conference, and I'm working on the press release. Want to take a look?"

Butch scanned through it. "Not exactly Ernest Hemingway, but it'll do," he said. "Still, the BOLO is working, isn't it?"

Joanna nodded. "From items in Roper's trophy case, we've cleared several—two in Minnesota, and others in North Dakota, Washington, Oregon, Nevada, New Mexico, Arizona, Missouri, and Tennessee," she said, counting off on her fingers. "He has verified them all, including his deceased step-grandmother."

"Why switch from a BOLO to a press conference?"

"Because BOLOs usually only go to cop shops. News stories may reach actual family members."

"Makes sense," Butch said.

"So I should send it?" Joanna asked.

"By all means," he replied. "Send away."

She added contact information to the bottom of the sheet. Then, in an accompanying note, she let Anna Rae know she was free to make any changes she deemed necessary. Joanna saved the document first, and then shipped it into the ethers.

"What are you going to do now?" Butch asked.

"I'm going to go into the bedroom, strip off my clothes, put on my nightgown, and go to bed."

"What about dinner?" Butch asked.

"I just now had breakfast," she said. "I need sleep way more than I need dinner."

CHAPTER 51

BISBEE, ARIZONA
Sunday, December 10, 2023

JOANNA FELL INTO BED AROUND SEVEN AND SLEPT FOR the next ten hours. By the time she woke up at five a.m., the PR storm had already broken. Anna Rae had sent out the press release, and Joanna's mailbox was overflowing with requests for interviews from four separate networks, all of them asking for hour-long sit-downs during the day on Monday, after the arraignment and before the press conference. Ditto from TV stations in Tucson.

At that point, Joanna's mother, Eleanor Lathrop Winfield, would have been turning handstands and booking her daughter in for full hair, nail, and makeup appointments. Joanna wasn't interested. She looked the way she looked, and that would have to do. She booked the network interviews for an hour and gave the Tucson stations half an hour each. Those already took a huge chunk out of a day where much of the morning would most likely be spent at the courthouse.

Several people requested information about the evidence photos. She forwarded those to Dave Hollicker. Anna Rae wanted to know if there was any response. Joanna let her know there was. Joanna was still lounging on the couch in her bathrobe when Dennis came out of his bedroom.

"You're not going to church?"

That was something that almost never happened.

"Nope," Joanna said.

"Why not?" he asked. "Is it because of that Roper guy?"

Joanna's first thought was that Butch must have said something, but Dennis quickly put that concern to rest.

"One of my friends lives just up the street from him on Country Club Drive. He said there were cop cars all over the place the other day and now it's covered with yellow crime tape. People are saying it has something to do with whatever happened to that reporter you don't like."

Joanna took a breath. "Yes, it has something to do with Marliss," she said, "but I'm not allowed to mention a suspect's name until after he's actually been charged with a crime, and you shouldn't either. The arraignment is set for tomorrow, but today I don't feel like going to church and having people asking me questions I can't answer. It's the law, yes, but it also seems rude."

"Will Dad be dropping us off? I'm supposed to hang out with Jeffy after church."

"I'm pretty sure he will, but he's making breakfast. Why don't you ask him?"

Moments after Dennis left for the kitchen, Sage showed up and the conversation repeated itself. No, Joanna wasn't going to church, but Sage wasn't interested in a ride. "If you're not going, can I stay home, too?"

Joanna wasn't prepared to fight any battles today. "That's totally up to you," she said. "Go if you want; stay home if you want."

"Thanks, Mom," Sage said, giving her a smooch. "What's for breakfast?"

"Go ask Dad," Joanna told her.

She was preparing for a quiet morning at home when her phone rang with a call from Detective Howell.

"Morning, Deb," Joanna said. "How are things?"

"Sorry to disturb your morning," was the reply, "but Marliss Shackleford's mother just called from Tombstone. She'll be here in about half an hour and wants to talk to you."

"No rest for the wicked," Joanna said, closing her computer and putting it aside. "I'll be there as soon as I can."

She was at her desk by ten past ten when Deb ushered Dianne Borison into the room. Marliss Shackleford's mother was not at all what Joanna expected. Pencil thin, wearing a designer suit and high heels, she could have been a doppelgänger for Jane Fonda, red hair and all. She was dripping with diamonds and condescension.

Joanna rose to greet her. "I'm so sorry for your loss, Ms. Borison," she said. "Won't you have a seat?"

"Thank you, but Mrs. Borison, please, if you don't mind." Before sitting down the woman examined both of the visitors' chairs as though expecting to find a horde of lice lurking there.

"Marliss was such a bright young thing, but she adored her father, and when Danny, my second husband, entered the picture, she hated him from day one until her dying day, as it turns out."

Dianne Borison sniffed and paused long enough to wipe a tear that was threatening to dislodge a chunk of mascara. "Marliss could have done anything, been anything. Instead she came to this hick town because her aunt, my first husband's sister Glenda, left her that run-down shack, little more than a cabin, really—in Briggs or Galena, whatever; I can never remember which is which—and went to work as a reporter for that two-bit *Bisbee Bee*. Why work for a rag like that or even a website when, if she'd played her cards right, she could have been working for the *Washington Post*?"

Joanna was astonished by the woman's unmitigated snobbery. The houses in Galena and Briggs were bungalows that had served as company housing back when the copper mines had been in operation. Most likely Marliss's uncle had worked for Phelps Dodge. He and his wife had probably lived in it as a rental and then purchased it once PD put the property up for sale. Marliss's yard may not have been picture perfect, but her place was definitely not a "run-down shack."

For the second time in as many days Joanna's heart ached for Marliss Shackleford. Butch's mother was a piece of work, but Dianne Borison topped Margaret Dixon by a long shot!

"How can I be of service, Mrs. Borison?" Joanna asked carefully.

"Well," she said, "Dr. Baldwin has released the body to a place called Higgins Funeral Home. I suppose you're familiar with them?"

"Very," Joanna replied.

"Several years ago, when Marliss and I were still on speaking terms, she sent me an email saying that if anything ever happened to her, she wanted to be cremated and have her ashes spread at a place called Juniper Flats, wherever that is."

"It's the highest point in the Mule Mountains," Joanna answered. "You came through the Mule Mountain Tunnel on the way into town. Juniper Flats is way above that."

"Sounds dangerous," Dianne said.

For someone in shoes like that? Joanna thought. *Absolutely.*

"Anyway," Dianne continued, "Mr. Higgins is going to do the cremation tomorrow. I've already purchased a beautiful urn, but he suggested that since Marliss had lived here in town, perhaps a small memorial service is in order. He has a time slot available on Tuesday afternoon at four."

"At the mortuary?" Joanna asked. "Why not at the church?"

"What church?" Dianne asked.

"Tombstone Canyon United Methodist," Joanna replied. "But even at the funeral home, I'm sure Marianne would be glad to officiate."

"Who is Marianne?" Dianne Borison wanted to know.

"She's a pastor," Joanna replied. "She was Marliss's pastor and mine, too."

"Are you telling me . . . Marliss actually went to church?" Dianne asked in disbelief.

Joanna nodded.

"How do I get in touch with this Marianne?"

Without having to look it up, Joanna wrote Marianne's number on a Post-it and handed it over. Dianne took the note and shoved it into a brand-name purse that had probably cost a bundle.

"There's one more thing," Dianne said.

"What's that?"

"Again, back when Marliss and I were still in communication, every time I talked to her, it was always Joanna Brady this and Joanna Brady that. It occurred to me that you were probably her best friend here in town, and I wondered if you'd mind giving her eulogy."

Joanna was flabbergasted. It had never occurred to her that she and Marliss had so much in common—grieving for an absent father, dealing with a controlling mother, and having to fight to find their own paths. And if in Dianne's conversations with her daughter she had come away with the notion that Marliss and Joanna were the best of friends, then the woman hadn't been listening to a word her daughter had been saying.

Joanna didn't hesitate, not for a moment. "Of course," she said. "I'll be happy to. Four p.m. on Tuesday at Higgins Funeral Home?"

Dianne nodded.

"Okay," Joanna told her. "I'll be there."

CHAPTER 52

BISBEE, ARIZONA
Monday, December 11, 2023

HAD SHERIFF JOANNA BRADY BEEN WATCHING THE NEWS that week rather than making it, she might have been aware that another winter storm was moving in off the Pacific. Her father, D.H. Lathrop, would have said, *It's raining cats and dogs.* On Monday morning, not only was it pouring rain, it was cold as hell, and the wind was blowing a gale. Joanna supposed that all the out-of-state visitors—and there were many—were ready to punch the noses of every single person—including their travel agents, who had told them how lucky they were to be going to "sunny Arizona" in the winter.

The traffic in Bisbee that day was horrendous. Everyone in town was headed for the same destination—up Tombstone Canyon to the Cochise County Courthouse on Quality Hill. When Bisbee was founded, the main drag was created in the most convenient way possible, by following the natural streambed that wound its way through a narrow canyon creating a roadway barely two lanes wide. When both Sheriff Joanna Brady and County Attorney Craig Witherspoon found themselves stalled in an impossible traffic jam minutes before they were due in Judge Cameron Moore's courtroom, Joanna took the lead. Positioning her Interceptor in front of Craig's Lexus, she carved out a third lane where there were only two.

When they reached the Iron Man statue and turned left, they discovered Chief of Police Bernard had deployed traffic cops. With their help, they threaded their way up the hill and into the two parking places that had been reserved for them. *Rank hath its privileges*, Joanna thought once again.

They had to push through an angry mob of people jammed into the square outside the courthouse. All of them, cameramen included, had just learned the courtroom was full and they wouldn't be allowed inside. As soon as Joanna saw the packed room, she resigned herself to having to stand. But then, once Craig took his place at the prosecutor's table, he turned to the man seated directly behind him and nodded, first at him and then at Joanna.

A uniformed bailiff stood up and motioned Joanna into his vacated seat. Once there, she noticed that Arturo Peña and Elena Delgado were next to her, probably also in bailiff-reserved seats. Some official arrangement must have been made to allow Xavier's mother to publicly cross the border.

What followed took only a matter of minutes. The roomful of people was asked to stand while Judge Moore entered the room and called things to order by announcing, "The first matter before this court today is the arraignment of Mr. Stephen Roper. Is he in attendance?"

Roper stood up. He was wearing an orange jumpsuit, jail-quality flip-flops, and manacles on both his wrists and legs.

Judge Moore seemed surprised. "I don't see your attorney in attendance, Mr. Roper," the judge said. "Is he on his way?"

"I fired his ass," Stephen said.

"Mr. Roper, this is a court of law. Please refrain from using that kind of language. If you do so again, I'll hold you in contempt."

Roper actually laughed. "What are you gonna do, put me in jail? Guess what? I'm already there."

Judge Moore took a steadying breath. "You are here on two separate but very serious charges. Are you intending to represent yourself?"

Roper nodded. "I am," he replied.

"Then I urge you to reconsider," Judge Moore said.

"Come on, Judge," Stephen Roper said. "Just ask me the question."

Judge Moore frowned. "What question?"

"How do I plead, guilty or innocent?"

Judge Moore looked down at the paperwork in front of him, then he cleared his throat. "You are charged with murder in the second degree in the death of Xavier Francisco Delgado. How do you plead?"

"Guilty," Roper said.

"In the death of Marliss Glenda Shackleford, you are also charged with murder in the second degree. How do you plead?"

That was the first time Joanna had ever heard Marliss's full name, and a layer of goose bumps covered her body. That's when she understood that Marliss's father must have filled in her birth certificate. Dianne never would have stood for her daughter being named after a much-despised sister-in-law. Joanna was so caught up in that realization that she almost missed Roper's response.

"Guilty."

To Joanna's surprise, there were no outbursts. The only sound in the room was that of Elena Delgado sobbing quietly into Arturo's shoulder.

"Then," Judge Moore continued, "you are remanded without bond to the Cochise County Jail to be held there until such time as you can be sentenced."

"Good," Roper said. "Then get me the hell out of here. I'm a cancer patient with an impaired immune system. Being with all these people is going to kill me."

Good riddance, Joanna thought. *That can't happen soon enough.*

CHAPTER 53

BISBEE, ARIZONA
Monday, December 11, 2023

BACK AT THE DEPARTMENT, JOANNA DID THE SCHEDULED sit-down interviews, one after another. The questions each time were almost identical, and it occurred to her she could have done just one, but the various network news stars had to have their allotted screen time. Once those were over, it was close to four and still raining, so, at the last minute, the decision was made to bring the press conference inside and into the largest space available—the public lobby. That meant there was enough room for people, but not enough for chairs, and the mic-filled lectern ended up being positioned directly in front of the photo of Joanna with her wagonload of Girl Scout cookies. That image quickly went viral.

"Good afternoon," she said, when it was finally time for her to speak. "I'm sorry about the weather and the crowded conditions, but I'm glad you're here. We need your help. Many of you were here earlier today for the arraignment of a local resident, Mr. Stephen Roper, on two charges of murder in the second degree. But here's the problem. In the course of investigating his two most recent crimes, we came to believe he wasn't a first-time offender. When we took him into custody, we discovered what turns out to be his trophy case—a cigar box filled with small items taken from his various victims. By our count, the total comes to ninety-nine.

"During police interviews, he has acknowledged committing twelve homicides that we currently know about. Details on those cases will be released once we ascertain all relatives of the victims have been notified. Mr. Roper arrived in Bisbee from Minnesota in the seventies and taught at Bisbee High School for decades before retiring in 2002. Disguising himself as a law-abiding citizen during the school year, he evidently spent the summers prowling the country, hunting for potential victims.

"Mr. Roper's crimes have a definite signature: He strangled his victims and left their fully clothed bodies in nearby rivers, lakes, or reservoirs. None of the bodies showed signs of sexual assault, but in each case he took a small token from the victim. Whenever tokens or trinkets were unavailable, often in the case of prostitutes, he kept track by making an X on a piece of paper in an old cigar box. There's a total of twenty-three X's—nameless victims where we have no way of connecting Roper to their deaths. But for the seventy-six items we do have, that's where you come in.

"Families of murdered victims never forget their lost loved ones. Everything about those deaths is imprinted on each of their hearts. For example, today we've connected an ivory-handled switchblade knife to Amanda Hudson of Grand Forks, North Dakota; a red bandanna to the death of Michael Young of Shiprock, New Mexico; a piece of yellow ribbon to the kite belonging to nine-year-old Calvin Dobbs of Beaverton, Oregon, who disappeared from the seashore in Cannon Beach.

"We have a whole collection of shoelaces—fifteen in all—that were found in Mr. Roper's cigar box. We know that one of those belonged to one of our current victims, Xavier Delgado, and we believe another is most likely connected to a seven-year-old girl named Lisa Daniels who went missing from Seattle's SeaFair Hydro races in 1983 and another to Lucianne Highsmith of Calloway County, Missouri, who died in 1977. Having a crime scene with a missing shoelace may not seem like a big deal, but if other details of crimes match up with Stephen Roper's modus operandi, those could allow us to find answers for other grieving families even decades later.

"So please, when you go back home, talk this up. If some of these details ring bells with one of your readers or listeners or viewers, please feel free to put them in touch with my department. Our contact information is listed on the press release. Now are there any questions?"

"You said he 'acknowledged' committing several other crimes. Will he be prosecuted for any of those?"

"Mr. Roper is currently seventy-eight years old. This morning he pled guilty to two counts of second-degree homicide. The standard sentence for second-degree murder in Arizona is ten to twenty-five years. Mr. Roper is not in the best of health. One twenty-five-year sentence would most likely be a death sentence as well, so I doubt he'll be prosecuted for other offenses, but at least the families will have answers."

"Is it true he was your English teacher here at Bisbee High School?"

"Yes," Joanna answered. "My senior year. He gave me a B+."

"But you didn't see anything off about him back then?"

"No, to all intents and purposes he was an upstanding citizen."

"Will we be able to see the evidence from the cigar box?"

"Yes," Joanna said. "My CSIs have set up a display in our crime lab, and digital photos of those items will be available upon request."

"I can see why he'd kill a little kid from Mexico, but why the reporter. What's her name again?"

"Marliss Glenda Shackleford," Joanna replied. "I believe she was following up on some aspect of the Xavier Delgado story. In the process she let him know he was under suspicion. After getting away with murder all this time, I think the very thought of being apprehended drove him into a state of blind panic."

Hands were still waving with more questions, but Joanna shut it down. "I'm sorry," she said. "That's all for now. I apologize that we had to do this under such adverse circumstances, but again, if any tips come in to you as a result of your reporting on this matter, please be sure to pass them along to us. Thank you."

She left the public lobby and headed for her office. Being in the limelight wasn't her favorite role, but under the circumstances, she felt as though both her parents, even her mother, would have been proud.

CHAPTER 54

BISBEE, ARIZONA
Tuesday, December 12, 2023

ON TUESDAY MORNING, JOANNA WAS AT HER DESK WORK-ing on Marliss Shackleford's eulogy when her phone rang with a caller ID number in Grand Island, Nebraska.

"Sheriff Brady here," she said.

"I'm Tom Malloy, the sheriff of Hall County, Nebraska. Saw your piece on *Good Morning America* today. You guys happen to find a green barrette in that asshole's trophy case?"

Once retrieved from the evidence room, the green barrette led back to a girl named Wendy Adams who had disappeared from the Nebraska State Fair in August of 1991. Because she was too small to ride the roller coaster, her two older sisters had left her alone while they took their ride. When it was over, Wendy was gone. And once again, after seeing the barrette, Roper confirmed he was responsible.

"Thanks so much," Sheriff Malloy said, once Joanna gave him the news. "But there's one more thing before you go."

"What's that?"

"I saw that picture of you on the news. You still selling Girl Scout cookies? There's nothing I'd like more right about now than a box of Thin Mints."

"Sorry," she said. "I'm afraid I'm all out of Girl Scout cookies. That ship has sailed."

But once Joanna was off the phone, she sat there at her desk acknowledging that Anna Rae Green had been one hundred percent correct. That nationally broadcast press conference really was doing the trick.

At three o'clock in the afternoon, Joanna showed up at Higgins Funeral Home in upper Bisbee. Even though she was an hour early, the chapel where Marliss's memorial service would be held was already full to the brim, and Norm Higgins's daughter and son-in-law were busy setting out chairs and loudspeakers in the lobby.

"Looks like it's going to be quite a shindig," Norm said, when Joanna tracked him down in his office. "I didn't think this many people would show up."

"I didn't, either," Joanna said. "Is her mother around?"

"Are you kidding?" Norm asked. "She's long gone. For all I know, she's probably already back in California by now. She paid for the cremation, the urn, and use of the chapel. When she found out that the ladies from Tombstone Methodist wanted to have a reception afterward, she sprang for a room for that, too, but then she said she had to get home to her husband."

"Without even staying for the service?" Joanna demanded.

"Seems like," Norm said. "Couldn't be bothered, but she left you a note."

Thank you for being my daughter's friend, and thank you for agreeing to speak at her service. I've asked Mr. Higgins to entrust her ashes to you. I'm afraid I'm far too old to go mountain climbing.

Dianne Borison

Joanna felt as though her head was about to explode. Dianne Borison hadn't listened to Joanna any more than she'd listened to her daughter.

"What a piece of work," Joanna muttered, wadding up the note and shoving it into her pocket.

"You can say that again," Norm replied.

Much to Joanna's surprise, Marliss Shackleford's memorial service in Bisbee was one of the most well attended in recent memory. People who couldn't get inside the building stood outside in the street, and Norm made sure there were outside loudspeakers as well. After the demise of the *Bisbee Bee*, clearly Marliss's ongoing web-based reporting on the Cochise County Courier website had filled a void in many people's lives, and they came out in droves to pay their respects.

Joanna's remarks were brief but to the point. "Thank you for coming to honor Marliss Shackleford," Joanna began. "She and I didn't always see eye to eye, but she was a reporter to the bone, and the reason she's not here with us today is that she was on the trail of an evil man who, unfortunately, is known to many of us in this community.

"My understanding is that she could have gone almost anywhere to practice her craft, but she chose to come here where she lived in a home she had inherited from her auntie, Glenda Shackleford. We were honored to have Marliss here with us for as long as we did. I can tell from the number of people in attendance today that Marliss's work touched many lives, and it is with profound regret that I come to say hail and farewell."

Several other people spoke as well before Marianne Maculyea brought the curtain down on the service. Knowing she was likely to be grilled by everyone and his uncle about the Stephen Roper case, Joanna almost bypassed the reception, but as soon as she caught sight of Ernie Carpenter, she was thrilled she hadn't.

Ernie saw her about the same time she spotted him. He hurried up and engulfed her in a hug. "Great job nailing that bastard," he said.

Joanna stood back and looked at him. He was in far better shape than the last time she'd seen him. Back then, he'd just gotten a serious prostate cancer diagnosis, and he and his wife, Rose, were setting off in an RV, intent on getting as far as they could before the grim reaper caught up with him.

"What are you doing here?" Joanna demanded.

He grinned. "Turns out I wasn't dying after all," he said. "That new treatment wasn't fun, but it worked. Finally, though, full-time RV-ing got to be old. Rose wanted to have a real kitchen again, and I wanted a shower I didn't have to step out of in order to turn around. Besides, being close to the grandkids seemed like a good idea. We rented a place out in Huachuca Terraces."

Suddenly, a light came on in Joanna Brady's head. "You wouldn't by any chance be wanting to go back to work, would you?"

"Me?" Ernie asked.

"Yes, you. Turns out I happen to have a cold case file with ninety or so unidentified victims. I don't know how much I could pay you . . ."

"Pay me?" Ernie echoed. "Are you kidding? You won't have to pay me a dime. I've been so bored, I'll be glad to do it for free. When can I start?"

"Tomorrow?" she asked.

"You bet," he answered. "I'll be there with bells on."

CHAPTER 55

BISBEE, ARIZONA
Saturday, December 23, 2023

AT TWO P.M. ON DECEMBER 23, BUTCH DIXON WALKED HIS beloved stepdaughter, Jennifer Ann Brady, down the aisle. He made it to the front of the church all right, but when the Reverend Marianne Maculyea asked, "Who giveth this woman?" he burst into tears and barely got the words out.

Within minutes Jennifer Ann Brady and Nicholas Richard Saunders were husband and wife, having exchanged their vows in a church overflowing with poinsettias. For her part, Joanna wasn't at all surprised when Marianne introduced the newlyweds as Jennifer Ann Brady and Nicholas Richard Sanders. Jenny kept her name, and Nick kept his.

After all, Joanna thought. *Jenny's a chip off the old block.*

It was a joyous event. Butch's collection of Mexican finger foods was a big hit, and the cake was downright spectacular.

THE FOLLOWING SUNDAY, AS THEY WERE GETTING READY for church, Joanna told Butch that they'd need to take separate cars because she had something she needed to do after church.

"Scatter the ashes?" he asked.

Joanna nodded and dragged her hiking boots out of the closet.

The road to Juniper Flats was little more than a rutted footpath, and it was also covered with a smattering of snow, but the Interceptor made the trip with no difficulty.

Once on top, she parked near the radio, cell, and TV towers dotting the summit, but she walked past them, over to the edge of the precipice. Once there, she unscrewed the lid from the urn.

"I'm sorry you had such a tough life, Marliss," Joanna said aloud. "If you'd lived long enough for us to grow old together, we might have become friends after all, but for now, this is the best I can do."

As she poured out the ashes, a gust of chill wind caught them and carried them off into the canyon below. Marliss Shackleford had chosen to make her life in southern Arizona, and here she would stay.

ABOUT THE AUTHOR

J. A. Jance is the *New York Times* bestselling author of the J. P. Beaumont series, the Joanna Brady series, the Ali Reynolds series, six thrillers about the Walker family, and one volume of poetry. Born in South Dakota and brought up in Bisbee, Arizona, she lives with her husband in Seattle, Washington.